CW01218688

Corno da Capo

Corno da Capo

The Life and Adventures
of an 18th Century Horn Player

A novel by

Richard M. Seraphinoff

Cover design and layout by Katherine Webb
Cover picture, Mozart Musikalischer Spaß, First edition, Offenbach, a/M: André, Paris, ca. 1797

ISBN 979-8-769-77013-5

Acknowledgements

I would like to thank several people who have read the manuscript of this book to search out the many grammatical errors and typos and make suggestions that have greatly improved the story and the characters. These include former Indiana University horn students (and natural horn players) Eleni Giorgiadis and Olivia Martinez, and my long-time early music loving friend, Alex Barker.

On the professional editorial side, Birdalone Music and Books publisher Viola Roth used her keen editorial eye to make many suggestions for the improvement of the text and refinement of dialogue and character development. Thanks also go to Birdalone Music for permission to use quotes from the 1994 translation of the Dauprat *Method for Cor-Alto and Cor-Basse.*

My good friend and fiction writer Robert Barclay, endured many evenings during the International Trumpet Making Workshops listening to me read chapters aloud, made many suggestions on writing style as well as historical and technical issues in the story, and was responsible for details of the city of London in the 18th century being correctly depicted. My brother Michael Seraphinoff, also a writer of fiction, historical, and biographical books, added his thoughts and insights along the way as well.

Former horn and natural horn student John Manganaro has been a constant source of information on the history of natural horn playing technique, sharing freely his own research and writing on horn technique of the 18th century. Natural horn player Pierre-Antoine Tremblay supplied French translations from treatises and books.

Musicologist Sterling Murray, author of the definitive biography of Antonio Rosetti, did much fact-checking and added important information to my depiction of that composer, as well as the Öttingen-Wallerstein court orchestra, and the Thurn und Taxis court orchestra in Regensburg.

Special thanks go to former IU doctoral student Katy Webb for her work on the cover design, formatting, and layout of the text.

Last, but definitely not least, I would like to express my sincere thanks and appreciation to my wife, Celeste Holler Seraphinoff, who in many respects was the model in my mind's eye for the character of Beate Pokorny. Celeste spent several years listening to me working out plot lines, helped in shaping the characters, and used her natural horn and period instrument knowledge and performing experience to help make the musical performance parts of the story more convincing. Finally, in the last stages, she spent many hours working on punctuation and editing of the dialogue, with the help of a well-thumbed copy of the *Chicago Manual of Style* and read the entire text out loud more than once to help me refine the speech of the characters and make it flow as though it was being said by real people. For her constant involve-ment and patience every step of the way over several years, I dedicate this book to her.

Table of Contents

Preface

From academic study to historical novel...

My initial intention in writing this book was to give horn players who are interested in the playing technique of the natural horn and the musical settings and styles in which it was played a better understanding of how the instrument developed from the simple and straightforward baroque horn, played without the hand in the bell, to the more sophisticated fully chromatic hand horn of the late 18th century.

It occurred to me, while considering how to proceed with this project, that three figures stood out as driving forces behind that development: Giovanni Punto, and the duo of Johann Palsa and Carl Türrschmidt, three of the most prominent horn players of the fourth quarter of the 18th century. All three were members of the second generation of the development of hand stopping on the horn, begun by players such as Josef Hampel, Jean-Joseph Rodolph, and others whose careers spanned the period of the 1740s to the 1780s. Following the careers of Palsa and Türrschmidt, whose lives and work as a horn duo are well documented, seemed like a perfect vehicle for the story of the development of the instrument during this important period. These two virtuosi crossed paths with Punto on several occasions, making it easy to incorporate his contributions to the horn's development into the narrative as well.

Carl Türrschmidt's life is well documented from his birth and studies with his father, through his working period in France and Germany, and on to the end of his life. But the figure of Johann Palsa is somewhat more obscure, with virtually no information on his early life until teaming up with Türrschmidt in Paris in 1770, leaving much room for speculation about how one of the most prominent and influential horn players of the period could appear on the Paris concert scene, essentially out of nowhere. Equally enigmatic is Beate Pokorny, one of the very few women horn players of the 18th century, whose existence is documented by only a handful of references to her performing at the Paris Concert Spirituel and in London.

The story grew in the telling, as the saying goes, and the initial idea for a book on the historical development of the horn, and biography of these prominent players all came together into a historical novel that I hope will be of interest not only to the natural horn specialist, but also to modern horn players, musicians and music lovers in general. The non-musically trained reader will be happy to know that none of the technical information on the horn or musical terminology is necessary to understand and enjoy the story.

Though this is a work of historical fiction, all the principal characters actually lived and worked in the places and time periods I've placed them, with just a bit of artistic license. Their adventures, conversations, and even the relationship between Johann Palsa and Beate Pokorny are pure speculative fiction. Because this story will be of particular interest to horn players and music students, persons, places, and events mentioned in the text are explained and documented at the end of the book in notes, excerpts from primary sources of the period, and brief biographies. These are included for the benefit of the reader who would like to see what is actually known about the principal characters, the sources I used as a starting point for the story, and which of the minor characters were real, and which are fictional.

Regarding the languages that would have been spoken by the characters; throughout the story, dialogue appears in which the characters would have been speaking French, German, or English. When the characters are supposed to be speaking French, they address one another using "Monsieur, Madame" and "Mademoiselle" and refer to the horn as the "Cor de Chasse". When speaking German, characters are addressed as "Herr" and "Frau" and the horn is called a "Waldhorn". When speaking English, "Mr., Mrs." and "Miss" are used, and horn is called a "French horn". Royalty and nobility speak using the royal "We" when talking to commoners in all three languages.

Richard M. Seraphinoff
Bloomington, Indiana
October 2021

Corno da Capo

Prologue

As I begin writing this memoir, I'm sitting in my comfortably heated, well-furnished, and spotlessly clean living room, in front of a cozy wood fire. I'm wearing comfortable clothes and shoes, and all my teeth are in their proper places and in excellent condition. All this is in stark contrast to the life to which I had become accustomed. I'm holding in my hand a small solid silver French horn mouthpiece which I watched being made in a shop in Paris twenty-two years ago, and have played on ever since until quite recently, though I am but twenty-eight years old. I feel twenty-eight years old physically, but I have nearly twice that many years of life experience in my memory. The story of my grand adventure, and how it all happened is one that I can't tell anyone at this point, but I feel I must write it down for posterity. I have very little hope of anyone giving it any credit, if it ever is read, but I know the truth of my story.

I'll be able to go back to work in a few months in the symphony orchestra in which I play third horn, and it will be a big adjustment going back after all this time, though in many ways a welcome one. The little silver mouthpiece is my only physical link to another lifetime full of memories. Many of them are extremely pleasant, and others less so, but none of which I would give up for anything in the world.

John Paulson
December 2020

Part I
Paris 1770 - 1774

Chapter 1

In the midway of this our mortal life,
I found me in a gloomy wood, astray
Gone from the path direct...
... How first I enter'd it I scarce can say,
Such sleepy dullness in that instant weigh'd
My senses down, when I left the true path...
- Dante Alighieri, The Divine Comedy, Canto I, 1321

I opened my eyes after what seemed like an eternity of unconsciousness. My head was pounding, and every bone in my body seemed to be making its presence known in the form of aches and pains. Everything was spinning around, and it felt as though my body was in motion, which was actually the case, since someone was dragging me, holding me under the arms, and I could feel my shoes moving over an uneven surface like a cobblestone street. A lot of voices were talking all around me, and I couldn't understand a word they were saying. The words were all jumbled nonsense.

"Is he a toad?"

"Nine! A limp duck!"

My brain began functioning bit by bit again, and the words were starting to make more sense.

"Ist er tot?"

"Nein, er lebt noch!"

As my head began to clear, I began to understand that what I was hearing around me was German.

"Is he dead?"

"No, he's still alive! But he's badly injured!"

My first thought, as more arms came to lift me up, was "Oh crap! I forgot to do my German homework, and I can't understand what the professor is saying." I had two years of German in college, and was rather proud of my ability to read, write, and speak with a fair degree of fluency in that language, which had come in handy on our orchestra's European tours, but what I was hearing around me now was not the standard kind of German one learns in school - and way too fast.

I was beginning to get my senses back, and the scene around me was the strangest thing I had ever seen in my life! I was looking up at a building with ornate stone carving on the front in the rue de Faubourg in Paris. Just seconds before, my friends from the horn section of our orchestra and I were looking up at this same building while crossing the busy street. Cars and buses had been going past in a continuous parade, and the noise of the city surrounded us. Now all was changed.

The rest of the buildings in the street and the people, and the entire scene looked like an engraving out of a Dickens novel. There were horses everywhere, and everything smelled bad. The road was indeed made of cobblestones, and the house into which I was being carried had a hand painted sign that I didn't understand, because it was in French. I hadn't the foggiest notion of what was happening, but I was still fairly calm, because I knew it was just a dream, and that I would wake up soon. But wow! - what a vivid dream, with colors and smells, and in some kind of odd German that I could sort of understand.

The several hands that were carrying me laid me down on a wooden floor and a red face appeared over me and said something in French. I guessed he was asking my name and if I was ok. I ransacked my brain for the little bit of French I knew, but couldn't find any of it, so I answered in German that I thought I was all right, and that my name was John Paulson.

"A foreigner - and such strange clothes!" I heard voices in the background saying.

I was still wearing my concert clothes from the performance we had just finished in the Salle Pleyel, the home of the Orchestra de Paris. My black tailcoat was dusty and torn in a couple of places, and my white tie was nowhere to be seen. I had a bloody nose, a painful throbbing in my side, and an ankle that seemed unlikely to support me if I tried to stand on it, judging by the pain.

The red-faced man went on in German.

"You were run over by a coach! Those damned nobles! They don't care who they run down. They won't slow down for anyone. No one saw you at all until the coach was already past. It was as if you appeared out of nowhere right under the wheels."

"I don't remember a thing," I said, stalling for time until I could figure out what was actually happening.

"Where do you come from?" he asked.

"I'm from America ... I've been traveling. I'm not exactly sure what happened."

"You must have been robbed in the street, and the robbers pushed you out into the traffic."

"Um... Yes, - that's probably what happened. I have a sort of vague memory of something of the kind, but I can't remember anything else."

"Were you traveling with friends?"

"No, I don't think so. Where am I?"

"In the rue de Faubourg, in Paris, of course."

"Then why are you all speaking German? I'm very confused."

"We are German musicians who work in Paris. We were on our way home from a rehearsal of the *Concert Spirituel* orchestra when we saw you roll out from under that carriage. I'm Carl Stamitz, this is my brother Anton, this is Johann Baer, and this is Herr Wendling.

"Are your clothes and other things at an inn nearby? Can we take you back to your rooms?"

"I don't remember where my hotel room is," I said, using a couple of words that would not become common in their language for about a hundred and fifty years, though I didn't know that at the time. As I started thinking more clearly, I looked around for my horn case.

"Where is my horn?" I had my horn with me when I stepped into the street, and I don't see it anywhere!"

"Horn? Are you a musician too?" asked Carl Stamitz.

"Yes, I'm a horn player."

"I see how it was," said the older gentleman called Wendling.

"Someone grabbed your instrument, pushed you into the street and ran; a common occurrence in the streets of Paris. We'll take you back to my house, which is not far. We all live in the rue Chantre, where a lot of other musicians live. A young man from Germany who plays the horn is staying with us at present, and he may be able to put out the word to the Paris horn players and the local music shops that a horn has been stolen. It may turn up yet."

They helped me onto my feet, and I walked a couple of blocks supported on each side by Baer and Wendling. The main memory I have of that walk was the intolerable smell of the people who held my arms and led me along. We turned a corner into a dark street full of dark houses - no lights anywhere - and stepped into the front door of a house that looked like something out of *A Tale of Two Cities*. We were in a dusty museum-looking sitting room that led into a kitchen with a smoking open hearth in which a pot was simmering. Herr Wendling looked at a disheveled boy of about ten, who was wearing wooden shoes that looked terribly uncomfortable, and a threadbare cap on his head.

"Hannes, go to all the inns and taverns in the neighborhood and see if this gentleman is a guest at any of them."

"Jawohl!" said the boy and clunked away at top speed out the door and down the street, sounding like a herd of impatient goats on a boardwalk.

At this point a man who looked much like Thomas Jefferson, ruffled shirt, waistcoat, and all, arrived on the scene with a black leather bag, and they informed me that he was a doctor. He looked me over in a rather unscientific way, asked a few questions that they translated for me and then they all talked together in French for a while. Then Carl Stamitz told me the doctor thought I may have a fractured rib, and a sprained ankle, in addition to some scrapes and bruises.

The doctor stopped my nose from bleeding, and told them I was not seriously injured, though still obviously a bit confused. He said they should put me to bed until they could figure out where to send me. The doctor looked at me one more time with a professional eye and said something else.

"He is asking if you would like him to let a little blood before he leaves," said Wendling. "He has a lancet and bowl all ready."

"No, no!" I said nervously, "That won't be necessary! I'm feeling better by the minute."

I limped into a back room with the help of Wendling and Anton Stamitz, and fell into a heap on a bed, whose mattress felt as though it was stuffed with straw and scrap lumber. They covered me with musty old blankets and left me to sleep, which I did almost immediately.

Chapter 2

First, good Peter Quince, say what the play treats on, then read the names of the actors, and so grow to a point.

- William Shakespeare, A Midsummer Night's Dream, 1596

I woke the next morning at sunrise to discover that the house I was in was not heated in any way. It was pitch black, cold, and the smell of cooking meat permeated the air. My first thought was, "Whatever is happening to me is still happening! What the hell is going on here? How did I get here, and how do I get back to where I'm supposed to be?! Dreams aren't usually this persistent, so something weird must be happening!" I lay there for a long time trying to gather my thoughts, but to absolutely no avail. I went over the events of the previous day in my mind and began to put them into a sensible order. It was all coming back.

The orchestra had just arrived in Paris for the last concert of a European tour. We had played in some of the most important European cities, and the orchestra had received excellent reviews everywhere. This was a standard program of romantic works, including the Overture to Der Freischütz by Weber, Brahms Piano Concerto no. 2, and the Saint-Saëns Symphony no. 3. Each of these pieces had important solos for the third horn and had been on my audition for the orchestra, making it a very meaningful program for me.

The Freischütz overture begins right away with a famous passage for the horn section. After the first chords played by the full orchestra, the strings lay down a gentle accompaniment, preparing the way for the entrance of the third and fourth horns with the main theme of the overture. The concert was in the Salle Pleyel, the home of the Orchestra de Paris, which has wonderful acoustics. With very little effort, you can project over the texture of the orchestra without sounding like you're working hard to do so. Katy, our fourth horn, and I have been playing together for three years, and she knows exactly how to tune and play together with me. This lyrical duet sets the stage for the entrance of the first and second horns a few measures later, filling out the quartet. It's one of the most beautiful and well-known horn passages in the orchestral literature, and we played it well that night.

The next piece, the Brahms piano concerto, also has some wonderful passages for the horns. In much of Brahms's music the horns function in pairs, so that the first and second play together, and the third and fourth are like a separate horn section. The third horn often has the lead voice, or plays prominent solos, and very satisfying solos they are!

The Saint-Saëns symphony is another piece in which the third and fourth horns have very independent parts from the first and second. Originally, the composer wrote the first two parts for the valveless natural horn, which was still very much in use in France late in the 19th century, and the third and fourth for the valved horn of the time. The first and second horns play rather simple parts, while the second pair have interesting melodic lines and some exposed solo passages. In one lyrical section, the first clarinet, first trombone, and third horn play a melody in octaves that blends together to sound like one big otherworldly instrument. A difficult passage for intonation and phrasing between the three instruments, but worth the effort.

That, in any case, is how those pieces look from the perspective of the people sitting in the horn section of the orchestra. The audience hears the entire package and enjoys the concert while each musician and section functions in their own little world of the technique of their instruments, fitting their parts into the texture of the music. Overall, it was one of the most rewarding concerts I've ever played.

After packing up our instruments, the four of us from the horn section left the Salle Pleyel and headed in the direction of our hotel.

"Let's get something to eat on our way back to the hotel," said Katy. "I'm starving, and thirsty."

We all agreed that a beer and some food would be just the thing to wind down from the excitement of the performance, and we started looking for a restaurant as we walked down the rue de Faubourg. We were just about to cross the street, when Chris, our principal horn stopped and looked upward.

"Look at the carving on that building across the street, it's really spectacular. It must be hundreds of years old!"

We all looked up as we stepped into the street, and somehow I tripped on the curb and plunged forward. Before I could catch myself, or even knew what was happening, I saw bright lights in front of me and everything went black. When I next opened my eyes, I was in the exact same place, but the entire scene was different.

I came back out of these thoughts and returned to my present situation. "OK, OK, get a grip on yourself and see it through, whatever it is. I somehow ended up in the same place where I had been, but the scene had changed, and it seemed like another time, or a movie set or something. It's all too elaborate and convincing for a movie set. They don't go so far as to make a set smell authentic, do they? How the hell does this work? It doesn't work! It's right out of some ludicrous science fiction novel! Stuff like this doesn't happen to real people! Stay calm. Somehow this will resolve itself, or at least start to make some sense. I'm just going to go with it and see what happens. If these are people from hundreds of years ago, they will be just as confused about the whole thing as I am, so I'd better be ready to talk my way around all their questions. I think they used to burn people at the stake who they didn't understand and couldn't explain."

I then began thinking about all the people who would be distraught at my disappearance. My wife, Beth, and our two young children were at home in the States, and someone would have to explain to them that I had vanished into thin air. What would happen to them if I wasn't there? Beth had a good job as an editor at a publishing company, so they wouldn't starve, but their lives would be changed completely. So many thoughts were whirling around in my mind. Would I ever see them again?

But at the moment my task was to find out where I was and what the date was. I mustered up all the courage and resolve I could, got up onto shaky legs, and found my way to the front of the house. "This couldn't really be happening, could it? There must be some rational explanation."

I was freezing and kept one of the blankets wrapped around me as I came out into the front room to be met by Wendlings' daughter, whose name was Elisabeth, a nice-looking blonde girl of about eighteen with a pleasant friendly face, and Hannes, who I had seen the night before.

Hannes was the younger brother of the Wendlings' cook, Katherina. With them was another well-dressed young gentleman who Elisabeth introduced as Carl Türrschmidt. They all stood up from their breakfast, greeted me very cordially, and asked how I was doing. I hadn't used my German to this extent for a while and was unfamiliar with many of the idioms and some of the words they used, but in answer to their questions, I told them I was feeling better than the previous day, but still very sore. The pain in my side was much less than the evening before, so I probably hadn't broken a rib, but my ankle was still throbbing.

"The doctor will stop by to see you again this morning," said Elisabeth, "but we still haven't been able to find out where you were staying or where your belongings are. Hannes went to every inn in the area and none of them knew anything about you. Do you remember now where you were coming from and where you were going when the accident happened?"

"It's beginning to come back," I said, "but it's all still rather unclear and foggy in my head."

"Well, maybe some breakfast will help to clear your mind before the doctor arrives. Katherina! Bring something for the gentleman to eat!"

Katherina, who I had not seen on the previous evening, was about twenty. She was dressed in an apron and cap like the sort of German *Hausfrau* that one sees in paintings from the 18th century. She had a board filled with bread and sausage, and a big lump of some kind cheese, as well as a steaming pitcher and wooden cups.

Herr Wendling and his wife had left earlier that morning for Lyon for a few days where they were taking part in a series of concerts. Wendling was the principal flutist of the famous Mannheim Orchestra in Germany, and Dorothea was one of the leading singers of the Mannheim Opera. This past year he had spent much of his time in London, working with J. C. Bach in a series of chamber concerts, and in between these, visiting Paris, where the rest of the family was living.

The bread was made of a very coarse whole grain, probably rye, and would have made an excellent building material, should you happen to run out of bricks. The cheese was something between cottage cheese and butter and had virtually no taste at all. Katherina told me with pride when she brought the food in that the neighbors had just slaughtered an excellent pig, and she had made the blood sausage herself from some of the meat. It was my first taste of blood sausage, and after the initial shock, and the thought of which parts of the pig were in it, it wasn't bad. The pitcher was full of incredibly bad coffee mixed about half and half with milk, which I drank out of one of the wooden cups. Carl Türrschmidt was drinking beer out of a metal cup with his breakfast, which wasn't a very appealing thought at eight o'clock in the morning, and especially since I still had a pounding headache. As it turned out, this was a weak beer with a low alcohol content that was brewed at home and was drunk at any time of the day with meals by most of the common people in Germany.

Having already finished their breakfast, Elisabeth and Hannes soon took their leave, and I was left at the breakfast table with the young German horn player, Carl Türrschmidt, who appeared to be in his early twenties. I found out later that he was just eighteen. He was slim, and rather tall, with dark hair that might identify him as coming from some of the southern parts of the German speaking Holy Roman Empire. His family was originally from the area known as Bohemia, German speaking at that time, but in modern times, part of the Czech Republic. He was a very pleasant and friendly guy, and we immediately fell into conversation, each of us trying to figure out who the oddly dressed stranger was on the other side of the table.

Chapter 3

I am always at a loss to know how much to believe of my own stories.
- Washington Irving, Tales of a Traveler, 1824

"I believe Herr Wendling said your name is Johann?" he said, trying to get the conversation off the ground.

"John, actually, - John Paulson".

"Very pleased to meet you. As Elisabeth said, I'm Carl Türrschmidt, from Wallerstein in Swabia. I arrived in Paris a couple months ago from Regensburg, where my family has been living for the past few years, and I'm trying to make a living with all the other musicians here in the big city. I haven't made great headway as of yet, but things are beginning to happen. Herr Wendling, who has been a resident of Paris off and on for many years, is an old friend of my father and was good enough to give me a room until I can afford a place of my own, which I should be able to do soon. Are you English?" he asked.

"No, I'm American."

"Oh, - right, from the English colonies, and therefore, English is your native language?"

"Yes, I learned German at school."

"Yes, of course. There are a lot of German speakers in the colonies. Herr Wendling said you are a horn player. Is that your profession?"

"It is. I play in an orchestra in America."

"No! Really? They have professional orchestras there?"

"Quite a number of them."

"Herr Wendling might have mentioned that I'm a horn player too," he went on. "He told me what happened to you last night. This is an unbelievable coincidence. What are the chances of having such an accident and being rescued from the street by some fellow musicians? It's quite amazing!"

"That is pretty amazing, I have to admit," I said, trying to figure out what to say next, "but it isn't the strangest thing about my arrival here by a long shot. I'm still very confused about it myself."

"Well, I was just about to ask you about that. What's the real story; why the funny clothes and all?"

"Carl, I have to ask you a couple of very strange questions. Please promise you won't think I'm totally crazy. You say we are in Paris, dare I ask what the date is?"

"Yes, certainly. It's Wednesday, October twenty-fourth."

"In the year..." I prompted.

"1770, of course," he said, laughing. "I've known guys who have lost track of a day or two, but one has to do some pretty impressive drinking to forget what year it is, and not know what city he's in!"

The room began to spin around just like on the previous day, and I put my head in my hands for a few moments to try to grasp the situation. I was sitting in a dusty 18th century room with a young man dressed in a brown waistcoat, white ruffled shirt, and knee-length pants with silk stockings who was telling me in some sort of archaic German that it was 1770.

I took a deep breath. "No, it's not like that at all. Something very weird has happened, and I've lost much more than a day or two. I think I've lost more than two centuries."

"I don't understand what you're talking about," he said, looking at me in the same sort of worried way that one might look at a perfect stranger who comes up to you and starts shouting in Latin.

With a sudden new resolve in my voice, I looked straight at him and began.

"Look, Carl, I don't know what else to do, so I'm going to be totally honest with you, in the hope that you can help me figure out what's happened, and what I should do. I'm not just a stranger from another country who had an unfortunate accident. Apparently, I've been accidentally sent through time from my own time to this one."

I thought this was the moment of truth, and that he would probably run out the door and call for help, and I would be in for whatever they did to insane people in those days. But he remained sitting and looked at me blankly, waiting for me to explain.

"Just a few hours ago I was playing in a concert with my orchestra in the Salle Pleyel. After the performance was over, I was walking back to our hotel with the other horn players, when an accident happened. I tripped on the curb in the street and fell, and then everything went black. When I opened my eyes again, I was in the middle of the same street, where your friends found me, but the entire scene was changed. That's all I can tell you. The rest is a total mystery, and I have no idea how or why I'm here, or what to do about it."

He stared at me for a few seconds.

"That's a pretty crazy story, but I'm sure it will all turn out to have a perfectly logical explanation, and the truth will come to you when you're feeling better. You're not really from some time two hundred years from now, you just got a bad bump on the head and are not thinking clearly yet. We'll get it all sorted out. Now tell me what you can remember about where you are from and what you were doing during your travels."

I was now becoming more certain of my story, and I was determined that I would convince him, because I needed someone in whom I could confide, and who could help me in this strange place, where I was totally unequipped to help myself.

"Ok, so here's how it is; I was born and raised in Boston, Massachusetts. Do you know where that is?"

"Yes, that's one of the larger cities of the English colonies," he said, obviously proud of his knowledge of the geography of the New World.

"Well, yes, but by my time the colonies had become a large single country called the United States of America, and Boston is a large modern city. "

"And may I ask, what is this 'your time' that you speak of?"

"The year 2019. I was born in 1991."

"Right... So, you say you play in an orchestra in America, in the year 2019?"

I could tell he was humoring me, trying to get some idea of just what sort of lunatic I was, and I was just as determined to prove my story.

"I play third horn in one of the best orchestras in the country. The orchestra employs almost a hundred musicians, and we are paid very well. We play three concerts a week, almost every week from September through the end of May. Then we do a summer series, and then a few weeks of paid vacation before the new season starts. All together I consider myself one of the luckiest musicians in the world, since I make a good living playing with other fine musicians."

"And there are a hundred musicians in this orchestra? How many horns?"

"There are six of us, but only four or five play at a time, as a rule. You wouldn't recognize our instruments, since they have changed a lot since your time... that is to say from the present time... which is long in the past in my time. Since the invention of the valve, the instrument is now totally chromatic, and we no longer have to change crooks and do hand stopping. It's a very usable musical instrument now, not primitive at all, like the ones of your time."

"Primitive?! The horn is one of the most refined and beautiful instruments there is. I come from a family of horn players who have brought our instrument to the highest degree of perfection. My father is the first horn player of the famous *Oettingen-Wallerstein Hofkapelle* of Prince Kraft-Ernst of Wallerstein. Primitive indeed!"

"No offence intended!" I added quickly, trying not to blow out of the water all the headway I felt I was making. "I'm sure I have very little idea of how refined the *Waldhorn* is in the most skillful hands, and I look forward to hearing it at its best!"

"I hope I can change your mind about the Waldhorn," he said, "but back to your story. What can you tell me to prove that what you're saying is true? You have to admit it's pretty far-fetched, and I dare say that you wouldn't believe a story like this if someone dressed in strange clothes walked into your house off the street..."

"Was carried in..."

"Ok, was carried into your house, and started telling you they were from two hundred and fifty years in the future, would you?"

I had to agree that it was a lot to ask. I sat a minute and thought, and then it occurred to me; I could prove everything by the things I had in my pockets!

"Here," I said, and quickly took off my watch and started emptying my pockets. "These things will convince you for sure that everything I've said is true."

I don't know why I hadn't thought of this earlier, but my pockets contained all the proof I needed; my wallet, car keys, my wristwatch, a gold-plated Holton Farkas DC horn mouthpiece, and the ultimate proof - my cell phone! I had recently bought a new state-of-the-art phone, and it was filled with music, photos, games, and videos. I started with the easy ones and showed him my keys.

"These are my keys. This one starts my car."

"Car?" he asked.

I made the mistake of using the modern German word *Auto*.

"Umm... a horseless carriage, I'll explain later, there's so much I need to tell you. This one opens the front door to my house, and this one opens the room at the university where I teach horn."

"You're a professor of horn too?"

"Yes, I give lessons at a university in addition to playing in the orchestra. This one opens my garage," I said, using another word that wouldn't become part of the German language for at least another century. "And this one is for the lock that keeps my bicycle from being stolen when I ride it to work with my horn strapped to my back." It occurred to me too late that the bicycle showed up sometime in the 19th century, and therefore the German word for it, *Fahrrad* had gone right past him with no effect. I had to remember to be careful to use words that I was sure were meaningful to him.

"Have you ever seen keys like that?" I asked hopefully.

"No, but I've never been to the New World, so I wouldn't know."

I picked up my watch.

"Of course you know what a pocket watch is, but have you ever seen one this small that you wear on your wrist? You don't have to wind it up because it runs on an electric battery."

"I've heard of Luigi Galvani and the electric battery. I read everything I can find on science and new inventions," he said. "Keep going. This is most interesting."

"Ok," I said, "believe me, I'm just getting started. This is my wallet, where I keep all my important papers and money. Here's my driver's license, and some credit cards. I'll explain later what they're for. Look at the date on this."

"It says 2023 here, I thought you said you came from 2019?"

"That's the date when I have to get a new one. The government requires you to get a new one every few years."

"The French government requires that we foreigners renew our papers every couple of years. It's just a way of making money off us."

"Some things never change," I said, smiling.

"All right, what are the rest of these papers? That one looks like a banknote."

"That's our American money. These are paper notes, $1, $10, and $20, and here are some coins, 10, and 25 cents. Dollars and cents are the units of money. Look at the dates."

"2014, 2017, 2018, and the coins are 1998, and 2007. Hmm..." he said slowly. "The picture on the banknote says "Washington." Is that General George Washington of the colonies? The Paris newspapers are full of reports of the friction between the colonists and the English, so we've heard of him."

"Yes," I said. "He became the first president of the United States sometime in the 1780s, I can't remember the exact year. The only date Americans usually remember is 1776, when the Declaration of Independence was signed."

"Right. I think I understand," he said shifting uncomfortably in his chair. "What's that, a horn mouthpiece?"

"That's right. Have a look at it."

"Strange!" he said taking it from me and examining it closely. "Heavy, turned out of a solid piece of metal, like a trumpet mouthpiece, and with a shallow cup and throat, like a trumpet. Pretty wide rim too. Is it made of solid gold?"

"No, it's made of brass and only has a thin layer of gold on the surface, known as plating."

He stepped out of the room for a minute and returned to hand me a mouthpiece.

"Here's mine. Quite different, isn't it?"

It was much lighter, being made of sheet metal, and was totally funnel-shaped with a narrow rim and rather wide inner diameter. It appeared to be made of silver.

"You play on this?" I asked, trying not to look too incredulous.

"Yes, it's a new one I got from Joseph Raoux, the horn maker in the *rue de Petit Lion*, when I first got to Paris. He's the most famous maker in France."

"Holy shit!" I burst out in English. "Raoux?!" I had bought a Raoux horn, made in the 1820s, from a Paris dealer in antique instruments on our tour the previous year, and it was displayed prominently on my mantel at home. I hadn't had time to sit down and figure out how to play very much on it yet.

"I mean – Yes... Raoux, I've heard of him," I said in German.

We looked at each other in silence for a few seconds, and then I went on.

"Now, my final bit of evidence for my story," I said, holding up my phone triumphantly.

"What is it?"
"This is a telephone."
"A what?"
"A communication device."
"A what?"
"A little machine that also runs on an electric battery, with which you can talk to people who are far away. It does some other amazing things too. It plays music."
"Like a music box?"
"Not exactly, I'll show you how it works. I won't be able to talk to anyone, because both people need to have one to talk to each other, and there won't be another one for nearly two centuries. But I do have some music and pictures I can show you. If you think about all the machines and devices that have been invented in the past hundred years, just imagine what the next two hundred years will bring, and what will be possible when people figure out how to use the powerful force of electricity."
I was trying to sound impressive, and he was clearly very curious about the shiny little device I was holding. I was praying that it hadn't been damaged the day before in my fall, or by what happened after. I turned it on, and to my immense relief, it appeared to be in good working order. The screen said, "No signal". I went to the web browser and it flashed "You are offline". Subconsciously I must have expected to find a signal in the middle of Paris, proving that the previous twelve hours had been a dream or an elaborate hoax. A wave of disappointment flowed through me as this new reality was once again confirmed. But I did have a lot of things stored on the phone and started with a few photos.
"Here's a picture of my horn section. That's me third from the right."
"A miniature painting!" he said in amazement. "*Scheiße!* It just changed into another painting all by itself! How did you do that?" he gasped.
I was scrolling through photos of the orchestra, my family, the European trip, and others when I stopped at a picture of a street in Paris, full of cars and people.
"What are those?!" he said, in a voice that was getting more and more excited.

"Those are the horseless carriages I mentioned. It has an engine that makes it move forward, and you can drive it wherever you want to go. And the pictures aren't paintings, they are a picture of the scene in front of you as recorded by this device. It gathers the light and sets it down into a picture that looks exactly as you see it with your eyes. It works very much like a human eye. It records what it sees, so that you can look at it again whenever you want. They are called photographs, and the process was invented in the 19th century. It's gotten a lot better since then."

"Is that your instrument? he asked, as I stopped on a close-up of me playing my double horn. "What sort of horn is that?"

"It's the fully chromatic valved horn I was talking about," I explained.

"It looks heavy, what does it sound like?"

"I can show you what it sounds like." I said, saving the video and music for the grand finale.

"You amaze me with all of this!" he said, shaking his head in bewilderment. I started a video of the first movement of the Mozart quintet for horn and strings, K.407, recorded at a recital I gave a couple of months earlier at the university where I teach. It was a pretty good performance, which was why I saved the video.

"This is far too strange!" Carl said in a shaky voice. "The picture is moving, and I can hear the music as though it's in the next room! If I weren't a modern person who is very interested in modern inventions, I would ask if this is some kind of black magic, but these are modern times, and I know that science can explain everything. Tell me how it's done!"

I felt like I was finally making him believe me.

"These are some of the inventions of my time. As you can see, our musical instruments have developed, and we have all sorts of machines and devices like this. Just about everyone has one of these. We are watching and listening to a recording of the sound that took place at a concert in February of 2019, and a moving picture that was recorded at the same time, so it seems like you are watching the concert all over again through a little window."

"And that's you playing the horn," he said. "I recognize you in the picture. It's a beautiful piece. What is it?"

"It's a piece by Mozart."

"These are orchestra horns by Anton Kerner of Vienna[1]. They're the best instruments you can get, and many of the finest players in Germany are playing on them. Show me how you hold your hand in the bell of your horn."

I put my mouthpiece into it and held it as though to play. The bell throat was tiny.

"That's about right," he said. "Let's hear what it sounds like."

The horn seemed to be roughly in E flat, and I started playing up and down the overtone series and playing arpeggios.

"Impressive," he said. "You're really strong, but that mouthpiece will never do. Much too bright and harsh, and much too loud. In a wind section that kind of sound would stick out like a wart on a beautiful girl's nose."

Carl's 18th century German slang and idioms were to be a constant source of entertainment for me the entire time we worked together. He took a small leather bag out of the horn box and looked at two or three mouthpieces.

"Here, try this one." "The inner diameter is about like yours, and the rim should be okay for you."

It was a funnel shaped sheet metal mouthpiece like his, but smaller. I played a few notes, and the sound was soft and dark, with no edge at all until you got rather loud. It had very little resistance, so you had to make the airstream more compact.[2]

"That's more like it! Do you know how to use your hand to correct the open notes that are out of tune?"

I knew the principles of hand stopping as all horn players do, but I had never learned to play the hand horn. I played up the scale and closed the F.

"It doesn't have to be that stopped," he commented. "Just close your hand enough to be in tune, but not so far as to get a nasal sound."

I tried it again and found that you could play a nice, rather open F with relatively little hand movement, once you found the right shape for the hand.

"Great! Most of the closed notes from the middle of the staff upward can be played with a lightly stopped sound like that, so they can match well with the open notes in a melody. Play the scale again, all the way up to the top C this time and open the hand wider for the A above the staff."[3]

I tried it, and it worked fairly well.

"That's right, you'll get used to it. It takes some practice, but someone with an embouchure like yours and good air support will catch on fast. The F sharp is played with the hand more open than usual, sometimes all the way out. Try that."

I did, and that worked well too, but so much hand movement was awkward for me, being used to keeping my hand in the same place in the bell of my modern horn.

"All right. Let's try a duet. We'll do something simple without any chromatic notes."

He chose a couple of pages from a paper folder in the stack of music and put one on each side of a wooden music stand with two desks facing each other. It was all in hand manuscript, and the piece was called *Menuett von Herrn Haudek.*

"Which part do you want me to play?" I asked.

"Well, obviously you are a *primo* horn player, and I am a *secundo*, so you will always play the high part," he said, as though he was explaining some simple concept, such as the use of a fork, to a small child.

We played the duet, which was straightforward. Carl's sound on this diminutive horn was pure and sweet, like a woodwind instrument, with articulations that reminded me of a cello. He was a superb second horn, matching intonation and phrasing perfectly with me. Playing next to him made me immediately scale down my sound and alter the tone color to be more woodwind-like. He was obviously a well-trained and talented player. We finished the piece and he turned to me. We were both evaluating each other's playing, and we were both surprised by what we were hearing.

"So you can play - and very nicely. I can't remember hearing a stronger player since the last time I heard Punto, but you have a lot to learn about how to play the Waldhorn. I think we can get you playing it as well as anyone soon with a little practice. High horn players are in shorter supply than low players at the moment, and there may be some opportunities out there for you. Let's play one more piece, and then go back into the kitchen and talk."

We played an adagio by A. J. Hampel that had a couple of stopped notes in my part, which I played as best I could. Carl's part had several stopped notes in low scale passages, and you could hardly hear the difference between the open and stopped notes. Little did I know that this was the start of something big.

Chapter 5

What's in a name? That which we call a rose by any other name would smell as sweet.
- William Shakespeare, Romeo and Juliet, 1595

After we finished playing, we went back into the kitchen and filled our cups from the pitcher of coffee. I could tell Carl was getting into the idea of not only helping me out of my predicament, but also of showing me how the horn was played in his time. Even at this early date I could see that he was the type who takes matters into his own hands. He saw this as the kind of challenge that most people would think was impossible on every imaginable level. His mind was already working out how to go about the plans he was quickly forming.

"Before we can think about getting you some work, there are some things we'll have to take care of, we'll need to get you some official papers so you can be here legally. We don't want you to end up in the Bastille if you can't prove who you are."

"Yes, we want to avoid that in any case." I said, thinking about all the potential for trouble.

"And we need to decide what your name should be while you're here."

"Do I need a different name?"

"It's best if we make you a Bohemian musician. You'll get the most respect that way, and a lot of help from the network of German speaking musicians, of whom there are many in Paris. No one here would take you seriously as an English or American colonial horn player. Let's see - John Paulson... A good Bohemian version of that might be Johann... um... let me think for a second... Palsa! That's it! From now on you are Herr Johann Palsa! And you were born in Jemeritz in Bohemia. That's a little out of the way place that no one here would question or be able to find out anything about."

"Fine. But if I'm supposed to be Bohemian, how do I explain my English accent when I speak German?"

"Yes, good point. It could be problematic if you talk with other Bohemian musicians, and there are dozens working here in Paris."

He thought for a while.

"Ok, so here's your story; Your family was from Bohemia, and shortly after you were born in... we'll say... 1752 - that would make you just about my age - they emigrated to the New World, as many German speaking families do these days. You grew up in Boston, and spoke English most of the time there, and if your German accent is not convincing for a Bohemian, it's because your parents died when you were very young, and you were raised by a family from... let's see, what does your German sound most like? - rather northern German, I would say... Hannover, that's it! A family from Hannover!

It sounded pretty thin to me, but he knew what would be believable, and keep people from asking a lot of questions.

"So, what we have to do," he continued, "is to get you a couple of letters of recommendation that we can take to a friend of mine in the foreign office and get you the proper traveling papers. If you have a little money to spend, you can get any kind of documentation you need here."

"By bribing people?" I asked. "We can't get away with that where I come from."

"That's the only way to get things accomplished here, whether your business is legitimate or not. The people who help you get the right papers aren't very concerned about whether you're telling the truth or not, if you can pay for it. Your story is mostly true anyway, you came here from America, and want to work, just like all the other foreign musicians in the city; nothing unusual about that. We just need to do it in a way that will get you accepted and respected quickly.

The only people who saw you so far are the Stamitz brothers, Baer, and Wendling and his family. I can now report to all of them that you're feeling better and remember exactly what happened. I'll go out this afternoon and get you some clothes that will make you look like a German musician, and we can tell them we located your baggage and had it brought here. Herr and Frau Wendling will be away for a few more days, so we have plenty of uninterrupted time to do everything we need to do."

"I'm leaving everything in your capable hands," I said, "but there is one thing I think we should absolutely keep to ourselves. All the things I've told you about my time, the inventions and the developments, and the music should stay confidential between the two of us."

"No problem there," he replied. I'm not ready to be locked up as a lunatic for talking about meeting someone from the 21st century. I'm still not even sure I'm not dreaming all this, so let's just say you're a horn player who has arrived in Paris, and I'm helping you to get on your feet. No one needs to know what we might talk about on our own time."

This was a big relief, since I was starting to think about the implications of letting out information about the future, and how that could change the course of history. I needed to do what I had done to convince Carl and gain his confidence, but I decided at that point that I would not divulge anything about my situation to anyone other than him. If I needed to spend the rest of my life here, I needed to become an 18th century person in every way, and as soon as possible to blend into their world and stay unobtrusive.

Chapter 6

Beware of all enterprises that require new clothes.
- Henry David Thoreau, Walden, 1854

Carl went out for a couple of hours, during which time the doctor stopped around and looked me over again. I couldn't understand or speak to him, but Katherina was able to convince him that I still didn't want him to draw any blood. He left shaking his head, certain that I didn't know what was good for me, and I limped back into the music room, where I played a while on Carl's horn and looked through his music again. The books were mostly duets, and about half of them were hand-written. The printed ones were by composers I didn't know, and many were printed in London and Paris. The majority were simple open-note pieces, but some of the hand-written music, which seemed to be compositions and arrangements of his own, looked more difficult and more interesting musically.

Then I became curious about the house itself and how the family lived and started looking around. By modern standards, there wasn't very much in the house. The room where I had slept had only a bed, a wooden bench, and a chest with drawers and a compartment with a door, on top of which sat a bowl and pitcher. The window, which looked straight out at the next house had embroidered linen curtains, and the floor was smooth but unfinished wood. Katherina was working in the kitchen, and I went in to see what it looked like. The open hearth, in which a wood fire burned, made the kitchen the warmest room in the house. It smelled smoky and the ceiling was quite black.

A pot about a foot in diameter and just as tall made of copper was simmering over the fire in the hearth, and in it was a delicious smelling soup she was making for supper. She was very talkative, and within twenty minutes, I knew that she was born in Mannheim, and had been working for the Wendlings for about five years and traveled with them wherever they went. I learned that Elisabeth was an aspiring opera singer, like her mother, and would continue her studies when they returned to Mannheim, which they would do in the spring. I heard all about how the Wendling and Türrschmidt families had known each other for years, and how Carl had shown up on their doorstep a few months earlier with a letter from his father, and they had taken him in. She also explained that Herr Wendling, who was about fifty years old, was one of the most famous flute players in the world, and his wife, Dorothea was a famous opera singer.

After hearing the entire history of the family and their travels in France, England, and Germany, I left her to her work and continued to explore the house. The dining room where we had eaten breakfast had a nicely made wooden table and several chairs. The only other piece of furniture in the room was a sideboard with shelves that held wooden serving boards, bowls and cups, and a box full of silver spoons, knives, and forks. I have to admit I was very curious about everything and looked in the drawers of the sideboard, which contained tablecloths and linens, a corkscrew, and a few other obviously handmade kitchen implements, some of which I didn't recognize.

The place wasn't terribly clean, though as I discovered later it was one of the cleanest houses I was to see for a very long time, including the houses of nobility and royalty. I asked Katherina where the bathroom was, using again a word that wouldn't enter her language until the 19th century and got a blank look in return. After explaining in much more detail than was comfortable what I meant, she showed me a pot in the chest in my room, and it was at that point that I discovered one of the most disappointing aspects of living in the 18th century. The bathroom and the toilet had not been invented yet, and you had to use a pot that sat in your bedroom until a servant took it out and emptied it into a pit behind the house. All houses had this method of getting rid of waste, and in a crowded city like Paris, it meant that every street in the city had an odor that made a New York subway station smell like a rose garden by comparison. Servants who were too lazy to take the pot around to the back of the house often emptied them out of the nearest window, and only occasionally looked to see if anyone was standing under the window. This was one of several revelations I experienced in the first couple of days of my adventure. The next happened a few minutes later when a boy showed up at the door with a pole across his shoulders with a bucket of water on each end.

"Who was that?" I asked Katherina.

"The water carrier, of course."

"Where does he get the water?"

"From the river I suppose. I've never asked him."

"Is that where you get all of your water? Someone delivers it in buckets?"

"Where else would we get it?" she asked, giving me an odd look.

I was saved from showing even more of my ignorance of the simplest things of daily life by Carl's reappearance. He was soaking wet, since it had rained while he was out; and not a nice summer rain, but a cold dreary rain, but it didn't seem to concern him at all. He was carrying two packages wrapped in brown cloth that he put down on the table, and as soon as Katherina had gone back into the kitchen, he started to untie them.

"Since you are just about my size, it was easy to pick out some clothes and shoes for you at a second-hand shop. Here, go and try these on."

Carl was built just about like me, but an inch or so shorter, and it was then that it occurred to me that he was the tallest person I had yet seen. I had absolutely no idea what to do with the clothes he took out of the package, and he was highly amused that he had to show me how to get dressed. The stockings were made of white silk, and had to go on first, because the pants had to go below the knee and cover the top of the stockings so that no bare leg was visible. The pants had a button up fly. While I was putting these on, he was looking curiously at my Fruit of the Loom underwear and inspecting my tux shirt and pants that I had taken off.

"What's this material?" he asked, feeling the cloth of my pants.

"It's probably a cotton-polyester blend," I said, knowing full well that it meant nothing to him. "It never needs ironing."

"Wherever you really come from is a very curious place," he said, helping me put on my new shirt, which had ruffles on the front. Then came a vest, or waistcoat, which I thought was way too long, but he assured me was very much in style in Paris at the moment, and then a green outer coat that came down almost to my knees.

"There. Now you can go out in public without attracting too much attention. We'll have to make sure you wear a hat until that ridiculous haircut of yours grows out a bit."

Carl's hair, as with most everyone else I had seen, was long, and pulled back in a short ponytail in the back. It was a very simple system, and almost maintenance-free, since all you had to do when it got too long was to cut off an inch or two from the end of the ponytail.

I looked in a foggy mirror on the wall and burst out laughing.

"I look absolutely ridiculous!"

"No, - you have now ceased looking ridiculous, and are starting to look normal."

"I have to pee in a pot in my room, and wear these ludicrous clothes," I thought. "What next?"

These were, of course, the tip of the iceberg in my transition into 18th century life.

On closer inspection, the clothes were definitely second hand, showing signs of wear and an unpleasant musty smell, and it wasn't too many minutes later that I discovered they were infested with fleas. This turned out to be a regular way of life for everyone of all levels of society. Every person and animal, and all clothing, bedding etc. had fleas and bedbugs.

I still wasn't feeling my best, but I was very curious about what was out there in the city, and since Carl thought it was safe for me to appear in public, we went out to see the sights. Though my ankle was still sore, and the black leather shoes with brass buckles on top didn't fit very well, I thought I could walk a little, and was so absorbed by everything I was seeing, that soon I totally forgot about the discomfort and pain.

Chapter 7

... when good Americans die, they go to Paris.
- Oscar Wilde, A Woman of No Importance, 1893

I had only a quick glimpse of the streets the night before, and I had been in no condition to really appreciate my surroundings. Now with fully functioning faculties, the scene around me was absolutely mind numbing. The streets were filthy, the wooden houses were in various states of disrepair, and there were tattered looking people and animals everywhere. It must have been an extremely interesting city for dogs, because the array of smells was vast. With every step some new smell accosted the nose, a few of them were interesting and bordering on pleasant, but the vast majority were downright foul and indicative of filth, waste, and decay. It hit my nose like a sledgehammer that day, and a year or two later I could walk the streets of Paris without noticing it at all.

Carl spoke French well. Though German was his mother tongue, he had been around nobility who had spoken French for most of his life, and was quite comfortable in the city, though he had only been in Paris for a few months.

"We'll have to get you some French language lessons," he said. "Yet another reason to be from the American colonies. There you would have spoken only English and German and would have a good excuse for being a well-educated person who doesn't know French. We'll get you equipped linguistically in no time".

We walked for quite a while and looked in at shops of various sorts, eating and drinking houses, and other businesses before it started to get dark. We met with beggars on just about every corner, and my impression was that the art of panhandling hasn't changed a bit over time. It was probably practiced in the same way in ancient Rome and Athens.

The entire time we talked about music, and the orchestra scene in Paris and at the courts of Germany. Carl had grown up studying horn with his father and had gotten plenty of experience in the Thurn und Taxis court orchestra in Regensburg, where the daily work involved accompanying opera, playing wind sextet music for dinners and other events, both indoors and out, and concerts with the full orchestra of twenty musicians. He had come to Paris on the recommendation of some of the other German musicians who had been there and was hoping to join a private orchestra that was being formed by a wealthy prince.

We found our way back to the Wendlings' house, where Elisabeth, Katherina, and Hannes were already sitting down to an evening meal. Carl and Anton Stamitz, who were violinists and composers, had also dropped in to see what had become of me, and we all sat around the table together.

This being a German household, we ate in the German style of the time, and had the same dense bread, beer, cheese, and sausage, as we did at breakfast, with the addition of a very pathetic looking cucumber, off which we all cut pieces. As at breakfast each person had their own wooden board instead of a plate. Carl explained that all my things had been brought to the house from where I had been staying, and that I was going to stay with them for a while, since I was in Paris looking for work, and that his father had known my family before they had gone to America, so it was all perfectly okay. Carl was enjoying the complicated story of my life that he was weaving together on the spot, and they seemed to accept it without too many questions. I was amazed at this, but Carl explained later that the musical world was a small one, and it wouldn't be unusual at all for his family to know mine. If you met any musician for the first time, within five minutes you could come up with a long list of people who you both knew and had worked with.

After supper we played horn duets a little while longer, and then retired to our separate rooms for the night. This was the end of my first day in this world, and alone in my room, the weirdness of my situation really started to hit me. Was this permanent? Had I been hit by a car and killed, and ended up here? If I was still alive, what had happened to the "me" in the 21st century? Would I ever go back? I fell asleep thinking about what my friends had thought when I disappeared before their eyes - or had it looked that way to them? And what had they told my family, and what were they thinking? Were they waiting for the return of my dead body, or were they wondering where I had gone? What had really happened at that moment? As would happen for years to come, the day had been filled with learning about this new world and how to navigate it, and the nights consisted of missing Beth and our kids, Ana and Chris, and thinking wild and frightening thoughts about what was happening to me, and them, and why.

Chapter 8

In Paris they just simply opened their eyes and stared when we spoke to them in French; we never did succeed in making those idiots understand their own language.
- Mark Twain, The Innocents Abroad, 1869

The next day, after the same type of breakfast as the day before, we went out again, but this time on serious business. Even though Carl had only been in Paris a relatively short time, he seemed to have made a number of friends. Our first stop was at an office, or at least he called it an office - it looked like an ordinary house to me - where we sat in a dusty sitting room and waited a few minutes before being led into another room, where we met with an older gentleman in a powdered wig.

"This guy is right out of the 1750s," Carl said, with a knowing look, and I looked back as though I understood, but I had no idea what he was talking about. Apparently powdered wigs were on their way out of style for daily use at this point.

After a little conversation, he and Carl worked together on a letter which he stamped at the bottom with a wax seal. Carl paid him some money, and after a little more friendly conversation and a cup of lukewarm weak tea, we left.

"So, what exactly just happened?" I asked, as we left the house.

"I just paid one *livre* for a document certifying that you are Monsieur Johann Palsa, a Bohemian lately arrived from the American colonies, and a qualified professional musician who has been recommended by Monsieur Johann Wendling, the well-known musician who resides in the rue Chantre. See the official notary seal at the bottom?"

"But Wendling doesn't know he just recommended me."

"Oh, he will after I explain everything to him. We'll get him to write the letter referred to here. The man we just saw was a notary, and he put his seal on this letter stating that everything in it was true, so we shouldn't have any trouble. Of course, he has no idea if it's true, but I paid him, so it's okay."

We then went to another house that looked just a bit more business-like and sat down in another musty smelling sitting room.

Carl told me we were about to see someone who he knew in the foreign registration office, who would take care of papers that I would need to travel or prove who I was. After a while we were ushered into the presence of a young man in a dull red waistcoat who offered us some tea that was even worse than the tea in the previous place.

Carl began to explain what we needed and showed him the notarized letter. After a while the red-coated man turned to me and spoke in almost unintelligible English.

"And you confirm that your name is Johann Palsa, and that you were born in Jemeritz in Bohemia in 1752?"

"Yes. Absolutely," I said.

"And the day and month of your birth?"

Without thinking, I said; "The 20th of June." which was my birthday.

"Good. June, 20^{th,} 1752," he said while writing. "And you affirm that you have lived in the American colonies until coming to Paris on October 24th of this year, one week ago?"

"I do."

"Well, I think everything is in order, Mr. Palsa, and we will draw up your papers."

He called in a clerk, and with Carl's help, he dictated a document, which the clerk wrote out in a fancy script. These were my official French government papers allowing me to live and work in France and to leave the country and return whenever I pleased. A few minutes, and one more livre out of Carl's purse later, I left the office with my new identity, and all the documentation I needed to prove it.

We walked toward the rue Chantre again and arrived back at the Wendlings' house with Carl talking the whole way about his youth in Wallerstein, and the high quality of the orchestra there. Carl's father, Johann Türrschmidt, had come to play in the Wallerstein orchestra in 1752, the year before Carl was born, and worked there until Carl was thirteen. That year the old count of Oettingen-Wallerstein died, and music stopped at the court. Many of the musicians still officially remained in the Wallerstein service but were loaned out to other orchestras. Johann Türrschmidt was loaned to the Thurn und Taxis orchestra in Regensburg and was still working there. The new ruler of the Oettingen-Wallerstein court was the old count's son Kraft-

Ernst, who had not yet come of age. He would not take full control until he turned twenty-five, and until then his mother was ruling as regent. There was some talk of his interest in starting musical performances at the court again when he did assume rule of the family and lands, and the Wallerstein musicians and their families were looking forward to the time when the orchestra would return home and start playing again.

The rest of the day we spent at home, and as soon as we arrived, we had some of the soup Katerina had made the day before. I wondered as we were eating it where it had been stored since I had seen it cooking the day before but didn't ask.

I had been feeling much better on this, my second full day here, but shortly after we ate, I started having stomach cramps, and soon my body decided it was time to get rid of whatever was in the soup. I couldn't remember diarrhea of that magnitude since a trip to Mexico a few years before. It occurred to me at that point that it was not only incredibly filthy here, but there was a whole new set of germs to get used to in the 18th century. I didn't realize that I was in for a few weeks of off and on bouts that would make me absolutely miserable for a couple of days at a time.

Toilet paper hadn't come into its own as a concept yet, so newspapers and old books were kept around for the purpose. Carl had an old, dog-eared copy of a French language tutor for Germans, and with this, I was able to deal with dozens of trips to my chamber pot, and at the same time, to start my study of French. I would tear out a page, memorize the vocabulary words or verb tenses, and then put it behind me, so to speak.

It was also on this particular afternoon that my serious horn lessons started.

Chapter 9

A chapter of technical information about the natural horn. Essential for the horn player, less so for the non-horn playing reader.

> *Limited, so to speak, to its open sounding length, the horn produces only the following natural sounds: tonic, median, dominant, minor seventh, and major ninth, these last two doubled at the octave, and the others tripled or quadrupled. These are also virtually the only notes used in orchestral writing.*
> *- L.F. Dauprat, Méthode de Cor-alto et Cor-basse, 1824*

Most horn players know how the horn was played in earlier times, using different crooks and hand stopping, but the full impact of what that means doesn't hit you until you have to do it yourself. As modern players, many of us get used to playing the double horn placing pitches more by feel than hearing them in the key of the piece, though we should know how our note functions as part of the harmony. To adapt to the horn of the 18th century, it was absolutely necessary to start hearing notes as members of the key in which you are playing, and of the overtone series of the crook on which you are playing. We played duets out of Carl's duet books, and he quickly learned that I could find pitches with total accuracy in F horn, but the further we got from the F crook, the more difficult it was for me to hear the pitches. As we played, we continually changed crooks to get me used to changing my pitch center on short notice, as you have to do when going from one aria to the next in an opera, for example.

The pieces we played for the next few days were simple duets, with only a few closed notes. In these we worked to play perfect intervals with each other, and I got to know which way each of the overtones needs to be bent, or "lipped" to be in tune. In the playing of the simple intervals of orchestra parts and duets, you just get used to the fact that first line E is too low, fourth line D is too high, and fourth space E is too low, etc. Here are the intonation tendencies of the overtones relative to equal temperament.

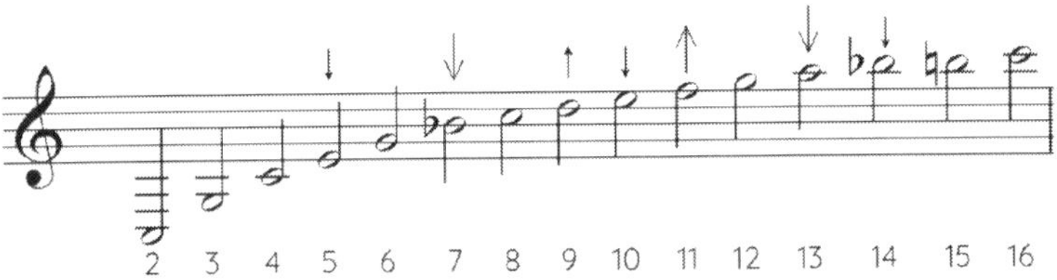

The out of tune overtones can be fixed with the embouchure and by opening or closing the hand more or less. After you get used to fixing each one of the out of tune notes, you work with your partner to play those intervals in tune on each of the crooks. At first, when we would play in a new key, we would play the following notes together to tune the intervals:

After I started to know the horn better and got used to which crooks and couplers to put together, and which tuning bits to use to get the pitch exactly right, I was able to get into whichever key we needed quickly, and we could start a piece without any testing of notes beforehand. You start to get the feel of each crook in your brain, just as we have the feel of the modern double horn programmed in so we can find notes out of nowhere.

The keys you could put together using the crooks and couplers for Carl's horns included Bb alto, A, G, F, E, Eb, D, low C, and low Bb. There were three terminal crooks (those with mouthpipes) for Bb, A, and G, three single coil couplers of different lengths, two double coil couplers, one triple coiled coupler, and several tuning bits that you could add for fine tuning, since the horns didn't have tuning slides. By using different combinations of the crooks, couplers, and bits, you could get to just about any key at any pitch level, though when crooked in some keys, the instrument was a bit awkward to hold.

This flexibility of pitch level was important, because if you went to another city, or even to another orchestra in the same city, you might have to play as much as a half step higher or lower than you were used to. There was no absolute standard of pitch anywhere, and it seemed to be the wind instrument makers and organ makers who set the standards in any given city and kept them consistent. Herr Wendling had several middle sections of different lengths for his flutes to deal with this problem. All the woodwind players seemed to be constantly working with reeds or putting wax in holes to tune their instruments, and everyone complained about the pitch all the time in every group we ever played with. For the horn players it was easy; put the parts together to get the right length of horn, and you are immediately in business.

These Anton Kerner horns from Vienna were state-of-the art orchestra horns, which Carl referred to as *Inventionshorns*, because they had crooks. Most horn players were still playing on fixed pitch horns without crooks in 1770, which meant that you, or the orchestra that employed you, had to own several pairs of horns in different keys, and if they weren't exactly in tune, you just had to make them play in tune with tuning bits or small single coiled "pigtail crooks" and by bending the pitch up or down.

Crooks were an important invention, because they eliminated the need for several horns, and made fine tuning easier in an orchestral setting, but soloists still preferred the stability, responsiveness and lightness of a fixed pitch horn. While soloists and orchestra players often played on different instruments, there were also two distinct styles of playing technique. The soloist held the hand in the bell and did sophisticated chromatic hand stopping, while the orchestra player played mostly with the hand out of the bell and did a lot of lipping of the overtones that needed to be corrected. This was often the case, but not by any means standardized, and everywhere you went the horn was played differently. Carl and a few others of the newer generation played almost exclusively with the hand in the bell, both as soloists and in the orchestra.

As we played duets, I noticed a few things happening to my playing. I was scaling down the airstream from that of a big orchestra player of the 21st century to that of an 18th century player who plays in small groups for small audiences in small rooms. To play in the upper range of these horns, the air had to be fast, but the overall volume of air was smaller, and therefore the sound was smaller and more compact. Over the next days and weeks, I began getting used to how close together the notes are between the 8th and about the

24th partials of the overtone series and got better at playing melodies with moving notes within that range. I was starting to take to the small first horn mouthpiece, and to get the singing woodwind-like sound that matched Carl, but I wasn't totally comfortable with the rim on the mouthpiece he had given me, and I needed to either get used to it or find another.

Mouthpieces in the 18th century were quite simple in their form. Instead of having a cup, throat and backbore like a modern mouthpiece, the early horn mouthpiece is a funnel or cone that continues to get smaller right to the end. The body is constructed of sheet metal, either brass or silver, and the rim is a separate piece soldered to the body. There is seldom an extra shank or sleeve over the end, because it usually goes into a rather small inlet in the mouthpipe of the crook. Players in the 21st century are used to thinking about high and low horn mouthpieces in terms of the depth of the cup and the size of the throat, but in early mouthpieces, the main thing that makes it more suited to high or low playing is the inner diameter of the rim. The same funnel shaped body can be cut off shorter or longer to make it a high or low horn mouthpiece. Rims varied greatly in their width and shape, but most often they were slightly flatter than modern rims and the inner edge was a bit sharper, which speeds up the response. As I found out when playing in an 18th century wind section, these mouthpieces made it easy to blend with the other winds, and the soft, round tone quality made it clear why the horn was always associated with the woodwinds from their first introduction into the orchestra.

Carl suggested we go to Joseph Raoux's shop and have a comfortable mouthpiece made for me. He was very interested in the design of the horn and mouthpiece and was always thinking about how the instrument could be improved. A lot was happening at this point in the history of the horn. Crooks were beginning to make it possible to play in all keys easily and to do fine tuning. Hand stopping, which was practiced in a rudimentary way by the previous generation, of which Carl's father was an important figure, was now becoming quite sophisticated, and was beginning to open up a whole new world of solo and chamber music to the horn.

I was quickly learning that Carl was a founding member of this new generation of horn players, led by Giovanni Punto and a few others, that was changing the way the horn was played, making it into a viable solo instrument, as well as contributing to making it an equal member of the wind section of the orchestra and a refined chamber instrument. In their hands, the technique of hand stopping was changing from a way to play certain notes of the overtone series in tune, and adding the occasional neighbor note, to a sophisticated method of playing the horn completely chromatically through the better part of its range.

Chapter 10

...music washes away from the soul the dust of everyday life...

Over the next few days I was just about as sick as a person can be and still function at all, but nonetheless we played horn duets when I was feeling up to it. I spent a lot of time in bed with a fever, and it got so bad that they sent for the doctor again. He gave me a truly nasty tasting mixture that made things even worse. I vomited and had stomach cramps until the stuff was completely out of my system, and at that point I vowed I would never consult a doctor again.

I also decided that if I was going to live through this, I needed to get used to the germs of the 18th century slowly, so I asked Katherina to boil water for me every morning for making coffee, and to bring all food to a boil that had been cooked the day before. At the end of that first week things started getting better and it was beginning to look as though I was going to live. We played a lot of horn, but I couldn't leave the house during that time, so it was a great relief when I finally felt well enough to go out and about again.

My first real trip out into the social life of Paris happened about a week and a half into my stay there. Carl proposed that we go to a concert at the Tuilleries Palace given by the *Concert Spirituel* orchestra. This concert series was one of the most respected in the city. It took place by royal permission during religious holidays and other times when the opera and other theaters weren't allowed to give performances.

The orchestra was made up of the best musicians in Paris, and many of them were from German speaking countries. They were either visiting Paris trying to get their music played and published, or had decided to settle there permanently, since there was more money to be made there than by being a member of a court orchestra elsewhere. Success, of course, was dependent on being a top-quality musician or composer, having good connections, and being good at marketing yourself. There were a lot of people who came to Paris and didn't do well for any number of reasons and had to go back to their court orchestras empty handed. It seems like everyone had to go there at some point to make a reputation, and playing at the *Concert Spirituel* was at the top of the business, much like playing at Carnegie Hall in modern times.

We made our way through the streets, most of which were frighteningly dark and narrow, and every time a coach came rumbling through the street, Carl would pull me into a doorway to keep me from getting run over. It was a dangerous business walking the streets of Paris at night, but after you got the ground rules down, and knew what to watch out for it was only moderately life threatening, but you didn't want to do alone if you could help it.

A couple of reasonably well-dressed guys didn't attract too much attention in the streets, though the better dressed you were, the more of a target you were for beggars and pickpockets. Poorly dressed people were subjected to all sorts of abuse, and the lack of simple human respect I saw in the way the poor were treated in that city while I lived there can't be described. Musicians were somewhere in the middle of the hierarchy when it came to dress, which made them too well dressed be constantly taken advantage of and abused, but not the highest priority for beggars and criminals.

We got to the palace and found the room called the *Salle des Suisses* well before the concert was scheduled to start and Carl paid five *sous* each for us to get in. A sou was a small coin, 1/20th of a livre, and three of them was enough to buy a good meal at a restaurant in Paris. The room was ornately decorated, mostly made of wood with painted panels and trim covered in gold paint or gold leaf. There were tapestries on the walls, and the perimeter was lined with furniture of an artistic and rich design. The room wasn't overly large, and the hard, straight backed wooden chairs that had been brought in for the audience seated about three hundred people.

The audience was loud before the performance, but I was sure things would quiet down when the concert started. As the performers came into the room, there was clapping and enthusiastic cheers, but to my surprise the pre-concert level of noise hardly subsided as the performers took their places to start the concert. They were just as loud and obnoxious as ever, and it wasn't until the music actually started that it quieted down a little, though throughout the concert people continued to talk. This was quite a refined, upper-class

Parisian audience, and therefore not the loudest and rudest I would encounter by a long shot.

To my modern eyes, the orchestra was small. The strings consisted of eight first and seven second violins, three violas, four cellos, and two double basses. The wind section was made up of two oboes, one of whom doubled on flute, two clarinets, two horns and three bassoons. The principal oboist's name was Besozzi, a popular soloist with the orchestra, and one of the clarinets I recognized as Johann Baer who I had met on the night of my bizarre arrival. The horn players had fixed pitch horns that sounded like they were about in F. There was also a harpsichordist who sat in the middle of the orchestra with his back to the audience.

The first and second violins sat facing each other on either side of the harpsichord, with the other strings crowded around the keyboard, and the winds behind in a sort of semi-circle. The two Stamitz brothers were in the string section, Carl playing principal second violin, and Anton as first violist. This, as I found out later, was one of the largest, and best orchestras in Europe, though at the time I thought it was rather ragged, not terribly well in tune, and obviously under-rehearsed. You could tell they were skillful, and very musical players, but the attitude seemed rather casual. In my own time, the whole thing would have been pretty good for a first reading at an early morning rehearsal after a long summer vacation in terms of precision.

The bassoons seemed to be playing the bass line along with the cellos and basses for most of the concert, which made things rather bass heavy. The violas appeared to be playing the bass line an octave up for the most part. It was also unclear who was actually leading the orchestra. It appeared to be a joint effort between the concertmaster and the harpsichordist, but there didn't seem to be very much rhyme or reason to it other than that the concertmaster started every piece, and the harpsichordist was responsible for giving cues and tempo changes, and leading recitatives in the opera arias.

The first piece was a symphony by Toeschi, a Mannheim composer, in which everyone played. It was a pleasant little piece in four movements, and the oboes and horns played pretty much the whole time making the texture a bit thick. The horns didn't play in the second movement, in which the second oboist was the soloist on the one keyed flute like the ones I had seen at the Wendlings' house. That movement, an andante in 3/8 time, was scored for flute and strings only, and there were some nice melodies for the flute, which he played with the greatest of expression, but not always the greatest of intonation. The thing that hit my ear as particularly strange that day were the trills, which were all a little too wide and appeared not to conform exactly to the key of the piece, but fortunately there were only a few of them. At that point I hadn't gotten used to the various quirks of the woodwinds of the time. These wide woodwind trills were part of the technique and personality of the woodwinds, and of the flute in particular. I learned to enjoy them as I learned about the instruments and music making of the time.

The minuet had a nice oboe and bassoon duet in the trio section, which Besozzi and the bassoonist played beautifully. Along with the flute solo, it was some of the best woodwind playing of the concert. The finale was a fast 6/8 in which the horns got a couple of hunting horn melodies to play, which was the only time during the evening that they played anything resembling a tune.

After the symphony there were a couple of recitatives and arias from operas that everyone in the room seemed to know but me. The soprano sang with a pleasant, but rather small voice with a subtle vibrato, though not nearly as much as a modern opera singer.

Next came a violin concerto composed and played by the concertmaster, which was performed with the utmost reckless abandon in the fast outer movements. He could certainly get around on the violin, but I thought it a bit overdone and showy for the kind of piece it was. His name was Nicholas Capron, and Carl assured me that he was not only the leader of the *Concert Spirituel* orchestra, but also one of the finest soloists in Paris. How the players in the orchestra followed him, especially in the middle movement, which was incredibly slow and highly ornamented, was a total mystery to me, but somehow they were able to follow him on nearly every rubato and highly ornamented cadence.

The next piece was a motet sung by a chorus of eight voices accompanied by the strings and continuo section, minus the bassoons. The strings appeared to be simply doubling the vocal lines and didn't have independent parts of their own. It sounded rather like 17th century sacred music, and out of place in this very classical orchestra program. Both horn players were playing viola on this piece. All the pieces and composer's names were announced by the performers, and this one was by Giroust.

Following the motet, there was a set of short solo pieces on the organ played by a Monsieur Charpentier, during which the orchestra left the room. After that, Carl and Anton Stamitz and a cellist played a quartet with the harpsichordist by J. C. Bach. The harpsichord part was as soloistic as the violin part and sounded like it would have worked better on a piano. This was, without a doubt, the most well-rehearsed piece on the program. After the concert we heard from the players that this quartet had been played a couple of times on this series already, and they had performed it elsewhere several times as well. All the musicians in the orchestra gave the impression of being good readers, but this piece and the violin concerto showed that many of them were also very virtuosic, if a bit rough around the edges.

It was an interesting concert, and my introduction to concert life in the 18th century, with its virtuoso players and ragged performances, and hundreds of different composers writing new music all the time, and almost never playing a new piece more than a few times.

We talked to some of the players after the concert; mostly to the horns and other winds. The horn players' names were Dargent, a Frenchman, and Mozer, who was German, and therefore I could talk to him in something other than the simplest broken French. They both played regularly with the orchestras of the *Paris Opera* and *Opera Comique* and did *Concert Spirituel* performances when the theaters were closed. They were horn players of the old school, who played without the hand in the bell, and though they played well, it was clear they were not part of the new innovative generation of which Carl seemed to be at the forefront. They were working horn players who played a performance almost every night and made a fairly decent living doing it.

Carl introduced me to them and to the other musicians as a Bohemian horn player newly arrived in Paris and looking for work. He was getting good at telling my story, and each time would embellish it a little more. This time he told them I had studied with Joseph

Matiegka, a famous horn teacher in Prague. Mozer was visibly impressed by this, and I was getting a little nervous that he would start asking questions that I couldn't answer. We managed to get the conversation off in another direction before it got uncomfortable, but later I asked Carl if we could write down some of the important things I needed to know about my newly invented history so I could talk intelligently about myself and be consistent with what he was telling everyone.

I was not only intrigued by the concert, but it was nice to hear a live performance of music of any kind. It occurred to me that day, as we were walking home, that one was not surrounded by recorded music all day as we are in the 21st century. If anything musical was happening, it was being sung or played by real people at that moment. If you walked past a tavern or inn, you often heard music being sung, or someone playing an instrument. Everyone seemed to whistle a tune in the streets or sing, because if you didn't, there was no music. In houses, people played and sang, and since it took skill that had to be acquired, music wasn't taken for granted. Even the very wealthy who could afford to hire the best musicians seemed to take pride in the music and put great value on it.

We walked back home through the pitch-black streets, having only a bit of faint light that came out of a window here and there to know where we were. It was a perilous trip, filled with near misses by recklessly driven horse-drawn vehicles, and the fancier the carriage, the faster it went, and the less it seemed to care who was in its way. It was raining and cold, and I was beginning to learn that your average 18th century person was used to getting uncomfortably wet and cold if they had to go out when it was raining. No thoughts of raincoats or umbrellas for the common people here. We didn't talk on the way home, since we were dodging carriages and walking against the wind, but we talked over the concert and the orchestra in great detail after we arrived home. Katherina made us a pot of hot coffee and some bread and soft cheese and we hung our coats and waistcoats by the kitchen fire to dry, but there was little chance of them being dry by the next day. The feeling of putting on slightly wet clothes the day after getting caught in the rain eventually became a familiar one, but was extremely irksome on the following morning, when we were both still chilled and damp.

Chapter 11
A visit to Joseph Raoux's workshop, and a lot of shop talk[4]

> *The Mouth-pieces commonly used are made of Brass, some are made of Silver, and some of Ivory, in the tone of which there is little material difference; but Silver I would give the preference to, as Brass, when first you apply it to your lips, has a disagreeable taste, and Ivory often splits, but Silver is generally sweet and wholesome.*
>
> *- New Instructions for the French-Horn, London, ca. 1770*

The next morning Carl and I played more duets, and I continued my serious study of the natural horn. I was getting more adventurous with my hand technique, and the chromatic notes were beginning to come easier and match better with the open notes. I was also getting more used to dancing lightly over the upper overtones, playing lyrical melodies and agile fast scale passages over Carl's accompaniments. I was doing my best to adapt to him in my sound, articulations, and the vocal qualities of his playing, and not to influence his playing with my modern concepts. This was his musical world, in which I was a guest, and it was my job to learn from him how to fit in.

We were starting to think together musically and play together comfortably, with perfect intonation and a similar concept of phrasing. So far, from Carl's playing, and what I had heard in the single concert I had seen, I was getting the impression that music was much more flexible here than in my time. There was always time to take your time if you were enjoying the phrase you were playing, or were arriving at a high point, or coming to a cadence. On the other hand, reckless abandon is the only way to describe most of their fast movements. At times the goal seemed to be to go so fast that the piece was on the edge of disaster. We had read a lot of different pieces, but on this morning we concentrated on a duo for flutes by Carl Stamitz that Carl Türrschmidt had adapted for horns but hadn't had the opportunity to play with anyone yet. As we were learning the piece together, and beginning to make it sound rather respectable, I could see that Carl was starting to form some ideas about the possibilities for us as a duo.

We decided it was time to find a mouthpiece for me that was more comfortable, and after our mid-day meal, we took a walk into the city and found the workshop of Joseph Raoux. The house, in the rue de Petit Lion, was normal looking from the outside, but the inside was fascinating. The business consisted of two large rooms on the main floor and living quarters on the floor above. It was filled with heavy workbenches, anvils mounted on blocks of wood, a large forge with a fire burning in it, large and small bench vises, sheets of brass, and important looking pieces of equipment. The walls were lined with rows of hand tools, including hammers, files, burnishers, shears, saws, and other interesting implements. In one corner there was a lathe that was powered by a large flywheel that was set in motion by foot pedals, like an old-fashioned sewing machine, and a winch and chain stretched over a long table for drawing tubes through dies.

The most fascinating part was how the shop and all its benches were arranged to take advantage of the natural light that came in through large windows. That was absolutely necessary, since there would only have been oil lamps or candles for artificial lighting, which wouldn't have been enough to do fine work. For that reason, they started work as soon as there was enough sunlight and kept working until it ran out.

That day, Joseph's son, Lucien-Joseph was in the shop. He was apprenticing at another shop at this point, but the ultimate plan was that father and son would join forces in a few years to establish a larger shop. There was one other worker, whose name was Michel, and a young apprentice, named Jean-Pierre, who was about sixteen. Jean-Pierre was polishing a horn bell that was clamped to a wooden board held fast in a vise. He was using a flat stick covered with cloth that he dipped from time to time in a pan of pumice and water, or maybe some kind of oil, and after that he would rub the surface of the metal with a highly polished steel burnisher to give it its final finish. I was surprised by the fine finish this produced. Michel was making tubes by wrapping strips of sheet brass around a steel rod and closing the seam with a wooden mallet. We were there for a couple of hours, during which time he made a whole box of tubes, working non-stop.

Joseph was a short muscular man of about forty-five with black hair and a well-trimmed mustache. A well-shaven man in the 18th

century shaved every few days, and unless this was the day, he would have some serious stubble on his face. Carl, who he already knew from a couple of previous visits, introduced me, and told him we would like to have a high horn mouthpiece made with a rim like the one on my Holton Farkas DC. I handed him my mouthpiece and he looked at it curiously for a while.

"Some kind of *Cor de Chasse* mouthpiece made for a trumpet player?"

"No, it's a horn mouthpiece made by a maker in the English colonies of America," Carl explained.

"Oh, for military music – fifes and drums, and that sort of thing," said Joseph. "I've heard they use horns and trumpets in their military bands. Well, we can certainly make a rim like that for one of the high horn mouthpiece bodies that we have already prepared, and we'll have your friend Monsieur Palsa sounding like Punto in no time. By the way, what's this American mouthpiece made of? Gold?"

"No," Carl replied. "Monsieur Palsa tells me that it's made of brass and coated with gold by a process used by instrument makers in the colonies."

Raoux looked at it closely again.

"I'd love to watch them do it. It's incredibly even. Looks like it wears well too."

Carl then showed him the high horn mouthpiece of his that I had been playing on, and Raoux took a caliper off the wall and measured it.

"The inner diameter of this one is a good size for a high horn player, about 5½ *pounces*. Your American mouthpiece is about 6 ½, or about halfway between normal high and low dimensions. I can make a rim with an inner diameter of 5 ½ but with the roundness of your 'Whole-tone Da Capo' or whatever it's called. But I think you'll be more flexible if I make the rim just a hair thinner than yours."

He went to a shelf and took down a wooden box filled with funnel shaped mouthpiece bodies without rims.

"Silver or brass?"

These were the first words of the conversation that I had definitely and completely understood.

"Silver please, it tastes better than brass," I said, realizing that I had just spoken my first complete and correct sentence in French to anyone other than Carl, during our first tentative French lessons.

He put a cast ring of silver into the chuck of the lathe and started it turning using the foot pedals. As he shaped the rim and cut a step into it to make it fit snuggly over the body, the valuable silver chips that came off the piece were collected in a sort of leather hammock that hung below. He took the rim and body over to the forge and put a grey colored paste on the places that were to be joined and stuck the pieces together. Then he set them on a small brick in the middle of the hot coals and heated them, directing the flames by blowing air through a pipe about a foot long that he held in his mouth. As the flames rose and were directed at the mouthpiece, it began to glow, and the metal in the paste mixture of flux and silver solder melted, joining the two pieces together permanently.

He took the mouthpiece out of the fire and cooled it in a tub of water, and then put it back on the lathe to shape the rim. He also polished both the outside and inside while it was turning using a cloth and pumice and a couple of scrapers of various shapes. When it was finished he took it off and handed it to me. I tried it, and after a couple of minor adjustments to make the outer edge feel more like mine, it was quite comfortable. This little silver mouthpiece was the one on which I played for the entire 18th century part of my career.

The Wendlings arrived home that afternoon while we were out and were surprised to find me still there. Carl immediately launched into the story he had manufactured for me, which he now had down to a science, and I was getting pretty good at it myself. Again, they all seemed to accept the whole thing without question, and I felt as though I was beginning to have a group of friends who could help me get established in this place. As weird as the situation was, this was reassuring, because what had seemed like some hideous and surreal dream for the past few days was now starting to feel like a new reality; a reality from which I was beginning to realize I might never go home.

Chapter 12

Such friends as the butcher and beaver became
Have seldom, if ever, been known.
In winter or summer, 'twas always the same,
You could never meet either alone.
- Lewis Carroll, The Hunting of the Snark, 1876

The next morning at breakfast Herr Wendling told Carl that he had received a letter with the morning post from the music director of the private orchestra of the Prince de Guéméné, who was in the process of adding winds to the string group he had established a year or two before to provide entertainment at the Hôtel de Rohan-Guéméné on the Place des Vosges in Paris, which was owned by his family. It was now going to be a full orchestra that would play weekly performances. Wendling had written to ask for an interview for Carl, and this letter requested that Carl meet that afternoon with the music director and play for him.

This was the moment Carl had been waiting for, and the main reason he had come to Paris. For this occasion, he had prepared a low horn concerto by Joseph Hampel, and a transcription of a flute sonata by Francisco Geminiani which he had arranged himself. After breakfast Carl left for his interview, and I spent the afternoon practicing my chromatic hand technique and getting used to my new mouthpiece. The upper range was even better than the one Carl had loaned me. It had a sweet sound that made the lyrical high parts of the duets sound very vocal, but I could also get around well on it when the music was fast and agile. The only downside, coming from modern horns and mouthpieces, was the slow speed of the attack, but I was getting used to that too, and learning how to get a more immediate response.

Around four o'clock Carl returned in about as excited a state as I had seen him. He had played for the concertmaster and the music director of the group, and they were extremely impressed with his playing. They had offered him the low horn position on the spot and said they would have a letter of agreement prepared with conditions and salary in a day or two. He had to be totally at the service of the prince whenever he was needed, but he would be free to play elsewhere during his free time. The trial period was three months, and then his position would be permanent. Services for the winds were to start in a few weeks, on the first of December. Carl expressed his appreciation of Herr Wendling's help in making the contact and getting an interview for him, and everyone was happy that it had all gone so well.

"But here's the best part..." Carl said, when all the congratulations were over. "They are still looking for a high horn, and I told them that an old family friend who is an excellent high horn player, and of fine character has recently arrived in Paris and is looking for work. Everyone knows Bohemian horn players are the best, and they said if we would come back tomorrow afternoon, we could play for them and if they like the way we sound together they would consider Johann for the other horn position. How about it? Do you want to go and play for them?"

I was speechless. I had been here less than two weeks, and was just getting used to the instrument, and I was being offered the opportunity to audition for a high-class private orchestra that most of the horn players in Paris would give their eye teeth to play with. Carl must have had a good deal of confidence in me to even suggest to them that they should hear me.

"Yes, certainly, and thanks for your confidence in my playing!"

"I think we'll really impress them as a duo," he said. "Let's play the Stamitz duo we practiced yesterday for Herr and Frau Wendling and see if they think we're ready for the concert stage."

We went into the music room, got out the horns and played the duo we had worked out. Wendling complimented us on our intonation and the way we matched each other musically.

"The two of you will definitely impress them tomorrow, and if I had to make a prediction about your futures, I would say that you could make quite a go of it as a horn duo if you stick together, work hard and put your minds to it. The sky is the limit for a couple of talented young players like yourselves. The idea of the horn duo is becoming popular these days and the horn is coming into its own as a chamber and solo instrument. You could get right in on the ground floor and make a name for yourselves."

Everyone I had spoken to so far had talked about what a great artist Wendling was, and how much influence he had in musical circles in France, England, and his native Germany. And now he was suggesting that Carl and I work together and try to make our mark on the world of horn playing. We spent the rest of the evening picking out some pieces to play along with the Stamitz duo, and listening to Wendling and his wife both practicing, he for the next London concert with J. C. Bach, and she for a *Concert Spirituel* performance of arias in a couple of weeks.

Carl and I were so excited about the possibilities of the next day that we decided to go out and have a drink and talk in peace.

"Let's bring the horns," Carl said.

"What for? I asked.

"You'll see..."

We went a few streets over to a tavern, and when we walked in the door, the owner came up to Carl immediately and asked if he had come to play.

"How about half an hour of *Petit airs* for a bottle of Bordeaux?"

"Sure thing!" said the owner. We unpacked the horns and duet books and went to the music desks at the far end of the room. We played short duets for about half an hour, and the patrons stopped to listen now and then, and even clapped after a couple of the more interesting ones. We sat down at a table and a girl brought us glasses and a pitcher of red wine, which may or may not have been from Bordeaux; it didn't taste like any kind of Bordeaux I had ever tasted.

"Now you see that a good musician never needs to starve or be thirsty," said Carl. "I've been here a few times in the last couple of months and played sonatas with a cellist or a harpsichordist for a good supper. Many restaurants and pubs will let you do that."

"So, Carl, tell me truthfully," I said, starting right in with what was on my mind. "Why is all this happening? I showed up here with an outlandish story of how I got here, and you have just gone along with the whole thing. In a little over a week you have helped me in every possible way, and now you're even helping me to get a position in an orchestra that must be a good one, if you are so excited about getting into it yourself. Why are you doing it?"

Carl's face suddenly became serious.

"You're right, it was an outlandish story, and it took a lot to get me to even consider the possibility of its being true. I'm still not sure, but the things you showed me were so convincing, and you were so sincere and genuine in your explanations that I was fascinated by it all. You were also such an enigma in your lack of knowledge of the world of today, that you either have amnesia, or you really are from some other world or time. Whatever it is, it's intriguing, but there is another side to the whole thing. When we played those first duets last week, I thought, okay, this guy can obviously play the horn, and he'll catch on fast and be a good orchestral player. But what has happened over the past couple of weeks has shown me that you can be one of the great high horn players of our time, and soon.

Wendling wasn't just giving us meaningless compliments. He doesn't do that. He calls things the way he sees them, and he saw right away that there is great potential for us as a duo. I'm a low player, as Punto and many other successful soloists are, but my dream has been to find and join forces with a really fine high horn player to take advantage of the trend of double horn concertos and duos that are coming into vogue.

So far, the high horn players I've met are mostly from the old school, and not refined enough for modern solo music, and often not the kind of people I want to spend my time with or can connect with musically. Then you came along, and you're not only a friendly and easy-going person, intelligent, interesting, and willing to adapt to anything, but you can also play the horn cleaner, stronger, and more musically than just about anyone I've met here. You've made incredible progress in learning how to play the *Inventionshorn*, how to do chromatic hand stopping, and how to play together with me as though we've been playing together for years - and all in a couple of weeks. Whether your strange story turns out to be true or not, I would be crazy to pass up the chance to give this a try and see what we can do together.

I was hoping to make a connection with a high horn player when I came here, and even brought two horns with me, since I knew that compatible instruments are essential to a horn duo, and the chances of someone here playing on something that I could get along with were pretty slim. You can use that horn as long as we work together."

"Carl," I said, "I'm overwhelmed by your good opinion, and I have to say I've been greatly enjoying playing with you too and have been pleasantly surprised by the way we seem to be able to work together. You know my position; I'm helpless in this place, and you've helped me to avoid any number of extremely unpleasant things that could have happened to me in this city if left to fend for myself. I'm pretty certain anyone else would have assumed I was a lunatic and steered clear. I'm still helpless, not knowing the language, and still very much in the dark about how to deal with life in your time and in this amazingly filthy and unsafe place. Sticking together and working together is not only a pleasant prospect for me musically, it's essential to my very survival here. I'm agreeable to whatever you want to try to do as a horn duo or as members of this orchestra, if they decide they want me."

"Oh, I don't think there will be any problem with that." he said. "When we play some of our pieces for them, they'll be ready to offer you a position then and there. I told them we had played a lot together, which is true now that we have played so much over the past two weeks." He filled both of our glasses again. "So, it's agreed, we'll do our best tomorrow and see what happens next. I've always been a hard worker and good at making connections and relating to people, and I get the impression that you are too, so maybe Wendling is right, and the sky is the limit for us."

We clinked our glasses together.

"Okay," I said. "Agreed! The Palsa - Türrschmidt duo is hereby established! But I don't know how I can repay you for everything. You've taken a big chance with me, but you've also spent a good deal of money on clothes, official papers and other things."

"Don't even think about that, Johann, you'll start making money in about two weeks, and you'll be able to pay me back easily at that point. We will certainly be offered a good salary for our positions with the prince."

We talked for a while longer and then went home to rest up for our audition the next day.

I spent an almost sleepless night, with conflicting thoughts bouncing around in my head. The possibilities of the future were exciting, but those were pushed to the side by thoughts of the life and family I had lost. What were Beth and our kids experiencing, and what were they thinking? I missed them terribly and was tortured by the thought of never seeing them again. Somehow in the back of my mind - and often very much in the front of my mind - I felt as though I could wake from this weird dream at any moment, and that feeling stayed with me every day for many years.

Chapter 13

> *The art of refining the tone on the simple horn is, in our day, brought to the highest level of perfection. One has the impression, when a horn duo performs, not to hear the sound of brass instruments, but rather that of a flute accompanied by a viola da gamba.*
>
> *- Ernst Ludwig Gerber, Historisch-Biographisches Lexicon der Tonkünstler, 1792*

The next day Herr Wendling was preparing to leave for London, and the whole family was at home. Carl and I went out in the morning (he wasn't willing to let me go out alone yet) to look for a couple of things I desperately wanted, including bicarbonate of soda, or baking soda, that I could use as toothpaste and some kind of toothbrush. No one here seemed to do much in the way of cleaning their teeth, but it was one 21st century practice that I wasn't going to give up. I also needed to solve the problem of getting some decent coffee. The way they brewed coffee here was absolutely awful, and I was sure they were adding other things to it. I had the idea that if I could get some fresh beans and roast them myself, I could figure out how to brew something I could drink.

We went first to a shop where they made brushes of various shapes and sizes and bought a couple of boar bristle brushes of a size that I could use as toothbrushes. We then went to an apothecary where they had bicarbonate of soda and got a supply of it that I could mix with salt and water to make a usable toothpaste. After nearly two weeks of not being able to clean them properly, it felt as though there was fur growing on my teeth, and it was a great relief to clean them well that day before we went to play. We also stopped in at a coffee and tea shop and bought a bag of green coffee beans, which we planned on roasting at home. I assured Carl that he would never go back to that nasty stuff he knew as coffee after tasting what I planned to brew.

We came home and had a bite to eat before going back into the city, and said goodbye to Herr Wendling, who would be on his way to London by the time we returned in the evening. We packed the horns and crooks into the wooden box, along with the music we were going to play, and headed on foot toward the Hôtel de Rohan-

Guéméné on the Place des Vosges, each taking one of the handles of the box and walking with it between us, looking for all the world like two pallbearers carrying a small casket to the cemetery.

We arrived at the Hôtel and were admitted to the main ballroom by a very haughty and well-dressed doorman. The string group was rehearsing there that afternoon, playing a symphony by Gossec, which obviously had wind parts that were missing. When they finished the movement, the concertmaster rose and came over to greet us. He introduced himself as Monsieur Paisible, and told us that the music director, Monsieur Petit, for whom Carl had played the day before, would be there to meet us shortly.

"While you are waiting," he said, "you could join us on this new symphony that Monsieur Gossec has written for the *Concerts des Amateurs*. It has parts for horns and flutes, and you can help us get a better idea of what it sounds like, since this is our first reading."

There were three first violins, three seconds, two violas, two cellos, and a double bass. Even though I was beginning to get used to the tattered and dirty look of most of the people I met everywhere, my first impression of this group was not terribly favorable. They were mostly poorly dressed and disheveled, but when I stopped to think about it, Carl and I didn't really look much better. They were, however, an excellent group of string players. The prince was putting a good bit of money into building this orchestra and was engaging the best players he could get by offering good salaries.

We got out the horns and crooked them in D. The parts were simple and straightforward, and easy to hear. It was the first time I had played the natural horn in an ensemble, and I immediately noticed a few things about how orchestral playing worked on this instrument. We had to try a couple of combinations of tuning bits before we felt like we were in tune with the group.

The D horns were easy to play and balance with a group of this size, but the part that was a bit of a surprise was just how much you needed to correct the open overtones to match the intonation of the strings. Written fourth line D had to be lowered and fifth line E had to be raised more than I thought I had been raising and lowering them when playing horn duets, and for a while it was a conscious effort that I had to remember to do. Our jobs were still the same; the first horn player plays in tune melodically, and the second horn plays perfect intervals with the first horn, but now I had to also play in tune with the players around me, and Carl had to be sensitive to the intonation of the bass line.

Two horns playing together unaccompanied will match each other's articulations and let the response happen at a comfortable speed for that crook, but with the strings, you had to be on your toes a bit more. It made the whole thing even more of a challenge, but also gave you a framework into which you could set your notes. It was fun, and we locked into what they were doing quickly. We played through the entire piece, including an andante middle movement that had some unaccompanied places for the horns and flutes. The concertmaster and principal second played the flute parts in those places so we could all hear what the music sounded like. At first I thought they must have a score, but they were reading from flute parts at that point. In all my time in the 18th century I never saw a printed score, only composers' handwritten scores that they would bring to rehearsals, though it was not uncommon to have printed parts, especially for pieces by foreign composers. Most of the time we were playing from hand-written parts of varying degrees of legibility.

The music director finally arrived, and the strings ended their rehearsal to go and have supper. Most of them had performances of one sort or another later that evening. Carl introduced me to Monsieur Petit, the director, as Monsieur Johann Palsa, the well-known Bohemian high horn virtuoso, newly arrived from the English colonies in America. Then Messieurs Paisable and Petit took us to a smaller room, well-furnished like a private drawing room, in which there was a harpsichord and music stands.

Monsieur Petit directed us to a two-desk music stand.

"Yesterday I had the great honor of hearing Monsieur Türrschmidt, and today we are very much looking forward to hearing the two of you together, Monsieur Palsa. What would you two gentlemen like to play for us?"

Carl stepped forward and bowed.

"We've prepared a duet by Carl Stamitz that I've arranged myself, and three short airs by Giovanni Punto."

We crooked our horns in E flat and checked our pitch. I was glad we had played with the group in the rehearsal room, because it took a little of the edge off what was beginning to feel uncomfortably like an audition.

We began playing the Stamitz duo and settled immediately into the comfortable feel we had gotten used to in this piece. The duo had three short movements, and a few high clarino passages in my part, but I was getting used to doing these, and beginning to figure out what kind of air speed and articulation made the high passages reliable.

We finished, and Monsieur Petit stood up and came toward us.

"I've never heard the horn played in such a refined way as the two of you play it; like a flute being accompanied by a viola da gamba, and the chromatic notes and moving melodic bass lines are truly astounding! Wait one moment before playing your other pieces."

He left the room for two or three minutes, and when he returned, he was accompanied by an elegant gentleman in a wig, three cornered hat, and a suit that looked to be brand new with a fancy shirt, gold stitching on the cuffs, gold buttons, and coat that was longer than the normal coats that the rest of us were wearing. He had highly polished black boots and a sword at his side. With him was a lady in an elegant dress with a hoop skirt that also looked like it could have been made that morning, and hair built up into a ridiculous structure that prevented her from moving very quickly. This was Henri Louis de Rohan, Prince of Guéméné and his wife Victoire Armande Josèphe de Rohan. This wealthy nobleman was highly respected at the court of Louis XVI, and rumor had it, according to what Carl had told me on the way there, that he was in line for the position of Grand Chamberlain of France, an important position at court, the purpose of which I never totally understood.

"Your Excellency, these are the two Bohemian *Cor de chasse* players, Messieurs Palsa and Türrschmidt. They were just about to play some *Petit airs* on their horns for us."

Carl stepped forward and bowed and I followed his cue.

"Your Excellency," he said bowing again, "we are greatly honored to have this opportunity to play for you and Madam the princess and hope you will enjoy these airs by the famous horn virtuoso Giovanni Punto."

"Please proceed," said the prince. "We are curious to hear your music after the report that Monsieur Petit has given us."

We went back to the music stand and the prince and princess sat down in two chairs that had just arrived, carried in by servants who seemed to appear out of nowhere, and disappeared just as unobtrusively. We began playing the first piece, a minuet which was simple enough, and I must admit, I was a bit on edge, having never been in the presence of nobility before, but Carl seemed to know exactly how to act around them, so I felt reassured. We finished the minuet, and the prince asked where we were from.

"We are both Germans. I am lately arrived in Paris from Wallerstein Germany, where my father is in the service of Prince Kraft-Ernst, of Öttingen-Wallerstein. Monsieur Palsa was born in Bohemia and has lived for several years in the English Colonies of America.

"Is Monsieur Palsa unable to speak for himself?" asked the prince.

"No, your Excellency, he doesn't understand French very well yet."

"How is it that he doesn't understand French?" asked the princess, speaking for the first time.

"In the colonies, German and English are spoken, so he never had the opportunity to learn, but he will learn quickly now that he is in Paris."

"Yes, we have heard that the American colonies are incredibly uncivilized," said the princess. "Please continue with your music."

I didn't understand any of this exchange at the time, but Carl filled me in afterward. We went on to an andante in which I had a lyrical scale-wise melody, and Carl played an agile flowing accompaniment. We were getting warmed up now and matching well. After this short piece we played our finale, a fast allegro that had a couple of slippery high passages, but to my relief they worked well.

"Remarkable!" said the prince, when we were finished. "We would like to have these young Cor de chasse players in our orchestra, and as members of our chamber musicians. They will be a great novelty for our guests, who no doubt, have never heard the horn played in this way, like a woodwind instrument. Monsieur Petit, please make all the necessary arrangements, and Messieurs Palsa and Türrschmidt, we will look forward to the great pleasure of hearing your music again soon. Good day."

At that they both rose and left the room, and the chairs disappeared as unobtrusively as they had arrived. I felt like a commodity that had just been checked out thoroughly and purchased. But we now had a gig, and it seemed like an extremely high class one at that.

"Now for the details of your engagement," said Monsieur Petit. "You will be available whenever needed for the full orchestra for concerts and social functions here at the Hôtel de Rohan-Guéméné, and at the prince's residence, and of course, when you are not needed to play horn you both may be called on to play viola."

"What's that about viola that he just said?" I whispered to Carl in German.

"Regular orchestra contract stuff, - it's okay."

"But Carl, I don't..."

"Shhhh, I'll explain it all later."

"In addition, you will be members of the wind group for *Tafelmusik* service when required, and also, as the prince just mentioned, members of the chamber musicians for private performances. At the prince's expense you will be fitted for new suits in a uniform fashion with the other musicians at a shop in the city, the address of which I am writing down for you now. These suits you will keep in good condition and wear whenever working in the service of the prince, and nowhere else. Your trial period, as with everyone in the orchestra, is three months, and your annual salary will be nine hundred livres each, which will be paid out in twelve equal installments throughout the year at the beginning of each month. When your services are not required, you will be free to play for anyone else, but the prince's services will be your first priority. The starting date for the winds is December 1st, and your first installment will be paid immediately to cover your expenses until that time. I think that takes care of everything, and if you would like to stop around again tomorrow afternoon, I'll have the prince's secretary draw up letters of engagement for you to sign and have payment waiting for you. I think you will find the prince's service a good one, and the orchestra a very rewarding musical experience. Monsieur Paisable and I will look forward to working with you.

We thanked them both, shook hands, and left the Hôtel feeling like we had just won the lottery.[5]

Chapter 14

At musical gatherings, in which quartets or other instrumental music was being played, when he wasn't otherwise occupied, it pleased him (J.S. Bach) to join in on the viola.
- J.N. Forkel, The Life, Art, and Works of J.S. Bach, 1802

We went out into the street and started off in the direction of the tailor's shop to get measured for our new suits before going back to the Wendlings' house. Carl was in a high mood and practically bounced down the street.

"We did it! Johann, do you realize what it means to not only play in the orchestra and wind band, but to be members of the prince's private chamber musicians too? It means chamber music with other instruments, but mostly it means horn duos! He really went for the duets and obviously wants to show us off as something special to his guests. A lot of important people dine with him and his family and visit their private residence. This could be really big for us, and we'll make a lot of good connections."

"And all we have to do is play horn duets for him?"

"That's right; and find new chamber music of any sort that has horn parts."

"But Carl, what was that he said about playing viola in the orchestra?"

"Oh, as I said, that's a regular thing for horn players to play viola now and then when the music doesn't have horn parts."

"But Carl, I don't know how to play the viola."

"What do you mean you don't know how to play the viola?!" he said, stopping dead in the street. "All horn players play the viola. What do you plan to do when your teeth fall out? That's too late to learn how to play another instrument."

"I don't plan on letting my teeth fall out. Remember all the baking soda, salt and brushes I bought this morning? And I have never played the viola, not even the tiniest little bit."

"I'm more and more convinced you really are from some other world. I've never heard anything like it! You're just going to have to learn. It's not hard, and we'll get you started so you can play simple orchestra parts in no time. I have one at home, and we can get another just about anywhere. My father will move to viola permanently in a few years in the Wallerstein orchestra after he can't play high horn anymore. Horn is a young person's instrument, and you still have to keep earning money when you get too old to play it."

"All right, you know best about these things," I said. "I'll get to work on it. But I can't believe that all horn players play the viola."

"Ask any one you meet. A few of them, like Punto play the violin or cello, or maybe the flute, but everyone can play the viola." The only thing easier to play is the double bass, but it's very impractical to travel with, though on cold winter nights a bass will burn longer than a viola.[6]

A few minutes later we arrived at the shop where we were to order our new suits for the orchestra. It was a rather shabby looking shop lined with shelves from floor to ceiling that had rolls of cloth of different colors and weaves. There were a couple of wavy full-length mirrors and a few chairs and some wooden platforms that the customers could stand on while being measured, as well as long tables for spreading out and cutting material. We could see into a back room where several men and women were busy making clothing. This was a new clothing shop where people who could afford new clothes went to have them custom-made. The written order for our suits that we had been given at the Hôtel seemed familiar to the shop manager, and he called for a tailor to measure us.

"Two more suits for the Prince of Guéméné's musicians. That makes six this week. We'll all be rich if he keeps adding to his orchestra at this pace!"

They took our measurements and told us to come back at the end of the week to pick them up. We stepped out into the street again and headed in the direction of the rue Chantre, carrying the horn box. As we approached the next corner, we saw little Hannes, the brother of Wendlings' servant, on the other side of the street, and Carl called to him. Hannes immediately bolted across the street to come to us, and as he did, a fancy coach, pulled by four white horses rumbled around the corner at top speed.

The boy was right in its path, and without a thought of the consequences for myself, I sprang in front of it pushing Hannes out of the way so the coach only grazed him, knocking him off his feet, instead of actually running over him, as it surely would have done. I miraculously made it out of the way in time and wasn't touched by the coach, but seeing the child sprawled on the pavement, and the coach going on its way, totally unconcerned, filled me instantly with rage, and before I knew what I was doing, I picked up a stone about the size of my fist that happened to be at my feet and hurled it with all my might after the speeding vehicle.

"No!... Don't!" shouted Carl, in absolute shock at what he was witnessing. But it was too late. The stone shattered the back window, and the coach came to a screeching halt. I ran toward Hannes and picked him up out of the street. To my relief he seemed to be uninjured, though a little shaken. Before any of us knew what was happening three men in fine servant's clothes jumped from the coach and made after us. We didn't have the presence of mind to run in the confusion, and in a couple of seconds they had grabbed us and were dragging us, still struggling, toward the coach. They apparently didn't notice Hannes or the horn box, and as we neared the carriage, I turned for a split second to see Hannes, who without a doubt knew exactly what was happening, and what sort of trouble we were in. He picked up the box and disappeared around the corner, knowing full well that he could help us best by getting away quickly.

Someone called for the police, and in seconds two officers of the Paris police pushed their way through the crowd. We were now in front of the coach, and emerging from it was a very large, well-dressed gentleman in a light blue suit, with a long coat, much of the same cut as the one worn by the Prince of Guéméné. He was followed by a young lady, also well-dressed and obviously aristocratic, who was crying and picking pieces of glass out of her hair and the skirts of her dress and shawl. The portly old man was in a rage and his red face looked like it was about to explode.

"Are these the vermin who deliberately broke the window of my coach and almost killed my daughter and myself with flying glass and stones? Officers, seize them and take them to the Bastille until I can press formal charges against them and have them punished to the fullest extent of the law! The nerve of these people, attacking a nobleman's coach in the street!"

"Let me go!" I shouted in French, and then in German; "He almost killed a child in the street, and I lost my temper and threw a stone at the coach!"

"Quiet! Shut up! urged Carl in low tones. "It's bad enough as it is. You're just getting yourself in deeper! Be quiet! I'll handle this."

"What is he saying?!?" bellowed the man, who we soon found out was the Comte de Guînes, French ambassador to England and an important man at the court of Louis XVI.

"My Lord," said Carl, "it was all an accident. My friend was trying to save a child who was knocked down in the street."

"Silence! There was no child in the street. These ruffians simply began throwing stones at my coach without the slightest provocation. Away with them!"

With that he turned from us, and he and the young lady got back into the coach, which the servants had swept out to remove any remaining glass from the window, and they drove away again at top speed. By this time two more officers had arrived. And by officers, I mean two more ragged men with five-day beards who smelled like they had just come from the pub, wearing dirty grey coats and three-cornered hats with a royal badge on them. One could have easily mistaken them for homeless beggars in a half drunken state. With one of these men on each of our sides holding our arms with a vise-like grip, we were hurried through the streets toward the east side of Paris, followed by a small crowd for a while who thought there might be more of a scuffle to see, but these tapered off gradually and finally gave it up. We knew it was useless to struggle and went along quietly, trying to talk to them, but couldn't get them to listen.

"We can explain how it all happened. It's all a mistake!" said Carl.

"Save it! You can explain everything to the judge when you go to court," said one of the men, who seemed to be in charge.

We finally came to a large stone building that looked like a medieval castle right in the middle the city, and a gatekeeper let us in. This was number 232, rue Saint-Antoine, the Bastille, and from what I knew about the French Revolution, I could have told them that it was going to be stormed by an angry crowd in 1789, touching off the French Revolution, but unfortunately it was entirely intact and impenetrable on this particular day in 1770. The building consisted of an irregular rectangle with eight towers, most of which were used as prison cells at this point. Each tower was at least a hundred feet high and connected by walls of equal height. The whole building was surrounded by a moat that must have been almost as wide as the towers were high. The Bastille was so huge and imposing with its stone towers and rows of windows with iron grates, that it totally dominated the east side of the city.

We went over a wooden bridge, through the gate, and through a corridor that led into a central courtyard that was open to the sky. *A Tale of Two Cities* and *The Man in the Iron Mask* came to mind immediately as I looked up at the rows of windows in the tower. We were met by a man in a military uniform with a sword and musket, who looked incredibly bored by our arrival. He led us into a small building in the middle of the courtyard that was connected to the outer walls and essentially cut the courtyard in half. Sitting at a desk was a man who was obviously a military officer. He didn't rise when we entered the room but gave us a quick look and went right back to his papers on the table.

"And what do we have here?" he asked in a voice even more bored than the soldier who showed us in.

"Monsieur," said the police officer who was in charge, "his lordship the ambassador Adrien-Louis de Bonnières, Comte de Guînes has ordered that these two men be kept under lock and key until he can make a formal charge against them."

"And what have they done to deserve the honor of the Comte's attention?"

"They were apprehended in the street, throwing stones at the Comte's coach and breaking all the windows."

"Just one stone and one window!" I interjected.

"I told you to keep quiet, if you want to get out of this alive," Carl whispered in German. "You're not making it any better for us."

"Take them to number 107 North Tower, where they will wait until we hear more about them," he said to the soldier who had brought us in. "And if I know the Comte, that could be a good long time, my fine young gentleman! Enjoy your stay!"

He looked back down at his papers, and it was obvious that the interview was over.

The city police left the room, and two soldiers led us out into the courtyard, where other soldiers were milling around. Some of them were playing a game with a leather ball about the size of a cantaloupe. We went across the yard and entered a wooden door in one of the towers and went up a spiral stone stairway to the third level. The stone walls were damp and cold, and the whole place looked very uninviting. There was a tapping as of someone hammering on something in one of the rooms we passed.

"What's that noise?" Carl asked one of the soldiers.

"It's your neighbor in number 105." he replied, "He's making shoes."

"Making shoes here?"

"Yes, the person who ordered his imprisonment, many years ago, allows him to make shoes to earn his food and clothing."

"I'm sure there's an interesting story behind it all, which no one will ever hear," said Carl.[7]

We went two more doors further down the hall and one of the soldiers took out a key that would have fit perfectly in a horror movie torture chamber scene. He unlocked a small wooden door with the number 107 painted on it in black, and pushed us in. The door closed again with a disconcertingly heavy sound, and the key turned in the lock.

The room was small, with a single window about two feet wide and three feet tall with an iron grate on it. It would have been hard to escape that way because it was about twenty-five feet down to the ground. The only objects in the room were a simple bench about five feet long, and three wooden boxes filled with straw, sitting directly on the stone floor that were obviously meant for beds. In the corner stood a heavy wooden box on which a tin pitcher full of water stood. That was the extent of the furnishings.

Carl had said little as we were being taken through the streets, into the Bastille, and into the room. Apparently he didn't want any of them to hear any conversation that could be used as evidence against us. But now that we were alone his thoughts burst out of him.

"Just what in the hell were you thinking?! Throwing a stone through the window of the coach of the French ambassador to England! You absolute idiot! What would have possessed you to do such a thing?"

"I did save Hannes from getting run over, that's certainly something!"

"Yes, and it was a heroic act that would have been cause for celebration, if you hadn't followed it up by taking the law into your own hands and hurling a stone at an aristocrat!"

"I got angry and lost my head. I thought poor Hannes was dead."

"We may both very well lose our heads if he stays as outraged as he was when he got out of that coach! If we're very lucky he'll just forget about us and we'll sit here and eat oatcakes and water and freeze our asses off until we die!"

"It can't be that bad," I said, trying to calm him down. "Can't we pay for the window and work this all out somehow?"

"You don't seem to understand the implications of a common person offending a nobleman, do you? They have absolute power to put people like us in places like this and enough influence to make sure they're convicted, if they ever get around to taking the thing to a judge. And God only knows what the law does to people who destroy the property of a Comte!"

"This whole system of nobility and common people is something I've never had to deal with, and I'm not properly equipped for it. I didn't mean to do what I did. It was just a reaction to the situation and the lack of concern for human life he was showing. How could anyone stand by and watch that happen?"

"Well, it does happen," said Carl, still looking daggers at me. "It happens all the time, and people just let it go and stay out of the line of fire, because they know how dangerous it can be to fight it. You can't afford to cross them."

"I'm learning that, and it's a lesson I'll never forget - part of my ongoing education in this place."

"And you're learning it at some expense to our careers, which may not happen now. It could take weeks or months for him to do anything! I'm serious. We could sit here, and no one will know what's happened to us, or where we are until the Comte takes action, which he won't be in a hurry to do, and may forget about us all together. Nobility can just throw people like us away. And in the meantime, we've lost the horns and we've probably lost the positions with the prince!"

He sat silently for a few seconds.

"You idiot!" he burst out again. "How could you get us into something like this? They probably won't even let us write a letter to anyone. Fortunately, I still have some money in my pocket, so we can get some decent food for a while, until that runs out."

"We have to buy our own food?"

"As long as we can, and then we'll be forced to eat whatever they make here. I'm sure it's only fit for dogs!"

"Carl, I'm truly sorry that I got us into all this trouble. I wish there was something I could do to get us out of it. But I can tell you that the horns are safe."

"What? How?"

"As they were dragging us to the Comte's coach, and all eyes were on us, Hannes picked up the box and ran in the other direction."

"Well thank God for that! If someone didn't grab him thinking he was a thief taking advantage of our misfortune, he may have made it home, in which case Herr Wendling knows about it now. He will certainly try to help us if he has any means of doing so. But it's unlikely he would know where to start looking for us, or who it was that sent us here. It's a slim chance but at least it's something to hope for. We can't do much of anything on our own behalf except wait."

"Let's just hope Wendling gets word and can do something," I said, trying to be hopeful.

Carl was beginning to calm down somewhat, and now it was my turn to begin to appreciate the full impact of our situation. We sat and talked it over a little more sensibly for the rest of the evening, speculating on whether Hannes had been able to get all the way home alone with the horn box, and what Wendling or anyone else could do to help us.

The light from the single window gradually waned, and before long we were in utter darkness, which was extremely eerie in that cold stone room. There was nothing else to do but try to sleep. Footsteps passed the door at regular intervals and voices could be heard from time to time, while the sounds of the city outside found their way in through the window. More unsettling was the sound of small feet scurrying across the floor inside the room.

"Carl!"

"Yes. What?"

"Did you hear that?"

"Hear what?"

"Something in the room."

"Yes, those are rats. Remember? This is a prison you've gotten us into. Go to sleep."

I'm sure I must have dozed off a few times during the night, but neither of us slept very much.

Chapter 15

Stone walls do not a prison make,
Nor iron bars a cage;
Minds innocent and quiet take
That for an Hermitage;
- *Richard Lovelace, 1649*

The sun poured in through the window in the morning, giving us a better view of our surroundings, but it didn't make the scene look any more appealing or comfortable. I was in a state of complete dejection, as it gradually sank in what a mess I had made of everything by one 21st century outburst of rage at injustice. It just happened to be aimed at exactly the wrong person. Carl was still in a foul mood, and not terribly sociable, which was completely understandable, since I had probably derailed all the plans he had been formulating since he decided to leave his home in Regensburg almost a year before.

"The only worse choice for a target would have been the king himself; but on the other hand, that would have resulted in your immediate annihilation, saving a lot of time and trouble for a lot of people, myself included!"

We sat for a couple of hours before a soldier brought in a board with some bread and an empty wooden cup that we used to drink water out of the pitcher in the corner. The morning dragged on at an incredibly slow pace, and we both sat staring blankly, wondering if this was how we were going to spend many weeks or months before something even worse would happen.

At about noon the door opened, and a soldier brought in a letter addressed to Carl, written in German. Carl took it beneath the window and looked at the folded paper, sealed with wax on the outside.

"Wendling! It's from Herr Wendling! At least someone knows we're alive!"

He tore it open and immediately began reading:

My Dearest Carl,

Hannes brought home your horns and informed me of what happened yesterday. Though Herr Palsa's reaction to the situation was a rash act, and one that could be very difficult to set right, please tell him that I appreciate his concern for the welfare of Hannes, and that his quick action probably saved him from injury or death. I immediately went to the street where this took place and was able, after much questioning of the shopkeepers, to determine that the gentleman whose coach was damaged was the Comte de Guînes, French ambassador to England, and that the two of you were taken to the Bastille. My daughter, Elisabeth, will bring food and a few other things over to you this afternoon.

I have postponed my departure to London until we can bring this unfortunate occurrence to a satisfactory conclusion. This morning I have written to several musicians who have some influence with the Comte, as well as Monsieur Petit, music director to the Prince of Guéméné, as, no doubt, the prince himself will also be involved.

In the hope of a speedy solution to your difficulties, I remain,
Your most interested and concerned friend,
J. B. Wendling

We sat for some time speculating about what anyone could do to get us out of this mess unscathed. At about five o'clock in the afternoon, we heard footsteps outside our room, and Elisabeth Wendling was shown in. We were overjoyed to see a friendly face, and the wicker basket she was carrying smelled delicious. Katherina had filled it with fresh bread, meat and cheese, and a bottle of wine, all of which were very welcome to two starving prisoners. Elisabeth filled us in on what had been going forward earlier in the day and what Herr Wendling had been able to do on our behalf.

It turned out that the Comte de Guînes was an amateur flute player, and his daughter played the harp. This information came through Monsieur Petit, who also said that he knew for a fact that the Comte had attended the Concert Spirituel each time Wendling had been a soloist and was a great admirer of his flute playing.

“My father thinks he and Monsieur Paisible may be able to get an interview with the Comte and see if they can convince him to drop the charges he intends to bring against you. He’s a cantankerous old mountain of unpleasantness with a legendary bad temper, but his passion is playing the flute, and he’s a huge music lover, so that may be our route into his good graces.”

Elisabeth stayed for a while longer, and when it was beginning to get dark she left us with promises that they would bring food again the next day along with any news. The evening wore on, and we eventually fell into a deep sleep in the total darkness and knew nothing more until the following morning.

At daybreak a soldier brought us our bread and water again, and we sat bored out of our minds and worried until the afternoon, when Herr Wendling himself arrived with Hannes who was looking as good as new. They brought us enough food for a couple of days and a few other things that would make life as comfortable as could be expected in a rat-infested 18th century French prison.

“I’ve been in touch with several people already,” he began. “The Stamitz brothers, Nicholas Capron, Giuseppi Cambini and a few others are writing letters to the Comte on your behalf, but he won’t receive them for a few days, since he is away from Paris until the end of the week. When he returns, it is even possible that the Prince of Guéméné will intercede for you with him. Monsieur Petit tells me that the prince was very impressed with the two of you and doesn’t want to lose you as members of his chamber musicians and orchestra. If that’s really the case, then there is a chance that we can resolve this without a lot of trouble. We’ll see how he reacts to all our appeals. He’s known for being unbelievably stubborn and immovable.”

“That means we’re here for a while in any case,” said Carl.

“At the very least another week, and possibly longer if he chooses to ignore us. It’s difficult to say. Herr Palsa, you shouldn’t feel too bad about how it has all happened. You did a good deed in saving Hannes from a terrible accident, and though it was a foolish thing to do, everyone who has heard the story admires you for being bold enough to do something we all have been tempted to do at some point, but didn’t because of the dire consequences we know so well.

You're becoming somewhat of a hero among the musicians of Paris, and the story will get you a good deal of respect and notice, if we get you out of this."

"Thank you, Herr Wendling," I said, "for your kind words, and for everything you've done for us."

"You're very welcome, and to pass the time, I thought you might want something to keep you occupied, so I brought some music manuscript paper and pens, in case the muse inspires you to do some composing. If everything works out as we hope, you'll need a good supply of duets for the prince's entertainments, and this would be a good time to start composing them."

Wendling said he or Elisabeth would come back as soon as possible, but he couldn't promise anything since the next few days would be busy for him, mustering up support for our case, meeting with the Prince of Guéméné, and ultimately with the Comte de Guînes himself.

"I have a couple of creative ideas that could break the ice with him, though I must say, it's pretty thick ice in his case. We'll do our best."

With that he and Hannes left, and that was the last we saw of him for the next four days, though we received daily messages.

They had also brought a couple of old blankets that were a little help against the cold, but it was still freezing, and the November air came in freely through the window, which had only a poorly fitting shutter that could be closed at night over the iron grate. We were a bit more comfortable too, with some decent food, wine, and something to occupy ourselves. Carl's mood toward me was slowly softening, and we began working on some ideas for short pieces for two horns. I had never done any composing, but it was becoming obvious that everyone here did, and nearly everyone had a concerto or solo pieces they had written, which they performed whenever they had the opportunity.

Since all music was new and composed in the current style, a lot of it had to be written. Some people published their music, and some of it was worth publishing, but the majority of pieces were meant for a few performances and then discarded for something new. There appeared to be virtually no lasting repertoire for orchestra, though individual soloists, like Punto, had a bundle of concertos and chamber pieces they played wherever they went.

"Punto has at least a dozen concertos, about half of which bear his name," said Carl. "He actually wrote a couple of them, and the others were done by some of the finest composers around; people like Antonio Rosetti, Carl Stamitz, and Franz Pokorny. Once at a concert in Regensburg, Punto announced that he would play one of his own concertos, and someone in the audience called out asking who the composer was. Punto replied that he has his music written only by the finest composers, and this one was orchestrated by Herr Rosetti, using themes Punto had given him. Often a soloist will say that it is a concerto of their own composition, for which Herr so and so has written the accompaniment."

"Don't the composers get offended when someone claims a piece is their own? I asked.

"Not at all, because when someone commissions a piece from a composer, and pays them for their work, the piece belongs to them, not to the composer. Punto is right to call them his concertos, since he paid good money to have them composed specifically for him."

I tried to wrap my mind around this way of thinking, but it seemed wrong from my 21st century perspective.

"Where I come from, the composer is paid to compose pieces, but they take great ownership in the piece, and get a percentage of the money that is earned from publishing it or from its performance. If someone else were to claim to have written it, or publish it without permission, the composer could take that person to court and be awarded damages from them for stealing the music."

"That seems almost incredible," Carl said. "Composers have no way of stopping someone from publishing their music in another city, and no hope of getting any money from the sale of it. The best way to protect yourself from that is never to give anyone copies of your music. Though, even that doesn't ensure it won't happen. I've heard of music printers going to an opera and writing down the arias as they are performed and then arranging them for voice and keyboard. There are a few who can do it on one or two hearings. Then unauthorized books of arias from the opera show up for sale in their shop. The current trend in Germany at this point is to make arrangements of pieces from the most popular operas for wind sextet or octet. A lot of publishers have people working for them who do nothing but arrangements of the newest pieces, and the composer doesn't get anything for them, unless he can get the jump on them by making and selling his own arrangements before anyone else can."

We each started working on bits and pieces of duets, and in the time it took me to think up a melody and figure out how to write it for two horns, Carl had composed four or five charming little minuets, airs, and fanfares in hunting horn style. He obviously had more confidence in my upper range than I did at that point in my natural horn career, because he wrote some things that I wasn't at all sure I could play.

"You'll figure them out," he said. "You're getting more secure in the clarino range every day."

We worked on these, using themes that Carl remembered from other composers, and making up some of our own as long as the light lasted, and it did take our minds off the question of whether Wendling and all our other friends could convince the Comte to set us free. A few of these little pieces were published years later in a book of some of our favorite duets that Carl collected together and had printed in Berlin.[8] Many of them stayed in our duet repertoire as we traveled all over Europe and were played on many important and memorable occasions.

The whole of my compositional output from our time in prison that was fit to perform consisted of three little pieces, a short Siciliano in g minor, a Minuet in F major, and an Adagio in c minor, all very simple pieces, but in unusual keys for the horn[8]. I would have done more, but ran into difficulties on the second evening. At the Wendlings' house, they were able to boil any water I drank, which meant that I only became violently ill, and not deathly ill. With what they gave us at the Bastille, where you couldn't put in a special request for boiled water, I became deathly ill.

I thought I had been in pretty bad shape the week before, but now I was sure my time was up. I lay in my box of straw for a couple of days with a high fever and chills and didn't remember very much about what was happening. I remember people coming to visit, and Carl talking about what Wendling was doing, and his interview with the Prince of Guéméné. I'm sure it was all very interesting, but I didn't care, I just wanted to be anywhere but there, and feel any way but the way I was feeling. Carl did everything he could to make me comfortable, and the Wendlings sent more blankets and food.

On the fourth morning I woke up to see him and Wendling sitting next to me talking and looking rather worried about my state.

"Your fever is still pretty high," Carl said. "How are you feeling today my friend?"

"Terrible, and it's tempting to ask the doctor to come by and give me one of his mixtures to finish me off."

"A military doctor came last night and looked at you. He said we should keep you warm and give you chicken soup, and that it would probably pass all on its own. We'll get you through this. The good news is that Herr Wendling has arranged a meeting with the Comte when he arrives back in Paris tomorrow, and it looks like the prince is going to either write to him or call on him too. In a day or two something will happen, and we can only hope it will be our release."

"I've dealt with a good number of aristocrats," said Wendling, "and I have an idea that might make some headway with him. I had begun composing a set of trios for flute, violin, and cello for Christian Bach's series in London, and I'm going to offer to dedicate them to the Comte. That should flatter him enough to get him into a magnanimous and merciful mood. The prince, as his social equal should be able to sway him too. I managed to get an interview with his highness yesterday and explained what had happened. Though he considers you, Johann, to be a very unruly and hot-headed young fellow, he very much wants to get you out of here so you can begin working for him. But you will only continue your positions with him on the strict promise that there will be no more trouble. You can't contradict a nobleman, so I didn't even try to tell him that you are nothing of the kind, but reassured him that, in future, the two of you will be the best-behaved members of his orchestra without question. He was highly impressed with you and considers you to be valuable acquisitions to his musical establishment; something new and novel. I don't think he would go to such lengths for any of his other musicians."

I fell back to sleep before Wendling left and had a very long and involved dream. I was at home with my family, and we were preparing to go on a trip somewhere by car. Beth and I were getting the kids ready, packing bags, and preparing food for the trip. We finally got everything packed in the car and started out. It was just like one of our family trips, which were always fun. The scenery was vivid as we drove through the countryside, the four of us singing songs and talking. The day was beautiful, and I was happy to be with them. Suddenly I saw lights flashing behind us and a siren, and I pulled off the road. The lights pulled off too and came up close behind as I stopped.

A police officer got out and came up to the window.

"Mr. John Paulson?"

"Yes," I replied. "Is anything the matter?"

"Please come with us Mr. Paulson."

"Why? What's happened?"

"You have been charged with identity theft, impersonating a Bohemian musician, and committing acts of vandalism while traveling under an assumed name."

"It wasn't vandalism! I was trying to save a child who was run over by a horse-drawn coach. I can explain how it all happened. It was all a mistake! And I didn't steal the name! Carl Türrschmidt made it up!"

"Save it! You can explain everything to the judge when you go to court. If convicted, you will be sentenced to twenty years of hard labor playing the viola in a theater orchestra with eight performances a week, no pay, and no vacations."

The kids were crying, and Beth was shouting. "Don't take him away from us! He didn't do any of those things!"

They pulled me out, put handcuffs on me and dragged me toward a horse-drawn police wagon. In it were sitting the four half drunken Paris police officers who had taken Carl and me to the Bastille. They were all laughing hysterically – and then I woke suddenly.

It was just approaching daybreak, and I lay for a long time, lost in dismal thoughts about my family, and wondering why this was all happening to me. The 18th century was a dangerous place. I had, within a few weeks, been terribly ill due to the unhealthy living conditions that I, as a 21st century person, wasn't equipped for and

I had experienced a few narrow escapes in the streets, which were full of all sorts of perils from criminals to coach drivers who weren't held responsible even if they killed people. I had been eaten by fleas and hadn't had a decent bath or clean clothes the whole time. And to top it off, I had to function in 18th century German and start learning 18th century French. "There are two possibilities," I thought. "I can either give up and let it kill me, or I can continue to find my way through the maze of this life and conquer it. I'm not the type to give up that easily, and I won't give up! I have a circle of friends here who I can depend on to point me in the right direction, and one who even understands where I'm coming from, though I'm not sure he's totally convinced I'm really from the 21st century. But he does seem to have become a true friend. I'll keep going, and stick with Carl, and deal with whatever this world throws at me."

I dozed off to sleep again and didn't wake up until the middle of the afternoon. I wasn't sure what day it was, but I was feeling slightly better, and was ready to eat something.

"Well, it looks like he's alive!" said Carl, and I also heard the voices of Wendling and his daughter talking. "You're looking better today. Here's some broth to sip on that will strengthen you. You'll need it because, if you are able to move, we may very well be going home today!"

"What?" I cried out and sat upright, which immediately made my head spin. I had to lay right back down again to keep from falling over. "The Comte is going to let us out?"

"I met with him today and learned that the prince had been to see him this morning," said Wendling. "The prince had made it very clear to him that he wanted you for his orchestra, and that there weren't two more valuable horn players in all of France. I then talked with the Comte for a while, and he insisted on playing the flute for me. I was surprised. He's a very good amateur player and goes to just about every concert he can that features the flute.

I showed him the set of trios I've been working on and told him I wanted to dedicate them to him.[9] All this worked on his ego, and he finally said that if he received a signed letter of apology from the two of you, and payment for the repair of his coach window, he would send a letter to the prison releasing you. Carl has already written the letter he requires of you, and if you could sign it, I will deliver it to his house, along with the money for the window. If all goes well, and he doesn't reconsider, the officer in charge should receive the letter ordering your release this evening."

Though I still felt awful, this was great news, and we both expressed our sincere appreciation of Wendlings' intervention with the Comte. I was still quite weak, and after a few minutes of just listening to them all talking, I slipped back into sleep and dreamed again of home. This time they were all more pleasant dreams of daily life; dreams I didn't want to wake up from.

I woke again to see the first morning light streaming in through the window. Carl was sitting next to me, already writing music.

"What's happened while I was sleeping?" I asked.

"Last night before Wendling and his daughter left, the letter from the Comte arrived, and we're free!

"Then why are we still here?" I asked, still in a bit of a fog.

"We decided it wouldn't be a good idea to try to move you last night, so they went home and I stayed here with you. They'll be back this morning with a coach to drive us home, so you won't need to walk any further than over the moat and out to the street. We should be home by mid-day!"

Chapter 16

One cannot hear anything more beautiful than the little duets that Herr Palsa and his partner Herr Türrschmidt play on two silver horns, especially those set in minor keys.
- J.N. Forkel, Musikalischer Almanach für Deutschland, 1784

Elisabeth and Anton Stamitz were shown in shortly before noon, and with Carl's help, they got me down the stairs, out of the Bastille, and into a coach that was waiting for us. I hadn't been in any sort of horse drawn carriage yet, and this was not a good first impression of this mode of travel. It was an incredibly jarring business driving over brick and cobblestone roads in a coach, and by the time we arrived at the Wendlings' house, I was hardly able to move under my own power. They got me inside somehow and put me directly to bed.

I shivered and baked by turns for the next couple of days and experienced terrible nightmares that mostly had to do with the fate of my family in my absence. These persisted until the fever finally broke, with the help of Katerina's chicken soup and hot tea. I had very little idea of what was happening around the house, but it seems that Wendling was getting ready to depart for London again, and his wife Dorothea was in the middle of a run of opera performances in Paris. Carl was also in and out on various bits of business, as well as overseeing my care. He said when the doctor came by to see me, I had threatened the poor man's life if he so much as touched me. I didn't remember anything about this, but it did convince me that even on the most subconscious level, I didn't trust 18th century medicine to do anything but kill a person, and quickly. They took care of me for the next few days, and gradually I started to be in my right mind again and was able to keep track of whether it was day or night. Finally, I was able to get out of bed for short periods, and Carl caught me up on what had been going on over the past few days.

He had picked up our new suits of clothes for the prince's orchestra, and we tried them on to see how well the tailors had done in fitting us. They fit well, but the most satisfying part of our new suits was that they weren't infested with fleas yet, but it didn't take long in that environment. The coats were dark green with green breeches, and white silk stockings. The waistcoat was a beautiful burgundy colored velvet, and our shirts were of an ivory color with fancy ruffles. Both the waistcoat and the long outer coat had silver buttons with the prince's insignia on them.

The prince sent orders that he wanted to see us in our orchestra uniforms and have a "talk" with us as soon as I was able to go out. This sounded a little ominous, but it showed us that he felt it was worthwhile to give us a good talking to about being responsible citizens. It was an indication that he wanted to keep us in his service, rather than simply dismissing us without a word, as any nobleman normally would do if one of his musicians got into serious trouble.

Carl had also been on the lookout for a place for us to live and had found a second floor set of rooms in a house in a small street near the corner of the rue Saint Martin and the rue Saint Antoine. He described it to me as a well-kept respectable house in which Johann Baer, the clarinet player, also lived, and said that on our way to our interview with the prince, we could stop by and see it. I thought I might be able to try that in a day or two, and we wrote to the prince's secretary to ask for an interview.

As I gained strength, we started playing again, and began working on our duo repertoire. We added the small pieces we had written in prison; about a dozen for Carl, and three for me, and worked them out so that we could play them well in tune with no guessing what the other was going to do. We also learned one more of the longer duos Carl had reworked from a set of flute duos by Carl Stamitz. After a couple of days of this I was beginning to feel like a horn player again, and it was a good thing we were back in shape, because on the morning of our interview, we received a letter from the prince's secretary asking us to bring our horns with us.

We were careful in dressing in the new clothes and making ourselves look as clean and neat as this period of history would permit. We even went so far as to have our faces shaved at a barbershop. I now know how a sheep must feel when it's getting sheared by a clumsy farmer, who hasn't the least regard for the comfort of the sheep. That barber would probably have worked with the same precision and care if he had been mowing hay out in a field or skinning an antelope. It was a brutal scraping, but we were clean-shaven when we left, and felt like we could be presented to a prince.

With our horn box between us, each taking a handle, we set out into the city early in the afternoon to see our new lodgings and make arrangements to move in. The house Carl had found during my illness was in a small side street, not much more than an alley, between the rue Saint Denis and the rue Saint Martin. It was recommended by Baer, who lived there, but it was not very appealing at first sight. It was a three-story wooden house, with very few actual right angles, and probably had been painted at some point in the distant past, but far too long ago to be able to see clearly if the color had been red or brown, or the dirty grey that it was now.

The owner, a widow named Madam Marais, who could have been anywhere between sixty and a hundred years old, lived on the main floor, Johann Baer had the top floor, and the second floor was now ours. Madam Marais showed us up the stairs, and we followed at a safe distance, because the creaking of the steps gave every indication that you wouldn't want to have too many people walking on them at once.

"What's in that box," she asked, "a cat or a dog? I don't want animals in my house. Filthy things!"

I didn't think she had much to worry about, given the dirty state of the house.

"No Madam," said Carl. "These are *Cors de chasse.* We play in the orchestra of the Prince of Guéméné"

"Even worse! Now on top of the clarinet, we're going to have horns blaring at all hours of the day and night!"

"Oh no madam!" Carl said, trying to calm her down. "We will be extremely careful to do our horn practicing only during the day, and these horns are not as loud as the hunting horns that are played outdoors. We play only pleasant music, not loud hunting calls."

It was clear she was expecting the worst, and with the sort of sounds your average horn or trumpet made at that time, the picture that came into most people's minds when you said someone was moving into your house with horns was not a pleasant one.

The second floor, where we were to take up residence, consisted of four rooms. The two rooms in the back were obviously meant to be bedrooms, and a larger sitting room in the front of the house would serve as a music room in our case. Adjoining the sitting room was yet another room with a hearth, and this was our kitchen. The rooms were partially furnished, with a bed, chair, and chamber pot cabinet in each of the small rooms, a wooden table and two chairs on a well-worn rug in the sitting room, and a larger table and a large cabinet with two doors and shelves in the kitchen. We spent a few minutes looking it over and talking about how we might make it into a comfortable living space. We then paid our first month's rent to Madam Marais and proceeded on our way to the interview.

We arrived at the Hôtel Rohan-Guéméné on the Place des Vosges in the late afternoon in plenty of time for our appointment with the prince. Monsieur Petit prepared us for the fact that this meeting was meant to impress on us the importance of being well-behaved respectable servants of the prince while in his service, and the lecture we received for the better part of half an hour that afternoon from the prince was one of the more humiliating experiences of my time in the 18th century. I thought at first that it wasn't going to be so bad, because I could only understand about a quarter of what he was saying, but once he realized that fact, he began turning to Carl after each point.

"Monsieur Türrschmidt, please repeat in German to your colleague what we have just said, so we can be sure he understands our meaning completely."

Having survived this verbal abuse, we promised to be exemplary members of his household and musical establishment in the future.

"We are sure you will," he said in conclusion, "because if another embarrassing occurrence should take place, we promise you we won't save you a second time but will be happy to let the Comte de Guînes, or anyone else who feels you deserve it, flay you alive and have you drawn and quartered! And now that we understand each other so much better than before, we would like to have you begin your service with us a little earlier than originally planned. We are hosting a small dinner this evening for about twenty guests, several of whom are visiting foreign nobility, and we would like to have you entertain us with about thirty minutes of *Petit airs* on your Cors de chasse. Please be at the east dining room at nine o'clock precisely ready to play. Before you leave, our secretary, Monsieur Dupont will show you where to stand when you play for us, and when and how to enter. We look forward to your performance this evening. Good day Messieurs."

And thus was our first performance scheduled. We went with Monsieur Dupont to the dining room to see where we would stand, and he explained that he would personally meet us at nine o'clock to show us into the room where the prince would introduce us to his guests. We were then to bow and begin our performance. Before we left the Hôtel, he also gave us the promised advance on our salaries that we had been unable to pick up the day after our audition, due to circumstances beyond our control, namely, being hauled off to the Bastille, or as Carl referred to it ever after, "That delightful little inn where the rats were so very friendly..."

It was a sizable sum; seventy-five livres each, and out of it I paid Carl the approximately twenty livres he had spent on me so far. I now felt financially self-sufficient, and with an income of nine hundred livres per year from the prince, and whatever else we could earn in our spare time, we could live like princes ourselves.

We had almost three hours to kill before playing, and went to a tavern to have a glass of wine and some food, and choose our program out of Carl's duet books and the pieces we both had written during our stay in the Bastille. Having eaten and worked out exactly what we would play, we went back to the Hôtel and warmed up and practiced the beginnings of a few of the pieces until time to play.

We were waiting at the door of the east dining room at nine o'clock, but we could hear from outside that several of the guests were delivering speeches and toasts, and our performance would have to wait until they were finished. According to my wristwatch, which I still wore underneath the fancy cuffs of my shirt and coat, it was after ten o'clock by the time they were ready for us. A 21st century battery-powered wristwatch is, incidentally, a highly superior way of telling time compared to anything that Paris had to offer in 1770, and the part that irritated me greatly, was that in about a year the battery would die, and the watch would become useless. We had, in the privacy of my room, watched and listened to everything stored on my phone until that finally went dead, and my watch would eventually bite the dust too. With those, my last physical links with the 21st century would also be dead.

Monsieur Dupont finally ushered us into the room, which had three long tables, covered with white table clothes, and filled with silver dishes, bowls, teapots, and other things. I can't remember ever seeing so much silver all at once. There appeared to be just about as many servants as guests, and everyone was still eating and drinking, while the servants hurried around busily. The guests were all in fancy dress of the time. The men had long colorful coats with ridiculously large cuffs with gold or silver buttons, and gold stitching, and all wore high black boots. The ladies wore large dresses that looked like they would be impossible to sit in, but they seemed to do it somehow. There must have been many thousands of livres worth of gold jewelry and diamonds in that room. We went to the front of the room and the prince presented us to his guests.

"My dear friends, it is with great pleasure that I introduce to you the newest members of my chamber musicians, the two Bohemian Cor de chasse players, Messieurs Palsa and Türrschmidt. They will now entertain us with a set of airs played on the Cors de chasse in a manner that is totally new and innovative, and as musically refined as woodwind instruments."

We came forward, bowed to the audience and began to play. We started with a fanfare, and then moved into some simple minuets and airs to warm up into the more complicated chromatic music we had prepared. Even at this early date, we were a fine duo, though nothing like what we were to become in the years after that, which was partly the result of several performances every week for over thirteen years for the prince, either as a duo, in the wind group, or as soloists with the entire orchestra.

It seemed to me that when we were playing, all the hardships of my new life, all the unfamiliarity, and all I had left behind in my old life were of lesser importance. Life was beautiful when the voices of the two horns were intertwined and complimenting each other, or when I was playing a singing lyrical melody, and Carl's accompanying continuo line laid down a solid foundation, or when the parts became a dialog, as expressive as a deep philosophical conversation. It was a musical experience as fine as any I had ever encountered, and a stark contrast to some of the music making I had heard there so far.

I wasn't at all sure if I would survive this 18th century in general, but musically speaking, I felt I had important work to do here, and Carl was the one who I wanted to do it with. We were so well matched and had such a similar approach to the music that there was no question that this was the start of something big. And it seemed that others were aware of the special qualities of what we were doing too. The listeners received us warmly that evening, and did something that was rare with *Tafelmusik*, which was the equivalent of Muzak of modern times; they stopped what they were doing and listened.

Having only heard the horn played by Carl, and just a small sample of simple orchestra parts at the Concert Spirituel, I was unaware of the actual state of horn playing during this time. I later learned how the horn was played in France, and other countries; most often as a strictly open note orchestra instrument, without the hand in the bell. Gradually I began to appreciate the fact that there were very few horn players who were able to do what we were doing that evening, and that our work would help to inspire a whole generation of players and composers and contribute to the establishment of the horn as a favorite solo and chamber instrument.

Chapter 17

Mein trautes Heim laß gesegnet sein!
(Let my cozy home be blessed!)
- Old German folk saying

After this first performance, we had some time on our hands until our regular service started on the first of December, 1770. We used it to establish ourselves in the new house and get life organized before starting work. We now had a good deal of money at our disposal to make life comfortable and get the things we needed, and the next few days involved visits to several businesses, some normal, and some quite unusual for the time. There were regular household items like copper pots and pans, knives, and a few other simple implements for the kitchen to buy, and then a few other things I felt I couldn't do without that you wouldn't find in most 18th century houses.

I couldn't stand the thought of the coffee that was available and had to figure out how to brew something decent. This involved finding a pan in which I could roast the green coffee beans I had bought a few days earlier, a mortar and pestle for grinding them, and a coffee pot and paper for making filters for brewing the coffee. After some practice, I learned how to make a cup of coffee that was as good as anything I could remember from my local coffee shop in my own time. After I had perfected my roasting and brewing techniques, Carl became a convert to my coffee, and for years we carried in our traveling trunks everything necessary to have good coffee every day.

For my own survival I found a shop that supplied scientific equipment, which at that point in history meant mostly glassware, scales, mineral spirit burners, and other simple lab equipment, and got the things that I needed to distill water. Carl thought it was all rather unnecessary, but I assured him that I knew a few things about what lived in the water of Paris that he didn't, having had high school biology, and that I would certainly die if I drank it, not having grown up with water that had been taken from a river that was also the receptacle of all waste, human and animal, and from every manufacturing process.

The system of clearing waste from the city was very simple.

Almost every street had a shallow gutter, or ditch that ran along its length. Waste was theoretically thrown into these, or in the case of animal waste, found its way there eventually from the street. A good rain would wash the streets and send everything offensive toward the river, where it mixed in with the water that was delivered to houses across the city. Most people avoided drinking water, and drank alcoholic drinks or tea and coffee instead. Nonetheless, dysentery and diarrhea were common, especially in the summer, when the flies were busy transmitting bacteria from filth to food, and the water was at its foulest.

We also bought linens, blankets, towels, plates, cups, and silver spoons. It wasn't until a few months later that we decided we needed to get a second set of clothes for regular use, though my 21st century upbringing insisted from the beginning on having some extra underclothes, or linens as they were called, that I could wash out at regular intervals. Many people had only a single suit of clothes, but we were lucky enough to have our uniforms for the prince's service, an everyday suit, and a second outfit for other important performances, which put us into a fairly high level of common society.

Though we spent a couple of days going around the city, all together we ended up with a bare minimum of items by the standards of a modern household, and everything that we acquired fit easily into a couple of trunks. Later, when we did a lot of traveling, there were very few of our personal possessions that we didn't carry with us. After a life of accumulating things in the 21st century, I was quite happy with the smaller number and nature of things I now owned.

Of personal grooming items, my newly acquired toothbrush, home-made tooth powder, a cake of soap, hairbrush, and a pair of truly bad scissors, the best that money could buy, were about all I needed. The soap was a real luxury item at that time, and I'm sure I bought more of it than any other person in Paris. I'm also sure that I was the cleanest person in Paris, since I appeared to be the only person I knew who used it regularly. People seemed to get along very well without bathing, but my modern training wouldn't let me go for long without washing myself. A true bath or shower was out of the question, but a daily complete washing with a cloth and soap and water wasn't hard to accomplish with the resources at hand.

Carl thought I was the most neurotic person he had ever met in that respect, since I even went so far past the limits of sanity, in his mind, as to wash the spoons, plates, and cups with soap and hot water after every meal. Luckily it was common to bring your own spoon and knife to a public restaurant or tavern, but I always got a few odd looks when I would pull out my own glass and say, "Can you please put my beer in this?" After the water, the main cause of disease in cities of the 18th century was bacteria spread by fleas and flies. The diseases they spread could be deadly, so it was essential to keep these risks to a minimum by keeping the house clean.

I didn't think it was necessary to hire a servant, but Carl insisted, assuring me that virtually everyone had at least one servant, so we hired a girl from the neighborhood to do cleaning and other things for us, and arranged for her to stop by every afternoon to do whatever needed to be done, and cook the mid-day meal, which was always the biggest one, and most likely to consist of a hot dish of some sort with meat.

Chapter 18

My musical training continues, and a short discussion of intonation in the classical orchestra wind section that will be of particular interest to natural horn players.

> *There are Horns called Concert Horns, which have the advantage of all other Horns, that they can play in any Key, by the help of pieces called Crooks, and Shanks, the adding of which to a Horn, makes the Tone lower, that is, an A Horn, may play in G, F, E, D, C, or B, by the addition of more or less Crooks and Shanks, and that is, the Horn can be put perfectly in Tune to the Pitch of other Instruments whatever Key they play in.*
>
> *- New Instructions for the French horn, London, 1770*

By mid-November, we had completely moved into the new rooms and said goodbye to the Wendlings, who had been so helpful to Carl on his arrival in Paris, and then to me after my own arrival. Up until the time when they left Paris to go back to Mannheim in the spring of 1771, we still often dined with the Wendling family, and spent many pleasant evenings playing music with them. It was several years before they returned to Paris, though we saw them the following year in Mannheim, but we had some fond memories of those early days with them in Paris.

Though there was every bit as much competition for work and fame among 18th century musicians as among those of the 21st century, I sensed a brotherhood of musicians in those days that was stronger than in modern times. Life was precarious and work for musicians was unpredictable because most court orchestras were fragile institutions that existed solely because an individual thought it was important to put their money and energy into supporting an orchestra. In the absence of that individual, the interest in the orchestra at a court could disappear overnight, and with no notice your means of support could be gone. In a world like that, you were always happy to hear that someone you hadn't seen in a while was still alive and well, and working, and when the situation deteriorated for someone, or they needed help in some way, the network of other musicians did what they could.

There was one more thing we needed to take care of before starting work, and that was to get another viola, and for me to start learning how to play it. We went to a few music shops and finally found a pretty good instrument made in Cremona, Italy, and bought it, along with some simple viola duets. We went home and I had my first viola lesson and started to get the hang of the alto clef. I now had three daily lessons that took up a good deal of our time; my continued study of hand technique and taming the slippery upper range of my Anton Kerner *Inventionshorn*, which was becoming a passion with me, and my study of the viola and the French language, both of which I looked at as utilitarian skills that would help me do my work and function well in life.

We combined all of them during the day by playing horn duets until we got too tired, and then playing violas, and the entire time conversing in French. We made a pact that we wouldn't speak German again until we were finished with our lessons. Carl was a persistent and strict teacher in each of those areas, and I made excellent progress on the horn, and tolerably good progress on the other two; proof that you learn best what you want to learn most.

We attended some concerts during that time, including some chamber music and another Concert Spirituel performance. The impression of the quality of music making in Paris in 1770 that I had formed at the first concert I had attended was reinforced by these performances. In the orchestra concert we heard even more of the typical kind of horn playing that Paris audiences were used to hearing. Dargent and Mozer were playing horn again, and this time we got a better picture of their playing. For this concert they needed F, G and D horns, which meant that each had three horns with them. The G horns were terribly sharp, forcing them to use several long tuning bits. They played with the hand out of the bell, and their playing was solid and pretty well in tune, though a bit rough around the edges. There were just a few simple stopped notes in the music, for which they inserted the hand in the bell, but they obviously preferred the sound of the open horn without the hand. I was skeptical as to whether they could have played some of our duets very effectively.

It occurred to me that I was just about to start work in one of the best ensembles in the city, and I had never played a performance in an orchestra on the natural horn. I knew it would be fine, since my ensemble skills from many years of modern orchestra playing would serve me well, and it wouldn't take me long to get into the swing of things, but it would still be nice to get some real-life practice before jumping into regular work.

It seems all you have to do is ask, and things happen. A couple of days after we had attended the Concert Spirituel again, Hannes showed up at our door in the afternoon with a letter that had been addressed to Carl at the Wendlings' house. It was from the first horn player of the *Opéra Comique*. He and his colleague in the opera orchestra had the opportunity to play in a concert of the newly formed *Concert des Amateurs*, directed by Gossec, but before they could commit to it, they needed to be able to provide subs for the opera for three performances, and he wanted to know if we could cover for them. This was just what we needed to see how I could handle the quick negotiation of crook changes, and generally fit into an orchestra in a performance. Carl immediately wrote back that we would be happy to do it and thanked him for thinking of us.

We got a reply that same afternoon that we should show up at the theater one hour before the performance on the following Friday and go over tempos with the continuo players.

"Do we get to see the parts in advance?" I asked.

"Not at all necessary. I'm sure they're straightforward, and we're good readers. He would have told us if there was anything we needed to know about in advance."

"Ok, I trust your judgment and knowledge of the orchestra world," I said, not fully convinced.

We spent the rest of the day practicing fast crook changes by playing short simple duets and changing crooks after every piece. We would choose half a dozen duets, map out in advance in which key each would be played, and then play them back-to-back with no testing of notes beforehand. This was an important skill, especially in opera, since there is almost always a crook change between arias, and it was impossible to test the new crook during the recitatives that occur in between. We used a tuning fork that Carl had to make sure we were tuned properly, which is a very inefficient way of doing things when you are used to using an electronic tuner to check your pitch. In the case of our duo practice, we figured out how many tuning bits and which couplers to use for each key from high B flat to low B flat, knowing that the absolute pitch of the tuning fork may not be where the opera orchestra will play.

The most important skill is the ability to find your next starting note from the last note of the previous piece. Often the tonality of the piece would be enough to get you started, but sometimes the horns would start right away in the beginning, and it was essential to hear the note before you play it. In the case of an opera, I would often write in the part "Fourth above singer's last note" and at the top of the next aria "G crook + coupler #3+ two tuning bits." The number of bits would change from night to night depending on the weather, since the range of temperature in a theater could be anywhere between 50°F and 100°F during this time of no heating or air conditioning.

We complain in the 21st century about a shift of a few degrees that makes tuning difficult because strings go up and winds go down when it gets cold, but modern musicians have no earthly idea what we went through in the 18th century trying to play in tune under the most appalling conditions of temperature and humidity. Somehow we did it though, and got used to fixing things almost without thinking about it. In a top-quality modern orchestra, one in which you play with the same people all the time, and at a very consistent level of pitch, and in halls with modern heating and cooling systems, of course you have to use your ears, but you don't have to think too much. You just do the same thing that has consistently worked before, depending on your colleagues' pitch in the same way they depend on yours. But in this 18th century musical world, neither the pitch level, nor the temperature, nor the people around you were dependable, and it was a constant struggle to find a center of pitch and function within it.

Certain keys, or tonalities, were less comfortable on each of the wind instruments, but intonation on the horn was equally difficult in all keys, since we were playing with the same overtone series on each crook. That meant the horns were often the foundation of the pitch in a wind section. We were almost always tuned to the tonic of the piece, and our tonic and fifth were notes that the other winds could depend on if we were doing our jobs correctly. The tone of the horn is also one that is easily heard, and the pitch is easy to discern. That's why, in a wind section, when the pitch was wavering, someone would always say, "Listen to the horns, they're laying down the pitch." And things would immediately stabilize.

These skills were our work for the next couple of days, and after doing this I was noticeably better at plugging into the full range of crooks on short notice. On the valve horn, we get used to the feel of a particular note, and you can find it out of nowhere, even if you don't have the pitch in your ear, solely by feel, and the fingering on the double horn is a tactile reinforcement that helps that process. E at the top of the staff on the F horn, for example, just "feels right" when your thumb and second finger are pressed down. On the natural horn tonality is the way to find pitches, and that is the case about 95% of the time, but you also get used to the "feel" of the note. After a while a G on the top of the staff on the D or low C horn really does have a feel that you can pull out of nowhere with a good deal of reliability with no pitch reference.

Chapter 19

The French are much indebted to M. Philidor, for being among the first to betray them into a toleration of Italian music, by adopting French words to it, and afterwards by imitating the Italian style in several comic operas, which have had great success, particularly, Le Marechal Ferrant, Le Bucheron, Le Sorcier, and Tom Jones.
- Charles Burney, The present state of Music in France and Italy, London, 1773

On Friday evening we got to the theater of the Opéra Comique at the Hôtel de Bourgogne more than an hour before the performance and met with the harpsichordist and leader of the continuo section. The opera being performed was *Tom Jones* by Philidor[10].

"Here are the horn parts," he said. "Not too much to worry about, but let's go over a few tempos and I can tell you who starts each number and whether your parts are prominent, or if you need to stay in the background. The overture is fast - one beat to a bar, and there are a few soli lines in the horn parts to watch out for. The first aria is in two and goes about this fast..." and so on through the entire score, until we got to the hunting scene, which was the most important number for the horns.

"There are a few places where you start alone with a hunting fanfare. I'll give you the cue and the tempo. It should be loud and outdoors-like, and you'll be trading the theme back and forth with the oboes and the singers. Just stay in tempo, read the ink and everything will be fine."

The parts were handwritten, and they weren't terribly legible. There were a lot of corrections, cuts, and additions that had been pasted over the original in places; very messy all together.

"Is this a normal looking opera part? I asked Carl when we had a moment to ourselves.

"Yes. These are about normal. The composer, staging director, concertmaster, and horn players have been messing around with the parts since they were written, which could be as much as ten years ago in some cases. Generally it's clear what you should play, but sometimes it gets confusing, and then the best advice is to lay out until you can figure out where you are."

The pit was long and narrow, with the harpsichord in the middle, so the keyboard player could face the stage. The musicians sat in two long rows on either side of the harpsichord, facing each other, with the strings facing the stage, and the winds facing the audience. The music stands each had two desks, like the duet stand at the Wendlings' house, but they sat on a narrow table between the two rows of musicians. The horns sat stage left, and the people across the table from us, with whom we shared our desks were the second violins. The oboes were next to us, and then the bassoons.

I thought it odd that this group, and the Concert Spirituel orchestra had three bassoonists in an orchestra that only had six first, and six second violins, but that was the bass heavy concept of the time. Our desks had candle holders on each side, and I and the violinist across from me had two candles to illuminate our music, which wasn't very adequate, given the poor state of the parts and the dark room. Theaters with no electric lights are dark places. The pit was not very deep, and the musicians were sitting with the stage just about at the level of their eyes, and those who stood, like the double bass players, had the edge of the stage at about shoulder level. This made it easy for the concertmaster and the harpsichordist to see the stage. The concertmaster was responsible for starting and leading the full orchestra pieces, and the harpsichordist was in charge of the recitatives and leading the continuo section. This opera was a popular one and had been running a while already, and it was obvious that everyone was very comfortable, and even a little bored with the music.

A few minutes before the downbeat, we took our places on hard wooden chairs and lit our candles from those of the harpsichordist. Several musicians, mostly the winds, looked up and started talking among themselves, and to us, when we came into the pit, and of course, I didn't understand what they were saying.

"They've heard the story of the stone through the window of the Comte's coach," Carl whispered to me. "You're a minor celebrity in musical circles these days."

"Herr Palsa!" said a bassoonist in German. "Let me shake your hand sir! It is truly a pleasure to meet someone who had the courage to speak out and take action against the callous behavior of the nobility. I'm happy to hear the two of you escaped relatively unharmed. Someday, and soon I predict, more people are going to take matters into their own hands as you did, and when that happens, we're going to see a massive upheaval in this country."

I thanked him for his kind words and sat down, thinking about the fact that the Bastille would be stormed on July 13th, 1789, sparking the French Revolution, and a lot of stones and other things would be thrown at people, making my act and its consequences seem rather minor.

We checked our pitch with the first oboe, and discovered it was substantially lower than we had anticipated, which required spending the next ten minutes figuring out different combinations of crooks, couplers, and tuning bits while everyone else was warming up in their own peculiar ways. Only the oboist seemed to take any interest in our scramble to get our crooks right, and gave us the pitches we needed. For the first act we needed to crook the horns in F, E flat, and D which we got in order just in time. Tuning the E crook would have to wait until intermission, since we didn't need it until the second act. This was all a little disconcerting, but we felt reasonably okay with the pitch by the time the overture started.

The overture began with a cue from the concertmaster and we were off and running. The music was straightforward, as promised, and we laid down our parts solidly. Our crook changing practice had paid off, and we negotiated each change well. For the most part there was some tonality to get us into the key, but a couple of times we had to start cold, and I could hear Carl hum the tonic of the piece next to me, just to be sure I had the pitch in my ear.

The hunting scene was exciting. Without a doubt more exciting than it was for the regular horn players, because we had never heard it before. Several sections started with unaccompanied horns and oboes, and the entire piece was a dialog between the winds and the singers. It would have been rousing music in any case, but it was almost surreal to be playing this high energy hunting music, sight reading, and having no idea who was going to be playing with you, or if you really were supposed to be playing alone at any given moment. It was a total study in trusting what was on the page and going for it with your musical intuition alone. We made it through unscathed, and got a shuffle of feet from the winds, something that I thought was a 20th century tradition in orchestras, but apparently it goes way back.

After that, the rest of the opera was tame again, with just a few delicate entrances and solo lines in some of the arias. Though there was nothing that was technically hard to play, it was actually a rather complicated opera for hearing pitches and changing crooks. It showed me that I was ready to take on about any challenge that orchestral playing could give me in terms of tonality and key changes.

The other two performances were also fun to play, but not nearly as exciting as that first reading in front of a live audience. Orchestral playing in the 18th century was often a seat-of-the-pants sort of business, and as we started our regular work in the prince's orchestra and chamber musicians, I slowly got used to the idea of feeling like I was sight reading most of the time, except for our duets, and eventually our double concertos, which were some of our most satisfying musical experiences.

Chapter 20

from C. Türrschmidt, 50 Duos, op. 3, 1795

At the beginning of December, after having established ourselves in our new house, we began our service in the orchestra and wind band of the Prince of Guéméné. Like most court orchestras in Europe during the second half of the 18th century, the prince's orchestra played concerts with the full ensemble of eighteen musicians, and in addition, the wind players functioned as a wind sextet for *Tafelmusik* service. This consisted of playing rather dull wind music for oboes, horns, and bassoons that no one actually listened to at banquets and other events.

What we did not do, which was part of the work in many court orchestras, was accompany opera performances, simply because it was expensive, and the prince was not particularly interested in opera. He did, however, have a great interest in chamber music, and gave regular private chamber *soirées* in which members of the orchestra played in various chamber music combinations for the prince's family and guests at his residence. Carl and I became favorites at these gatherings, due to the unusually sophisticated nature of our horn duets for that period of history, but we also got to play chamber music with the other musicians, and sometimes with guests from outside the orchestra.

The full orchestra played a performance at the Hôtel just about once a week and spent a couple of days preparing the program before each one. Since the prince didn't have a composer as music director, we played music from a great variety of composers. Many of the orchestra members had symphonies and concertos they had written or acquired, and they often suggested them to our director, Monsieur Petit, and he just as often programmed them.

Some of our first double concerto performances were done for the prince, using music that Carl had either brought with him to Paris, or received by mail from his father in Regensburg. We also played from more printed music there than anywhere else we played afterward. There was a lot of music publishing in Paris, and the orchestra purchased many of the most recent orchestral works for us to play.

Our first week consisted of the preparation and performance of a symphony by Gossec, the one we had read with the strings on the day of our audition, another symphony by Toeschi, a sinfonia concertante for two violins by Giuseppe Cambini, and an oboe concerto by J. C. Bach. We also began working daily with the wind section of oboes and bassoons learning wind sextets by Haydn, Dittersdorf, Toeschi, J. C. Bach, and many others. Even the best composers had to turn out this sort of music by the truckload, and it was seldom their most inspired efforts, since it wasn't meant to be listened to, but rather served as a wallpaper of sound to accompany a feast. Near the end of the month we started doing Tafelmusik service, and it was some of the most boring and least rewarding music making of my life.

The woodwind players consisted of two French oboists and two German bassoonists. We were a pleasant little international group of musicians, and we kept our spirits up by reminding each other that we were receiving a handsome yearly salary for playing this predictable, uninteresting, and often badly composed music. A fringe benefit of playing at dinners and other social events was that the servants and musicians got first dibs on the leftover food.

The first chamber concert in which we played was for an audience of not more than a dozen in an ornate sitting room at the Hôtel where the prince entertained his guests. The pieces we played in this concert were a quintet by Joseph Haydn for violin, cello, two horns, and harpsichord, and a set of horn duos including some written by Carl and me. These were special musical occasions where the listeners would actually listen, and even occasionally talk with us after the performance. When this occurred it was the only time the barrier between nobility and common musicians broke down somewhat, though it was still very important to remember that we were playing and talking to our social superiors, something I was getting better at doing and accepting as time went on.

One thing I had to get used to in these concerts, and sometimes even in more formal concerts, was the audience's request that we play a piece again. It would most often happen with our horn duets. We would finish a piece at a small gathering, and someone would say after the applause, "That was such a charming little minuet, would you be so kind as to play it again for us?" This was a request that one could not refuse, and especially if made by the prince himself, who frequently did it at our orchestra performances.

The work schedule ranged from minimal, with days off, to being downright brutally overworked at times, and we always had to be available, even when the schedule changed on short notice. But it was predictable enough that we could, with some degree of certainty, sub for players in other groups, and take on extra performances here and there.

Though the pitch level in the Paris groups was relatively consistent, we found that some of the combinations of crooks, couplers, and tuning bits were awkward, and as we had the money, we went to the Raoux shop and had several new crooks and couplers made for the Kerner horns to be able to play in some of the common keys with only a single crook. We especially wanted the best one-piece crooks for our favorite duet keys, which were E and E flat.

We gradually began to fall into a routine with our work and daily life, and I found myself slowly becoming an 18th century musician and person, but always viewing this 18th century life through my 21st century eyes.

Chapter 21

Why do the German Virtuosi feel compelled to go on concert tours? – Because of the need of two things: bread and fame.
- Allgemeine Musikalische Zeitung, Aug. 11, 1802

Time passed quickly, and by early 1772 we were beginning to make a name for ourselves as a duo in the musical life of Paris. In our early days with the prince's orchestra, he seemed to want to keep us to himself and made it difficult for us to play as soloists with other groups. But as time went on, his attitude changed, and he was convinced by a few of his close friends that letting us play as soloists elsewhere was greatly to his advantage, since his name and fame would spread with each of our performances. It was around this time that we did some of our first Concert Spirituel orchestra performances, and some of our first solo performances in other slightly less prominent venues, like the Concerts des Amateurs.

That spring we had the opportunity to further our solo careers due to a break in the schedule of the orchestra. At the end of a morning rehearsal, Monsieur Petit stood up and made an important announcement.

"Messieurs, we have just received word that the prince will travel to Italy for several months beginning in May of this year. A small number of you will travel with him, including myself, four string players, and flute. The remainder of the strings and winds will remain behind. During his absence, those remaining in Paris will be free to spend their time as they choose. Your salaries will, of course continue to be paid, and you will receive word when you are expected back to work. Should you go on tours to other cities, please stay in contact with the prince's secretary, who will inform you of the prince's plans for returning to Paris. We will keep you informed as his travel plans firm up, and the duration of your leave is determined."

"Did you hear that?" said Carl. "This is our golden opportunity to set up our first tour!"

"Yes," I said. "Now I'll get a chance to see something other than this big filthy city, which has been getting on my nerves lately."

I was ready for a break from life in Paris. It was not a nice place. A brothel had moved into the house next door to us, and drunken customers could be heard at all hours of the night, making noise and fighting. The tavern on the other side of us was also getting rougher in its clientele, and we rarely went there of an evening to have a glass of wine anymore, but we still ordered food in quite often when the schedule was too busy to cook. Though I had gotten used to it, the constant filth and stench of the streets was getting old. I had also lost a tooth and two week's work, for which I had to pay a sub, as a result of trying to stop a couple of thieves from robbing a woman of a parcel in the street, an act Carl put right up near the top of the list of my most stupid moves, next to throwing the stone through the Comte de Guîne's coach window.

"You should have known they would fight back, and you could get hurt. It was only a woman's shopping bag, you should have just let them have it," he had said, shaking his head at my strange sense of justice, which I couldn't seem to alter. We were ready for a road trip.

"So how do we go about setting up a tour?" I asked, as we left the Hôtel carrying our horn box. "In my time, soloists had, or I should say, will have, booking agents who contact the concert series and orchestra managements to set up concert dates for them. Who is going to do that for us?"

"We don't have anything like that," said Carl, who was now used to me referring to my own time and comparing it to how things were done in his. "We have to do it ourselves. We start by getting a map of France and the Holy Roman Empire; I saw one in a bookshop last week. Then we start charting out where we want to go and write letters to people we know in those places and see what they can do for us. If we don't know anyone in a particular city, we go there anyway and try to arrange things when we arrive."

"Just like that? We show up somewhere and expect people to arrange concerts for us?"

"That's how it works sometimes. Of course, we have to try to pave the way, and make some connections to nobility and local music directors, but there are times when you just 'show up' as you say, and hope for the best."

We bought our map on the way home, spread it out on the table to decide where we would like to go, and quickly formed a plan. Our idea was to go first to Metz, and then Strasbourg, and then cross the border into the Empire and on to Mannheim, Würzburg, Bamberg, and possibly as far as Hof in Bavaria. If we made it that far, we might come back by a southern route that would take us through Nürnberg, Stuttgart, Karlsruhe, and back into France. Then we made a list of people to write to, asking for their help in organizing concerts, or asking who we could contact to get to the right people. Carl knew people in many of those places, and we started writing letters that evening. We had about six weeks before the orchestra would cease playing, so there was enough time for letters to go back and forth, and to make a few contacts before setting off. Carl wrote to his father too, confident that we could play with the court orchestra of Thurn und Taxis in Regensburg, and the Wallerstein Hofkapelle, if we were able to make it that far in the time we had. Over the next few days we talked with other German musicians and got more contacts to write to and try to drum up invitations.

Within a couple weeks we started receiving replies, and quite positive ones. With the state of travel, and the unreliability of the mail, no one would dream of actually setting a date for a performance months in advance for a musician who was traveling from another country. Most of the responses read; "We would be happy to have you play here. Get in touch when you arrive, and we'll see what we can put together." Others were only lukewarm; "The court orchestra here hasn't funds to pay guest soloists this year, but if you contact the *Kapellmeister* of the Count of -------- he may be able to point you toward something in this region..."

Carl's father wrote back almost immediately saying he had talked to Baron von Schacht, the *Musikintendant* in Regensburg, and we could count on a solo performance there.

Chapter 22

In the past, a first horn hardly went anywhere without a second horn, and vice versa. In the concerts they would give, each would first play a solo appropriate to his "genre", then they would come together in a duo concertante which would often be a piece most pleasing to the public. All the charm of their playing came from their habit of studying and deciding together on the dynamics, articulations and the expression.
- L.F. Dauprat, Méthode de Cor-alto et Cor-basse, 1824

By the first of May we had made a few contacts and were convinced the trip would be worthwhile. In those days, you couldn't just book a ticket on a coach to Strasbourg. You had to book your passage to the next large city, and when you got there, you could see what they had to offer in coaches going to your next stop. The passenger coaches had regular stopping places, and would only travel a few miles a day, more or less, depending on the weather and condition of the roads.

We started our journey from Paris, and our first stop was in Metz, which was about four days away by coach. During those years, it was easy to leave Paris, which was not the case fifteen or twenty years later, as the revolution was getting underway. Then you had to have all your papers in order and be ready to show them to anyone who asked, and even then, there was every possibility that you could be detained by some over-zealous official at the border. In the 21st century it would have taken about two hours to drive the one hundred miles to Metz, but the coach, drawn by four horses, was only able to make it halfway to Reims on the first day, stopping every few hours at posting houses to change horses.

We were packed into the small interior of the coach with two other passengers and countless mail bags. Our horn box and one traveling trunk for the two of us was strapped to the top of the coach, outside and exposed to the elements, which didn't make us very happy. The only protection for the trunks was a piece of oilcloth we had brought along to tie around them, but even that couldn't keep the contents dry if exposed to the rain all day on top of a coach. Fortunately, it was the first week of May, and the weather was beautiful.

The first evening's stop was in the middle of nowhere, out in the country. The countryside was clean and fresh, and it reminded me that I hadn't smelled fresh air for nearly two years, since I hadn't set foot outside of Paris all that time. The roads had ranged from moderately bumpy to almost non-existent, and it felt like our bones had been jarred out of their proper places by the time we stopped. The inn was a rather small house with stables for horses surrounded by farm fields and cow pastures. My first impression of life in the country was that the cows and other farm animals looked absolutely emaciated compared to the picture of cows I had in my mind from my own time. The proprietor and his family all lived in the house and had a couple of rooms for guests who came through on the coach.

The room they offered us was relatively clean, but very rustic, with straw beds and little else. This was roughing it for us, since by this time we had very comfortable beds in our house in Paris. We ate with the family in the kitchen, sharing with them a meal of bread, vegetable soup, and home-made beer. The family was friendly, and in appreciation of their hospitality, we played some duets for them before bedtime. Everyone, including the stable hands, gathered in the sitting room, and the smallest son, who reminded me of my own son, Christopher, was proud to hold the music and act as music stand for us. We didn't let on to him that the dim candlelight wasn't good enough to read the music by and we were playing the pieces from memory.

Our experience the next night, just outside the city of Reims, was not nearly as pleasant, other than the sight of its magnificent Cathedral. The inn where we stayed was filthy, and we paid far too much for the two eggs, stale bread, and sour wine that they were able to give us.

"I never thought I would be homesick for our old room at the Bastille," I said to Carl as we lay down to sleep that night.

"Don't worry, you haven't seen anything near the worst of life on the road yet. Good night, and don't let the bedbugs bite."

This saying, that people of the 21st century often use without any real appreciation of its true meaning, was a sincere wish that you didn't get too many bites from these vicious nocturnal pests on any given night in the 18th century.

We made it to Metz on the fourth day, and there we were met by the musicians with whom Carl had been in contact by mail. The only thing they were able to organize was a concert at the house of a rich businessman. Our reputation had preceded us, and this gentleman was thrilled beyond measure to be able to invite all the most important people in town to a concert given by prominent Paris musicians. We arrived on a Monday evening, and the concert was scheduled for Wednesday evening, so we had Tuesday to get together with the other musicians at one of their houses and prepare some pieces. At this point, we didn't have much of a touring repertoire built up. Several years later we would travel with a bundle of parts for double concertos and chamber music, all carefully copied out, with an innovation of my own that I never saw anywhere else in the 18th century - rehearsal letters or measure numbers. With our own parts, in later years, we could sit down with a group anywhere and efficiently prepare a concert in a single rehearsal. On this trip, however, we were equipped with only three double concertos, one by Franz Pokorny, another by Leopold Mozart, and a third by Francesco Barsanti, which was quite out of style, as well as a few chamber pieces of various instrumental combinations. We also had all our duets, many of which we could play from memory by this time.

The local musicians were a mixed bag, in terms of skill. The group consisted of two violins, a cellist, two oboes, and a harpsichordist. No violists were available, but that was okay, because the viola parts in the concertos were expendable, since they mostly just doubled the bass line at the octave. On the quartets we brought with us, a set of six by Carl Stamitz, there was only a single horn part, and the two of us took turns playing the viola part on a borrowed instrument.

Our concert consisted of the Pokorny and Barsanti double horn concertos, two of the Stamitz quartets, the quintet by Haydn, and too many unaccompanied horn duos. It wasn't the quality of concert we were used to, but went well enough, and our host was lavish in his praise, and in his payment to us. We earned as much from this first concert as we had spent so far on the trip, and a little more. We were breaking even so far, which wasn't always the case on a concert tour.

We left the next day and proceeded on through Nancy and Strasbourg, and over the border into the German speaking Holy Roman Empire, where our first stop was Karlsruhe, giving similar concerts in each city, with varying degrees of success musically and financially.

I hadn't been in any German speaking countries yet, and the flavor of everything was different - the food, the houses, the people, and the language. Carl's German, and that of most of the German musicians in Paris with whom I talked on a daily basis, was excellent, and totally understandable, but it seemed that being in the country now the dialect changed every twenty- five miles, and I had to stay on my toes to understand and be understood wherever we were.

"These dialects are really difficult for me," I commented, as we left Heidelberg on our way to Mannheim.

"Once you get used to them," Carl said, "the regional dialects are one of the most beautiful things you'll experience when traveling. Each one has its own songs and stories. You have to get them first-hand though, because if you write them down, they lose a lot of their charm. Still, someone really should try to collect them together before they get lost and forgotten."

"A couple of brothers by the name of Grimm will do that around 1800 and publish a big volume of fairytales from all the German speaking lands. I studied them in my German classes at school."

"You're going to drive me stark raving mad if you keep this up," he said laughing. "The really frustrating thing about talking to you, is that I'm sworn to secrecy about all of the outlandish things you tell me, and I can't tell anyone what an absolutely bizarre person I have to live and work with."

One of the differences in the way people lived in Germany was the way they arranged their living quarters. We stayed overnight at a couple of places where the house was known as a *Bauernhof*, in which the animals lived on the ground floor, and the family lived directly above them. This makes for a good heating system in cold weather, because twenty cows and a dozen pigs put out a surprising amount of heat. The trade-off is an unbearable smell and the accompanying noise.

After a couple of nights in houses of this kind, we arrived at Mannheim in a driving rain, and immediately got rooms at an inn near the Elector's palace. It would be a couple of days before our clothes and possessions, and our very bones felt dry again.

Chapter 23

...indeed there are more solo players, and good composers in this, than perhaps in any other orchestra in Europe; it is an army of generals, equally fit to plan a battle, as to fight it.
- Charles Burney, The Present State of Music in Germany, The Netherlands, and the United Provinces, London, 1775

Mannheim was a town of about twenty-five thousand residents, and the seat of the Elector of the Palatinate, Carl Theodore. It is situated at the confluence of the Rhine and Neckar Rivers, and is much like an island in that the two rivers surround the town. The Elector and his court were housed at the palace, which faces the town, with the river Rhine at its back. The streets were laid out in sensible squares, and the houses were well maintained and neat. Most of the businesses had to do with the support of the court, and supplied food, made clothing, and procured or manufactured any number of items that were necessary for the support of a court of about fifteen hundred persons. Many of the houses were government offices of various types. The money that supported the town and the court came from taxes paid by the population of the region.

The next morning, after a good breakfast, the likes of which we hadn't had for quite a while, including bread, cheese, sausage, boiled eggs, tea, and fruit at our inn, we sent a message to Herr Wendling that we had arrived. Since this was May, the court was at its summer residence in the nearby town of Schwetzingen. The entire orchestra spent the months of May through October there, and some of the musicians even owned houses in the town. Wendling was a member of the inner circle of chamber musicians, and flute teacher of the Elector, and was therefore wealthy enough to have houses in both Mannheim and Schwetzingen.

We walked around the center of Mannheim and saw the gates of the palace and other sights until noon, and then came back to our inn where we found Herr Wendling waiting for us.

"Greetings, and welcome to Mannheim, my dear young Waldhorn players! I trust the trip by coach was tolerable?"

"Tolerable, but I wouldn't go any further than that," said Carl. "We drove through rain and mud most of the day yesterday."

"I think most of my bones have been jarred out of their joints, I added.

"You'll be comfortable at our house in Schwetzingen, where you can get a few days of rest and some music making, both of which will bring you back to life in short order. But first you would probably like a little tour of the palace and the famous *Rittersaal* where the orchestra plays."

"It's my first visit to Mannheim," said Carl, "and I've heard for years about the palace and concert hall. We would like very much to see it."

We walked to the palace, and Wendling, being one of the most prominent musicians of the orchestra, knew everyone there, and we were admitted immediately. After going through the main gate, we proceeded down the walk past two large fountains and through the entrance to the middle courtyard. The palace consisted of three courtyards, each surrounded by wings of the buildings. The middle court was the largest, and at the far end was the largest building, which housed the grand concert hall known as the *Rittersaal*, the opera house, the chapel, ballrooms, meeting rooms, and many others. We went first to the *Rittersaal*, which is a rectangular room with an elaborate inlayed wooden floor, marble and wood paneled walls, and a ceiling that had to be at least forty feet high, painted with scenes of angels and animals, from which hung half a dozen chandeliers with countless candles that lit the room at night.

"This is the room where the Elector holds his weekly *Academia,* or orchestra concerts," said Wendling. "The orchestra stands in the middle of the room on a low green carpeted platform - only the cellos and harpsichord sit - and the audience is seated all around. The Elector sends out invitations to these concerts, and these invitations are highly sought after. The Elector and other important guests sit in front of the orchestra and play cards and drink tea, coffee, and chocolate. The concerts start at five o'clock and go at a leisurely pace until after nine o'clock. The programs are a mix of symphonies and overtures, mostly by our Mannheim composers, solo concertos played by our soloists or guests, and arias and vocal pieces.

Too bad you can't be here during the Carnival and Lent seasons to play with us in this beautiful room. We love having visiting soloists. I hope we can get Christian Cannabich, who is organizing the summer programs at Schwetzingen to work you into one of the concerts. Rumor has it that one of our horn players, Anton Dimmler, has written a piece in honor of your visit."

"A new piece?" said Carl. "That sounds interesting. How did he know we would be here?"

"When you wrote me in April, I immediately told our horn players that two of the finest Waldhorn players in Paris would be visiting. They were very enthusiastic - all except Georg Franz, who "doesn't approve" of the modern trend in horn playing that players like the two of you and Punto are developing. Musicians and audiences everywhere are enthusiastic about the horn becoming a high-class solo instrument, but I guess there will always be a few old-fashioned players who don't want to give up the traditional way of doing things."

"I hope we can change his mind while we're here," said Carl. "We are very much looking forward to playing with the orchestra."

We toured the rest of the palace, and saw the opera house and chapel, where the orchestra also played, and then went back to our inn to get our trunks and set out in a hired wagon for Schwetzingen and the summer residence of the court.

The town of Schwetzingen was small, with the Elector's residence being the focal point. It was a beautiful afternoon, and there were people everywhere on the streets and in small town squares. We saw several small bands of musicians playing outdoors as we made our way to the Wendlings' house. In other houses in the street, you could hear people practicing on various instruments. It was like a musician's colony where music was in the air all the time.

The Wendling family lived in a neat wooden house in the same street as many other musicians, and were neighbors of Ignaz Holzbauer, the composer famous for his operas, and Friedrich Ramm, the principal oboist of the orchestra. When other more formal concerts were not taking place, there were often chamber music gatherings at the Wendling or Holzbauer houses. Wendlings' daughter Elisabeth was now beginning to make a name as an operatic soprano, and Frau Wendling was as busy as ever with her own singing career. They showed us to a couple of guest rooms that were quite comfortable, with beds the likes of which we hadn't seen since leaving Paris.

When the family was gathered together for the evening meal, Wendling told us of the plans he had laid out for our visit.

"I've arranged for you to play with us on a chamber concert in the bath house of the summer palace garden, where we play several times a week. I'm sure you can do a set of duos, and if you have any other chamber pieces with you, we can probably fit one or two into the program. We'll be rehearsing this evening at the Holzbauers' and tomorrow morning at the bath house."

"We can do any number of duos, and possibly a quintet by Haydn for horns, violin, cello, and harpsichord," I said. "How would that work in the program?"

"Fine!" said Wendling. "Karl Toeschi will be playing violin, Innocenz Danzi will be the cellist, and Ignaz Holzbauer will play the clavier. I'm sure we can convince them to do a piece with you. The Elector will be there, and I hope he will be impressed enough to invite you to play in the next orchestra concert this coming Friday evening. I would have asked Kapellmeister Cannabich, but it's well known that he absolutely hates the horn and doesn't in any way consider it a viable musical instrument, so it's best to go through Carl Theodor himself. If the Elector says you'll play a concerto with the orchestra, Cannabich won't be able to prevent it."

"I get the sense that there's a bit of orchestra politics that one needs to learn how to navigate to be successful here," said Carl.

"More than you can possibly imagine," said Wendling, looking knowingly at his wife, Dorothea. "And if I'm not mistaken, here comes some of it now, about to knock on our door."

In half a minute, Katherina ushered in the two men that Wendling had seen through the sitting room window. Both were carrying cloth bags that obviously had fixed pitch horns in them, and the older of the two was carrying a score.

"Carl and Johann, may I introduce Anton Dimmler. and his son Joseph, two of our esteemed horn players," said Wendling. Anton was a high horn player and Joseph was one of the *Accessisten*, a younger player still in his apprenticeship, or trial period in the orchestra.

"Welcome to Schwetzingen!" said Anton Dimmler. We've been looking forward to your visit ever since Herr Wendling told us of your plans last month."

"Very pleased to meet you," we both said in unison while shaking their hands.

"We're looking forward to meeting all of the horn players," added Carl.

"We have a good group, and I'm sure you'll like them, though I do have to apologize in advance for one of our group, who is a bit unsympathetic to current trends in horn playing," said Dimmler Sr.

"A bit unsympathetic is understating the case," said the younger Dimmler. "My father is talking about Georg Franz, who thinks that crooks are an invention of the devil, and that playing the horn with the bell in the air, as we do in the orchestra here, was approved by God almighty in heaven, and any other way of doing things, including chromatic hand stopping, is an affront to himself personally. He comes with the territory. A fine horn player, but rather stuck in his ways."

"But back to more pleasant things," said Dimmler Sr. "In honor of your visit to Mannheim, I've composed a little concerto for you. Here, you can take a look at the score. I would be greatly honored if you would be willing to perform it while you're here."

"We're very grateful to you for going to all the trouble of writing a concerto for us. We'll give it a try, and hopefully we can learn it by the weekend," said Carl.

I was already looking over the score, and was a bit skeptical about learning it by the weekend. It was for horns in E, and was relatively straightforward horn writing, but there were a few difficult passages for each of us.[11]

"If we can't get it on the program for the formal concert, we can organize a performance here in our house, or on the town square," added Wendling. "There is always a way to get music played even if the powers that be won't put it on a program."

We talked with the Dimmlers for a while, and two other horn players showed up to welcome us - a low horn player by the name of Georg Eck, and Franz Lang, another first horn player. All four of them were wearing the standard Mannheim orchestra uniform of a gray coat with red cuffs, light colored breeches, red stockings, a white neckerchief or scarf, and a black three-cornered hat.

After dark we went to the house of Ignaz Holzbauer to rehearse for the chamber concert. There we met Danzi, the principal cellist of the orchestra, concertmaster Toeschi, and Holzbauer, and several others who came and went during the evening. Innocenz Danzi was the father of Franz Danzi, whose woodwind quintets all horn players know. He was a small dark Italian man who spoke with a heavy accent and was the brother-in-law of Karl Toeschi. The Mannheim orchestra was like a big family, with all sorts of complicated intermarriages, and everyone seemed to be related to everyone else in some way or other.

We rehearsed the Haydn quintet, which went together easily. These people were very skilled at making things sound good on the first reading. This was because they spent most of their time reading and performing music on short notice.

They went on to rehearse a quartet for flute and strings written by Wendling, and an oboe quartet by Toeschi, played by Friedrich Ramm, the oboist, who we would get to know better in later years in Paris. There were a few other pieces by Holzbauer, Franzel, Cannabich, and others. I was surprised to find that, other than wind band music written for Tafelmusik service, there was very little chamber music that included horn parts among the hundreds of pieces that the resident composers had written. This was because the orchestral horn playing in Mannheim, though very well done, involved almost exclusively open notes, with minimal use of the hand for the occasional stopped note or to correct intonation on sustained notes. This style was well suited to the wind band music, but not to soloistic chamber music.

Chapter 24

To a stranger walking through the streets of Schwetzingen, during summer, this place must seem to be inhabited only by a colony of musicians, who are constantly exercising their profession: at one house a fine player on the violin is heard; at another a German flute; here an excellent hautbois, there a bassoon, a clarinet, a violincello, or a concert of several instruments.

- *Charles Burney, The Present State of Music in Germany, The Netherlands, and the United Provinces, London, 1775*

The chamber concert the next evening was in a building called the *Badhaus,* or bath house in the palace garden. It was an ornate room lined with statues and fancy furniture, and the musicians stood in the middle of the room with the audience seated and standing all around. Like most 18th century concerts, people came and went the whole time, and talked throughout the performance. Shortly before the beginning of the concert Carl Theodor, the Elector and his wife arrived, and sat at a table with some other important people. They immediately began drinking tea that had been set out for them and playing a card a game called *L'Omber*, or *L'Hombre*, using a deck of cards that I recognized as regular playing cards, with kings, queens, jacks, etc., but hand colored.

The Elector was a middle-sized man with thin hair and a pleasant face. He was wearing clothes that didn't particularly distinguish him from the other well-dressed guests. He wore a loose-fitting red coat, white breeches, and very simple shoes. This was in stark contrast to the French aristocrats with whom I had come in contact and turned out to be the norm with nobility in German speaking countries, except on more formal occasions, at which time they pulled out all the stops and dressed up in high style. Carl Theodore was an enthusiastic amateur flute player and received lessons almost daily from Herr Wendling. His wife, Elisabeth-Augusta was taller than the Elector, and had a bright round face and a large nose. She was surrounded by two or three ladies in waiting, and they laughed and talked pretty much continuously during the concert. The ladies were also well-dressed, but in a simpler style than their French equals. The really noticeable difference was that the ladies of the German courts didn't feel obligated to wear the elaborate hair styles popular in France at that time, which I thought very sensible of them.

This rather long program had pauses between the pieces during which the audience ate and drank, and the musicians mingled with them. It was a very loosely organized affair in comparison with chamber concerts of the 21st century. There were no printed programs for these concerts, and the concert order was determined shortly before the performance. Our Haydn quintet was a piece we had done numerous times, and the others read it beautifully with us. Our set of duos came about two thirds of the way through the program, and as we were preparing to play, I noticed the arrival of the four horn players, and a fifth, who I assumed was Georg Franz, who we had not yet met.

As we often did in a mixed concert program, we played six short pieces by various composers, and always one or two by one of us. They went well, and as usual, the audience became substantially quieter as we did our pieces, using chromatic notes that had probably never before been heard on the horn in Mannheim. The Elector was clearly very interested in what we were doing, and the horn players, who were all within our sight were also impressed and listening carefully. Georg Franz stood with his arms folded in disapproval of what he was hearing. We left the center of the room after acknowledging the applause and sat down at a vacant table where the performers had left instrument cases. Within half a minute we were joined by the Elector himself, who was a very friendly and approachable man. He valued the musicians, artists, writers, and scholars at his court, supported them well, and treated them certainly not as equals, but with a degree of respect and regard that we would never have received from our own employer, the Prince of Guéméné in Paris.

"Welcome to our summer residence gentlemen!" he said smiling as he sat down next to us. "What a pleasure to hear the latest trends in horn playing as it is being practiced in Paris, - and done with such perfection of execution, expression, and perfect intonation! Just like well-played woodwind instruments!

"Thank you, your highness," said Carl. "It is our great pleasure and honor to come to Schwetzingen and perform with some of the finest soloists in Europe who are in your service."

After these formal compliments went back and forth, the conversation lightened up, and he wanted to know all about our instruments with the crooks, and the method of playing completely chromatically on them.

"We've heard reports of what Punto and a few others are doing with the horn, but until now we have not had visiting horn soloists who are doing this type of playing at Mannheim. We would certainly feel we had missed a grand opportunity if we failed to have the pleasure of hearing more from you during your visit. Do you have any music that you could play with the orchestra for the next *Academia* on Saturday? It's unlikely we have any solo concertos for horns in our library. It isn't the sort of playing our horn players do. They are rather traditional in their approach to the instrument."

"We have a few pieces with us," I replied. "Possibly a piece by Leopold Mozart of Salzburg would fit into the program. And on our arrival yesterday morning we were presented with a concerto written for us by your own horn player, Herr Dimmler, the elder."

The Elector beamed with enthusiasm.

"We know Herr Mozart's music well, since he has paid us a number of visits over the years, bringing new compositions each time, and as you know, many of our musicians contribute compositions to the programs. A concerto by Herr Dimmler would be a welcome addition."

At this point Carl Theodore waved at a tall well-dressed gentleman standing across the room, listening to the oboe and string quartet that was being played. He immediately came over to us, and at a gesture of the Elector sat down at the table.

"Gentleman, may we present Kapellmeister Christian Cannabich. Herr Cannabich, these are Herrn Türrschmidt and Palsa, the celebrated horn duo from Paris."

Cannabich, who had just arrived at the concert, and had not heard anything we had played, greeted us in a rather uninterested way and turned back to Carl Theodore.

"The orchestra has been under the direction of Herr Cannabich ever since the death of our beloved Johann Stamitz in 1757, and under his direction it has continued its reputation as the best orchestra in Europe. Herr Cannabich, we are highly impressed with the skill of these two young Waldhorn players and would like them to play two concertos in the Academia this coming Saturday. They have a piece by Leopold Mozart, and a new concerto by Anton Dimmler. When can they join you to rehearse these pieces?"

"We begin preparing the music tomorrow morning your highness, but we already have quite a full program."

"It won't tax the listeners a bit to add a couple of short pieces," said the Elector. "We don't want the Schwetzingen audience to miss hearing these talented Waldhorn players."

"Bring your orchestra parts to my house this evening," he said turning to us for the first time, "so I can look them over beforehand, and we will do our first reading tomorrow morning at ten o'clock in the *Zirkelsaal*. That's the large circular room in the Orangery. Your highness and our esteemed guests, I bid you good night."

He rose and left us looking at each other inquisitively.

"Herr Cannabich always reserves judgment until he hears someone play." said the Elector. "You can be sure he will become a big supporter after he hears your remarkable way of playing the horn."

Later that evening we took our orchestra parts to Herr Cannabich, who didn't seem particularly interested in having them. He took them from us without comment, and we found our way back through the streets of Schwetzingen to the Wendlings' house. It was a beautiful warm clear evening, and the stars were brilliant in the sky.

"Not terribly warm and friendly, is he?" I said.

"I think it's just that we play horn," replied Carl. "Everyone told us yesterday evening that he hates horns. It should be a fun time rehearsing with him tomorrow!"

We had spent a good deal of our spare time learning the new Dimmler double concerto and felt as though it was ready to try with the orchestra. The next morning we showed up at the *Zirkelsaal* just before ten o'clock to find the orchestra taking their places and tuning. The orchestra was a well-groomed group who were all dressed in the Elector's orchestra uniform. They were also better behaved than any other group I saw in the 18th century. Christian Cannabich was a strict disciplinarian, both musically and in the group's appearance and deportment, and it made the orchestra concerts at Mannheim some of the best in the world.

"Gentlemen, we will start this morning with the horn concertos, and then rehearse the symphonies by Herr Toeschi and Herr Haydn before we break for lunch. We have a lot to do, so let's get started."

We tuned our E flat crooks to the pitch given to us by Friedrich Ramm, the oboist. The pitch was just about where it was for the chamber concert the day before, so it wasn't difficult to find. The Mannheim Orchestra played slightly lower than we were used to in Paris, but it only took a couple of tuning bits to get there, and we could use our favorite one-piece E and E flat crooks.

The orchestra was a bit larger than the Concert Spirituel Orchestra, having nine first and nine second violins, and in the bass heavy style of the time, four each of violas, cellos, and basses, as well as pairs of winds. As they started the opening tutti of the Leopold Mozart double horn concerto, it was obvious they were a tight group; more precise, and with better intonation than most of the Paris orchestras, and with more energy. This made sense, since in Mannheim, the orchestra was together year-round, with the same people in the same seats, as opposed to our more freelance attitude, even in the Paris Opera orchestra, where subs were business as usual. The Concert Spirituel Orchestra was contracted for each set of concerts, and though the same players were generally used, they only played during holidays when the theaters were closed. Our own small private orchestra was the exception, since all the players had to be there for all services as their top priority, and it was reflected in the quality of the performances.

As we arrived at the first solo section, Cannabich stopped the orchestra. "Fine, fine, let's jump to the next orchestra tutti. Gentlemen, you can get together with the continuo section at the end of the rehearsal to go over the solo sections while I am working with the violins."

"But can't we just read through the piece to give everyone an idea of how it sounds?" I said, a little taken aback at his lack of interest.

"We simply don't have time. I have two new symphonies to rehearse, and both are much more complicated to put together than these simple horn pieces. I'm sure you know your parts, and we will follow you strictly."

We went through the whole piece in this way, and we could see that Josef Toeschi, the assistant concertmaster, and Holzbauer, the harpsichordist, both of whom we had played with on the previous evening, were visibly annoyed at his attitude toward us. But there was no room for negotiation with him. He was in charge, and it was clear that he didn't care to rehearse our pieces very much.

Both the Leopold Mozart concerto and the new piece by Dimmler were accompanied only by strings, and none of the wind players were present. Had they been there, I'm sure they would have come to our rescue. We hardly played a note in the full rehearsal, but Holzbauer and Danzi, the principal cellist, and a couple other continuo players stayed after to play through our solo sections, and we were able to at least make sure the parts for the new concerto were correct.

Later that evening we talked it over at supper at the Wendlings' house.

"I knew he was going to be difficult, but that was absolutely uncalled for. It was the height of rudeness to not allow us to play through the pieces even once," said Carl.

"It's sad," said Wendling, "but as I told you, there are always political doings behind the scenes here. You just happen to be horn players, to whom he pays little attention anyway, and when the Elector announced to him that you would be soloists, he took an instant dislike to you, and decided to make the experience as unpleasant as possible. It happens to all of us from time to time." Frau Wendling stepped into the dining room at that moment.

"I got on his bad side for several months last opera season, and rehearsals for Holzbauer's newest opera were absolutely miserable. Holzbauer finally got him to let up, and we eventually made our peace, but it was extremely unpleasant for a while."

"Though he insists on the highest level of precision in the orchestra, he doesn't mind setting up a soloist for a bad performance if he doesn't like them," added Wendling.

During the evening several musicians stopped by, and each apologized to us for the unfortunate rehearsal of the morning and said they would do their best to make the concertos go well.

The next day we were not invited to rehearse again, nor did Cannabich ask us to participate in the dress rehearsal on the morning of the concert. Another private rehearsal with Toeschi, Danzi, and Holzbauer, who were now determined to help us have a good performance, made us feel better prepared and took some of the edge off a tense situation.

Chapter 25

Hail, gentle Dawn! mild blushing Goddess, hail!
rejoic'd I see thy purple Mantle spread o'er half the Skies.
Gems pave thy radiant way, and orient pearls from every shrub depend.
The Horn sonorous calls, the Pack awak'd their Mattins Chant, nor brook my long delay.
- William Flackton, The Chace, ca. 1740

Saturday morning, the day of the orchestra concert, was bright and clear. After breakfast, there was a knock at the door of the Wendlings' house. Katerina opened the door to reveal Georg Franz, one of the horn players, who we had been told was not a fan of ours. On this beautiful morning he was all friendliness and eloquence.

"Gentlemen! I fear I was unable to properly welcome you to Schwetzingen upon your arrival and thought I might come around this morning to formally greet you and invite you to go out with us today to see the Elector's hunt, which will take place this afternoon. I will be playing the hunting calls today and would be honored to show you how we horn players accompany the party and sound the signals."

"Thank you for your friendly offer, Herr Franz," I said. "We didn't have anything planned today before the orchestra concert, so a little fresh air might be nice. What do you say Carl, shall we go along for the ride?"

"Yes, by all means." he replied, though I thought he didn't sound his usual enthusiastic self.

"Excellent," said Franz. Meet me at the stables of the palace at eleven o'clock and we will join the hunting party. I'm sure you'll enjoy getting out into the fields and forest today and experiencing the fresh air and excitement of the hunt!"

"That was awfully friendly of him," I said after he had left.

"Hmm.... I don't like the feel of this," said Wendling, who had heard the entire conversation from the kitchen. "I just have a feeling he's up to no good. That was very out of character for him. I've never seen him act so friendly to anyone here, let alone horn playing guests."

Well, there can't be any harm in going along," said Carl. "We can always leave them to the hunt and come back if it seems uncomfortable, or if he starts an argument about horn playing styles."

We changed into our outdoor clothes, and hurried over to the stables, where we found a rather large group of the most important people of the court, all ready to set out for the hunt. The Elector was not among the party that day, so we didn't know a soul among them. Georg Franz was already there on horseback and had two hunting horns with him.

"Good morning!" he said, waving to us. Herr Steidel, the stable master will fix you up with horses, and we'll be on our way. I brought an extra horn in case you want to try your hand at a call or two."

The stable master must have been told in advance that we would need horses, because he was bringing them out at that moment.

"Are you two gentlemen comfortable with horses? I have two rather spirited animals here for you, if you're ready for them," he said.

I had done some riding as a boy, but it had been quite a few years since I had been on horseback. Carl seemed to be all ready for a good ride.

"I haven't been out riding for a while, but we used to do hunting service in Wallerstein with my father, so I've spent a lot of time on horses."

We both mounted, and Franz handed Carl the other horn, which he put over his shoulder in a way that showed he was familiar with these things. Franz handed me a small book.

"Since you may not be familiar with our hunting calls in this region, I brought a book of them so you can see the purpose of each of the signals."

Soon we were underway, and it was a fast-moving group of riders, accompanied by a pack of very excited dogs and several servants on foot. We headed out of town and were soon in the fields and patches of forest. "Spirited" was a bit of an understatement in describing our horses. They were downright wild, and mine, in any case, didn't at all want to go in the direction I wanted him to go. Carl was having similar troubles, but he seemed to have a lot of experience with horses and was doing okay. Georg Franz sounded the opening call, which in the book was called *La Point du Jour*. This was the signal for the hunt to begin, and after that, he would play calls as the hunters in the party would separate and need to communicate with each other. Some had to do with movements of the party, and some with animals that were sighted, or directions to the servants and dogs. All were played just about as loud as possible, to be heard at a distance.

We followed along, and I was enjoying hearing Franz's explanations of how the horn player fit into the proceedings, and learning the calls, with which Carl was already quite familiar. After about an hour, Franz came up beside me and handed me his horn. "Here, do me a favor and play the next couple of calls while I go back to fetch something I dropped on the trail. I'll be right back." And with that he rode off in the direction from which we had come and disappeared into the thick forest.

"What was that all about?" asked Carl, riding up next to me.

"He asked me to play the next couple of calls while he goes back for something," I said. "He'll be back soon."

"I hope he comes back soon. We shouldn't be blowing our brains out on hunting calls on the day of a double concerto performance."

At that moment someone called for a horn signal.

"I'll get this one, I know most of them from memory," said Carl, and he played the call, which needed to be strong and projecting.

A few minutes later, Franz had not returned, and the leader of the hunt, a nobleman by the name of Baron von Zedtwitz, decided that the party should divide in two and surround a herd of deer that had just been spotted.

"This group will go to the left, and I'll take the rest of you to the right. One horn player will go with each group so we can communicate. Off we go!"

"Carl! What am I supposed to do? I said as the two groups were organizing.

"Just read the calls out of the book. The Baron will tell you which ones you need to play. One of us will usually sound the call, and the other will respond to show that they heard it and understand."

That's all the time we had to talk about it, and we were off. The next hour was spent playing loud calls out of the book, and Carl playing back to me from what seemed way too far away for comfort. The horns Franz had given us were standard pitch E flat hunting horns, so the calls were not too high, but they had to be loud, and the horse was often in motion when they had to be played, because if you stopped to play you were totally left behind in the dust. This was all quite tiring, and when the two parties were finally reunited, Carl and I looked at each other, and we knew exactly what had happened, and how we had been tricked by Franz.

"That filthy rotten bastard! shouted Carl. "I knew this was some kind of set-up, and now I see his plan. He left us high and dry out here to play hunting calls all day to make us worthless for the concert this evening! What a low-down dirty trick to play on someone. I'm sure we won't see any more of him today. We should have known what was going on when he arrived with an extra horn and the book of calls for you. It should have been obvious too when he showed up alone this morning. There are always at least two horn players on the hunt, so they can play back and forth to each other when the hunters separate. And then to top it off he arranged for the two wildest horses in the stable to be given to us!"

"Waldhorn players!" cried Baron von Zedtwitz. "We need you to sound the call for a stag sighted. Play and then we'll be off after it!"

"But your honor," I said, "we can't play hunting calls all afternoon. We have to play in the concert tonight."

"Tut, tut my good gentlemen, there will be plenty of time to rest and clean yourselves up before the concert, but now we must be off! The hunt is up, the dogs are in rare form, and everyone is ready to go! Away with you!"

Knowing that one doesn't question or contradict a baron, we had no choice but to stay with the hunting party and sound the calls when needed. For the next few hours, we took turns wearing ourselves out playing loud calls, and when the parties would separate, we had to play back and forth. At about four o'clock the party had taken a couple of deer, and they decided to call it a day and go back to dress for supper and the concert that evening.

We came back to the Wendlings' dirty and exhausted, and with embouchures that were totally worn out from playing the hunting signals. Herr Wendling was outraged when he heard what had happened.

"I've heard of some very underhanded tricks played on visiting musicians, but this one top anything I've experienced. The Dimmlers, father and son stopped by to see you, and were surprised to hear you were out on the hunt. Georg Franz and Dimmler junior were supposed to be the horn players today, but Franz told the younger Dimmler early this morning that he wouldn't be needed today, and the young man, like any horn player, was happy enough to get out of a hard day of outdoor horn playing and riding and didn't question him about it. The Elector shall hear about this!"

We had a quick supper with the family and got dressed for the concert at the Zirkelsaal in the palace, which was to start at six o'clock.

Chapter 26

Warm up? I never cool down!
- Dale Clevenger

The concert hall was decorated for the occasion, tables were set for the Elector's family and his guests in the front, and chairs for the rest of the concert audience, all of whom attended the concert for free, but only with an invitation from the palace. The orchestra was already warming up, and the room was filled with the noise of the guests arriving and greeting one another. As soon as we entered the room, Wendling pushed his way through the crowd to the Elector's table and had a few words with him. Though we couldn't hear what he was saying, it was clear that Carl Theodor was upset by it, and pounded his fist on the table when replying.

Wendling returned to us where we were putting our horns together with a satisfied smile on his face.

"I explained everything, and the Elector said that if today's abuse of his guest soloists gets in the way of a fine performance, Herr Franz is going to have some explaining to do tomorrow."

"Much help that!" said Carl, after Wendling, with his flute in hand, had gone to his place in the wind section. "I don't know about you, but I'm absolutely wasted, and if I'm able to get anything out of this horn, it will be by some miracle of a merciful God."

"My face is pretty much like chopped meat too," I said. "Have we ever played a concert under worse conditions; exhausted, with almost no rehearsal, a new piece we've never performed before, and that in front of the Elector of the Palatinate and his entire court?"

We knew there was no point in warming up, since the whole thing was going to be a disaster and an embarrassment, so we just sat dejectedly at a table on the side waiting to play.

The concert began with the overture to the opera *Lo Speziale* by Joseph Haydn. Then the orchestra played the new symphony by Josef Toechi which was pleasant enough, and then an oboe concerto played by Friedrich Ramm. That was followed by some arias from the latest opera by Holzbauer. The orchestra was playing well, and despite our own predicament, it was fascinating to listen to them in top form, and at the height of their fame as one of the best orchestras in Europe.

Finally, about two hours into the concert, it was our turn to play. Kapellmeister Cannabich addressed the audience.

"Your highness, and our esteemed guests, may I introduce our next soloists, the visiting Waldhorn players of the Prince of Guéméné from Paris playing a concerto for horns by Kapellmeister Leopold Mozart of Salzburg."

We stepped out to our places in front of the orchestra, and Cannabich looked absolutely gleeful as he started the piece, knowing that he had done everything in his power to make our lives miserable. He would have been even more beside himself with joy if he had known that we had been out playing for the hunt all day and were almost incapable of playing the horn.

As the opening tutti was coming to a close, I looked over at Carl, and he had the most determined look I had ever seen on his face. I could tell he was going to do his damnedest to get through this and it inspired me to do the same. We nodded to each other and I put my horn to my lips, which felt like they were about to start bleeding.

I don't know how it works, but with all our experience appearing as soloists over the previous two years, we had learned how to move into a special performance zone that was all ours. It was like a trance in which we could do everything at as high a level as we were capable of, and at the same time, feeling a totally open line of communication with our audience. At this moment we were there, and being tired and all the other things that should have made this the worst performance of our lives were completely forgotten in an instant. We were doing what we did best accompanied by this fine ensemble. They too were doing their best for us, and the excitement mounted as we played each solo section.

The Leopold Mozart double concerto was a product of the previous generation, having been written in the 1750s, which meant it was a little old fashioned next to the current music that was being played that evening, but what it lacked in contemporary style, it made up for in virtuosity, with daring passages in the *clarino* register for me on the E flat horn, and the wildest acrobatic second horn tricks for Carl. We had played this piece many times, but I couldn't recall it being this exciting or clean ever before.

The piece ended to loud cheering and applause from the audience and the orchestra. Somehow the impossible had happened and the performance was a great success. The original plan was for the two horn pieces to be played back-to-back, but as we were acknowledging the applause, Cannabich came up to us with his violin under his arm.

"Gentleman, after that fine performance you deserve a break. We will rearrange the program and play another orchestra piece before going on to the Dimmler horn concerto."

We really needed to rest, and went back to our table while the orchestra played a short piece by Ignaz Fränzl, another of the Mannheim concertmasters. We were surprised that Cannabich had given us a bit of slack and let us rest before the next piece. His approach to us was quite different when he told us they would play another piece before ours.

The playing of the Dimmler concerto was like child's play after the success of the Mozart concerto, and we were in top form again. The orchestra urged us on as we played one difficult solo section after another and brought the piece to a brilliant conclusion to the wild applause of both audience and orchestra. Carl and I hugged each other, and amidst the noise of the applause I whispered to Carl.

"If we can pull off something like this, we can do anything, anywhere, anytime!"

We made our exit from the concert stage and sat in a state of disbelief at what had just happened. The orchestra played the new symphony by Joseph Haydn, which a modern program would have called the *Trauer Symphony*, No. 44 in e minor. This was the end of the concert, and as the audience was dispersing, a smiling *Kapellmeister* Cannabich approached us.

"My dear Waldhorn players! My sincere apologies for the events of the past few days! I have never been impressed with what I have heard from the horn, and of course when the Elector insisted on your playing in tonight's concert, I had no idea of the quality of artistry and perfection of execution you would bring to the performance. I hope you will forgive me for my groundless assumptions about your instrument and yourselves and believe that after tonight's performance, I look forward to the opportunity to work with you again in the future under more comfortable and friendly conditions. And to show you the sincerity of my apology, I promise to write a double concerto for you."

We thanked him for his good words, though we were both still a little skeptical of this man who had done all he could in the rehearsals to thwart us. As far as I know, he never wrote a concerto for horns. As Cannabich left us with more words of praise, the Elector himself approached us and beckoned us toward a side door that led into a private sitting room.

"Gentlemen! What a pleasure to hear you a second time! Before this week, we would not have believed that the Waldhorn could be played with such perfection and expression. We are truly impressed with your skills on that instrument, and would like to make you an offer that we hope will be hard to refuse. Our regular horn players do a fine job as orchestral players and for Tafelmusik service and the hunt, but we would be honored if you would consider joining the Mannheim orchestra as soloists and chamber music artists. We would allow you to go on concert tours for a reasonable number of weeks out of the year and offer a higher salary than the Prince of Guéméné is currently paying you. Will you consider such an offer, and attach yourselves to one of the best musical establishments in all of the Holy Roman Empire?"

This was all quite sudden and unexpected, but from the look we each saw on the other's face, it was obvious that we were of a single mind. Carl spoke first.

"Your Highness, we are greatly honored by your good opinion of our performances, and by your offer to go into your service. The Mannheim Hofkapelle is without a doubt the best orchestra we've heard or played with, and it would be a great pleasure to play more with such a fine group of musicians. I hope we can come back and perform here again in the future, but as to a permanent appointment, we are under obligation to our employer in Paris, and can't possibly break our contracts with him at this point. We are also very much attached to the musical scene in Paris, and plan to stay there for as long as the prince will have us in his orchestra."

"We understand your position completely," said the Elector, "and we respect your allegiance to your employer. If you are ever at liberty to come and work for us here in Mannheim, we could guarantee you a fine musical experience and a good salary."

"Thank you, your highness." I said. "Should we find ourselves in a position to leave Paris, we will certainly accept your generous offer, but for the present, Paris is our home and our base of operations."

We talked with Carl Theodor a little longer, who didn't seem at all offended at our refusal of his offer, and then said our goodbyes to him and some of the other musicians who were still in the concert hall. We then headed back to the Wendlings'.

Carl was visibly relieved when we left the palace.

"That was a close call. I wouldn't sign up to work in this den of vipers for the biggest salary in the Empire!"

"I'm with you there," I said. "I've seen a few dysfunctional families in my time, but this one takes the prize. Why do you suppose there is so much behind the scenes backstabbing and political stuff happening here? It makes freelance life in Paris look like one big happy family."

"Remember, this is one of the best and highest paid orchestras in the Empire, and pretty much everybody would like to have a seat in it. If you are a member, you do everything you can to get positions for everyone in your family. You saw all the Cannabiches, Wendlings, Holzbauers, Toechis, Danzis, etc. on the orchestra roster. I counted five Wendlings alone, between the singers and instrumentalists in the Hofkapelle. That sort of intermarrying and nepotism will definitely lead to some pretty weird goings on behind the scenes. I think we just escaped with our sanity."

Chapter 27

Beer is proof that God loves us and wants us to be happy.
- Attributed to Benjamin Franklin

When we arrived back at the Wendlings' everyone was preparing to go to a nearby inn for supper after the concert. We went as a group to *Der Goldene Adler* and took over a long table in a private room. After plates of steaming bratwurst, sauerkraut, and freshly baked bread were set before us, Wendling stood up with his beer mug and made the first toast.

"Friends, this evening we are celebrating the successful visit of these two fine Waldhorn players from Paris, who I knew when they were just beginning their careers there. Here's to the duo of Palsa and Türrschmidt, the finest horn duo in all of Europe!"

From that point on the evening was one long string of toasts and speeches, and all were in high spirits on this, our last night in Mannheim.

At about eleven o'clock in the evening, when everyone was full and contented, Joseph Dimmler came down to our end of the table and started giving us a detailed description of the various beers that could be had at the inns in Schwetzingen. He was clearly very familiar with all of them.

"The *Adler* makes a good beer, as you can see, but the best beer is made at a little place called the *Blaue Eule* which is over on the other side of the town. You really should step over to it and give it a try before the evening is over."

"It's getting pretty late, and we will need to get some sleep before leaving on the coach tomorrow morning," I said, "so we may have to try the beer at the Blaue Eule another time".

"It isn't all that late," said Carl, "and Joseph's description of the beer intrigues me. What do you say we take a walk over there and have a glass?"

"The two of you can go and taste the beer," I said. "I'm exhausted and have scheduled an appointment with a featherbed and pillow back at the Wendlings' house".

They left for the Blaue Eule and the rest of us slowly found our way home and went to bed.

Our plan was to leave Schwetzingen in a hired wagon in the morning with our trunk and horn box and catch a coach that was leaving Mannheim just after noon. I woke the next morning at about seven o'clock to find Carl in the bed next to mine. I hadn't heard him come in, but I had gone to sleep almost immediately, so I wasn't surprised. Carl woke shortly thereafter, and didn't look terribly well.

I, of course, had to give him a bit of a hard time about his night out - I mean what are friends for anyway?

"Well! Look what the cat dragged in! Did they put you guys out with the trash this morning, or did you find your way home under your own power?"

He groaned. "The beer was everything that Joseph Dimmler promised. So good that I hardly remember how I got home. I'll pay for it the rest of the day, but it was worth it."

We got dressed and went down to breakfast with the family, and just about halfway through our third cup of coffee, there was a knock at the door. Wendling got up to see who it was, and a man in the uniform of the town police stepped in.

"Is there a Herr Carl Türrschmidt staying here?"

"Yes, I'm Carl Türrschmidt, what can I do for you?"

"You can come with me to the *Rathaus* where you will appear before the magistrate to answer a charge of assaulting a city official last night at about one o'clock in the morning at the *Schwarze Pferd* inn. You are under arrest Herr Türrschmidt!"

"The Schwartze Pferd! That's just across the street from the Blaue Eule," said Wendling. "Did you go there too last night with the younger Dimmler?"

"It's possible," said Carl. "The whole evening gets a little fuzzy in my memory after the first couple of glasses at the Eule. But I don't remember getting into a fight of any sort, or even talking to anyone other than Joseph Dimmler. I can't imagine there is anything to this story. There must be some mistake."

"No mistake," said the officer. "A drunken gentleman got into an argument with Herr Fischer, an official in the Burgermeister's office, and gave him an impressive black eye. He ran away after hitting him, but when Herr Fischer asked his name, the gentleman in question turned back before bolting out the door and said that he had the honor of being hit in the eye by Carl Türrschmidt, the visiting Waldhorn player from Paris."

"Unbelievable," said Carl. "I don't remember anything about it, but I had drunk a lot of beer, and maybe it did all happen that way, and I actually got into a fight with this man! This is terrible!"

"Come along quietly Herr Türrschmidt, and there won't be any trouble."

"Where will he be taken? And may we come along to try to clear this up?" asked Wendling.

"To the *Rathaus*, and you can come along anytime you want, but I must take him now. Good Day!" said the officer. They left and we all looked at each other in utter bewilderment.

"I can't understand it,' I said. "This would have been totally out of character for Carl, sober or drunk!"

"Get your coats, and follow me to the Rathaus," said Wendling. "We'll get to the bottom of this!

Apparently Schwetzingen was a very peaceable little town, because Carl's arrest appeared to be a big event for the officials at the town hall. A crowd had gathered to see the criminal who had been taken into custody, and there was a lot of excitement as Carl was taken into the waiting area outside the magistrate's office, where Wendling and I found him upon our arrival. At that point a messenger came in with a note from the chief magistrate saying he would not arrive at the *Rathaus* for at least an hour.

"This doesn't look good Carl," said Wendling. "I've sent for a lawyer friend of mine in Mannheim, who I hope will arrive before the magistrate, and we'll see what advice he can give us."

Carl was already in pretty bad condition this morning, and the excitement of being arrested only made it worse.

"What are they going to do to me? I've never committed a crime before, though I have been in prison, as you remember, as a result of Johann's well aimed stone at the Count of Guînes' coach. But this time I really did it, and I know they are going to put me jail and ruin our tour, and when the Prince of Guéméné hears about this he'll have us flayed alive, and we'll be out of a job. He said he wouldn't help us if we got into trouble again, and would dismiss us if we did!"

The secretary of the magistrate arrived, took out a pair of silver-rimmed glasses, put them on, and looked Carl over for about half a minute before speaking.

"Herr Türrschmidt, I am Hermann Friedl, secretary to his honor Herr Nicholai, the chief magistrate of Schwetzingen, who will see you as soon as he arrives. He will not be in a very good mood, since he has had to cut short his breakfast to come and hear this case. The gentleman who you assaulted last night, Herr Fischer, will be here this afternoon at your formal hearing before a jury of townspeople. He will identify you as the perpetrator, and his lawyer will enter the charges. Depending on the mood of the magistrate and the jury, you may be sentenced to anywhere between four and eight weeks in the city jail and to pay a fine not to exceed twenty-five florins.

"Twenty-five florins!" said Carl. "Eight weeks would be most of our tour and we'll be lucky if we could have made that much money on the entire trip!"

Wendlings' lawyer, a nervous little man by the name of Friedrich Koch arrived, carrying a black leather briefcase and everyone tried to explain all at once what was going on, which only confused the poor man until he seemed at his wit's end.

"Wait, wait!" he shouted with his hands in the air. "Can some single person please give me a simple version of the problem at hand in simple, straightforward language?!"

"It's very simple," said Wendling. "Our friend Herr Türrschmidt has been accused of assaulting a town official last night in one of the inns of Schwetzingen. It is not entirely clear if the incident actually happened as reported, and Herr Türrschmidt can't remember having fought with anyone."

"This could be serious, Herr Türrschmidt," said Koch furrowing his brow. "This sort of incident is rare in Mannheim and Schwetzingen, and normally when something of this sort comes up, the penalties are severe, to make an example of the offender and discourage drunken and disorderly conduct. We'll try to make a case for the good character of the defendant; he is of good character, is he not Herr Wendling?"

"Oh! Absolutely the best! And an old family friend! He is also one of the finest Waldhorn players in the world, and in the middle of an important concert tour with his colleague Herr Palsa."

"His concert tour may be cut short for a while if Herr Nicholai, the chief magistrate of Schwetzingen, is the one who will hear the case," said Koch.

Carl emitted some unintelligible sounds with his head in his hands.

"Whatever I did, I didn't mean to do it! It must have been just an accident. I would never hit anyone if I was in my right mind!"

This scene was interrupted by the entrance of Herr Nicholai.

"And what sort of low-life drunken ruffian dares to start trouble in the peaceable town of Schwetzingen, tearing me away from my family and my breakfast at such an hour on a Sunday morning?!"

Herr Friedl the secretary, who looked like he was about to burst into song in a Broadway musical, was beside himself with joy that he was able to convey the details of this important case to his superior.

"Your honor, the defendant is one Carl Türrschmidt, a wandering musician who arrived in town a few days ago," he said in a high excited voice.

He then went on to describe the incidents of the previous evening in greater detail than any of us had heard before, making Carl look like the worst brawling criminal that could be imagined. The magistrate took notes the entire time, occasionally looking at Carl as one would look at a mad dog that had just attacked someone in the street.

"I want an officer on each side of him at all times. He may be drunken and dangerous still, and I'll not have the safety of myself and the people of this town put into jeopardy by the possibility of an escape!" shouted the magistrate. "Bring him into the courtroom, and someone fetch Herr Fischer from his home to identify him and file the charges."

A makeshift jury was being assembled from somewhere. God only knows where they were finding them on a sleepy Sunday morning, but the officers were bringing townspeople into the courtroom. The magistrate sat at a desk and Carl was made to stand before him with chairs around the room for the rest of us, and the jury and witnesses. The case was presented to the jury again by Herr Friedl, who was feeling more self-important than ever, and elaborating even more about Carl's offences. The case was discussed in great detail for about half an hour, and the situation looked like it was going from bad to worse for Carl, when a rather indignant looking gentleman, fairly well-dressed and sporting a black eye of very impressive proportions was ushered into the room.

"Herr Fischer!" announced the secretary, as the man approached the desk of the magistrate.

"Herr Fischer," said the magistrate, "we have just about wrapped up this case, and we only need to hear your version of the events of last evening to conclude the proceedings. Will you, first of all, be so kind as to identify for the jury the man who assaulted you last night at the *Schwartzer Pferd* Inn?"

"Your Honor, I would be happy to identify the scoundrel and witness his punishment to the fullest extent of the law!"

"Herr Türrschmidt, please step forward!" sang out the secretary almost gleefully.

Carl took a couple of steps forward to the middle of the room, very tentatively on shaky legs.

"That's not the rascal!" said Herr Fischer more indignantly than ever.

"Not the rascal?!" shouted the magistrate rising from his chair as if propelled by some unseen force.

"Certainly not!" exclaimed Herr Fischer. "The man who struck me last night was shorter, had darker hair, and was older than this gentleman, and said he was a Waldhorn player. I was in the *Schwartzer Pferd* most of the evening, and the gentleman before you did not set foot in the *Schwartzer Pferd* last night.

"What sort of farce is going forth here?" bellowed the magistrate. "Someone started a fight with Herr Fischer, and I'm going to get to the bottom of this!"

"Georg Franz," I heard Wendling muttering under his breath at my side. "It has to be Georg Franz." Wendling rose, and approaching the magistrate said aloud, "Your honor, I think I may know who was behind this, and who has implicated our good friend Herr Türrschmidt in this affair. If you will summon Herr Georg Franz, Waldhornist of the Mannheim Orchestra to come before you, I believe he may be able to help us clear up everything and completely clear Herr Türrschmidt of all charges."

The magistrate was still staring daggers at Carl, who looked more bewildered than ever, and without taking his eyes off him said;

"Very well. Herr Friedl, send for the horn player Georg Franz, and we'll hear what he has to say."

We waited in silence for a few minutes, during which the magistrate fussed with papers on his desk, gave a few orders to his officers, and generally looked as though he was building up steam to be vented at the next person who provoked him.

Eventually the door opened and Georg Franz strutted proudly into the room, obviously expecting to be called in as a witness, and fully prepared to do as much damage as possible to Carl's case. It apparently hadn't occurred to him that Herr Fischer might be present, or maybe he thought Fischer had been too inebriated to remember any details about his combatant. He went straight to the front of the room, right up to Herr Nicholai's desk and addressed him in a self-satisfied voice.

"Can I be of any assistance to your honor in identifying this itinerant horn player who has caused nothing but trouble since he and his partner, who I see is also here, arrived in Schwetzingen?"

At that moment, Herr Fischer jumped out of his chair.

"That's the man who gave me this black eye last night at the *Schwartzer Pferd!* he exclaimed."

As all eyes turned to him, it was obvious to Franz how matters stood, and before anyone could say a word or stop him, he shot out of the room.

"After him!" shouted the magistrate in a rage that made him look as though he was about to explode. Three or four officers were on their feet and out the door after him in a flash.

I'm sure they must have eventually caught up with him and brought him back to the court, but he had a good head start on them. In the meantime, Wendling, Fischer, and I explained the situation to the jury, and Carl was set free, though the magistrate was still skeptical of his innocence, and needed to vent his frustration at the situation a little more.

"Is there anyone else present who has any complaint or charge against the defendant?" he asked the room hopefully. Getting no reply, he went on, "Then I suppose, Herr Türrschmidt, I have no other choice than to drop the charges, which I do against my better judgement, and I never want to see you in my court, or in the town of Schwetzingen again!"

Carl had just begun to tell him that he needn't worry about seeing him there again, because he had no intention of ever setting foot in Schwetzingen or Mannheim again, when Wendling took him by the arm and gently led him from the room, for fear of more trouble erupting from behind the magistrate's desk.

The morning was turning bright and beautiful, and we all went back to the Wendlings' house for a second breakfast before loading our trunk and horn box into a hired wagon to take us into Mannheim to the coach.

"Farewell until we meet again my dear young Waldhorn soloists!" said Wendling at the coach in Mannheim, shaking both of our hands. "We will expect you back again to play with the orchestra someday under better conditions. Though there were many obstacles, you gave fine performances here."

We thanked him sincerely for all his help and encouragement, sent greetings back to his family and to the musicians who had come to our rescue for the orchestra concert, and climbed into the coach. The coach pulled away and we stared at each other in silence for a few minutes.

"Promise you'll shoot me if I ever suggest stopping in at Mannheim on another tour," said Carl, and curled up in the seat to sleep off his hangover. We never heard the final fate of Georg Franz.

Chapter 28

from Turrschmidt 50 duos op. 3, 1795

We hadn't received any word from the orchestra manager of the Prince of Guéméné in Paris about when we needed be to back to work, but it was always possible the post had not kept up with us, despite our efforts to let them know where mail could be sent as we traveled from place to place. We had fully expected to have a letter waiting for us at the Wendlings' in Mannheim, but when no correspondence arrived there, we decided to cut our travels short and slowly start working our way back toward Paris. Though it was a disappointment, for Carl especially, since he hadn't seen his family for several years, we would have to visit Regensburg and Wallerstein another time. We traveled through the Holy Roman Empire and back into France, playing concerts along the way wherever we could make connections with the local musicians and courts.

The trip was expensive, and by the time we reached Paris, we had just a little less money in our pockets than we did when we left three months earlier, which Carl considered to be a successful tour. I thought getting your bones jarred in carriages on nearly non-existent roads, suffering through every imaginable kind of weather, sleeping and eating in filthy bug-infested inns, playing with musical groups of widely varying levels, mostly bad, and not breaking even financially wasn't a very successful tour, but he was familiar with these things, and I wasn't.

We moved back into our rooms in Madame Marais' house, evicted all the creatures that had moved in during our absence, and got life up and running again. The prince wasn't expected back in Paris for a few weeks, and we were still at liberty for a while, so being a couple of ambitious young horn players, we started making more connections around Paris, and especially with the organizers of the Concert Spirituel, the most prestigious series in town. Since our reputation was beginning to grow from our work with the private orchestra of the Prince of Guéméné, a couple of opportunities to play as members of the Concert Spirituel orchestra came up soon after our arrival home. This was a big step, but what we really wanted was to start specializing in the new double concerto literature that was just coming into vogue, and to cultivate a reputation as soloists in Paris.

The opportunity to play as soloists for one of the biggest and most important audiences in Paris finally came up in April of 1774. This was partly due to the fact that wind soloists were becoming more popular on that series. They had engaged some of the biggest names in Paris as well as visiting wind players from the continent for that season; people like our friend Johann Baptist Wendling, oboists Gaetano Besozzi and Friedrich Ramm, bassoonist Georg Ritter, and Johann Baer, the clarinet virtuoso. When we received the invitation, we had to decide what we would like to play. Our Leopold Mozart concerto was far too old fashioned for this high-class Paris audience, as were a couple of others we had picked up, and some of the newer ones, such as the double concerto by Anton Dimmler that we played in Mannheim, weren't of a quality that we felt good about, compared with some of the other pieces that were being programed on the series by prominent composers. We needed something really up to date as well as virtuosic and musically substantial.

We were racking our brains about this when we arrived home from a wind band performance one afternoon to find a package by our door that had been delivered earlier that morning. It was from Carl's father in Wallerstein, and it contained a handwritten set of parts to a new double horn concerto by the first oboe of the Öttingen-Wallerstein Orchestra, Josef Fiala, who had only entered the service of Prince Kraft-Ernst the previous year.

"Well," said Carl. "It looks like our troubles may be over! This might be our Concert Spirituel solo debut piece. I had written home to ask if my father had any pieces to suggest, hoping they might have something new that would appeal to a Paris audience."

He opened the letter in the package, which was written in the bold and elegant hand of his father and began reading.

My Dearest Carl,
Here is a piece that you might be able to convince the concert organizers in Paris to program. It's a double horn concerto by our new principal oboe, Josef Fiala. He's written some very nice music for our orchestra, and this one was written at my request for the purpose of sending it to you to introduce his work to the Paris audiences. It's very much in the current style, and quite a showpiece for both high and low horns - with opportunities for double cadenzas, which I'm sure the two of you will enjoy composing. Herr Fiala will be very interested to hear if you are able to play it at the Concert Spirituel, and if it is well received in Paris.

The family is doing fine, and music is thriving in the Öttingen-Wallerstein Hofkapelle since the new Prince, Kraft-Ernst has taken the reigns this past year. He is quite enthusiastic about his orchestra, and has brought in several new musicians, including a talented new low horn player, Johann Nisle who plays as well, or even better than our previous esteemed second horn player, Josef Fritch, who decided to stay in Regensburg, when the rest of us returned.

We look forward to seeing you sometime when you are able to get away from your duties to make a visit home. We would all enjoy meeting Herr Palsa, whose reputation for fine high horn playing comes to us with every visitor who has been to Paris.
With greetings and love from all here, I remain,

Your most proud and affectionate father,
Johann Türrschmidt

He looked up from the letter, obviously homesick and missing his family. "Awfully nice of him to get his colleague to compose a piece for us. The next time we can escape from this cesspool of a city we need to go to Wallerstein to see them and play with the orchestra. There are some great composers there and we could probably bring back a heap of new pieces. My father had already said that Franz Pokorny, who I know well from our days with the Thurn und Taxis Hofkapelle at Regensburg, would talk to their Kapellmeister about putting us on a program with the orchestra there, and probably write a concerto for us."

"We can only hope the prince will get into the habit of taking extended trips away from Paris every summer, giving us the opportunity to make a trip like that," I said.

We started learning the new concerto that afternoon. It was not only very much in the latest style, but was also a major challenge technically for both of us, with virtuosic scale passages and singing melodies above the staff for me, and acrobatic arpeggios and leaps for Carl - classic high and low horn tricks of the time. I, of course, already knew the piece from a well-known recording from my own time by the Tylšar brothers, Zdeněk and Bedřich, horn players from the Czech Philharmonic. I made the mistake of mentioning this as we started looking at the first movement.

"Carl, I know this piece! I grew up with a recording of it made in the 1980s by a famous horn duo from Prague."

"You're going to drive me crazy if you keep telling me that you already know half the pieces we play while the ink is still wet! Sometimes I still can't believe your whole outlandish story. I keep thinking I'll wake up from this ridiculous dream and wonder what I ate last night that put such things into my head! How can I believe you already know this piece?"

"Okay," I said. "You've just set the first movement on the music stand, and haven't turned to the other movements, right?"

"Right..." he said with a skeptical look.

"Twenty *sous* says I can sing the themes of the other two movements to you before you open up the music."

"And twenty sous of mine says you can't! It's brand new, it just arrived, and neither of us has seen it yet!"

"The second movement is in 3/4 time in the key of A flat major, and it goes like this," I said singing the theme. And the last movement is in 2/4 in E flat major and goes like this... and I have a great first movement cadenza that the Tylsar brothers wrote for their recording that I can write out for us to play. It's not plagiarism if theirs hasn't been written yet, right?"

"All right – you win," said Carl, looking at the other movements for the first time. "Put the twenty sous on my tab, but you have to admit that it's all very weird, even after five years of knowing about you and your strange story. It gets on one's nerves to know all of this and to have to keep it a secret."

"You think it gets on your nerves?" I replied, just a little too irritably. "I'm the one who had to give up my entire world, my life and family, who I miss terribly, and even my name when I came here, - and not of my own choosing I might add! The only redeeming quality of this filthy brutal 18th century of yours is the music we get to play together!"

At that point we both looked at each other, realizing that we both had been letting our emotions get out of hand.

"Alright – calm down Johann. We both know you didn't choose to come here, but now that you mention the music we play, you have to admit we're making the best of it all. Your horn playing and musical talents, and musical personality have made it possible to do amazing things that I couldn't have done with anyone else I know."

"Sorry I got a little upset," I said. "You've made it possible for me to survive and thrive and fit into this century. I owe you more than twenty sous for everything you've done for me. Friends and musical partners for life?"

"Friends and musical partners for life!" he said.

In true 18th century style, we shook hands, having gotten all that out of our systems, and proceeded to learn the Fiala double concerto in E flat major, practicing together as we always did.

We rehearsed the new concerto with the Concert Spirituel orchestra under the direction of concertmaster Monsieur Gaviniès, a fine violinist and leader, and gave a couple of very respectable performance in April of 1774. The reviews in the Paris papers were enthusiastic, as were the audiences at the concerts. It was a turning point for us in the eyes of the musicians and the concert-going public of Paris. We were no longer just "*Les deux Cors de Chasse de la Prince de Guéméné,*" we were becoming known as the prominent "Pals Tierschmiedt" Duo. The French never could wrap their minds around our Germanic names, or spell them properly.

One of the disadvantages of being a horn soloist at that time was that, unlike the way we do things in the 21st century, the soloists played in all the other pieces on the program as well. In a typical Concert Spirituel program, we would be expected to play a Haydn Symphony, then in the accompaniment of a violin or oboe concerto, then in a couple of opera arias, then step up to the front and play our double horn concerto, and immediately sit back down in the orchestra and end the program with a Mannheim composer's latest symphony. It was never dull, and often quite taxing.

But this was an age of soloistic wind playing, and in addition to true solo concertos, the idea of the "Sinfonia Concertante" was much in vogue. The double concerto was a form that was favored by German composers, and most of the concertos played at the Concert Spirituel and elsewhere came from the continent, while the Sinfonia Concertante was popular with French composers. These types of pieces were not exactly solo concertos, but rather symphonies that had prominent solo parts for several instruments. A few are still part of the repertoire of modern times, such as the Mozart Sinfonia Concertante for winds, or the similar "Concertante Symphony" by Haydn for violin, oboe, bassoon, and cello. There were hundreds of pieces like this by French composers, or people who liked to think of themselves as French composers, like Giuseppe Cambini, who was a master of the genre.

The closest German equivalents were composed by Michael Haydn and Leopold Mozart, who loved to write symphonies and serenades in which a movement or two were devoted entirely to specific solo instruments, and winds and brass were often the featured instruments. It was a golden age for wind soloists, who half a century later would be absorbed into the wind texture of a larger orchestra and be featured as soloists much less often. We were in the thick of this golden age, and what a spectacular time to be a horn soloist! All music was new music, and over the following eight years in Paris, several composers wrote double horn concertos and concertante symphonies that featured the two of us.

Another result of our rising reputations was that everyone knew we could be called on short notice to sub for anyone who was sick, or feigning illness at the last minute to do another gig that paid more.

This resulted in filling in at various times with just about every private orchestra, the Paris Opera, and the many other concert societies and theater orchestras that came and went during our time in Paris. There was only one group that neither we, nor any of our fellow Parisian musicians ever played with, and that was the musicians of the court of the king of France.

This was a group of fine musicians who played exclusively for small audiences at court, and the rest of us hardly knew of their existence, because their performances were not open to the public, and they weren't allowed to play anywhere else. No one ever seemed to know what was happening musically at the court.

Occasionally we would be called on to sub at the Paris Opera, which had a very old-fashioned orchestra, using an instrumentation and approach that was in style fifty years before, and very "French". Every other orchestra in Europe was led by a violinist who played the whole time while leading the group, but the opera was still using a time beater or *batteur de mesure* who beat time on the floor with a stick to keep things together. And believe me, they needed it! It was the most ragged ensemble I had played with since high school. The orchestra was divided into what they called the *Grand Choeur* or tutti ensemble, and the *Petit Choeur* meaning the small group within the orchestra that accompanied the recitatives. The *Petit Choeur* was mostly bearable, but the full group played with terrible intonation and very little sense of precision or musical nuance. The big criticism of the opera orchestra was that they were extremely conservative, and played adamantly in the old fashioned French style of Jean-Philippe Rameau and his contemporaries. They didn't approve of the modern "Italian style" as everyone referred to it, and didn't do any of the expressive elements of that style, such as the crescendos and diminuendos of the symphony composers of the 1770s. This was the big musical controversy in Paris at the time, with one style for the court and the opera, and another more modern style for the rest of us.

The private orchestras were the highest quality ensembles, and the nobility and wealthy who supported them spent huge sums of money to have some of the finest musicians in Europe in their service. These flourished up until the 1780s when the deteriorating financial situation in France made it no longer feasible for even the very wealthy to support their own private orchestras. The financial difficulties of our own employer, the Prince of Guéméné, led to his disbanding the orchestra, and our being out of a very cushy gig in 1783.

The other theater orchestras were of varying qualities, ranging from the *Opéra Comique* and *Comédie-Françaís* that were at the top of the heap to small theaters and opera companies that sprang up and died at regular intervals each year around the city. The orchestra of the Opéra Comique was a very fine one, employing a lot of German musicians, and they played actual operas by actual opera composers, while many of the small theaters had terrible orchestras, small noisy audiences, and did performances cobbled together from arias and dance numbers from unrelated operas so that they made no sense, and resembled a Vaudeville show more than an opera.

The Concert Spirituel was the top series of the many concert societies, public orchestras, and chamber music concerts. These included the *Concert des Amateurs*, directed by Gossec, the *Sociéte du Concert d'Émulation*, the *Concert des Amis*, and many others, and we played with most of them that were functioning during the 1770s and early 1780s. Whenever we would get a new double concerto or chamber piece, we would approach the director of one of the societies or series, and they would often program it on the next performance. We could get a lot of mileage out of a new solo piece by doing it with our own private orchestra and with two or three of the other Paris concert societies. It was a rich concert life that flourished during the 1770s with good financial support, and only started to erode into the 1780s as money became scarce, life got more difficult, and tensions rose between the aristocracy and the common people.

Part II
1775 - 1780

Chapter 29

from Horn Concerto in E, 1755

Another year passed quickly, filled with regular full orchestra and chamber music concerts as well as tedious work with the wind band every week at the Hôtel Guéméné for the prince and his guests. And when the schedule allowed, we did solo performances with the Concert Spirituel and on other concert series. We were two extremely busy horn players, and during this heyday of music in Paris, we did well financially and saved a good deal of money. This was necessary during a time when there was no public assistance for those who were no longer able to work. There was no age that was considered "retirement age" and everyone but the nobility, wealthy businessmen, and landowners worked until they couldn't, and then were dependent on family and savings. We were fortunate enough to make more than we needed to survive, while the majority of professional musicians spent their careers barely keeping their heads above water, and often dying in poverty.

As we had hoped, word came to the orchestra in April of 1775 that the Prince of Guéméné would again spend the summer months in Italy, and the orchestra was free to do as they pleased during that time, while still receiving our regular salaries. For several of the members of the orchestra, that meant working with other groups in Paris, but for a few of us, it meant, once again, going on tour.

Carl wrote immediately to his father, telling him we would be in Wallerstein by the middle of June, and Türrschmidt the elder, as he was known among horn players and musicians, must have written back on the day he received his son's letter, because we received his reply exactly four weeks later, which was probably some sort of record for a reply to a letter to Germany. The reply was enthusiastic, and Türrschmidt had already talked to Antonio Rosetti, the composer and double bass player of the orchestra, requesting that he compose something for us for a concert in Wallerstein.

After some of our experiences on the first tour, I was less enthusiastic.

"We've played at a lot of smaller courts and cities where our concerts were well received, and a couple – Mannheim comes to mind - where what we are doing on the horn was not universally liked. How do we know that the other horn players in Wallerstein and Regensburg are going to welcome us with open arms?"

"This is a completely different scene, my home turf," said Carl. "My father and all of his colleagues in Regensburg and Wallerstein will be totally blown away when we play there. We'll knock their socks off!"

I use these English idioms to give some idea of the colloquial way Carl spoke when we talked among ourselves. He was a master of the most current *Umgangsprache,* or German slang of the time, which he used as artistically as he played the horn.

"I certainly hope so. If we have another Georg Franz and Mannheim Orchestra experience, I'm swearing off tours forever, and sticking with our quiet comfortable life in Paris."

"Relax Johann! After they made Georg Franz and the Mannheim crowd, they broke the mold. This trip is going to be a blast!"

No German speaker today would have understood the idioms Carl was using in his excitement. It reminded me of an instrument ad that ran in the musician's union paper in the 1980s. A famous jazz trumpet player is pictured with his trumpet saying, "This horn is the baddest!" Many of our figures of speech that are here today and gone tomorrow are seldom preserved for posterity, and French and German musician slang of the late 18th century is completely lost to the world, except in one secret repository, unknown to the rest of the world: my brain.

We wrote to people in a few more places along the route we planned to take through the various German kingdoms of the Empire, in the hope of playing at a few of them, and got a couple of responses before leaving on the first of May.

The roads and travel by horse-drawn coach had not improved since our last trip through the Holy Roman Empire, which Voltaire remarked was neither holy, nor Roman, nor an empire by this time. It would only hold together as an official institution for another thirty years or so. We bumped along for days on end, stopping off at towns and cities along the way, playing concerts wherever we could, with whatever ragtag orchestra or city band we could get in touch with, sometimes for nothing more than a meal and a place to sleep. Though at other times, when playing with a nobleman's small court orchestra to impress his guests with high class musicians from Paris, we would receive a handsome gift of gold *Gulden* coins or silver *Thalers*.

The money in the various parts of the empire made no sense at all, and I was never convinced that I was getting a fair deal when we would go to a local counting house to exchange *Gulden* for *Kreuzers*, or *Thalers* for *Florins*. You would walk into a money changing house, and the banker would say "One *Gulden* or sixty *Kreuzer* is trading for 5/12ths of a *Conventionsthaler*, or 1/24 of a Cologne Silver *Mark*, which will get you fourteen *Reichsthalers*, which is what you'll need as you travel east from here, but after you cross the border from Bavaria into Austria, they won't accept those, so you'll want to have a good supply of *Ducats* that you can trade for whatever is used in each locality." ...and on and on until your head spun.

"They make their money by confusing you to death," said Carl. "And in total exasperation you end up saying, 'Just give me whatever they're using here for whatever these are that they were using where we just came from.' It's worth your sanity, and the cut they get from you, not to ask for explanations."

Carl was a philosopher about these things and enjoyed the challenges of traveling. It would have taken all the fun out the trip for him to travel from Spain to Finland and need only Euros the entire way.

Near the end of May, after hardships that were considered mild at the time, but would have been the death of many a 21st century traveler, we arrived in Regensburg, a very important city in the governing of the Holy Roman Empire. It was smaller than I had imagined, from Carl's description, having about 15,000 residents.

"So, Carl, what makes Regensburg such an important city?"

"Lots of things. Many people think of Regensburg as the second capital of the Empire, the actual capital being the court of Emperor Joseph II in Vienna. But our prince, Karl Anselm, fourth Prince of Thurn und Taxis, is his right-hand man. He's the Postmaster General of the Imperial *Reichspost*, and became head of the House of Thurn und Taxis a couple of years ago. The prince's daughter Maria Theresia, who is about eighteen, was married to Prince Kraft-Ernst of Wallerstein last year, making an even stronger connection between the houses of Thurn und Taxis and Öttingen-Wallerstein. Prince Karl Anselm is in the middle of a big scandal at the moment. His wife, the Duchess Augusta of Würtemberg, tried more than once to assassinate him, and Prince Karl is trying to get her banished and kept somewhere under house arrest. It's a pretty dangerous business being a monarch or nobleman. You couldn't pay me enough to accept a princedom. I'll stick with something safe like being a horn soloist, where the critics aren't using real musket balls, or knives, or poison."

Carl knew the city well, having lived there from the age of thirteen to eighteen, and knew exactly where we needed to go to find Franz Pokorny and his friends from the Hofkapelle after we arrived by coach at an inn in the center of Regensburg.

"We'll go directly to Castle Trugenhofen, which is in Oberdischingen, not too far from here. That's where the court and the orchestra spend the summer. They spend most of the year at the prince's residence in town, but they will all certainly be at Trugenhofen by now."

We hired a small wagon drawn by a single horse to take us and our things to the castle, with Carl describing all the sights along the way, and by early evening were knocking at the door of a thatched roof cottage near the castle in the town of Oberdischingen. The door was opened by a small young woman of about eighteen or nineteen with more long flowing dark hair than I had ever seen on a single person, a pair of small thick oval shaped glasses, and a beaming smile.

"Carl!" she squealed.

"Beate!" he answered at a similar pitch of voice. And they embraced each other like brother and sister.

"Come in! Come in! It's so good to see you! Father! Anna!" she said turning toward the interior of the house. "Carl and his friend, Herr Palsa have arrived! Oh! I'm so sorry - you are Herr Palsa aren't you? So nice to meet you! Right this way," she said, leading us into the kitchen of the cottage. This was my first impression of Beate Pokorny, and it was a pretty accurate picture of her personality[12]. I hadn't gotten a word in yet, when a rather short thickly built man with a wide face and thick bushy eyebrows, spilling out from behind glasses of equal thickness to his daughter's, appeared out of the kitchen. He was followed by another girl of about fourteen with bright eyes, a pleasant face, and similar thick hair, all in braids, who was carrying a tortoise shell cat, so that she looked like a dark haired "Heidi". This was Anna-Maria, the younger of Franz Pokorny's two daughters.

"Come in my fine young travelers," said Pokorny, who appeared to be in his late forties, but robust and active. "Welcome to Regensburg! We've been expecting you for the past few days. I hope the trip and the roads weren't too bad this time of year."

"Pretty normal," Carl replied. "And the inns along the way were the usual too, but somehow we survived, and here we are! It's so nice to see you all again! And may I introduce you to my good friend, and one of the finest high horn players in all of Europe, Herr Johann Palsa. Herr Franz Pokorny, Beate, and Anna-Maria.

I shook all their hands and thanked them for their friendly reception of us.

"And my goodness," Carl went on, "how the two of you have grown up since I saw you last. What would it be, six years ago?"

"At least," said Beate. "It seems like ages. But we've been getting reports about your great success in Paris all along. Most of the musicians here thought leaving Regensburg at the age of eighteen and going to Paris was madness. Many said you would be back in a few months, but father and I knew you would make it and land a good position in an orchestra there. And how exciting to be in one of the best private orchestras in Paris!"

"The success has been due to my partnership with Johann. We think musically like a single person and play very much the same. We knew from the first time we played together that playing as a duo was what we wanted to do. And how have you been progressing with your musical studies? Still at it?"

"As diligently as ever! I've been studying horn, violin, and viola, and one of these days I'm going to convince all the old stick-in-the-mud court orchestra members that I could be a member of the Hofkapelle."

At this point Franz broke into the conversation. "And I would prefer that a nice-looking young woman of eighteen would get married and settle down, rather than practicing music several hours a day in the hope of breaking into the music profession, which just isn't suitable for a woman. A very nice violinist from our orchestra, the grandson of my old teacher *Konzertmeister* Riepel, has asked me for her hand, but she would have no part of it, and I, being a modern father, will allow her to marry as she wishes, subject to my approval, of course."

Beate was turning several shades of red with embarrassment at this point, and I could tell that we had already hit upon the family controversy. Franz Pokorny was one of the concertmasters of the Thurn und Taxis Orchestra and one of its most prominent composers, having studied with Johann Stamitz, Holzbauer, and Richter in Mannheim before coming to Regensburg. Though he was a modern composer in the latest style of symphonies and concertos, he was an old-fashioned orchestra musician and father, and quite adamant in his opinion that his daughter shouldn't try to compete in the exclusively male business of professional music.

"Yes father," she said sweetly, rolling her eyes so that only Carl and I could see. "We'll discuss that later. Let's go into the kitchen and prepare a meal for this hungry traveling horn duo. I'm sure they would like to wash away the dust of the road first though."

We spent the evening eating and talking, and I felt quite at home immediately with the Pokorny family. Carl went through the whole story he had manufactured of why I didn't sound quite Bohemian, explaining that I had grown up in the English colonies of America, and as usual everyone accepted it without question, which always amazed me. After supper, Franz went into his music room and brought out a folder of music manuscript paper labeled *Waldhorn-konzerte* and opened it.

"Now down to some business," he said. "I have three concertos for two horns that I composed some years ago, before Carl's time in Regensburg, and you are welcome to make copies of the parts to take home with you, but I wanted something more up to date for you to play here, and to take back to Paris. So I've composed a new concerto that I think you'll enjoy playing. Prince Karl Anselm has several concerts and chamber music evenings planned over the next two or three weeks, and I can suggest to our *Musikintendant*, Baron von Schacht, that we play it on one of those programs."

"There is one small detail, Herr Pokorny," said Carl. "We should have a look at it first and see if we can learn it in time."

"Oh, I'm confident the two of you will learn it in no time; there's nothing in it you haven't seen before."

I had opened the new piece and was looking at the solo parts. There were plenty of technical challenges for each of us, and I thought the sooner we could start practicing it the better.

"We will just have to work out one little problem," added Franz. "I've scored horns and flutes in this piece because both of our oboists are out of town, but now our first horn player is away for a couple of weeks caring for a sick parent, and only Herr Fritch, the second horn is available."

Beate's face lit up immediately.

"I could play..."

"No, no, my dear, Baron von Schacht would never hear of it. Imagine what people would say if I allowed my daughter to play the Waldhorn in a public concert with the Hofkapelle!"

"But these parts are dead easy Papa," she said taking the part marked Corno I off the stack. "I could sightread it without my glasses!"

I discovered much later that Beate couldn't find her way to the front door of the house without her glasses.

"That's not the point! It is not appropriate for young ladies to play the Waldhorn. You play the harpsichord and violin so nicely, and those are instruments that can be played at home. Stick with those and leave the horn to the orchestra players."

"But I like the horn best, and someday I'll get to play it somewhere other than in the attic when no one is around," she said, winking at Carl and me.

Chapter 30

And, after all, what is a lie? 'Tis but the truth in masquerade.
- Lord Byron, Don Juan, 1818

The next few days were spent learning the new concerto, copying parts for all of Pokorny's horn music to take back to Paris with us, and playing in a couple of chamber music evenings, as well as visiting Carl's old friends from the orchestra, who were very curious about how he had been getting along in Paris, the musical capital of Europe.

We began rehearsing with the orchestra the next week, and like most orchestras of the 18th century, this one had its own distinctive personality. 21st century orchestras have their stylistic differences and approaches but are relatively the same in how they play. By comparison, 18th century court orchestras were all over the map. This group played within a relatively narrow dynamic range, and were rather conservative in their expressiveness, in comparison to the Mannheim orchestra, but played with a good deal of precision and respectable intonation. In addition to Pokorny, the other concertmaster, who was playing a concerto on this program, was a French violinist by the name of Joseph Touchemoulin. There were a few other soloists in the orchestra, including the first flute player, Fiorante Agustinelli, who was also scheduled to play a concerto that week.

The second horn player, Josef Fritch, was a friendly guy, who used to play next to Johann Türrschmidt in Wallerstein. The two of them had been "loaned' to Regensburg when music ceased in Wallerstein. When the Wallerstein Hofkapelle started up again in 1773, Carl's father returned to Wallerstein, but Fritch chose to stay in Regensburg. Unbeknownst to Franz Pokorny, Fritch had been giving horn lessons to Beate off and on for the past few years.

As we began rehearsing the new double concerto, which we were certain would go over well in Paris, there was some talk about who would play the other orchestra horn part. Josef Fritch said he would arrange for someone to come in from a neighboring town to play, and the director of the group, Baron von Schacht, left it in his hands.

We rehearsed three times, and each time, we expected to see the visiting horn player, but he didn't show up. This was a little disturbing, since the last movement of the new concerto, the usual rondo, had an adagio section in which the two solo horns are answered by the two orchestra horns that imitate them softly. The lines were simple but touchy, because they were unaccompanied and needed to be perfectly together and in tune. Everyone was getting a bit nervous about the absence of this mysterious young man who Fritch had engaged to play, but Fritch assured us he would be at the concert, and that we would rehearse the adagio before the concert with the four horn players.

The castle was made up of several buildings, and the orchestra concerts took place in the one called the *Kapellenbau*. The room was not terribly large, and could accommodate around one hundred fifty people, including the orchestra of about twenty musicians. As in Mannheim and a lot of other courts, the concerts were attended only by the prince, his family, and his invited guests.

About half an hour before the concert began, Fritch approached us and said, "Carl and Johann, come with me please, the substitute horn player has arrived, and we need to go over the adagio in the last movement of your concerto."

We followed him into the next building, the theater where operas and plays were performed, and waiting for us in the dark theater, in the orchestra pit, was a small young man wearing a three-cornered hat, a green waistcoat and breeches, and carrying a horn. As we got closer, it became painfully obvious that it was Beate, dressed as a boy.

"Do you really think you're going to get away with this?" said Carl.

"I'll slip in just before the piece starts, and I'm depending on the fact that neither father's nor Baron von Schacht's eyes are very good at a distance. Von Schacht will be at the back of the room with the prince and his family, since he doesn't play in the orchestra, and father will be wearing his music reading glasses, with which he can't see past the music stand. I could probably get away with playing on one of the other pieces as well," she added.

"I think we'll be pushing our luck with the horn concerto," Carl said. "The three of us will cover the rest of the program and keep you out of trouble as best we can. Now let's play through the adagio in the third movement."

We played the passage a couple of times, and Beate and Fritch matched us, and matched each other well. She played with a fine sound, and good control, so apparently the lessons with Fritch had given her some solid horn technique.

We went back to the Kapellenbau, and Beate disappeared out of sight to wait for the concerto. The concert opened with a symphony in A major by Pokorny (one of his roughly hundred and fifty symphonies) in which Fritch and I played the horn parts. It was an energetic piece with a few prominent horn moments, and one very high soloistic passage in the trio of the minuet. Then Carl and Fritch played on the violin concerto, and the flute concerto was accompanied only by strings, after which came the new double horn concerto in F major by Franz Pokorny.

It was well-written for the horns, with nice melodies and challenging virtuosic passages for both horns. This piece ended up being a part of our solo repertoire for the next sixteen years. The tutti horn parts were simple all the way through until the final adagio in which Carl and I played gentle melodic lines using only simple open note horn intervals, and the orchestra horns echoed them back to us, as if from a distance. Fritch and Beate played beautifully, with perfect intonation. Beate was a fine second horn. Then there were a couple of arias from the latest opera by Holzbauer from Mannheim, and the concert ended with a symphony by Rosetti, who we would meet a few days later in Wallerstein. Carl and Josef Fritch played on the symphony.

The entire concert, and especially the new horn concerto, was a big success, and we celebrated afterward with a supper at the Pokorny house with a few of the musicians. Baron von Schacht, who we had gotten to know during the past two weeks, joined us for the evening. He was a rather pompous, know-it-all type, and was lavish in his praise of our playing, but curiously silent on the subject of the piece itself. Later we found out what this was all about.

"He's not a fan of my music," said Franz, "He fancies himself a composer, though many suspect that he gets his pieces from other composers, reworks them to make them more mediocre, and passes them off as his own. He seems to think we are in competition with each other, which couldn't be further from the truth, as far as I'm concerned. He was even caught recently filing some of my most recent symphonies in the library and making new title pages for them with the names of other composers[13]. If he outlives me and stays here, I'm sure all my pieces in the library will be attributed to other composers, but I don't care. They'll all be long out of style and no one will ever look at them again anyway. He's harmless."

As von Schacht was getting ready to leave, he asked, "Who was that young man who played the second horn part in the orchestra on the double horn concerto?"

Josef Fritch came to the rescue.

"Sir, it was a horn player from the wind band at Schwandorf, not too far from here."

"A fine young player with much promise," said von Schacht. "We should keep an eye on his progress."

With that he left, and Pokorny turned to Carl and me. "I have no idea who that visiting horn player was, but I have my suspicions. If you know anything about him, please have the goodness not to tell me!"

The next day, we went to Josef Fritch's house with Beate and Anna-Maria, and we all had a good laugh about Beate playing for the first time with the Hofkapelle, and then we played horn trios by Josef Hampel that Fritch had, and I discovered that Beate Pokorny was actually a very talented low horn player. Anna-Maria could also play the horn, and played a couple of low parts quite well. Franz Pokorny's daughters had been studying horn for several years without his knowledge and were on their way to gaining some very serious skill.

"You and Carl have been so friendly and accepting of my horn playing, and it's been such a great honor to play with you, two of the finest horn players of the present day," Beate said to me, as we were saying our farewells before leaving for Wallerstein. "Maybe we will get to play together again someday."

"I hope we can meet again soon," I said.

"Father talks of going to Paris someday to get his music played and published there, and if he does, Anna-Maria and I will come along. Until then, auf Wiedersehen Herr Palsa!"

Chapter 31

Every traveler has a home of his own, and he learns to appreciate it the more from his wanderings.
- Charles Dickens, A Christmas Carol, 1843

It was a rather short trip by coach to Wallerstein, and we were there by the next afternoon. The town was much smaller than Regensburg, with only a few hundred residents, but it was a busy place because it was a market town, with produce and other goods coming in from the surrounding countryside and going out to nearby towns and villages all the time. Wallerstein was the seat of the house of Öttingen-Wallerstein, which had been in existence for about five hundred years already by this time. The current ruler was Prince Kraft-Ernst, who took the reins in 1773, after the death of his father, and the big news in the region was that the emperor in Vienna had elevated Öttingen-Wallerstein to a princedom the previous year, which meant the twenty-five-year-old Kraft-Ernst could legitimately use the title of "Prince". He had recently married seventeen-year-old Maria-Theresia, daughter of Karl Anselm, fourth Prince of Thurn und Taxis, and the mood of the court was high after the celebration of this royal marriage and the ascension of Kraft-Ernst to the princedom. With this new level of importance came the need to impress the neighboring nobility, and part of that was the establishment of a high-quality court orchestra.

Prince Kraft-Ernst had spent the previous two years, with the help of his *Musikintendant,* or music business and artistic director, Ignaz Beecke, assembling the best musicians he could find for his orchestra. Local musicians who had been "loaned" to the Thurn und Taxis orchestra in Regensburg, like Carl's father, had been called back to Wallerstein in 1773, and several new players were added to the orchestra from elsewhere, enticed to leave their current posts by generous salaries from Kraft-Ernst. The prince now had an impressive and well-trained orchestra of about fifteen musicians. Among the group of new musicians was the young Bohemian double bass player Antonio Rosetti. Although he was initially hired to play double bass, he turned out to be a fine composer whose music was beginning to be recognized and respected in other parts of the Empire.

We arrived in the afternoon to find the market in full swing with carts, horses, and people everywhere. The coach dropped us off at an inn called the *Obere Wirtschaft* which was run by a friendly older man by the name of Johann Neher, who recognized Carl the minute he stepped in the door. The two of them talked together for a few minutes in the local dialect, which I could barely understand, though I got used to it over the next couple of weeks.

"The prince and the entire court, including the orchestra, have already moved out to the *Lustschloß* at Hohenaltheim for the summer," said Neher. "His Highness, Kraft-Ernst is very proud of his orchestra, and has put a sizable amount of money into getting the best musicians he could find. If you don't like music, you shouldn't work for the prince, because everyone in his court, including servants, are required to be at every performance of the Hofkapelle, which take place as many as three times a week."

"We'll need to go directly out to Hohenaltheim," said Carl. "Can we get a wagon to carry our baggage? It's a bit of a walk with trunks and our horn box."

"No problem! I can have a wagon ready in a few minutes. And Carl, I'd appreciate it if you could check out the new composer and contrabass player Antonio Rosetti for me. He's very interested in my daughter, and I don't know if I want Rosina marrying him if he turns out to be the typical court musician who goes through his money like it was water and is always in debt. No offence to yourselves, of course, who I'm sure don't fall into that group, but I've heard he's in debt already though he receives a good salary from the prince. He seems like a nice Bohemian boy, but I don't like the way he's taken on an Italian name to put on airs in the music world."

"We'll give you a full report on Herr Rosetti when we meet him," said Carl. "My father has asked him to write a concerto for horns for the concerts in the next couple of weeks, so we'll be getting to know him well."

"Thanks Carl, I really appreciate it, since things seem to be moving along uncomfortably fast between the two of them."

And while Herr Neher was arranging for a wagon to carry us on to the summer residence of the court, we walked down the *Haupt-*

Strasse, or main street of the town, which led uphill toward the princely residence at Schloß Wallerstein, parts of which dated back to the 13th century. On the way there and back Carl pointed out all the landmarks of his youth including the house where he had been born and lived for the first twelve years of his life.

The Lustschloß, where the court spent the summer months, was a small castle south of Wallerstein, consisting of two wings, a chapel, stables, and a garden with a few other surrounding buildings. There was only a single road leading to Hohenaltheim, which was in the middle of nowhere, and not much of a town. The fifteen members of the orchestra lived mostly with families in private houses nearby, though many servants and court staff had apartments in the residence where the prince and his young wife lived.

We pulled up in front of the castle as a group of musicians was leaving a sort of greenhouse full of fruit trees at one end of the English-style garden. They were all carrying instruments, and among them two horn players, who turned out to be Carl's father Johann Türrschmidt, and the second horn player, Johann Nisle. The elder Türrschmidt recognized Carl getting down from the wagon and came out to meet us, followed by the others. This was the wind section, which had been playing for some early evening occasion, and were all dressed in court orchestra suits of green coats and breeches, with white stockings. Herr Türrschmidt was about fifty years old, and built much like Carl, though a little shorter, with salt and pepper grey hair.

"Here he is friends, my oldest son, Carl, all the way from Paris, and his friend and duo partner Johann Palsa."

After embracing Carl, whom he had not seen for six years, and shaking hands with me, he began introducing the wind group of the Hofkapelle, none of whom Carl knew, since they had all joined the orchestra in the past two years. In addition to Nisle, the second horn, there was Josef Fiala, the oboist who had written the double concerto for us that we had played in Paris the previous year, and his second, Franz Fürall, the two bassoonists, Joseph Meltel and Franz Jandoffsky. With them was a small thin young man in his mid-twenties, with dark hair and eyes, carrying a double bass. This was my first glimpse of Antonio Rosetti, who over the next few years would cross paths with us several times and supply us with some of our best double horn concertos[14].

"We just finished a Tafelmusik performance and were on our way to our house to have supper. Your mother and Theresia are preparing a meal in honor of your arrival. We knew you would be here this afternoon, because we received a letter from Joseph Fritch in Regensburg by the post yesterday that said you were on your way."

We went to the Türrschmidt family's house, which was a neat cottage with a thatched roof, and there we met Carl's mother, his sister Theresia, and brother Joseph, who was about sixteen. Joseph was also a budding young horn player under the tutelage of his father. We were joined by the wind players and Rosetti. He wrote most of the music they played, and often played along himself. That evening we got to know the wind players. Fiala and Fürall, the oboists, were young and enthusiastic. Alois Ernst, a flute player, was only about sixteen, but a fine player and fully accepted into the group as a professional musician. Türrschmidt and Nisle, were older and seemed more comfortably established than the others. Joseph Meltel and Franz Jandoffsky, the bassoonists, were both house servants who played in the orchestra in addition to their household duties as livery servant and cook. Some of the violinists also fell into this category of "servant/musician".

Antonio Rosetti was a quiet man who listened more than he talked, and always looked a little distracted, as though he was working out a theme for a new composition.

Herr Türrschmidt and Nisle had a thousand questions about horn playing in Paris, the musical scene, and what we had been doing there. Both of them were of an earlier generation of horn playing in Germany and Bohemia, who learned to play with the bell down and did some hand stopping, but hadn't developed it into a totally chromatic system. They were very curious to hear about the latest developments.

After the others had departed, and only the Türrschmidt family, the two of us, and Rosetti were left, Carl's father poured another mug of beer for each of us.

"Carl, my boy, and Johann, if I may call you Johann on such short acquaintance - I already feel like you're part of the family – for your stay here in Wallerstein, I've asked Antonio if he would be so kind as to compose a little something for you to play with the orchestra. In his typical enthusiasm, which I've had the opportunity to get to know very well over the past couple of years, he has written three pieces! The first is a grand double concerto in E that will show off your talents as a duet team, and the other two are solo concertos for each of you, both in E flat. Prince Kraft-Ernst has been looking forward to hearing you and has promised that we can organize an evening of music for horns just as soon as you can learn the new pieces and we can rehearse them. Unlike other court orchestras, we don't have an official Kapellmeister, so whoever has composed the piece leads the rehearsals, which recently has been Antonio, since we have been playing a lot of his music."

Rosetti spoke now, almost for the first time that evening.

"We're lucky that we're a small group, and no one person is in charge, unlike places like Mannheim, which is a total dictatorship under Christian Cannabich. You'll find things much more easy-going and friendly here. I think our compositions are also better than at a lot of other courts. We have Josef Reicha, our cellist, and Fiala, in addition to myself, and we compose symphonies, serenades, and wind pieces. Janitsch and Hutti, the violinists, write concertos for themselves in a never-ending competition to see who can play the most notes as fast as possible in a single piece."

"We've experienced the weirdness of the Mannheim orchestra," I said. "What a relief to find a friendly group to play with here!"

"Get a little more beer into us, and we'll tell you the whole hair-raising story of how we escaped with our lives from Mannheim!" Carl added.

"You'll find our group here just as good, but without the underlying stress," said Rosetti. "The prince leaves things in our hands and those of Ignaz Beecke, the Musikintendant, who oversees the programs and looks out for our best interests with his Highness. And now gentlemen," he said producing a folder of handwritten orchestra parts, "new horn concerti for everyone - made to order!"

He handed each of us a solo part to our new solo concertos, and we each began scanning the pages to see what great musical challenges he had given us. Both solo pieces, and the double concerto in E major looked interesting and skillfully written. They were full of the latest in solo horn technique. After five years in this seat-of-the-pants musical world of the 18th century, I was still getting used to the idea that wherever we went people would hand us highly virtuosic pieces that they expected us to learn in a few days before playing them in concerts for royalty and nobility. Neither Carl, nor his father, nor Rosetti showed the slightest sign of skepticism about taking on the new pieces.

“Yes!” I said “They look like great fun. I can’t wait to get started on them. Can you give us a couple of days before we start rehearsing?”

“Just let us know when you’re ready to start,” said Rosetti. “We have concerts several times this week and next in the Orangery, and I’m sure we can convince Musikintendant Beecke to program an evening of Waldhorn music.”

Chapter 32

We each have a magic line between backstage and onstage. How good is the magic you're casting on yourself when you cross yours?

- Jeff Nelsen, Fearless Performance

We spent a couple of days resting, meeting Carl's childhood friends and relatives, and practicing the new pieces. During this time, I sensed a certain uneasiness from Carl about his solo concerto, which I had never seen in him before. We had both learned our respective concertos and the double concerto thoroughly, but I couldn't help noticing Carl practicing even the simplest passages from his concerto over and over, as if he didn't trust them to work. When you live with someone and hear every note they play every day, you notice when they start practicing in an unusual way, and it's an indication that something is bothering them.

"Carl, I'm sensing that each day as we learn these new pieces, you seem to be getting more and more agitated about something. It couldn't be the difficulty of the pieces. In all the double concertos we've played together over the past five years, you've had plenty of things as difficult to play, and you usually toss them off like child's play. Why all the stewing and pacing around, and practicing like your life depended on it?"

He sat silently for a moment.

"OK, here's what's going on, and I know it's all in my head, and you'll think I'm being a silly child for thinking of it, but this concert is really freaking me out because I've never played a solo concerto all by myself in front of an orchestra."

"That's the only way a solo concerto can be done," I said, trying to cheer him up.

"Yes, but that's the part that's getting to me. I've always been a second horn, and a second horn plays next to a first horn, who's the center of attention. When I'm the second voice, I can do anything with full confidence, because I'm part of a team, and the attention is on us rather than just me, and for some reason, my head is fine with that. Being the only horn in a chamber piece is okay, because the audience is focused on the entire group, and I don't feel like the success of the performance is totally my responsibility. But when I'm the only soloist, everyone is watching just me, and if anything isn't perfect, it would be my fault."

"But Carl, it isn't about who's at fault if the music isn't perfect, and we don't play music to be perfect or to prove anything. We certainly want to do our best and bring the music to a high level, but we can't worry about whether it's perfect. We'll make ourselves crazy if we get obsessed with always trying to be perfect."

"I know all that, but this goes a lot deeper than just wanting to play as well as I can. I left here at eighteen years old, and I was a pretty good horn player already. Now I've made it in Paris and have a lot more experience and skill than when I left, and somehow I have it in the back of my mind that I have to prove to my father and Prince Kraft-Ernst, and to the rest of the orchestra that I am worthy of the reputation that my father has built up in everyone's mind. He's made such a big deal about me to Rosetti, and everyone else here. That on top of the fact that I don't like to be the sole center of attention when I play is totally messing with my mind and making me feel more nervous than I can ever remember being about any performance."

"Carl, you know in the end you'll play as beautifully as you always do, and you'll think to yourself, 'Now what was I so upset about? It all went very well!' and we'll all celebrate the great success of our concert together. You're not in this alone. We're all playing together as a group effort, as always, and your concerto is just your moment to shine, as you do in your solo passages in our double concertos. This solo moment is just a bit longer, that's the only difference."

"You're absolutely right, and I know it's all true, but I spent my entire youth trying to prove to my father and everyone here that I was a fine horn player, and that I was good enough to leave and make a big career in Paris. And it's hard to get past those kinds of feelings when they start to rise up in your head."

"Carl, you're doing what we all do from time to time. You're letting the way you felt and looked at the world around you when you were a child determine how you are feeling and viewing the world around you now as an adult, and as one of the finest horn players in Europe."

"I understand that, but 'he' doesn't seem to understand it," he said, pointing at his forehead.

"That's true," I said. "As adults we can understand things intellectually, but there can still be an underlying attitude or feeling that is hard to shake off. When I was a student at a place called Indiana University, I studied with a guy who was not only a fine teacher and player, but he specialized in something called "Fearlessness Training", and the whole point was to build our confidence and replace those thoughts of fear and inadequacy that we all have with more constructive thinking and a more positive outlook."

I went on to tell Carl about my experiences learning a positive attitude and how we, in the 21st century, used positive affirmations, imagery, and the formation of a better self-image, to melt away the things that get in the way of doing our best. These were concepts that no one in the 18th century, at least to my knowledge, ever talked about. It was all new information for Carl, and he took it all in like a sponge.

"We start looking around ourselves as young children, trying to make sense of our surroundings, and figure out how we fit into this world, and what we should do about it. Whatever we decide about how we fit in remains the basic way you think about the world and your place in it from then on. Some of us feel like we have the world by the tail, and it's a friendly place made for our success, while others learn early on that they should be apprehensive about all interactions and protect themselves from possible dangers. But the good news is that it doesn't have to stay that way. Our outlook can be altered. Go back into your childhood and remember some of the early impressions you had about the people around you, and how you were raised, and how you related to them. I think you might get some insights into the way you view yourself in relation to the rest of the world. Both musicians and audience are on the same side, working toward the same goal, and that goal is very simple; performing nice music to make people happy."

We talked for quite a while that afternoon and on the following several days, and each day I could see that Carl was wrapping his mind around the idea of rewriting the story of how he related to music and the people he played for, and with. I know from my own experiences in making friends with the idea of being a performer, which didn't come naturally to me either, that a positive outlook was not something that could be switched on immediately. It had to be developed a little at a time.

Familiarity also breaks down some of the blocks that keep us from performing comfortably, and over the course of rehearsing each of our new Rosetti solo concertos and the double concerto, I could see him getting more comfortable, and feeling more like he had earned and deserved the place of soloist in front of the orchestra.

The concert that featured the new horn pieces was to take place on a Wednesday evening in the Orangery in the English garden, which was a greenhouse sort of building where the prince could have oranges and other tropical fruit growing year-round. We decided it would be best to program the high horn concerto first, and then the low horn concerto, followed by a new symphony by Josef Fiala, and then the double concerto to end the concert. As usual some other pieces of music, an overture by Holzbauer, the Mannheim opera composer, and a cello concerto by Josef Reicha were added to make an entire evening of it. Concerts were long-winded affairs in this period and would be stretched out with long pauses between pieces to last from six o'clock to ten o'clock in the evening.

The horn playing of the elder Türrschmidt and his second, Johann Nisle was rather old-fashioned, but clean and strong, and we had heard it at its best in the concerts that took place in the first few days of our visit to Wallerstein. Türrschmidt and Nisle played in a little more rustic manner than the new generation, holding their horns rather high, but with the hand in the bell to correct intonation when necessary. The idea of playing chromatically had been in their vocabularies for some years, but was still a novelty, and not something that was done on a regular basis. Our way of playing went a few more steps in the direction of a totally chromatic hand stopping technique, and we played in a style that was more woodwind-like rather than brass. The horn players, other orchestra members, and even Prince Kraft-Ernst and his Musikintendant, Franz Beecke were very interested to hear us play our new concertos.

Rehearsals with the Öttingen-Wallerstein Orchestra were not at all like the Mannheim orchestra under Christian Cannabich, the more friendly but organized leadership of the orchestra of the Prince of Guéméné, or the Concert Spirituel, where the concertmaster was in charge, working together with the harpsichordist to lead the group.

In Wallerstein, it was a free-for-all, with Rosetti, the unofficial Kapellmeister, whoever might be concertmaster that day, and Franz Beecke, who didn't play in the orchestra, all making suggestions about how to play the music. As in most 18th century orchestras, the composer, who was generally part of the group, got the last word on tempos and character of the music, but in Wallerstein, that didn't stop anyone in the orchestra from offering their ideas in rehearsals. That meant rehearsals were more laid-back than in other places and took a little longer than they might have under more strict leadership, but we were able to rehearse any passage as much as needed to feel comfortable.

The Orangery was an interesting setting for an orchestra concert. It was a large house with finely manicured grass for a floor, and mostly windows, so that the atmosphere was that of the tropics, complete with tropical temperatures in the daytime. The orchestra of about sixteen musicians stood in the middle of the single large room, on a wooden platform about six inches off the ground, just high enough to raise them noticeably above the audience. The audience sat around the musicians on all sides, with Prince Kraft-Ernst, the Princess Maria-Theresia, and other family members directly in front of the orchestra. All members of the princely household, and many of the town residents were there, making an audience of nearly a hundred listeners.

Musicians and audience started arriving well before six o'clock, and servants brought in drinks and cakes, but everyone knew the concert didn't start until the prince and his wife arrived, and were well situated at their table, and food and drink had been served to them. Only then did Musikintendant Beecke give the signal that the concert may begin. Antonio Rosetti introduced the first piece, an opera overture by Holzbauer, and said a few words about the composer and the opera. This was a spirited piece that used all the Mannheim elements of dynamics and articulation to make a dramatic effect. Carl and I sat behind the orchestra as they got warmed up on this first piece, and despite all the talking and internal work Carl had done over the past few days, he was on edge about this, his first time playing a solo concerto, and one written especially for him to be played with his hometown orchestra for his family and prince, and members of the noble house of Öttingen-Wallerstein.

After the overture it was my turn to play my solo concerto, and just as I stepped up in front of the orchestra, it occurred to me that I too had not played a solo concerto on the 18th century horn yet. And then I thought about the fact that the only time I had ever played a solo concerto with orchestra was in school, as the result of winning a concerto competition. This momentary panic attack stayed with me during the opening tutti, but as I listened to the beautiful lines Rosetti had written for me, I became absorbed in the music. The pieces that Rosetti wrote for us individually and together were some of the best music of the period for horn and would be equaled or surpassed only by those of Mozart and Haydn. I also became absorbed into the setting in this indoor tropical jungle, and the fact that I was playing as a soloist with one of the finest ensembles in Germany, in the presence of nobility, and that over the past six years, I had become an 18th century horn player and person. I had never quite had this feeling before, always feeling like a reluctant guest in this time and place.

When the first solo section started, I felt as though I could play with perfect ease. This was truly my own personal way of expressing the music, and the natural horn technique was now a part of me. I think it was a good performance – I don't remember, but that wasn't the point. The significance of this concert for me was that it was a turning point in my transition from guest to permanent resident in this time, and from that day onward it was my time and my world. I never forgot where I came from, and I still missed my old time, my family, and my friends terribly, but this was the new normal. I was a horn soloist in the year 1775, enjoying all the benefits of a rich musical life, working with fine musicians, and using my music to make people happy, if only briefly in this brutal 18th century.

This high horn concerto and the low horn concerto for Carl have both survived into the 21st century and have been issued in modern editions. There were so many other concertos by Rosetti that didn't make it into modern times, the manuscripts being destroyed or lost somewhere along the way. Two or three other solo concertos that I have never seen in any modern editions or heard mention of in modern times were in my own personal collection of music in the 18th century. I wonder what became of all that music.

After the almost spiritual experience of playing this concerto, I went back to my seat to find Carl unable to sit still during the opera arias that were sung between the solo horn concertos. He was quite agitated in anticipation of his first ever solo concerto performance, and all the emotional energy that came with it, which he had explained to me in our conversation a few days before.

"Carl, remember the affirmations you've been working on. Now tell me who you are and what it is that you do."

"I'm Carl Türrschmidt, and I am one of the finest low horn players in France or Germany," he said as though he was reciting from a book.

"That's right, and how do you know that's true?"

"I know it's true, because for the past six years I have very successfully played as a soloist with the most important musical groups in France and Germany and received praise and admiration from audiences, and the respect of my fellow musicians wherever I go."

"And why do you think you are here today about to play this concerto?"

"Because I have earned my prominent place in the world of horn playing through my own hard work and persistence, my love of music, and because I have much to express through my instrument."

"Good. Now go out there and play the concerto that Antonio has written for you. You're going to enjoy showing off his work and yours to your family and friends here tonight."

The piece that Rosetti had written for Carl was not an acrobatic showpiece, like the low horn concertos he would write in the 1780s for another low horn player, by the name of Franz Zwierzina, who specialized in those sorts of flashy technical tricks. This one was full of technical difficulties, to be sure, but every difficult passage was crafted to make a musical point, and this concerto was elegantly decorated with tasteful ornaments that brought out the best in Carl's horn playing and musicianship. Rosetti had depicted Carl's musical personality perfectly in this piece, although he had never met him before this week, going only on the description of Carl's playing related to him by his father. This is one of the more musical and well-thought-out of Rosetti's horn concertos, and Carl got a lot of mileage out of it over the next fifteen years as we took all our repertoire on the road.

During the opening tutti, which is very long, I could see him fidgeting a little, but as soon as he started playing, he took ownership of the piece, and his confidence grew as he forged ahead. Each movement had cadenzas to play, and the last movement had opportunities for about five of them, called an *Eingang,* a short single-breath ornamentation of the cadence before the next rondo theme. Each one of the cadenzas was more brilliant than the last. Although I had heard Carl do some amazing things in the past, I had never heard him play so boldly and soloistically before. He was coming into a new maturity as a horn soloist before our eyes and moving into the type of presentation of the music that would make him a superstar of the horn during his lifetime and keep the memory of his artistry alive for many years thereafter. I hate to use the phrase, and never have liked it when others used it, but I can't think of a better way to put it than to say that Carl played his ass off that day.

He came down from the raised dais after his concerto and shook both of my hands simultaneously, almost dropping his horn.

"Johann, you were right! I can play solo concertos! I was apprehensive when it began, but after I got started it was the easiest horn playing I've ever done! Thanks for all your encouragement and ideas for washing your mind clean that you got from your teacher! It's amazing stuff!"

"I knew it would be a great success," I said, "and the work that went into making it that way was actually yours alone. You deserve all of the applause and admiration for your performance, and you also deserve this glass of wine to refresh yourself during this next symphony, before we play the new double concerto."

We sat and listened to the next piece, a pleasant new symphony by Josef Fiala, and silently pondered over the musical and personal epiphanies that we both had just experienced. When this piece was finished, we again took to the stage and played Rosetti's concerto in E Major for two horns, which was the first of several double horn concertos he would write for us. It was full of fun and challenging high and low horn passages, with a lot of chromatic writing, and sections in which each horn got a chance to play complicated solo passages. It was not a concerto for a first horn accompanied by a second horn; it was a concerto for equally important high and low voices.

The performance was a great success, and the prince, the orchestra and many of the guests crowded around us afterward to see what made it possible to play the chromatic notes so easily. Everyone was astonished to find that they were normal Anton Kerner orchestra horns, exactly the same as those played by Johann Türrschmidt and Nisle. Carl's father was beaming with pride as he hugged us simultaneously.

"The two of you, both as soloists, and as a duo are, without a doubt, worlds beyond what anyone else is doing today. Johann, your singing high range, your clean and easy facility, and your musicality are without equal. And Carl, my son; you were a fine player when you left for Paris six years ago, but the maturity of horn technique and musicality, and the commanding presence as a soloist that you've developed since then puts you at the very pinnacle of low horn players. I couldn't be prouder of both of you!"

These were powerful words coming from one of the finest players and teachers of his generation, and we were both touched by the fact that he gave them out so freely, since I had heard from Carl about his strictness as a teacher of the horn. Apparently nothing was ever good enough to be called a finished product, and he always pushed his students for more.

Prince Kraft-Ernst himself, who appeared to be not much older than ourselves, was also very complimentary.

"We are very pleased to hear your fine playing this evening, and hope you will visit again soon, when your duties to the Prince of Guéméné will permit. As you know, our fine *corno primo*, Herr Türrschmidt the elder, is now over fifty years of age, and still playing marvelously, but horn playing is a young man's occupation, and in a few years, he will want to retire to the string section of the orchestra, at which time our Musikintendant, Herr Beecke, will be looking for a young and talented duo like yourselves. At that time you will hear from him asking if you are at liberty to come to Wallerstein to become members of our Hofkapelle."

"Thank you, your Highness, for your kind words," said Carl, "and for your invitation. Though I have moved to Paris, my heart is always back in my home country with my family and the noble house of Öttingen-Wallerstein. It would be a great honor someday to follow in my father's footsteps and be part of one of the finest musical establishments in Germany."

We made our farewells to all at the Orangery and headed back to the Türrschmidt family's house, which was only about a hundred yards away.

"Carl, did you mean that, about wanting to come back here to play in Wallerstein someday?"

"Of course not. We have much more important things to do in Paris and elsewhere than to play in an orchestra in a little one horse-town in the middle of nowhere for one nobleman and his family, even if it is one of the finest around. But it's important to be polite to nobility, and I'm sure he knows too that it's very unlikely that I would do that."

"I do like the musicians here a lot better than other places we've been," I said. "Antonio Rosetti struck me particularly as someone I'd like to know better."

"Probably because he's a fellow Bohemian," said Carl with a smile.

"And I owe it all to you for having made me a Bohemian. He writes good music too. As good as a lot of Mozart's stuff."

"Leopold?"

"No, Wolfgang, his son."

"Oh, right. You keep going on about Leopold's *Wunderkind* of a son. He's making a bit of a splash, but we'll see if he actually amounts to anything."

"Yes, time will tell."

Chapter 33

Sah ein Knabe ein Röslein stehen,
Röslein auf der Heide
War so jung und Morgenschön
Lief er Schnell es nah zu sehen,
Sah's mit vielen Freuden.
Röslein, Röslein, Röslein rot,
Röslein auf der Heiden.
- Johann Wolfgang von Goethe,
Heidenröslein, 1789

A young boy saw a little rose
Standing in the meadow,
young and beautiful as the morning.
He ran up close to see it
And gazed upon it with joy.
Little rose, rose so red
Little rose in the meadow.

Breakfast at the Türrschmidt house the next morning was quite a celebration, and joining the family was a young woman of about twenty, who I had seen at the concert the night before. Carl introduced her to me as Rosa Steinheber, or "Röslein" which means little rose. She was a nice-looking girl, with the dark hair and dark eyes so common in this part of Europe. She had a pleasant smile and seemed very friendly and good natured. It came out during breakfast that this was Carl's old girlfriend from a few years back, and that they were getting to know each other again during our visit. At Carl's suggestion, and the enthusiastic agreement of the Türrschmidt family, we decided to stay a few more days and take part in a couple of chamber music concerts for the prince at the castle. We spent a bit of time in the afternoons rehearsing trios with Carl's younger brother Joseph for one of these concerts. Joseph was a good low horn player, and eventually went to Paris to play professionally as Carl had done.

Röslein was the daughter of Johannes Steinheber, violist in the orchestra, and director of music and organist in the church in Wallerstein. Röslein sang in the church choir and was one of their soloists. Carl spent his evenings at the Steinheber house, or out in the countryside taking walks with Röslein in the beautiful summer weather. After years of the foul smells of Paris, it was a treat to be out in the clean air, and I went out as well to explore the fields and woods of the area, see how folks in the country lived, and made a couple of visits to Wallerstein itself.

Carl and Röslein were obviously falling in love with each other and were inseparable over the next week, and it was very difficult for him to make the decision that it was time to go back to Paris. But we had received a letter from the orchestra saying that concerts would begin again at the end of August, and to be on the safe side, we needed to start on our way back home.

There was one small local sensation that occurred during the week before we left, which kept the town talking and gossiping. The innkeeper of the *Obere Wirtschaft*, Johann Neher, who we had met when we arrived in Wallerstein, showed up after an orchestra rehearsal one afternoon, and confidentially announced to a very surprised Antonio Rosetti, that his daughter Rosina was expecting a baby, and that, with the permission of Prince Kraft-Ernst, he had already made arrangements for the wedding between the two of them, which would take place on a Sunday afternoon in two weeks in the garden at the *Lustschloß* in Hohnenaltheim. When word of the happy occasion trickled down to the members of the orchestra and their families, everyone congratulated Rosetti, who took it all good naturedly. He stopped by the Türrschmidt house later that evening, to say his farewells to Carl and me, since we were leaving the next morning. He was quite philosophical about his upcoming and unexpected marriage.

"Well, I hadn't planned on marrying so soon, being in a bit of debt at present, but circumstances sometimes alter one's plans, and she is a very nice girl, so here's to a new chapter of life!" he said, raising his beer mug. "Johann and Carl, I hope you don't mind if I send you some new horn pieces to play in Paris. I will send them to you, and also to a couple of publishers there. If you can perform them, I'm sure I can get them published and bring in a few badly needed florins. I may make a trip to Paris myself at some point and try to make some connections in the music publishing and concert world."

"We're always happy to have new pieces to play." I said, "One of our horn player friends is Jean Sieber, who is also the owner of one of the big music engraving and publishing businesses in Paris. Being a horn player himself, he likes to publish horn music, and we can make sure he hears anything you send."

Antonio, who was always in debt, and would remain that way for most of his life, looked truly appreciative.

"I can't thank you guys enough for playing my music so beautifully, and for doing what you can for me in Paris. Getting your music played and published there is the only way to make it big and gain the respect of people back home. I hope to see you there soon!"

Though he was writing some of the best music of the time, Rosetti was still just the contrabass player of the orchestra, and the prince seemed reluctant to promote him to the position and salary of Kapellmeister. A big success in Paris might prompt him to do that, and with his upcoming marriage, he was going to need more income.

We left the next morning, after a farewell breakfast with Carl's family, and hired a wagon to Wallerstein, accompanied by Carl's brother Joseph, and Röslein, who wanted to see us off at the coach. There we left them after a very long farewell between Carl and Röslein, which probably had everyone in the town talking for the next two weeks. We sat back in the coach, and Carl had a dreamy far-away look on his face.

"So, Carl, what's the plan for you and Röslein? You're obviously crazy about each other."

"She's the one I want to marry, Johann, and we've already talked it over. We decided that I would ask her father for her hand next spring, after she's studied a bit more and performed more, because she wants to try her luck in Paris as a singer. She has a beautiful voice, as you heard a couple of times in the church in Wallerstein. I think she could work in Paris."

"That's a long time to wait, Carl. Why couldn't she come with us now and study in Paris, where there are lots of good teachers?"

"Oh, that would never do! It's more normal and proper to take your time in these things and get everything arranged, and make sure that both parties are truly ready to make the commitment, and their families are supportive. Hasty marriages only happen in situations like our poor old friend Antonio has gotten himself into. No, I'll take my time and do things in the regular way. I don't want to do anything impulsive."

We slowly made our way back toward France over the next few weeks, and eventually to Paris, playing along the way wherever we could get something organized. As usual, we got home having not quite broken even financially, but it was a great trip, with major shifts in both of our thinking. Carl had proven to himself that he was a fine soloist in his own right, and had fallen in love, and I had come to the conclusion that I was in this time to stay, and felt, finally and completely, like I belonged there.

Chapter 34

Come live with me and be my Love,
And we will all the pleasures prove
That hills and valleys, dales and fields
Or woods or steepy mountain yields.
- Christopher Marlowe, The Passionate Shepherd to his Love, 1599

We were soon back into life as usual after our return, and if anything, even busier than before as the orchestra started preparing for the concert season in the fall of 1775. One evening in the autumn, after a performance with the orchestra, we arrived home late to find a letter that our landlady, Madame Marias had slipped under the door. We were soaking wet from the walk home, since it had been drizzling the whole way, and the only thing that remained dry was our horn box which we covered with a piece of oil cloth when the weather was bad as we carried it between us through the muddy streets. We got a fire going in the kitchen hearth to dry off, and warmed up some soup that had been in a pot over the fire left from earlier in the day and sat down to see what the letter was all about. For most common people, it was a rare and exciting event when a letter arrived. This one appeared to be from Germany and was addressed to "Herrn Carl Türrschmidt". Carl stood in front of the fire, which was the only light in the room, opened the envelope, and began to read. I was busy getting out bowls and spoons and was surprised when Carl fell into one of the kitchen chairs, and even by the dim light of the fire was visibly pale.

"Carl, what is it? Is everything alright in Wallerstein? Nothing has happened to anyone in your family?"

"No, no. Everyone's okay. It's not from my father, it's from Röslein's father, Herr Steinheber."

"Röselein's father? Why is he writing to you? Read it to me!"

My Dear Carl,

Welcome to the family! We look forward to your upcoming marriage to my daughter Röslein. I should explain in more detail so that you don't wonder at this way of opening my letter to you. You see, my dear future son-in-law, the circumstances are these; Röslein, who has become in the last month or so, very visibly and undeniably pregnant, tells us that the child she is expecting could only belong to you. The fact that there is no question in her mind about the matter will be, I'm sure, as great a consolation to you as it is to me. After a very frank and friendly discussion between your father and myself, we have decided that the only sensible and honorable course to follow will be for the two of you to be married as soon as possible.

Röslein also indicated to us that during your visit in July of this year, the subject was discussed, apparently in great detail, between yourselves, and you had agreed that by next summer, you intended to ask me for her hand; so I believe the decision your families have come to is not an unpleasant prospect for either of you. It would have been better for all if the entire affair could have been done in the usual order - proposal, marriage, and then beginning to raise a family - but since the two of you decided to alter the traditional way young people proceed in cases like this, we will all make the best of it.

The baby is due in April, and in order to make your child legitimate, and save face with our families and the community in Wallerstein, I will bring Röslein to Paris as soon as possible, while the weather is still conducive to travel, and while Röslein's condition is also such that she can still travel with some degree of comfort and safety for the unborn child, neither of which would be the case after the end of November.

I have asked Prince Kraft-Ernst for a leave of absence from my duties in the orchestra and as church music director, and he has agreed to appoint Antonio Rosetti to the post of temporary church music director, and a violist will be found to take my place in the orchestra while I am away accompanying Röslein to Paris. The prince would not agree to pay for my replacements, and I myself am in no position to take a couple of months away from my duties and pay for a substitute, so I'm afraid, my impulsive young future son-in-law, the burden of paying the costs of my replacements, and our travel and accommodations in Paris, will fall directly on yourself, as the person responsible for the situation at hand.

We will be leaving in the next few days when all necessary arrangements have been made and look forward to seeing you in a few weeks in Paris.

With warmest regards, I remain,
Your soon to be father-in-law,
Johannes Steinheber

"He doesn't leave the subject very open for discussion, does he?" I said.

"No." said Carl, "He and my father have pretty much decided everything for us."

"Carl, I seem to remember you saying that hasty marriages only happen in cases like our poor old friend Rosetti got himself into, and that you planned to take your time and do things in the regular way, not wanting to do anything impulsive."

Carl gave me one of the most sheepish looks I've ever seen on a horn virtuoso.

I could see that this was not the time to make jokes or tease him about the situation.

"Sorry old friend, I couldn't resist the temptation, but in all seriousness, how did all of this come about, and what happens now?"

"Well - it was just one of those things... It could happen to anyone. We were out in the forest between Hohenaltheim and Wallerstein, it was a beautiful summer day, we had been making our plans for the future and had decided that we would spend our lives together, and were very happy, and she looked so beautiful and young and attractive, and one thing led to another, and well, you know how these things happen. I'm not sorry, because I fully intended to marry her, - just not quite as soon as this."

"What's wrong with it happening now? Unlike Rosetti, you're not in debt, and make a good living in the service of the prince and are fully capable of taking good care of Röslein and your child."

"No, that part is fine. The thought of not seeing Röslein until next summer was unbearable. This letter arriving out of the blue with such news was a shock, but now that I think about it, things have actually worked out better than I could have asked for. I'm very happy that she'll be here in Paris in a few weeks. But there will be a lot to do in the meantime. We'll need to have a place to live. I mean, we can't all live in this house. It's too small. And did you hear all the expenses that Herr Steinheber expects me to pay? His replacements for who knows how long, their travel and lodging, and I don't know what all else connected with having a wedding and setting up a new house. It could wipe out all of my savings!"

"I don't think it's quite as bad as all that. Yes, it will cost a bit, but it's worth it to have Röslein here with you now, and start life immediately, rather than waiting for the better part of a year. And we can find a good solution for the housing question. For the moment we will all have to live here. There isn't enough time before they arrive to do anything else, but we'll figure something out soon. And the costs won't be as bad as you're imagining. We've been saving money faster than anyone else we know, and I would bet that the solo performances we have lined up for this coming year will more than pay for all of the expenses Herr Steinheber can come up with."

We talked far into the night, until the fire had burnt low, and it was way past time to go to bed, but in the end Carl was coming around to the idea of this new turn in his life.

We had no way of knowing exactly when Röslein and her father would arrive in Paris, but in anticipation we got busy making our house ready as best we could for the introduction of a new resident, and ultimately a new baby. We had a stroke of luck in that our upstairs neighbor, the clarinet player Johann Baer, was away in London from the first of November onward, and promised us before he left that we could use his part of the house, upstairs from us, to house the Steinhebers. This would avoid the cost of finding an expensive temporary lodging for them for an extended stay. When people traveled across the continent by coach, they usually stayed for a while, and we couldn't be sure how long Herr Steinheber would remain in Paris after Carl and Röslein were married.

Sometime around the end of November, as we were spending a Saturday afternoon alternately practicing, cleaning the house and preparing a goose that we had bought at the butcher that morning for our evening meal, the sound of a carriage stopping noisily in front of our house drew our attention. Carl went over to the window to look down into the street and see who it might be, and rushed back immediately, threw on his coat, and ran toward the stairs.

"They're here! Röslein and her father have arrived!" he said bounding down the stairs, and into the street.

In about two minutes they were all coming up the stairs, carrying boxes and trunks, and Carl looked like he was about to burst as a dozen different emotions were all trying to flow out of him at once. He was so excited and confused that he started introducing us to each other.

"Johann, this is Herr Steinheber, and this is Röslein, Oh! But, of course, you all know each other from Wallerstein, and the pleasant few days we spent there after our concert!"

At that point Madame Marais entered the room.

"Messieurs Pals et Tierschmied, if you please, I will show your German guests up to Monsieur Baer's rooms, and where to put the trunks and boxes."

She led Herr Steinheber up the steps, leaving us alone with Röslein, who was still quite overwhelmed with emotion, having just seen Carl for the first time in months, and having just arrived in this new foreign city.

"Oh Carl! I'm so sorry it has all come to this, and we are forced to have such a wedding so quickly. It's all my fault! Can you ever forgive me?"

"No, my dearest Röslein, it was my fault! Don't even think about blaming yourself!"

"But do you still want to marry me?"

"Of course I do *Liebchen*! We decided that when we were in Wallerstein, and I've not changed my mind since then. I'm as completely in love with you as I was on the day we took leave of each other in Wallerstein. And do you still want to marry me?

"From the time we renewed our childhood friendship this summer, I knew I wanted to marry you, and I know that I will always want to be with you."

Carl took her in his arms and kissed her, and they held each other in a long embrace.

"But how is your father taking all of this? Is he upset with me? I wouldn't blame him if he were."

"Oh no!" On the contrary, I can't remember Father being in such a good mood as he's been on this trip. He has always wanted to visit Paris, and this was his chance to make the trip. Prince Kraft-Ernst has given him money to buy sheet music for the orchestra while in Paris, so he has another official duty to perform here that will keep him busy. No, - he is quite happy with how things have turned out. Antonio Rosetti is also very happy about our current situation, because he gets to make some badly needed money on top of his regular salary by subbing for father as church music director. He is now married to Rosina Neher, and they are looking forward to the birth of their first child."

"I remember the circumstances," said Carl. "There must be something in the air in Wallerstein that makes people fall in love."

"And something that compels them to get married on short notice!" I said grinning.

Both blushed like embarrassed teenagers, and I thought this might be a good time to leave them alone and see how Herr Steinheber was getting along upstairs.

Carl and Röslein were married in a small ceremony a few days later at the chapel in the Hôtel de Rohan-Guéméné, in the presence of a small group of musician friends and her father. Our employer, the Prince of Guéméné, let us use one of the small dining rooms in the Hôtel for the ceremony and for the wedding breakfast, which was held afterward, and everyone was in high spirits. Carl and Röslein were happy that they didn't have to wait to get married and were genuinely looking forward to the baby and to starting their life together. Herr Steinheber was happy, because his daughter was now safely married to Carl, whom he had not only known from childhood, but also trusted to be a good husband and provider to his daughter. He was also glad to be in Paris, meeting and making connections with famous musicians, and hearing lots of music played in the latest style.

Though I was happy for Carl and Röslein, I was the only one who had any regrets or apprehensions, since Carl and I had been like brothers up to this point, going where we wanted, and centering everything in our lives exclusively around music and horn playing. I wondered how this turn of events was going to affect the thriving

Palsa-Türrschmidt duo, but I shouldn't have worried. Carl was in higher spirits now than I had ever seen him, and that seemed to translate into even more artistry in his playing, and Röslein became part of both of our lives.

In the 18th century childbirth was a dangerous business. If anything went wrong, the lives of the mother and child were at risk, and Carl and Röslein both wanted to do everything in their power to ensure a healthy baby. They consulted a doctor, who said activity was the best way for her to stay in good shape for the birth. She asked if continuing to sing was a good idea, and the doctor said that singing would encourage breathing, which was good for the muscles and the mind. As a result of this advice, Röslein wasted no time in starting her musical studies with a singing teacher in Paris.

Röslein's father stayed for about a month after the wedding and enjoyed Paris at Carl's expense. Carl also paid the rent on the upstairs rooms, and for the doctor who came around occasionally to see how the mother-to-be was doing. After Herr Steinheber departed, another fortunate turn of events solved the housing situation. Our friend Baer sent a letter from London saying he had accepted a post as principal clarinet in the Dresden court orchestra, and would stop in at Paris only long enough to gather his belongings and leave for the Electorate of Saxony, and that Carl and Röslein were welcome to his rooms at Madame Marais' house. We could now all live permanently in the same house, and there, in April of 1776, Carl's son and heir, Carl Nicholaus Türrschmidt was born, with the assistance of a midwife who lived in our street.

"Johann, you should think about getting married someday," Carl said to me one sweltering summer evening, as we were walking home through the crowded streets, dodging speeding coaches and watching for pickpockets and beggars.

"But Carl, I am married, and have two small children, though it appears that none of them will ever see me again or know what happened to me."

"You can't be married to someone who won't be born for two hundred years! Eventually you're going to have to let go of your old life and live this one. You said yourself after our trip to Wallerstein that you now feel like you belong here."

"I certainly feel like I'm still married to my wife Beth and I miss her and my children Ana and Christopher very much. Somehow it seems unthinkable to consider getting married now, and it isn't even really a question in my mind, since there isn't anyone who I have been particularly interested in romantically."

"You just wait. When the right young lady comes along, and you find yourself attracted to her, and she to you, and the prospect of spending your lives together and having a family is presented to you, then we'll see how you feel about it."

We arrived home to find Röslein singing the baby to sleep and cooking a pork roast over the fire in the hearth in the downstairs rooms where Carl and I had lived for the past few years. Though Carl and his family lived upstairs, we cooked and ate together in the lower level where I lived.

"Welcome home my two Waldhorn virtuosi!" she said, kissing Carl affectionately. "In a few minutes we'll have a nice hot supper and a glass of wine, and I can tell you about my singing lesson today and hear about your wind band performance."

It was such a cozy scene, so much like the memories of my own family, that it made me homesick and sad that I would never see them again. Though the thought was always with me, that night I remembered more than ever how terribly I missed Beth and our kids.

Chapter 35

The elector has a good band, in which M. Ponta (Punto), the celebrated French horn from Bohemia, whose taste and astonishing execution were so much applauded in London, is a performer.

- Charles Burney, The present state of Music in Germany, The Netherlands, and the United Provinces, London, 1775

Around the first of December 1776 word started to spread among the musicians of Paris that Giovanni Punto, the most celebrated horn soloist of the century, was going to visit Paris, and Joseph Legros, director of the Concert Spirituel, had already scheduled a solo concerto spot for him on the Christmas day program.

At the previous Concert Spirituel performance, in which we took part, Legros mentioned having scheduled Punto for the date in December.

"But what if he doesn't want to play a solo concerto while he's here? You haven't actually talked to him yet, have you?" asked Carl.

"My dear Türrschmidt, have you ever heard of Punto turning down a solo performance? You'll see flocks of pigs flying over the frozen wastes of Hell before you'll see that! I'm sure he'll be happy to play, as always."

"That's true," said Carl. "If there's a solo spot with an orchestra that needs filling, he's always the first in line."

"By the way," added Legros, as though it was an afterthought, "how would the two of you like to play a set of duos in the concert on the previous day, the 24th?[15] We would need you for the orchestra too. We'll be doing a new symphony by Carl Stamitz."

His invitations always sounded as though he had just thought of the idea that very second, but in reality, he had his programs thought out well in advance and virtually no one ever turned him down when invited to play.

"Yes," I said. "We would love to play some duos. We'll make sure we're free that day. The prince is getting better about sharing us with the world now.

"Marvelous!" cried Legros. "It will be a week of the top horn soloists in all of Europe! Just the thing to please the crowd during the holiday season."

As the time approached, rehearsals for the December 24th and 25th concerts began, and I was really looking forward to meeting the great Giovanni Punto, the horn player for whom Beethoven would write his Sonata Op. 17 about twenty-five years later. He would spend the intervening years pursuing one of the most brilliant solo horn careers of all time. On the first day of rehearsals we arrived at the Tuilleries Palace and found our way into the Salle des Suisses just in time to hear the end of a rollicking rondo for solo horn and orchestra, in hunting horn style. We only heard the last few notes of the horn and then the closing tutti section.

The horn soloist was a tall, neatly dressed man of about thirty in an elegant red coat and waistcoat with a rather long ponytail of thick blond hair. His features were chiseled in a Kirk Douglas kind of way, so that if someone had told me he was an up-and-coming Hollywood movie star, I would have believed them.

"It's him!" whispered Carl "It's Punto! You're in for a real treat now. He's three of the most entertaining people you'll ever meet."

He played the last note and ran across the room to embrace Carl.

"Mon cher Carl! Wie geht es Dir? Es ist so long since I've seen you, mein guter Freund. Ist hier votre amis Monsieur Palsa, von dem ich so much have heard?"

„Jawohl!" said Carl in German, barely able to get a word in edgewise before Punto went on.

"Signor Palsa! Je suis enchante Dich kennenzulernen. Von dem Padre of Carl in Wallerstein, I have gehört von your größen Erfolg ici zu Paris."

I was absolutely astounded at the man's way of expressing himself. He was speaking about a mile a minute in a merry mixture of French, German, and English. For the sake of understandability, I will translate his amazing jargon into proper English from here on.

"It's a pleasure to meet you too," I said. "I've heard so much about you for many years."

I wasn't lying, since I knew more about him than he knew himself; for example, the story of the commissioning of the Beethoven Sonata in 1800, and Mozart's admiration for his playing, which I had read in some horn history book or other. And that he would live for another twenty-seven years before dying on a concert tour of his native Bohemia, and the Mozart Requiem would be performed at his funeral.

"My dear Carl," he went on, without missing a beat, "the last time I saw you, you were about sixteen years old, and playing second horn with your father in the Thurn und Taxis court orchestra in Regensburg."

"I remember it well," said Carl. "You played a concerto by Franz Pokorny and impressed the pants off everyone."

"I was in Regensburg and Wallerstein a couple months ago and saw Franz Pokorny. Do you remember little Beate, his daughter who plays the horn?

"Yes, - she's a couple years younger than I am," said Carl. "We played together as children. She was always very talented, and can play several instruments well, but of course her father wouldn't let her study seriously with any of the court orchestra musicians. We were in Regensburg just last summer and saw the Pokorny family."

Carl then related the story of our trip to Regensburg and Wallerstein, and of Beate dressing in men's clothes and playing in the concert, unbeknownst to her father, who was leading the orchestra.

"I believe Beate is the only woman I've ever met who could get away with a trick like that," Punto went on, laughing. "She has turned into the most handsome and accomplished young lady you will ever meet and plays the horn surprisingly well. I also saw your father in Wallerstein. He is overjoyed to be back there playing for Prince Kraft Ernst, though you have probably heard that the court has gone into mourning, and music has been called to a halt for the foreseeable future, due to the death of the prince's wife, Maria Theresia."

"I had a letter about it from my father," said Carl. "There isn't much for the musicians to do now other than play in church, and my father has been playing viola more than horn these days, since there are no Tafelmusik services for the winds. But they all still receive a pension from the prince that keeps them alive, and when the court comes out of mourning, there will be orchestral and chamber music again."

"I talked with him while I was there," Punto continued. "He is very proud to hear the reports of what the two of you are doing as a horn duo here in Paris. At the inn where I am staying I have a letter for you that he asked me to deliver. I also bring congratulations and best wishes from all the Wallerstein musicians on your recent marriage. Your father seems very happy about it and said he could not think of a better match for you than Rosa, the daughter of Johannes Steinheber."

"Thank you! I'll look forward to hearing the latest news from home. We have to rehearse for the concert now, but it would be so nice to spend some time together while you're here and catch up on things."

"I'm leaving Paris for London the morning after my concerto performance, but tomorrow evening, after your duo performance, we could have a late supper and spend the evening together."

"Wonderful!" Carl said. "We can go to our rooms where we can sit comfortably and have supper brought in from the inn down the street."

"That would be delightful. I'll look forward to hearing you both tomorrow evening and meeting after the concert. *Adieux until then meine liebe Freunde!"*

We took our places in the orchestra and rehearsed the new symphony by Carl Stamitz. Both Stamitz brothers were playing, and Carl was very animated in his directions to the orchestra about how he wanted the long crescendos and other innovative Mannheim school elements of his new piece to be performed. Carl Stamitz's horn writing, while not always easy, was much tamer than that of his father, Johann Stamitz, one of the inventors of the classical symphony. The elder Stamitz apparently had some serious high horn players in the Mannheim orchestra back in his day and didn't mind sending them up into the stratosphere to tread on the tiny little bits of eggshell that exist in that exotic land above the 16th partial of the natural horn.

There were also horn parts in a flute concerto that was played by Herr Wendling, who at this point was back in Paris. When the rehearsal ended, we stayed for a few minutes to try out our set of duos in the acoustics of the Salle des Suisses.

On the way home we talked about Punto, and I told Carl what I had known about him from my reading as a university student.

"Punto was, even in my time, still regarded as one of the greatest horn soloists of all time, right up there with the best of the 20th century, like Dennis Brain, Herman Baumann, Barry Tuckwell, and a few others," I said, as we traversed the dangerous streets with our horn box between us.

"Never heard of any of them," said Carl.

"I wouldn't think so. They won't be born for nearly two hundred years. But every horn player knows about Punto, and especially the story of his commissioning Beethoven to write him a sonata for horn and pianoforte for a concert in Vienna around 1800. Since then it's been a standard piece in the horn repertoire."

"Beethoven?"

"He's also not known yet. He's probably five or six years old now, but he will be one of the greatest composers of all time." By this time, Carl was so used to my talking about composers and performers who hadn't been born yet, that he had ceased to show his astonishment long ago. He just went with it good humoredly.

"I've played sonatas with pianoforte a few times," he said. "It's a good combination."

"I thought the Beethoven sonata was the first one ever written. Whose sonata did you play?"

"Oh, no one actually writes sonatas for horn and pianoforte, though it would be nice if someone would. The ones I've played were sonatas for violin or flute by J.C. Bach and Geminiani. That sort of thing is done all the time. There isn't very much solo music for the horn, so if you want to play with keyboard, you have to rework music for other instruments. Punto is rather a specialist at that when he goes on tour."

"He also seems to be a specialist with languages," I added, "except he doesn't seem to know how to keep to one at a time. How did he get so mixed up with the languages he speaks?"

"Punto has been all over Europe and learned little bits of the language everywhere he goes. He always uses language very expressively, but hardly ever correctly. He was born in Bohemia and spoke a local dialect there that wouldn't be understandable to any German. Then he was shipped off to Prague to study horn at the age of twelve, and later to Dresden by Count Thun, in whose house he worked. After he left the count's service, which is a story I'll leave to him to tell, he spent time in Italy, England, France, Germany and God knows where else, and the result is that he speaks about seven languages poorly, and uses whatever word comes to mind at any given moment. Though oddly enough, he always seems to use words that you understand. When talking to him in previous years he mostly mixed together German, French, and Italian to me, but knowing that you speak English, as well as German and French, he mixed those three together when talking to you today. He's a total enigma in that way and has probably all but forgotten his mother tongue in the meantime. Some people call him the 'man without a language'. Nonetheless, he loves to talk away an entire evening, and it's always interesting and entertaining. He's played with everyone you can think of and knows important people in just about every major city in Europe."

"I plan to pick his brain on a few details about the horn," I said. "Didn't he study with Josef Hampel, the guy who invented hand stopping technique?"

"He studied first with Josef Matiegka in Prague, then with Jan Schindelarž in Dobříš and then with Hampel and Karl Haudek in Dresden. Hampel didn't invent the idea of using the hand in the bell; the concept had been known before that, but he did make it into a good system, and taught a lot of players how to do it. I'm sure Punto will be happy to tell you the whole story."

"You've told a number of people that I studied with Josef Matiegka, does Punto know that? It could be awkward if he hears the story and asks me about him," I said, thinking about how I would get out of an awkward conversation, since I knew absolutely nothing of Matiegka or Prague.

"Don't worry, he probably hasn't talked to anyone who would have told him that, and if he does ask you about your studies with Matiegka, all you have to do is mention that you remember the three dogs and a cat that were always in the room when he gave lessons, and it will start him off into a ridiculous story that he loves to tell."

Carl filled me in on more of Giovanni Punto's peculiarities as we walked home. On the way, we picked up a few bottles of wine at a little wine shop in the rue St. Antoine, run by a disagreeable man named Defarge,[16] and stopped by the inn on the corner of our street to order a dinner for us for the following evening to be picked up after our performance at the Concert Spirituel. We ordered a leg of lamb, bread, a dish called *cassoulet* that was made with beans, an onion and potato soup, and a couple of pastries. We were well equipped for an interesting and entertaining evening with one of the greatest artists I have ever met.

Chapter 36

Punto (Giovanni) - A great Master of the Waldhorn at Paris, who came to Germany in 1785, and performed there at the most prominent courts, where his artistry and skill won him universal admiration.

- Ernst Ludwig Gerber, Historisch-Biographisches Lexicon der Tonkünstler, 1792

The next day we had a short wind band performance in the morning for the arrival of some foreign dignitary at the Hôtel de Guéméné. It was an unusually cold December 24th, and we played the usual mindless wind sextet music for about an hour, first outdoors, and then in the Hôtel, and then went home to prepare our rooms for our important guest. We already owned four each of silver spoons, knives, and forks, copper cooking pots that hung in the hearth, four wine glasses, and bowls, known as porridgers, in addition to my invaluable coffee making equipment, but since Röslein's arrival, she had added a few other touches, such as a teapot, a table cloth, and embroidered napkins, all of which went together to make a very pleasant and inviting kitchen in those days.

We changed out of our uniforms and into our other set of concert clothes, and late in the afternoon set out for the Tuilleries Palace. The Salle des Suisses was ice cold, even though it was filled with people. There were no thermometers to say how cold it was, but I would be willing to bet it wasn't much above fifty-five degrees in the room that evening. 18th century musicians were used to these kinds of conditions, and temperature was just one of the many challenges we had to deal with in making our instruments function properly. For everyone, from commoners to royalty, being uncomfortably hot or cold most of the time was just part of life.

The new symphony by Carl Stamitz was the centerpiece, and otherwise it was a program of the usual arias, choral pieces, and a concerto, but there were often chamber pieces, and our duos were the representatives of that genre on this particular evening. Our set of *Petit airs* consisted of six pieces, each of two or three minutes in length. By now we were well-known soloists at the Concert Spirituel, and the crowd went wild with their applause, not allowing us to leave until we had played a couple of duos a second time. We played very well that night - just about note perfect, which was quite a feat, considering some of the daring high horn playing Carl had given me in his arrangements, and the highly acrobatic low horn feats in his own parts.

We left the room after our pieces, since the last item on the program was a choral piece, and as we did, we were met by Punto, who had been standing at the back of the crowded room.

"Bravo! Das war ein manifique performance, mon Amis! Josef Hampel would be proud to see that the art of hand stopping he worked so hard to promote and teach has been brought to such a high a state of perfection!"

We wrapped ourselves in cloaks and scarves and thin leather gloves that weren't much protection from the cold and went out into the streets.

"Is Hans Joachim along with you this time?" asked Carl.

"Who?" I inquired.

"Oh, Hans Joachim travels everywhere with me. I think he went back to fetch something and meet a couple of friends he ran into. He'll catch up with us," said Punto.

This was mysterious, since no one had mentioned that Punto was traveling with anyone. We proceeded through the streets and made our way to the inn on our corner to pick up the food for our late-night meal. There seemed to be some commotion going on in the butcher's shop across the street, and as we were going in the door of the inn Punto stopped short.

"Excuse me for a moment, friends. I just saw Hans Joachim and his friends go into that shop, and something tells me I had better go and see what they're up to. People don't always understand his playful little pranks..."

This worried me a little, since the butcher was shouting obscenities at someone and there was a crowd of people and animals gathering.

"We'll get the food," said Carl, "and meet you here after you've checked on whatever is happening over there. That's our house, next to the inn."

"I'll be right back," said Punto, hurrying off.

As we came out carrying a basket full of our freshly cooked supper, Punto caught up with us at the house door.

"Everything is alright," he said, out of breath. "They tried to steal a steak, and since they were already out the door with it when I got there, there was no other choice than to pay for it. The butcher was a bit upset, but it's okay now."

"Up to his old tricks, is he?" said Carl.

"He'll be coming along presently," said Punto slipping in the door behind us. "I'll leave the door ajar for him."

I hadn't seen this colorful friend of his yet, but I was beginning to wonder what sort of disreputable character he was. We went upstairs where there was a fire in the hearth and moved our table and chairs into the kitchen, since it was too cold to eat in the sitting room. Röslein had already started the fire, knowing that we had an important guest that evening. The kitchen was just beginning to warm up a little and we were about to sit down to eat, when the shrill voice of Madam Marais, our landlady, came up the stairs like a bolt of lightning.

"Messieurs Tierrsmied et Pals! Come down here immediately! There are three dogs in the hallway eating something, and they are making a terrible noise. Do you know who they belong to?"

"We don't know anything about any dogs, Madam Marais," Röslein called down the stairs.

"Wait, wait!" cried Punto dashing for the door and down the steps. "It's okay Madam, I'll take care of this."

There was some barking and slamming of doors, and in a minute he was back, with a large yellow dog in tow, who was wearing a green silk scarf around his neck.

"He isn't very happy at the moment. I sent his two friends packing, and they took the last bits of the steak with them. We'll find a little something for you old Hans. Nice scarf, by the way! Where on earth did you find that? Not stolen, I trust?"

With this mystery finally explained we sat down to our supper and wine. Hans Joachim joined us in devouring the leg of lamb, and then curled up and fell asleep by the fire. Having polished off the meal in record time, as well as the first bottle of wine, Röslein went off to put Carl Nicholaus to bed upstairs and leave us to our conversation with Punto. We were now comfortably warm in front of the hearth and refilled our glasses.

"Herr Punto, there is so much that I want to ask you about yourself and the state of horn playing in all the places you've been," I said to get him started.

"Please call me Jan," he said emptying his glass. "That's my actual Bohemian name, - Jan Václav Stich, or in German, Johann Wenzel Stich. I took on the name of Giovanni Punto a few years ago when I left my hometown in a hurry.

"I had just started to tell Johann about that on our way home," said Carl, "but I'm sure he would like to hear the whole story from you."

"I was born in Zehušice, a little town near Čáslav in Bohemia, and like the rest of my family, went into the service of Count Johann Josef Anton Thun-Hohenstein, an important Bohemian nobleman. My father was a coach driver, and my mother, siblings, and I were house servants. The count had a small orchestra, and I started to learn to play the violin at an early age, and at about twelve, began playing the horn. As I started to get better on the horn, the count sent me to Prague to study with Josef Matiegka. I've heard from Carl's father, that you studied with him too."

"Just briefly," I replied. "Only for a few months." Carl kicked me under the table, and I went on; "What I remember most is his dogs and the cat that were always there during my lessons."

"Oh yes!" interjected Punto, "I remember one particular lesson, when the animals got out of hand..."

He then launched into a long story about the cat bringing a rabbit into the house, and the three dogs going after it, knocking over furniture and making a huge mess of things. The cat eventually cornered the rabbit, and was protecting it from the dogs, which turned into a cat and dog fight of impressive proportions, and while they were at it, Punto was able to open the door and the rabbit got away unharmed. It was a good story, and it also diverted the conversation, so that we didn't have to discuss a man about whom I knew nothing.

"After a time with Matiegka, Count Thun sent me to study with Jan Schindelarž, and finally to Dresden to Karl Haudek and Josef Hampel. Haudek showed me that anyone, whether they are a *corno primo* or *secondo* by nature, can play high horn when necessary just by using the right concepts and directing the energy properly, but being naturally a low horn player, I learned the most from Hampel, who was doing more with the hand in the bell than anyone else at that time."

"I've always heard that he invented hand stopping," I said. "Is that true, or did others do it before him?"

"The best horn players have always known that you can fix bad notes by putting the hand into the bell, but it was seldom used because they felt it was more important to have the clear sound of the open horn with the bell held upward, and composers, even to this very day, have only written the simple open notes in orchestra parts. Haudek and Hampel played with the bell up exclusively early on, but later on they started to develop the use of the hand for soloistic playing. Only in his later years did Hampel keep his hand in the bell most of the time in more soloistic slow movements, and then with quite an open sound. As the style changed from the melodic type of horn writing of the early years of the century to the current way of scoring horns in the texture of the wind section, everyone became more concerned about intonation and blending with the winds, and slowly a few orchestra players have started to use the hand in the bell sometimes for that purpose. But that doesn't mean everyone does it; these modern changes come slowly. By Carl's father's generation, in the 50s and 60s, a few of the players in the best court orchestras were playing with the hand in the bell, and some could play some chromatic notes with a bit of facility. Isn't that right Carl?"

"My father and his partner Joseph Fritch played with the hand in the bell much of the time, and did so as far back as I can remember in Regensburg, but as you said, with a very open sound, and they still don't do a lot of chromatic playing. My father found that the hand in the bell made the upper partials more stable, and as a result high horn accuracy got a lot better when they started playing that way."

"In the early days, back in the 30s and 40s, audiences heard some pretty rustic horn playing, even from the best players," added Punto. "High horn playing was a slippery business back then, and the low players were very limited in what they could do. Low horn playing really came into its own as an art with Hampel. Before he started to make hand stopping into a real system, there were few low horn specialists, and very few low horn concertos.

We've come a long way since his time, and now all the people who studied with him, our generation who are playing soloistically, are doing it with a high degree of facility and making some very elegant and sophisticated music. But there are still a lot of places where the horn is played exclusively with the bell in the air in orchestras and wind bands. I was in England a couple of years ago, and no one in the audiences had ever heard the horn played with the hand. They were impressed, but the English horn players thought it ruined the open sound quality of the horn. They prefer to try to lip the out of tune notes into place as well as possible, and preserve the hunting horn character. In my opinion, that's not the way to make the horn into a viable chamber and solo instrument in today's musical world. And though most orchestra players still play with the bell up, I don't think it will ultimately be the norm in orchestras in a generation or two."

"In any case," he continued, "I went back to Bohemia and into the service of Count Thun for a few years. It was incredibly boring work, shoveling horse manure during the day in the stables, and playing horn in his orchestra and wind band at night."

I wasn't very familiar with the lives of court musicians at that time, and his story of doing hard manual labor and playing horn seemed unbelievable, but that was the case in many small courts. Only in the larger court orchestras were many of the musicians engaged to play music exclusively.

"After about four years of that," Punto went on, "I decided it just wasn't good enough to keep doing it for the rest of my life, and left town one evening with four other orchestra members who were also ready for a change. We had saved our money and hired a fast coach for our getaway. Our departure wasn't discovered until the next day when we didn't appear for work, but by then we were far away, and soon were over the border and out of Bohemia. The count, who felt that we belonged to him, since he had invested a lot of money into our musical educations, sent men out to try to bring us back, but they never caught up with us.

There were a couple of close calls, and in Munich I heard from someone who had talked to the count's men, that the count had ordered them to either bring me back, or at least knock my teeth out so I couldn't play the horn anymore. It was at that point that I decided another name would be a good idea. I hit upon the idea of

Giovanni Punto, as an Italianized version of Jan Stich. Get it? Punto – Stich? Pretty clever, eh?"

"Absolute genius," said Carl, "but how did you get the solo career going so fast?"

"The first thing I did was to get a little aristocratic support. The Elector at Koblenz took a fancy to my playing when I organized a benefit concert there, for my own benefit that is, and he offered a good salary and plenty of time to tour if I would commit to a small amount of time playing with his band and doing chamber music for him. I also started commissioning new music by good composers to start building up a repertoire of things I could do on short notice wherever I happened to be. Much of it was composed by Antonio Rosetti in Wallerstein. You must have met him when you were there last summer?"

"We know Antonio very well," I said. "Carl's father asked him to write a solo concerto for each of us, and a wonderful double concerto that we've been getting a lot of mileage out of lately here in Paris. He certainly knows how to write for the horn; very difficult stuff, but quite idiomatic, and well worth the effort."

"The quartets and solo concertos he's done for me are also the very best in contemporary solo horn music, said Punto. "His pieces, as well as a few by Carl Stamitz, Joseph and Michael Haydn, and some of my own, are my main repertoire. "After Rosetti has heard you play once, he knows exactly what would suit you best in a solo concerto.

I do a lot of transcribing too. In London I did some concerts with Christian Bach, Wendling, and Abel, and for a few of the performances, we did nothing but transcribed pieces; quartets by Bach for oboe and strings played on the horn, quartets for flute, oboe, horn, and bassoon arranged from Boccherini string quartets - that sort of thing. It's great fun to take a sonata for flute, or violin, or whatever and rework it into a horn piece. Some of the things I've gathered together I've published here in Paris, but many of them, especially the transcriptions, wouldn't be playable by more than a handful of us, so there obviously wouldn't be any point in printing many of them; you would never make any money.

I predict that in another generation, horn players from one end of Europe to the other will be doing chromatic hand stopping and will be able to do all the things we're doing now. But until then, those of us who are doing solo playing will have our own private repertoires of concertos and chamber pieces. I'm sure you guys have collected a good number of double concertos and duos that are strictly your own."

"We sure have," I said. "We now have double concertos by Rosetti, Leopold Mozart, Pokorny, and Josef Fiala. Carl's father has promised to send us yet another new one by Rosetti as soon as they've performed it in Wallerstein. We also have a few books of duets - mostly things we've arranged or written. In fact, I think your duos are the only actual printed horn duets we've ever played in public."

"I have some new ones I can give you, and I would be honored to hear you play them," interjected Punto. "I've only played them with Rodolph, so they need to be played by a really flashy duo like yourselves."

"We'll do our best with them and would love to see any other two-horn pieces you might have," said Carl. "We're always in the market for new things to play."

It was true that we were all hungry for new music, and whenever horn players met, there was a lot of trading of pieces. This often involved writing out by hand entire concerto scores quickly that you had borrowed from a horn player who was in town for just a few days. I was getting good at music manuscript, and I could see that we would probably spend the next few days or weeks copying pieces that Punto was going to loan us until he returned to Paris.

We talked until far into the night – until the fire had died down and all the wine was gone and parted on the friendliest terms. Punto and Hans Joachim left at about three in the morning, and we all felt as though we were part of a small secret brotherhood of solo horn players who were shaping the future of the art.

Chapter 37

Punto bläst magnifique!
Punto plays magnificently!
- W. A. Mozart, letter to his father, Paris, 1778

Christmas day, 1776 was again bitter cold and, as a result of our evening with Punto, I woke up with the most appalling hangover I could remember since my undergraduate days. We only had one musical service that day, and that was a performance at Notre Dame Cathedral of a Christmas morning high Mass for singers and orchestra that started at ten o'clock. Fortunately the horn parts were simple enough that we could play them in our sleep, since we were totally worthless as horn players that morning.

We went home after the Mass to sleep off our headaches and speculated how Punto was feeling after the previous evening's festivities, since he had an important solo performance that night.

"I'm sure he'll be fine," Carl said. "I've seen him put away more wine than that and play like a god afterward."

"I'm skeptical," I said, "but after meeting him, and hearing about him for years, I can't wait to hear him play the horn and see if he's as amazing as they all say."

The Christmas night concert was a rather long program. It started with an energetic symphony by Carl Joseph Toeschi from the Mannheim orchestra, a set of Italian arias sung by Mademoiselle Georgi, a popular singer in Paris, a clarinet concerto composed and performed by our old upstairs neighbor Johann Baer, who was back in town, Punto's horn concerto, and a violin concerto played by Giovanni Jarnowick, a violinist who was currently all the rage in Paris. The concert ended with a choral piece by a French composer by the name of Langlé. Carl and I slept through a good deal of the symphony, still being a little under the weather. I don't remember any of the arias, but we woke up to hear Baer, who played beautifully that night. We then fell back into a deep slumber for the duration of the violin concerto and woke up just as Jarnowick was bowing to the cheering audience.

After Nicholas Capron, the concertmaster, had tuned the orchestra once more, Legros announced that Monsieur Punto, the celebrated Bohemian horn player would now play a concerto of his own composition. Flutes and horns joined the string orchestra that had played in the previous piece and the room became quieter than I had ever heard at an 18th century concert hall. The side door by the orchestra opened, and Punto entered the room looking like Julius Caesar entering Rome after a brilliant victory. His bright red coat was neat and clean, he was freshly shaven, his shirt noticeably cleaned and pressed, and he didn't in the least look like he had been up half the night before, eating and drinking to excess. He smiled brightly at the audience and took his place in front of the orchestra.

Capron gave a preparatory gesture, and the opening tutti began. I smiled as I heard the first theme because the piece that was announced as Punto's first horn concerto was a piece that I knew as the Rosetti E major concerto, a popular piece in my own time. Herman Baumann had recorded it in the 1980s and I had listened to it countless times in my youth. I knew every note of this piece intimately. During the tutti, Punto stood with his eyes closed and face pointed heavenward. As the tutti was coming to an end, he opened his eyes slowly and surveyed the room as though to say; "You are all in my power – prepare to be spellbound!"

We were sitting near the front of the room, just a few feet away from him.

"Isn't it the most outrageous thing you've ever seen?" whispered Carl. "He's like a magician, he has the audience wrapped around his little finger and he hasn't played a note yet!"

The audience was indeed riveted as the horn came to his lips and he started the first theme of the exposition. He became at least an inch taller as he started to play his opening statement, and it was immediately clear who was in charge of the orchestra now. It was a sweet vocal sound, round without any edge, but very open and clear. There was an audible vibrato on longer notes, but it wasn't so much an element of his sound as an ornament that he used to add emotion to the phrase, much as an actor might put a little emotional quiver into their voice to express a dramatic scene. His phrasing was expressive and eloquent, articulating clearly in a very linguistic way, and shaping the phrase in ways that you wouldn't ever have thought of, but were so obvious and satisfyingly when you heard them. He pulled the listener along as though he was a Shakespearian actor forging his way to the climax of a scene.

By the end of the exposition, which was more melodic and lyrical than technical, I was totally drawn in by the sound, the phrasing, the expression, and the stage presence. He had the dramatic expression of Hermann Baumann, the beautiful shimmering vibrato of Peter Damm, the lightness of articulation and agility in his scale passages of Dennis Brain, the technical perfection of Frank Lloyd, and on and on through the entire list of the greatest horn players I knew. This man was without a doubt one of the finest horn players and musicians I had ever heard.

He made a few changes and additions to the solo part that I was unfamiliar with, adding tasteful ornaments, and altering the lines of this essentially low horn concerto to go effortlessly into the upper range briefly. His conversational way of talking back and forth with the orchestra gave the impression that, even though he had the entire situation in the palm of his hand, he considered the orchestra to be of equal importance to his voice and kept the dialog going in an exciting volley that reminded one of the dialogue in a theatrical piece. The orchestra was drawn into the sheer fun of the thing and were playing up to him and sounding better than I had ever heard them sound in the seven years I had known and played with them.

The last page of the first movement gets rather acrobatic and covers a wide range; down to G below low C, with wide leaps and arpeggios in triplets and sixteenths, all of which he tossed off effortlessly as though saying to the orchestra, "I'm in the home stretch, catch me if you can!" Then all came to a grand halt, and he began his cadenza. This was pure Paganini, complete with wide leaps, covering a range of pedal G to somewhere around high E, from a resounding fortissimo to an almost inaudible pianissimo, and ending with a solemn, hymn-like procession of multiphonics, a specialty of his, that were dead in tune in three part harmony, followed by a string of rapid scales that ended brilliantly in a trill that said; "That's all folks, and now back to reality!" I don't know if that cadenza lasted fifteen seconds or three minutes, but I do know that no one in the room took in or let out a single molecule of breath during it.

When the movement ended a few measures later, it was as if a curtain had come down, ending the action of the first act of the play, and we all woke up surprised to find ourselves in a room surrounded by other people who we hadn't previously noticed.

The second movement started after this brief respite, and his whole approach changed. This movement is a short aria in a very simple vocal style that takes advantage of the colors of the stopped notes of the horn in written c minor (sounding e minor). He was now an operatic voice singing a sweet love song with a gentle string accompaniment, and you could almost imagine what the words might be as he sang you into a state of intoxication. It was after the short cadenza at the end of the movement, which he did in a single long breath, that it occurred to me that I hadn't noticed the stopped notes, even though I knew very well that there were scales in written E flat major and c minor that included E flat, F, and A flat in the middle range, and D flat, E flat, F and A flat at the top of the staff. They were all clear and open, or at least he had made them seem so.

His horn was much like ours in size, but with fixed mouthpipe, no crooks, and no tuning slide, and it was made by a different maker, Carl Stärtzer in Vienna. The bell was slightly larger than our Kerner horns, and the sound was a bit broader. When I got to try his horn later, it occurred to me that Carl and I could benefit from a little more room in the bell throat of our horns, and from that time, the three of us started talking about our ideal design for a solo horn and an orchestra horn, with the intention of having custom instruments made someday.

Again, in the rondo, marked *alla chasse*, he moved into another character, and it was all excitement and pyrotechnical tricks beginning to end. After each rondo section there was a fermata that gave the soloist the opportunity for a short *Eingang* cadenza that re-introduced the theme. There were about five of them, and each one got more elaborate and ornate than the last one, but he always played them in a single breath, so as not to let up on the tension of the cadence that led back into the Rondo. Nonetheless he managed to fit everything you could imagine into them, including more multi-phonics.

Though he was a refined musician, expressive soloist, and absolute master of his instrument, he still enjoyed his hunting horn roots, and opened up the sound in the hunting themes to a full outdoor fortissimo in true showman style. He forged ahead to the finish, urging the orchestra on in a mad race to the end. He finished the last notes, and held the horn out at arm's length, much as a violinist ends a piece with a flourish of the bow. The audience absolutely ate up this final gesture and leapt to their feet immediately. Punto bowed triumphantly, but at the same time graciously, and with true gratitude for the appreciation of his fans. He left the room and returned three times, and finally had to repeat the second movement before the audience would even think of letting him go.

We met him outside the Salle des Suisse, where Hans Joachim was waiting for him, and I have to say, I felt like a student greeting and congratulating my superstar idol. Punto himself had turned back into a normal human being and was the same man we had dined with the night before.

"Let's go somewhere where we can have a good old fashioned German beer," he said. *"A foaming pot is just que nous avons besoin d'après so ein lustiges Konzert!"*

We went to a pub and drank beer until far too late, and the conversation quickly turned to horn design.

"I couldn't help noticing that your horn has a larger bell throat than ours," I said. "Do you think that makes the stopped notes more even?"

"It helps," he said, "but I think the shape is more important. If the hand can make the tube longer when it closes, it will lower the pitch more without having to close all the way and get to the nasal, edgy sound that we don't want to make. What do you think Carl? You've played a lot of different horns."

"I'm beginning to form some ideas," Carl said, draining his beer glass. "I think horns with a larger throat, bore, and bell diameter are the wave of the future. The string sections of orchestras everywhere are getting larger, and the composers are writing thicker textures. Our horns, whether we are soloists or tutti players, are going to have to get bigger too."

"And another thing that has to happen," Punto added, "is to find a better way to fine tune the horn, especially for those of us who travel. You never know what sort of pitch level you're going to find when you arrive to play with a group. Did you notice that Capron re-tuned the orchestra before my concerto? I have one of the best E horns I've ever played on, but it was too high for the pitch level of the orchestra here, so at the rehearsal, I said to him; 'Monsieur Capron, I can disappoint you in one of two ways; I can either play with about six wobbly tuning bits to match your pitch, and miss every second note, or I can ask that you tune your orchestra up to match me, thereby assuring you as fine a performance as I am capable of delivering. I leave the choice to you!"

"Did he fly into a rage and refuse to re-tune?" asked Carl, all ready for a good story of a battle of wills between two temperamental artists.

"No," said Punto. "Capron smiled and said, 'We want you to sound your best,' and asked me to give my "A" to Monsieur Lebrun, the first oboe, to pass on to the strings."

"Only you could get away with saying that to Capron," said Carl.

"To avoid awkward little problems like that," Punto went on, "we should get someone to make a decent-playing horn with a slide. Have you seen the *Inventionshorns* made by Werner in Dresden, and Haltenhof in Hanau? Josef Hampel worked with Werner on the design. It had some problems, like the fact that the mouthpipe taper is far too short for the lower keys, and therefore when crooked in E flat, D, or C, it has way too much cylindrical tubing, which messes up intonation terribly. The advantage is that the tuning slide allows you to adjust the pitch as much as a quarter step higher or lower if you need to, avoiding all the tuning bits and pigtails we normally use."

"Jean Sieber, from the Paris Opera orchestra, has one of those," I said. "I subbed a couple of years ago with them and had a chance to try it. It was nice in the upper keys, but the lower you go below F horn, the worse it gets."

"Yes, I've tried it too, and the lower keys are an acoustical disaster," said Carl. "But I think there are ways around that problem, so that you can have a better proportion of conical and cylindrical tubing. If you were to have a fixed mouthpipe horn like those, you would have to make it with the proper tapers to play in the middle keys, and it would only be useful for solo playing. But as to the orchestra horn, I think we could design an instrument with a slide and terminal crooks that would make orchestral playing a lot easier."

We talked over this and other horn matters for a couple of hours and solved all the acoustical problems of the instrument in our heads, though it was another four years before we got serious and started designing the horn that would be known as the French *Cor d'orchestre*.

Having drunk far too much beer, we parted with Punto and Hans Joachim, who were leaving for London at six o'clock the next morning and wouldn't be back for a couple of months. Carl and I somehow found our way home through the dark dangerous streets, which were almost deserted due to the bitter cold, and talked of Punto and his amazing performance the whole way.

Chapter 38

Lost time is never found again.
- Benjamin Franklin, Poor Richard's Almanac, 1748

Early in the year 1777, the prince's orchestra was playing one of its regular weekly performances at the Hôtel. It was a typical program of symphonies and concertos, in which we were scheduled to do one of our Rosetti double concertos. This particular piece had become a favorite on the programs, appearing at least a couple of times each year. By this time, we were featured as soloists about once a month during the regular season of performances and had a few pieces that we knew well and with which we were very comfortable.

Minutes before the concert was to begin, Carl came into the room.

"The prince's guest, Benjamin Franklin, the Ambassador to France from the newly formed United States of America is in audience, and he says he wants to meet you after the concert."[17]

"To meet me?! Why?"

"I was with Monsieur Paisible, and we were introduced to Ambassador Franklin. Monsieur Paisible began telling him where each of the musicians was from, and he mentioned that you had grown up in the colonies, in Boston. Franklin was immediately interested in meeting a musician from Boston, since he apparently knows the city well."

"But Carl, you know how problematic and awkward that could be, since the Boston I know is a very different Boston from the one he knows."

"I know, but there was absolutely no way of avoiding it. How could I possibly tell him you couldn't see him? Things like this are going to happen, and we just need to make sure that you can talk your way through it. When we meet German musicians I've always been able to get you up to speed and help to answer awkward questions, but when it comes to America, I'm afraid you're on your own."

"I'd better start ransacking my brain for everything I know about the American Revolution. At least I can tell him that I left Boston in 1770 and ask a lot of questions about what's happened in the last six years, which will divert attention from my own lack of knowledge about the colonies. Fortunately I've read a little over the years on colonial times in America and the revolutionary period."

"You are the strangest enigma of a man I've ever met Johann, and I'm not sure if knowing you and your story makes me one of the most privileged people on earth, or just simply a candidate for the madhouse. Let's go take our places in the orchestra."

The symphony that night was by Haydn; one that I knew as no.15, from my boxed set of Haydn symphonies in my own time, but here it was simply called Sinfonia in D by Signor Haydn. It's a lovely piece, the first movement of which begins with an adagio in which the strings play a flowing melody answered by two very pastoral horns in D, played softly, and then proceeds into a fast tempo with a return to the slow part at the end. After that came a violin concerto played by our principal second violinist, and composed by another violinist from the Concert Spirituel orchestra by the name of Leduc. This piece was accompanied only by strings, which gave us a rest before our concerto.

It was a particularly good night for us, and our performance of the Rosetti double concerto in E was very nearly flawless. This piece, three or four other Rosetti double concertos, and those of Josef Fiala, Franz Pokorny, and Leopold Mozart that we played were all pieces that somehow survived and made it into the 21st century horn repertoire. Years later I would often stop to think about how weird it was to have known these pieces from recordings by the Tylsar brothers, Herman Baumann, Klaus Wallendorf, Sarah Willis, etc. in my youth, and then to meet the composers and play the premier performances of them myself, and in many cases to have been the person who inspired the composition.

An even more intriguing thought is that there were just as many pieces that didn't make it to the 21st century, which were every bit as good; pieces that I could, to this day, probably play from memory if Carl and I were together on the stage again. Our touring repertoire later included concertos by Hoffmeister, Josef Reicha, Baron Theodor von Schacht and several others. My mother had always said, "That horn of yours will probably take you to some exotic and far-away place, and we'll never get to see you." If she only knew.

The last piece was a symphony by Carl Ditters, a German violinist who really did grow up in a place called Dittersdorf. It wasn't anything to write home about, which is an ironic figure of speech in my case, since I would have loved nothing more in the world than to be able to write home.

We left the ballroom where the concert had taken place, and outside, talking to the prince and his wife, surrounded by a small crowd, was a tall bald old man with small oval eyeglasses in a blue coat of an unusual style, holding a three-cornered hat. I recognized him immediately. It was as though he had stepped right out of his picture on the $100 bill. It was Ben Franklin! He was talking animatedly in French to the great entertainment of the people around him.

We waited at a distance until the people started to disperse before approaching him, and the whole time I was thinking, "Of all the excessively bizarre things that have happened to me thus far in the 18th century, this takes the prize! I can't believe that I'm standing here looking at Benjamin Franklin!"

He noticed us, still with our horns in our hands, and almost ran to us saying in English, "The French horn players! Sirs, what a pleasure it was to hear you play in such an astonishing way on your fine instruments! I've always been a great admirer of the French horn, but this evening's performance was worlds beyond anything I have ever heard from it previously! And which one of you is Mr. Palsa? I must say my eyes are not what they used to be, and I could not see your faces clearly from a distance."

"I'm Johann Palsa," I said. "And it is a great pleasure to meet you, Mr. Franklin, having heard and read so much about you. This is my colleague Mr. Carl Türrschmidt, and we thank you for your kind words about our performance. It is always a pleasure to play for visiting dignitaries."

He shook both of our hands, and was looking at me strangely, puzzled I assume by my English. By this time I was getting fairly convincing with my 18th century German, and sounding like a well-spoken foreigner in 18th century French, but I had heard very little 18th century English until that moment. It wasn't exactly what I knew as modern British English, and it was not at all American English as I knew it. In fact, my first impression of it was that he sounded rather Scottish, though it wasn't exactly that either. Whatever it was, I was trying to imitate him as much as I could and failing miserably.

"Your concertmaster tells me you grew up in Boston."

"Yes Sir, I left in 1770 to come to Paris and have been here ever since."

"I don't recognize your accent as that of Boston or anywhere in America, Mr. Palsa, where do your people come from originally?"

"My family is Bohemian, and we lived in Boston for a number of years, though I was raised by a family of relatives from Hannover after my parents died."

"Oh, I see," he replied, "so there were quite a number of different influences on your speech from your youth. I am always fascinated by speech and can usually place people geographically by the first few words I hear them speak, but you were a mystery. Now I see that you are one of those very international figures, as musicians often are, who speak several languages, and all in a way which is not actually spoken anywhere. I must go at present but would be very happy if you two young gentlemen would call on me at my residence at Passy. That's outside of the city, on the road to Versailles. I'm having a little musical evening next Tuesday, and if you are not working, I would be honored if you could come and take part. Giuseppe Cambini, Carl Stamitz and his brother Anton and several other prominent musicians will be among the company."

I turned to Carl, who hadn't followed most of our conversation, and asked him in German about Tuesday evening.

"We are free on Tuesday and would be honored to attend and take part in the music."

"Ich bitte um Entschuldigung!" Franklin said, begging Carl's pardon, and continuing in perfect German. "Herr Türrschmidt, I didn't realize that you didn't understand our conversation. We will continue in German so you won't feel left out."

This was a relief, because I knew if I talked to him for more than a couple of minutes, I would get myself into some linguistic fix that would be hard to explain my way out of. At a gathering at his house, French and German would be spoken, and I should be safe.

"Here is my calling card, with the address," Franklin said. "I'll expect you at seven o'clock in the evening on Tuesday next."

Chapter 39

A slip of the foot you'll soon recover, but a slip of the tongue you may never get over.
- Benjamin Franklin, Poor Richard's Almanac

I was both apprehensive and excited about the invitation to dine and spend an evening with Ben Franklin. My curiosity however was much stronger than my apprehension. On Tuesday evening, after playing a Tafelmusik service with the wind band for a luncheon given by the prince, we went home and changed out of our orchestra uniforms and into our best suits and hired a carriage to take us and our horn box out of the city to the Paris residence of Franklin. I had always heard that he had spent time in Paris, but didn't know the details, so this was my chance to obtain some first-hand information about what was happening in America at the time.

The house was a stand-alone two-story stone house in a more rural looking suburb or village, but lavishly decorated with fine carpets and furniture in the latest French style. A servant ushered us into a dining room with a finely set table filled with silver tableware and serving vessels. By this time in his life, Franklin was a wealthy man and could afford the best.

The company consisted of a few prominent musicians, including the Stamitz brothers, Monsieur Petit, a couple of string players from our orchestra, and the very colorful and entertaining Guiseppe Cambini, a tall handsome Italian violinist and composer. On this occasion, as I had heard him do several times before, he told the highly unlikely story of how he and his fiancée had gotten to France. He claimed they had been kidnapped by pirates on the Mediterranean Sea and released in France only after a huge ransom was paid by a wealthy French music lover. Carl and I liked him because he had always written good horn parts for us when we played in his orchestra works. He cranked out fairly good music by the truckload and was a favorite at the Concert Spirituel, where he specialized in the concertante symphony, which was very much in vogue at that time, and featured instrumental soloists in various combinations.

Among Franklin's guests there were also a few dignitaries, nobility and ambassadors, and several well-dressed women who seemed to be Franklin's guests, but who appeared to be there unaccompanied by any of the gentlemen, which was highly unusual in 18th century society. As it turned out, Franklin had quite a fan club of wealthy women with whom he spent a great deal of his time in Paris.

It became apparent as we were seated for supper in the dining room that there was a table for Franklin and his important guests, and the musician's table. We had a typical musicians' conversation at our table, talking about all the latest gossip at the Paris Opera, trashing the court musicians and the old-fashioned music they played, and hearing about the goings on in all the other performing groups in Paris. Guiseppi Cambini was in rare form, moving seamlessly from one outlandish story to the next, the Stamitz brothers told jokes and funny stories about their adventures, and we all had a good time as the finest wines of France flowed freely.

The "grown-up table", as Carl referred to it, was more subdued and refined in its conversation, and soon Franklin joined the musicians at our table, where it was obvious we were all enjoying ourselves immensely. The conversation was in French, and Franklin was just as much at home, and just as eloquent and funny in that language as he was in English and German. He could, within seconds of meeting someone, find common topics of interest to build a conversation around, and insert humorous anecdotes that fit the conversation at just the right moments. He was an expert conversationalist, but he also had the advantage of being an excellent and attentive listener and made the people he was conversing with feel like they were talking to an intimate friend who they could trust, whether they were nobility or a group of working musicians, like ourselves.

"Gentlemen!" he announced, after all the food and wine had disappeared. "Let us retire to the drawing room where we can all enjoy some music. We have been looking forward to the rare treat of an evening of chamber music with some of the finest artists in Paris. I am especially curious about the methods employed by our two fine Cor de chasse players, who seem to make their instruments sing like the most refined vocalists! Port wine from London and dessert will accompany the music."

We were able to taste the port, which was delicious, and freshly baked cakes as the musical part of the evening began with a violin sonata by Guiseppi Tartini, played by Cambini, with Monsieur Petit at the harpsichord. Then we got into the act, playing a piece for horns and strings by Joseph Haydn, with the title "Abendmusik". It was charming and straightforward music that was good accompaniment for eating, drinking, and conversation.

Then the usual thing happened; Carl and I played half a dozen of our favorite duos - little minuets, expressive andantes, and agile allegros - and the room immediately became quiet and everyone listened to the horns. Few had heard this kind of horn playing, and when we were finished they wanted to look into the bells of the horns to see what sort of concealed mechanism made them play chromatically. We explained how it was all done simply with hand-stopping. Franklin was very interested in the acoustics of the horn, and understood the overtone series well. He was fascinated by the effect of the hand and the colors and chromatics it could produce.

We then played a couple of quartets by Carl Stamitz with very flexible instrumentation, for mixed winds and strings, and some new wind arrangements of Boccherini string quartets, done by Othon Vandenbroeck, a Dutch horn player who worked in Paris. We played them that evening with a violin playing the flute part, clarinet and horn playing their proper parts, and cello playing the bassoon part. Substitutions of instruments happened all the time in both chamber music and orchestra music. If you didn't have clarinets, oboes would do, violins could play flute parts, a viola could play a horn part, an oboe or clarinet could sub for a missing trumpet, and bassoon and cello were almost completely interchangeable. In a pinch, the keyboard player could play anyone's part.

Following those, Cambini and Anton Stamitz played a new duo for violin and viola that Cambini had probably written that afternoon for the occasion. I sat down in a corner to enjoy another glass of port, and within a few seconds Franklin sat down next to me and started a conversation in English, which I was hoping to avoid that evening.

"Tell me, Mr. Palsa, about your youth in Boston. I lived in that city for several years and know it well."

I didn't want to show my ignorance, having lived in the modern suburbs of Boston about two hundred fifty years later, so I tried to think of the oldest area of the city that I could be sure was there in the 1770s.

"We lived on Salem Street, near the Old North Church," I said thinking this would be a safe bet.

"You must mean the Old North Meeting House, but that isn't in Salem Street. Christ Church of Boston is in Salem Street, but I've never heard it referred to as the Old North Church, since it was built not more than forty years ago."

"Yes, yes, I meant Christ Church, - of course," I said with a nervous laugh.

"I don't remember any dwelling houses in Salem Street near the Christ Church, only businesses and merchants' shops," he went on, much to my annoyance. Where was your family's house?"

"Oh, we lived in an apartment above one of the stores."

"Apartment? Store? I have never heard of any shops in that street with living quarters above them! And for being so very fluent in English, you seem to have some very odd notions of its vocabulary!"

"We spoke German most of the time at home," I said trying to rescue the situation.

"By which you must mean high Dutch. Where were you educated?"

I ransacked my brain for the name of the oldest school I could think of that wouldn't be too far away from Boston.

"At Yale sir. I did my undergraduate degree there."

"Oh, so you have studied theology, since to my knowledge they don't teach music or the humanities at Yale College?"

"Yes - I studied music later in Boston and played with an orchestra there," I said, realizing too late that I was headed into more uncharted and dangerous territory."

"For a young man in his twenties, you would seem to have had an unusual amount of interesting and varied experience. I am unfamiliar with any organized orchestras in Boston. Where did this orchestra play?"

I couldn't think of anything plausible that I could name as a concert hall from that period of history, nor did I know if there were actually orchestras in Boston, or what and where they would have played.

"We played often in churches around the city," I said unconvincingly.

"I see...," was the reply, and I knew he wasn't buying my story. I decided to try to steer the conversation in a new direction, and asked a couple of questions about the war, which, as far as I could remember, was at its height at this point. I could tell he wanted to talk about the conflict with the British, but first he wanted to grill me a little more to find out just what sort of imposter I was.

"The war for independence from the crown continues, which is why I am here in France, trying to solicit financial and military aid for our cause. There seems to be little support here in Paris for our efforts, or awareness of the situation in the colonies. What is the impression among the people you know, and what sort of information about the conflict is currently being talked about in your circles?"

I thought this might be a good time to bring out some of my knowledge of the American Revolutionary period, which unfortunately wasn't much more than your average sixth grader learns in school.

"In Paris we've heard many reports of the invasion of the British troops and the fighting. I was especially interested in the story in April of last year of the hanging of the lanterns in the tower of the Old.... um, that is to say, Christ Church to warn the people of how the British troops were arriving, if by land or by sea, and of Paul Revere riding through the night to deliver the information to Lexington."

"My dear young man!" said Franklin, his eyes growing larger. "How could you possibly know the story of the lanterns, and of Mr. Revere and Mr. Dawes riding that night to Lexington!? Only a very few patriots, myself included, are privy to the information of how that cleverly planned warning signal was sent to prepare the militia for the arrival of the British, and who was responsible. We are still at war, and if the British get hold of that particular information, it could be very damaging, not to say life threatening, for Messrs. Revere and Dawes, and especially for Mr. Newman, the sexton of Christ Church who hung the lanterns in the tower. From whom did you hear of this?"

I was now in a very tight spot, having opened a large and dangerous can of worms in my effort to look like I knew what I was talking about.

"In a letter from home sir... My uncle is a member of the militia in Boston, and certainly word traveled among the soldiers of how the message was relayed."

Franklin took off his glasses and looked at me seriously. "I think you had better inform your family that they should be more careful in sharing the information they have heard. The lives of many patriots are at risk, and if you and your family are true supporters, not to say fighters, in the cause of the colonists, and the establishment of the United States of America, you will need to proceed with the utmost care, and not speak casually to anyone you meet about confidential and potentially dangerous information! The very idea of hearing this from a Bohemian musician in Paris as casually as though he had learned it in his youth from a school primer!"

He was beginning to get quite red in the face, and I needed to try to explain before he got into an even greater state of indignation.

"I beg your pardon Mr. Franklin. I understand that this is very confidential information, and I meant no harm, knowing that you are an ambassador from the newly formed country. I can assure you that I and my family are completely loyal to the American cause, and I haven't spoken to anyone else about anything having to do with the revolt."

"I should hope not sir!" He paused to take in breath before going on.

"Much of your history that you've related to me this evening isn't very convincing, and I shouldn't wonder if you've never set foot in Boston, based on your apparent ignorance of the city, how the people there live, and even of the English language as it is spoken there. Nor do I believe that you attended Yale College or the absurd story of your playing in an orchestra that performed in churches!" He put his glasses back on and his voice became calmer and more subdued.

"But I'll tell you what I do believe; I believe you are truly a supporter of our cause, otherwise you would not have been so quick to speak openly to me, who you certainly know as an important American ambassador and patriot. I also believe that you are a naïve and inexperienced young man, but I suspect there is something much deeper to your story than you are letting on, possibly something of great importance to our newly formed government and the war effort. I ask no questions; these are delicate times, and sometimes diplomacy and even spying must be done under the cover of assumed identities and manufactured stories.

As I said, I will ask no more awkward questions, but I will give you some advice that may serve you well in the future. Whatever your business may be, don't be so naïve as to talk openly about it, even to people who you think you can trust - and get your story straight so it doesn't expose you to uncomfortable and unanswerable scrutiny. And if you are going to pass yourself off as a Bostonian, make a more careful study of the English language. I don't know where you've picked up some of the nonsensical jargon and idioms you've been babbling to me, or that very unconvincing accent of yours, but it will never do! Any American colonist or British subject will see through it immediately. Again, I ask no questions, but if you need assistance at any point, I am here to give advice and support to anyone who is on the side of our efforts."

I was about to say something to this – I'm not sure what, when he cut me short.

"Not a word sir! At this point I think it would be best to speak no more of these matters, and for you and your friend to play a few more of those charming *Petit airs* on your French horns, which you do so tastefully and skillfully – a skill that I am also sure you didn't learn in Boston! Wherever you are from, and whatever your secret is, it is safe with me. Good evening sir!"

He rose and rejoined the rest of the guests, leaving me alone to gather my thoughts and wrap my mind around what had just happened. I drank off my glass of port to calm my shaken nerves before going back to where the music was being played to find Carl and play a few more duets.

It was a very close call; one of the most awkward moments of my entire time in the 18th century. Franklin, who was one of the most observant and intelligent men I've ever met, had taken all the very inconsistent information I was giving him and assumed that I was hiding something very different from what I was actually hiding. He had also assumed that if I was talking openly to him, I was a member of the American cause, which in fact I could honestly say I am, and that the inconsistencies were part of some deeper intrigue related to that cause.

As Carl and I were leaving the house at the end of the evening, Franklin was there to bid us farewell.

"Thank you my fine young Waldhorn virtuosi for coming and taking part in the entertainment this evening," he said in German to us both, shaking our hands. "And please remember my advice Herr Palsa," he said, winking at me and holding his index finger to his lips.

"What was that all about?" asked Carl when we had settled down in our seats in the hired carriage.

"Oh, nothing in particular; he just ripped to shreds the story of my youth in Boston, and believes I'm on some sort of under-cover mission on behalf of the United States of America, and that I'm making a total mess of the whole thing. He wasn't impressed with my 21st century American English either."

Carl shook his head as he had done so many times before.

"I can only say that life with you is never dull, Johann."

Chapter 40

Time passed quickly and Carl and Röslein's son Carl Nicholaus grew and thrived and was now two years old. I lived in the second floor, and Carl and his small family in the third floor of Madame Marais' house, where we had been since the winter of 1770. I was now quite accustomed to 18th century life, the way music was played, and the very different role that music played in society, but now and then something would come along that would still put me into a state of astonishment, and sometimes awe, as though I had just arrived in this time. One of these surprises arrived in Paris at the end of March 1778 in the form of the twenty-two-year-old composer and piano virtuoso Wolfgang Amadeus Mozart[18].

Word got around that he was in town and working hard rubbing elbows with nobility and all the concert producers in Paris. The composers immediately recognized his genius and the creativity of his writing and felt threatened by him, while the musicians, who were not in competition with him, loved his compositions and clamored for more. We were quite busy with our service to the Prince of Guéméné, and hadn't run into him yet, which I suppose was a good thing, because it gave me some time to prepare myself for meeting one of the greatest composers, and most awkward immature adults I've ever met.

Our chance came when we were invited to take part in the Easter season run of the Concert Spirituel, which went from April 10th to 24th, 1778, with a concert almost every day. The prince agreed to loan us to Legros, the director of the series, and we played as tutti wind players in the orchestra accompanying some of the top soloists of the day.

Among the all-star cast was Punto, who was now a favorite at the Concert Spirituel, and some other old friends including flutist Johann Wendling, bassoonist Georg Ritter, and oboist Friedrich Ramm, all principal players from Mannheim, who happened to be in Paris on leave from their employer, the Elector of the Palatinate. It was to a nobleman's advantage to let his court musicians go to Paris to make a splash, because the reputation of the employer would be celebrated and furthered as well as that of the musicians themselves.

Each program started with a symphony and included arias, a couple of concertos, sometimes a concertante symphony with multiple soloists, and the obligatory choral pieces to qualify the concert with the government as having a religious theme for the religious holidays. During this run, one of the centerpieces was a sinfonia concertante by Giuseppi Cambini, whose music was extremely popular in Paris around this time. Wendling, Ramm, Punto, and Ritter were the soloists, and the piece was well received by the audience each time it was performed. Each of these soloists also performed their own solo concertos on those and other performances, with Punto performing solo concertos billed as being of his own composition at least six times over the course of two weeks. Two of these I knew for certain were written by our friend Antonio Rosetti.

Symphonies of Gossec, Toeschi, Sterkel, Haydn, and Cannabich were played, and rumor had it that the young Mozart was itching to get his music on some of the programs. He was lobbying heavily with anyone who would listen to him, but the programs had been determined long before Mozart arrived in Paris, and the only piece he could get Legros to include was a single aria on the concert of April 21st.

By this time Carl was beginning to get tired of hearing me talk about the young Mozart, and the fact that, of all the composers whose music we played, his name would be the one that would endure the longest, and his music would stay in the standard repertoire for centuries. The concept of a standard repertoire of orchestra music was totally foreign to Carl. To the 18th century orchestra musician, all music was new, and very little music got played more than a few times.

"You're always talking about the standard pieces your orchestra in America played. Don't the audiences and the musicians get bored with the same pieces over and over again?" he asked me as we were walking through the muddy streets on our way to the Palace of the Tuilleries for the concert of April 12th. "I mean, say this Beethoven fellow, or your Brahms, or Tchaikovsky, or whoever of the people you've told me about, write fifty symphonies each. Do you just keep cycling through them until everyone knows them by heart? Is there never any new music?"

"No, you don't quite understand how it all works," I replied. "Beethoven only wrote nine symphonies, Brahms four, and Tchaikovsky six, but there have been a lot of other composers, and we pick the best of the best from over two hundred years of music. It's actually a lot of pieces, and you can go a few seasons in an orchestra without repeating any of them."

"If these composers only wrote a few symphonies, how did they make a living? Did courts and patrons in your time put up with the fact that their composers weren't writing new music all the time?"

"They were all writing a lot of music all the time, but in the 19th, 20th, and 21st centuries, music wasn't supported by royalty or nobility. After 1800, many orchestras had to start supporting themselves, much like the Paris Opera does, by selling tickets to the public for their performances. In my time, orchestras give only public concerts to large audiences, sometimes two or three thousand people, and they pay the musicians and management and organize the concerts through the ticket sales, donations from individuals and businesses, and some money from the government. And we do have new music. Sometimes an orchestra or opera company will pay a composer to write a new symphony, or concerto, or opera, but more often, we play older music that is part of the repertoire."

Carl still couldn't wrap his mind around how all this worked.

"It sounds like a difficult situation if royalty and nobility no longer want to support music. If an orchestra has to support itself, it must be hard to pay the musicians and composers just from the ticket sales and the donations of strangers. No wonder you have to recycle old music, but how does the audience feel about that? Don't they feel cheated and want something they haven't heard before?"

"The audiences are happy to hear all of these greatest works of the last two hundred years, with a smattering of new music. And they get so used to the repertoire that they actually look forward to hearing famous works again. Unlike concerts today, people of the 21st century go to a large concert hall and sit in seats, and don't do anything but listen. If someone is having a conversation with another person during a piece, people all around will ask them to be quiet so everyone can hear the music better. People really do get to know the music and want to hear it again."

Carl shook his head.

"Sounds like a completely different way of thinking about music, and much less fun and spontaneous. And you say this Mozart is one of your big composers?"

"His music is everywhere. We horn players like him because we have four complete horn concertos and a couple of rondos for solo horn that he wrote for us, and they're great pieces."

Carl's musical world depended on the patronage of nobility and the wealthy, and any other way of producing or performing music didn't make sense.

"So, you see, Carl, I've been hearing and playing Wolfgang Amadeus Mozart's music from my childhood onward, and I'm really anxious to meet him and see what he's all about."

The first glimpse I got of the *Wunderkind* was that evening, the 12th of April. He had been in the audience listening to the Cambini Sinfonia Concertante and came up to the four soloists almost immediately as the applause died down. He was small and full of energy, bouncing around like an excited ten-year old, and looked as though he had suffered a disappointing bout of smallpox at some point in the not too distant past. Cambini was there too, and as Mozart congratulated them, the well-dressed and slightly portly Italian composer looked as though, at any moment, he could do a W. C. Fields imitation and say, "Go away kid, you bother me!" Mozart was not at all deterred by Cambini's obvious annoyance at his presence, but persisted in talking to the soloists. From what Punto told us later, he promised on the spot to write an even better sinfonia concertante for them at his earliest opportunity. The ever-astute Punto saw that the situation was deteriorating fast, and approached Mozart.

"Amadeo! Please come with me. I have a couple of friends I'd like you to meet." He practically dragged the young Mozart away from Cambini and the other soloists and brought him over to us.

"May I introduce you to the Cors de chasse of the orchestra of the Prince of Guéméné, and the finest horn duo of the present day, Herr Johann Palsa, and Herr Carl Türrschmidt."

Mozart bowed low in an over-done theatrical way and shook our hands. "Carl and Johann! Of course I've heard of you! Your double concertos and *Petit airs* for horns are known everywhere. You don't mind if I call you Jojo, do you?" he said to me. He pronounced it like "Yoyo". That's what a five-year-old in Germany might be called by his older brothers if his name was Johann.

"Oh, not at all!" I said, at a loss as to how to proceed in this very awkward conversation with one of the greatest composers in the history of western civilization. Carl and Punto, standing next to me were both trying not to laugh.

"Where I come from, in Salzburg, we don't stand on ceremony. We're quite familiar and friendly, and always use first names, even on first meeting, except of course with royalty and nobility, because they pay us to be polite and behave well and write and play good music for them."

"How long have you been in Paris?" I asked, not being able to think of anything else to say.

"My mother and I got here at the end of March. Papa sent us to Paris so that I could find a position as Kapellmeister or opera director. But so far, I've only been able to find a few pupils to teach and played for a couple of noblemen who had no knowledge of music or artistic taste whatsoever. I'm also giving composition lessons to the daughter of the Duc de Guînes, Ambassador to England, who is incidentally, a fine flute player. Do you know him?"

"We had a brief encounter with him about nine years ago," said Carl. "We didn't make a very good impression on him and he had us thrown in the Bastille for a while."

"Oh dear!" said the Wunderkind. "I do hope it doesn't come to that in my case. He's asked me to compose a concerto for flute and harp for him and his daughter, which I'm working on. Maybe that will please him enough that he won't act so harshly. The Bastille! Oh dear! My father would be furious if I ended up there. I'll definitely be on my guard around him."

There was another awkward silence during which piece after piece of his that he hadn't written yet was going in and out of my head.

"Say! Are you guys good friends with Legros, the director? I've been working on him to get a piece or two of mine onto one of the programs, but so far he hasn't committed to anything."

"We know him pretty well," I said, "but he makes his programs well in advance and it's very difficult to get him to alter them. The best thing to do is to give him some pieces to look at and hope he'll decide to do them in the next set of concerts. You could also start by approaching some of the smaller series in town to get on their programs first."

"No, my father advised me to go directly to the top and not to bother with lesser groups. I need to break right into the Concert Spirituel, and right away."

It seemed like the conversation would go on forever, but at that moment we were rescued by Josef Legros himself, who came up and greeted the young composer very eloquently.

"Monsieur Mozart! So nice to see you at our concert this evening! I'm so sorry we couldn't program one of your pieces this week, but I believe we will have space next week for one of the arias you gave me. We can talk about it this coming Sunday afternoon at my house. I'm hosting a dinner for the orchestra and soloists, and it would be wonderful if you could also join us."

"Thank you for the invitation! It will be a grand opportunity to meet some of the most important musicians in Paris and make some more connections. Jojo and Carl, I'll look forward to seeing you there too. And to commemorate our meeting, I'll write you a set of *Petit airs* for two horns. But I shouldn't keep you now; the second half of the concert is about to begin. Until Sunday, *Adieu mon Amis!*"

"*Adieu* Wolfie!" I couldn't help saying as we went back to take our places in the orchestra.

"Quite the young networker, isn't he?" I said to Carl.

"He learned from the best! His father, Leopold Mozart, has been marketing him and his sister since they were young kids. He dragged them all over Europe showing them off to royalty and nobility. Little Wolfgang, at about six years old, sat on the lap of Marie Antoinette and played the harpsichord. This time his father sent him to Paris with his mother, who I've heard is in fragile health, and Wolfgang is basically on his own, and trying to take Paris by storm single-handedly."

Chapter 41

Mozart Duo# 10, K. 487/496a

The two weeks of concerts were a big success, and we had a great time playing in the orchestra with all the most prominent soloists and orchestra musicians of the day. At the end of the second week of performances Legros had us all to his house for the promised dinner and evening of chamber music. You wouldn't think that these famous musicians who had just played ten concerts in twelve days would want to spend an evening playing chamber music, but that was the way of things in the 1770s, a time where the only music was live music, and who better to provide the music for a party than some of the best musicians in Europe. The food was of the best available, the wine was from Bordeaux, and Legros's well-trained servants made all the guests feel like royalty. True to his word, the young Mozart was there to rub elbows with the top of the Parisian musical scene.

After dinner, to accompany the desserts and wine, there were string quartets, piano trios, arias, duos of all sorts, and soloists. And "Amadeo", as many called him, was everywhere talking to everyone. He approached us as we were having a glass of wine and cake and pulled some sheets of music out of his waistcoat.

"Carl and Jojo, my Waldhorn friends! As promised, I whipped up something for you over breakfast this morning; a little set of duos. Will you give them a go for us this evening?"

Punto and Wendling had joined us and were looking over the handwritten manuscript of the duos.

"Yes, please play them for us! They look like absolutely charming little minuets and airs. We would love to hear what Herr Mozart has written for you," said Wendling.

We got out our horns and read through a couple of the pieces. The first one was an andante that was very elegantly composed, and idiomatic for the horns, showing a good deal of knowledge of what the instruments could do, including which stopped notes were most effective musically. Next we read a playful little minuet with agile accompaniment that had a trio section that modulated into the relative minor key; something that you didn't often see in 18th century horn duets.

We ended up playing all six duos at Legros's house that evening, and they, along with another set of six that he wrote for us many years later, became part of our regular duo repertoire. We played them all so often that, to this day, I could write out both parts from memory.

"Bravo!" cried Mozart, as we finished the last of the duos.

"Magnifique! Wunderbar! Brilliant horn playing, as always!" added Punto. "And Herr Mozart, you are truly an inspired and skillful composer!! I hope to hear much more of your music while you are in Paris!"

This inspired Mozart to sit down at the pianoforte and play a couple of his sonatas for the enjoyment of the guests. Everyone was taken in, both by the compositions and by his virtuosic playing. He was a truly remarkable pianist, technically clean and precise, and elegantly expressive without being over-done. He was in rare form, and several people were crowded around taking it all in, among them Punto, Wendling, Ramm, and Ritter, the four soloists who had played Cambini's sinfonia concertante a couple days before.

"Gentlemen! I promised a few days ago to write another sinfonia concertante for you, and here is what it will sound like..." said Mozart, never ceasing to play. "It will start with an opening tutti like this in the strings...." He played a pleasant opening theme. "And then transition into this second theme, and then the soloists all together will enter like this!" He played through solo sections for each instrument and combinations of instruments alternating with orchestra tuttis all the way through a first movement, which I assume he was composing on the spot, and the listeners were nodding and commenting enthusiastically.

The four soloists watched and listened, obviously impressed at his ability to improvise an orchestra piece before their eyes, and excited about the possibility of playing it. He sketched out two other movements spontaneously at the keyboard and finished the spirited rondo finale to the loud applause of everyone. I've played the piece known as the Mozart Sinfonia Concertante in E flat for Winds on modern instruments in my own time, but what I heard the young Mozart play at Legros's party was not that piece. Whether he finally wrote out what he did play that day I never found out. Many years later in Vienna he told us that he did, and that it didn't get played in Paris because of some behind the scenes treachery of Giuseppe Cambini. What took place next that evening would suggest to me that it was true.

Mozart saw that Cambini had joined the group around the pianoforte and was looking annoyed at the ease with which the young composer was composing off the top of his head, the genius of the melodies, and the form of the piece. Mozart obviously wanted to try to save the situation and turned to Cambini when the applause had died down.

"Monsieur Cambini, I've always admired your work. I was in Mannheim a couple of months ago and heard one of your string quartets. It was a very nicely composed piece. If I'm remembering correctly, it went something like this...." He began playing. Cambini looked pleased that his piece had made such an impression on the young virtuoso that he could remember it and play it from memory. After playing part of the exposition Mozart stopped, unable to remember exactly how the second theme went.

"Oh, please go on, it's a wonderful piece," said Punto and Wendling almost in unison. Mozart started to play again at the second theme but a cloud came over Cambini's face, because what Mozart couldn't remember he was making up out of his head, and it was obvious that it was an improvement on Cambini's own second theme. Mozart was getting carried away by his own creativity and went right on into a development section using bits of the two themes and some very interesting modulations. Cambini was looking more and more offended.

"Monsieur Mozart! That's not exactly what I wrote!"

"Possibly not Signor Cambini," said Friedrich Ramm, the oboist, "but you must admit, it's very clever music. I think he's making great improvements to your piece!"

Everyone laughed as the oblivious Mozart forged ahead to the end of the movement as he would have composed it. A stony-faced Cambini bowed low to Mozart and addressed him stiffly in Italian.

"Signor, my compliments to your genius." He turned and walked away looking very dignified. Mozart, who looked as though he had just awakened from the musical trance his improvisation had put him in, looked around in bewilderment as it slowly dawned upon him that he had just deeply offended one of the most influential composers in Paris, and in all probability ruined his chances of getting any of his own music played.

Another friend and colleague of ours, Jean-Joseph Rodolph, a horn player, composer, and teacher with whom we had played trios not long before at the Concert Spirituel, was also at the gathering of musicians at Legros's house and took pity on the unfortunate Mozart who was making enemies almost by the minute. He was standing with Carl and me by the table on which wine and deserts were elegantly displayed, listening to a virtuosic trio for flute, violin, and cello that Johann Wendling had composed, and was playing with a couple of string players from the orchestra.

"That poor young man is an amazing talent, both as a pianist and a composer," said Rodolph. "It's a pity he's so naïve about how to deal with people and make his way in the musical scene. I wish I could help him to get on his feet somehow."

The young composer had risen from the pianoforte and came over to us again.

"Herr Mozart," said Rodolph, "I have a number of connections with the musicians at the court of the King. I happen to know that there is currently an opening for organist at the king's chapel, and I'm almost certain that if you applied to the court, and they heard you play, the position would be yours. The salary would be handsome, and you would be well taken care of and a prominent member of the king's musicians."

"Thank you, Herr Rodolph. That's very kind of you to mention it, but I'm not so sure a position like that would suit me. We all know that whoever enters the king's service is quickly forgotten in Paris and is never allowed to play anywhere else. I need to play before the public, and compose symphonies, chamber music, and sonatas that will be recognized by the world for their quality, - not drab church music that would only be heard by the royal family. And I hate playing the organ. Thank you, but I don't see how I could possibly survive that sort of life for more than six months!"

"Then I wish you the best of luck in the free-lance scene," said Rodolph, as he walked away leaving us again with the clueless young virtuoso. The flute trio was over and Mozart turned to us.

"Carl and Jojo, let's play something together."

"We don't have anything with us for two horns and pianoforte," said Carl.

"Oh, no matter, we'll make it up as we go! How about the andante from the duets I made for you? You play it as is, and I'll accompany, and then you can play it again a couple of times and I'll make up some variations. Put your horns in D and let's give it a try!"

We crooked our horns in D and played the duet through with Mozart improvising the accompaniment, then we started again from the beginning and played it over again three times, and each time he improvised a virtuosic variation over our melody, first in scale-wise triplets, then in arpeggiated sixteenths, and finally a variation of fast-running chromatic lines. It was astonishing how the music just flowed out of him perfectly formed as though he had spent hours working out each passage. By the second variation people were again crowding around us to listen, and clapping after each variation. When we finished there was a great round of applause. Mozart was right in his element, doing amazing things and getting heaps of praise.

"Bravo my Waldhorn friends! We must play a concert together sometime! When I've landed a good position, or start my own concert series, you'll be some of the first for whom I'll compose a concerto!"

For the rest of the evening we watched as he alternated between dazzling everyone with his improvisations and sonatas and offending and annoying people.

We left with Rodolph, who had wanted to help the unfortunate young man, but by now had changed his opinion.

"Little shit!" he said, getting into a carriage that the three of us shared back to our own part of the city. "I know his father in Salzburg, and if he could see his son acting as we witnessed tonight, he would take him over his knee and give a good spanking as one should with such poorly behaved children. The sooner he makes a mess of his prospects in Paris and goes home the better, as far as I'm concerned, and I'm sure Giuseppi Cambini and a number of others would agree with me whole-heartedly!"

We ran into Mozart again only once more in Paris, when Legros finally programmed one of his symphonies at the Concert Spirituel. This piece later became known as his "Paris Symphony". We heard later that his mother had fallen ill and died, and by the end of the summer he was on his way home to Salzburg without having landed a position or won fame or financial success in Paris. It was nearly ten years before we encountered him again in Vienna.

Chapter 42

From C. Türrschmidt, 50 Duos, op. 3, 1795

Every musician and composer in Europe who was anyone, or wanted to become someone, came to Paris at some point in the late 18th century. Among those who flocked there in search of fame and fortune in the spring of 1779 was Franz Pokorny, concertmaster and composer of the Thurn und Taxis Orchestra in Regensburg, along with his two daughters, Beate and Anna-Maria, who we had met back in the summer of 1775.

Carl and I were among the few contacts they had in Paris, so we heard from them almost immediately when they arrived in the city. You needed to know people to get to the right people, and we and Punto were the connections who could introduce him to Joseph Legros of the Concert Spirituel, and other concert organizers. We went to welcome the Pokorny family immediately upon receiving a note saying where they were staying, which was not too far from our place.

"I decided it was time for a change of scenery, and Prince Karl-Anselm was good enough to let me go for a few months to see what I could accomplish here in the musical capital of the world," Franz

Pokorny said, as he welcomed us into the neat little set of rooms he had rented for their stay in Paris. "My daughters wouldn't hear of me coming alone, so they are here to watch over me and experience the big city."

At that moment the two Miss Pokornys came in from shopping with their arms full of loaves of bread, a goose, bottles of wine, and other food items. Anna-Maria was now a fully grown young woman of eighteen, and Beate was in her early twenties.

"Carl and Herr Palsa!" exclaimed Beate. "I knew we would meet up again! How are Röslein and the baby? News travels slowly between Wallerstein and Regensburg, and it was a while before we even heard that you were married. Are you playing double concertos for the Paris audiences? And Herr Palsa, how are you?"

As usual she was talking and asking questions much faster in her excitement than we could keep up with, but presently she settled down a bit and we were able to catch them up on our lives in Paris and hear about theirs in Regensburg.

"I have been trying for years to get them both married and established in life," said Franz, "but they won't hear of it, though they've had some good offers. Instead, they spend most of their time practicing music; violin, pianoforte, and Waldhorn. And I ask you, what can two young ladies possibly think they can do with the Waldhorn? They can't play it professionally, but that doesn't stop them from practicing like they were preparing for a career in the court orchestra."

"So, the family struggle goes on?" I asked. "I seem to remember that they were both getting pretty skillful on the horn already four years ago when we saw you last. I hope you don't think that bringing them to Paris will cool down their enthusiasm, with all of the musical activity going on here."

"We're planning to take advantage of every opportunity to play that we can get our hands on while we're here," said Beate. "There must be someplace where we can play with people, and we'll find it if we have to search the entire city of Paris!"

It was decided that we must stay to supper with them, and as the preparation of the goose and cooking of potatoes was making progress, Beate turned to Herr Pokorny.

"Papa, we didn't know we would have as our guests this evening the world's most famous Waldhorn duo, so we didn't buy any cake. Could you go down to the bakery and get a cake for dessert while I finish roasting the goose?"

She followed him to the door and made sure he was down the stairs and out of the house before turning around with a serious look.

"Now, Papa is out of the way for a few minutes, and we can talk freely about some important business before he returns. Carl and Johann - if I may call you Johann..."

"By all means!" I said smiling.

"We desperately need your help."

Carl and I looked at each other wondering what sort of crisis was going on in the Pokorny family and how we could help them.

"We need to get our hands on a couple of Waldhorns and get back into shape playing them. There must be some way in a modern city like this that we can get the chance to play with an orchestra or in some chamber music. In Regensburg we were able to borrow horns from Josef Fritch who owned a couple of extra instruments. We spent a good deal of time with him and made a lot of progress in our playing."

"Beate should say that she has made a lot of progress," interjected Anna-Maria. "We have both been practicing a lot, but Beate is the one who could really become a soloist. Father is hoping that being away from home amidst the excitement of Paris we will forget about playing horn, and instead become proper young ladies and do things that proper young ladies should do."

"And the Waldhorn," continued Beate, "is not high on his list of things that proper young ladies should do, so we need your help."

"We only have our own Kerner instruments," I said, "but Giovanni Punto usually has a couple of spare horns in addition to his own, and we can talk to him when he's back in Paris next week. Maybe he would even be willing to give you lessons."

"Oh, that would be wonderful if we could learn from Giovanni Punto! We met him three years ago when he played with the Hofkapelle in Regensburg. He was amazing, and so friendly. He inspired us to practice all the more. But if we have lessons father is to know nothing about it. He would be dead set against the whole idea."

By the time Herr Pokorny was back, Beate had extracted a promise from us that we would help them get instruments to play, and ask Punto if he would give Beate, at least, lessons. Anna-Maria was content to play the second parts of duets, but Beate wanted to play as a soloist, and was excited about the possibility of working with Punto.

On the way home we talked about how to organize lessons for Beate without her father knowing, and whether Punto would be willing to help them.

"I don't know about this," said Carl. "I've never heard of a woman seriously studying the horn. As Franz said, what is the use of her studying horn at a high level when she would never be able to work in an orchestra?"

"But Carl, how do you know she could never play in an orchestra? She played very well when we were in Regensburg and she filled in for the second horn in the concert we played there. Why shouldn't she play professionally? Just because it's not normal doesn't mean she shouldn't try. In my time about half of the horn players I know are women, and no one thinks it's unusual."

"Your world must be a pretty strange place with orchestras populated by both men and women! And audiences and other musicians take them seriously?"

"Sure they do. Why wouldn't they? Men and women play equally well. The way everyone in this time thinks about women lasted right up into the 20th century. But over the next hundred years things slowly began to change. Women were given the right to vote in the early part of the 20th century."

"Vote?" asked Carl.

"Haven't I ever told you about how we get to vote on important issues and to elect government leaders?"

Carl gave me one of his looks of disbelief.

"Sounds dangerous to let the common people decide things by a vote of the majority when a prince or monarch, with all of his experience in governing could make more informed decisions."

"By my time, we no longer had monarchs who have absolute power. There were still some countries that kept their kings and queens, but they also elected governing bodies who actually made the laws and upheld them. The United States of America is just getting started, and I don't know how they've organized their government yet, but eventually they will have a president, a congress of elected representatives of the people, and a court system to interpret the laws."

"Sounds complicated. Does anyone understand how it works?"

"It's complicated alright, but it gives the people a voice in the government. And women take part in the government, and in every business. But even in the early 21st century women still have an uphill battle to get their voices heard and get equal pay and respect."

"Well, as you've seen over the past ten years, it's different here. Beate probably plays as well as most of the professional horn players in Paris, but that doesn't mean anyone will let her play."

"We'll see," I said. "Something tells me Punto will be up for the challenge of promoting her if he thinks she's playing at a high level."

"I'm all for helping her, and I hope she'll be successful, but I'm skeptical about the whole thing," Carl said, shaking his head at my unorthodox ideas.

Chapter 43

He was like a cock who thought the sun had risen to hear him crow.
- George Eliot, Adam Bede, 1859

Punto was already giving lessons to a couple of students who had come to Paris specifically to work with him. One of these was the young and talented Jean Dubois, a Frenchman who was already starting to gain some notice in this city that was dominated by German speaking horn players. Punto had high hopes for him as a soloist and talked in glowing terms about his playing when we went to see him a few days later to bring up the subject of Beate having lessons and finding instruments for the sisters.

"What a delightful idea to give Waldhorn lessons to the Pokorny sisters, and especially fun if it has to be done clandestinely! Franz Pokorny will never be the wiser!"

Within minutes Punto had hatched a plan for meeting with the sisters, and we saw his excitement mount as he was keen on anything unique and involving pretty young ladies. Franz Pokorny would be told that his daughters were going twice a week to an imaginary lady in a fictional street to have piano lessons. Carl, who was supposedly a good friend of this made-up teacher, would vouch for her high social standing and character, and the quality of the instruction they would receive. Since it would not be appropriate for young ladies to go to a gentleman's residence to have lessons, even if their father didn't know about it, it was decided that, as close family friends, we could invite the sisters and Punto to our house twice a week, and they could have their lessons in the third-floor apartment. This was still stretching things a bit, but if Franz ever did get wind of their coming to our house, there was a perfectly good excuse in their coming to visit us and Röslein, and little Carl Nicholaus.

Punto owned a few horns, and loaned a pair of Anton Kerner orchestra horns to Beate and Anna-Maria, and throughout the summer the sisters had regular lessons. Punto was intrigued by the idea of finding out how much he could teach them, and would accept no money, saying that he was truly indebted to them for giving him the opportunity to make the experiment. Beate was by far the more enthusiastic student, and studied solo concertos and difficult chamber music, while Anna-Maria was content to play the accompaniments in duos and trios. Both made great strides in their playing over the following months.

It was during this summer that Punto's other student, Jean Dubois, began to get some work in some of the Paris theaters and concert series. We had heard about him from Punto, but hadn't had the pleasure of meeting him yet, when he called on us at our house one afternoon. Punto was giving the Pokorny sisters lessons that afternoon and had told Dubois that he could meet him at our house to go out to supper that evening. Jean Dubois was a rather tall handsome Frenchman, with wavy black hair and dark eyes who obviously thought a great deal of himself and his talents as a horn player - and thought the rest of the world should acknowledge that fact too.

"*Messieurs!* It is such a pleasure to finally meet you, and to make the acquaintance of two other members of the current trendsetters in horn playing! Led by my teacher, Punto, our generation is setting the stage for a revolution in horn playing that will change the way people think about our noble instrument!"

He appeared to be about twenty years old, and I wouldn't have immediately called him a member of "our generation", nor had we heard him play the horn yet, so my first impression was not a good one, and I could see that Carl was not impressed either.

"Nice to meet you too," said Carl, with an audible stiffness in his voice. "We've heard a lot about you from our dear friend Punto. What can we do for you, Monsieur?"

"Monsieur Punto asked me to meet him here this afternoon so we can dine together and then go to a performance at the Paris Opera in which I will be subbing for the first horn player."

At this point, Punto and the Pokorny sisters entered the room, having finished their lessons, and Punto greeted his star pupil with an embrace. "Jean! I would like you to meet my two charming students, the Miss Pokornys, both of whom are making great progress in their study of the horn."

Dubois stepped forward, briefly shook Anna-Maria's hand, and then bowed deeply and kissed Beate's hand.

"*Je suis enchante, Mademoiselle!* I look forward to getting to know you better during your stay in Paris. Will you and your sister do me the honor of being my guests for a chamber concert in which I'll be playing on Friday?"

"Thank you, Monsieur," said Beate graciously. "We always want to hear fine horn playing, and we have heard a lot about your talents from Monsieur Punto. We will ask our father if we can go to the concert."

"I will personally send my thanks to him if he will allow you to attend!" said Dubois, never taking his eyes off Beate.

The conversation went on rather awkwardly for a few more minutes before he and Punto left together, leaving us and the sisters to discuss our new acquaintance.

"Charming, but quite full of himself," said Beate.

"I think he's downright creepy," added Anna-Maria.

"I started to dislike him the moment he set foot in the room," said Carl.

"I have to say, he didn't strike me as someone I wanted to develop an immediate friendship with," I said, confirming what we all were thinking.

Röslein, who had come in carrying Carl Nicholaus joined in on the conversation. "Who was that handsome well-dressed young gentleman who just left with Giovanni?"

"Someone who we are not going to invite to dinner," said Carl, and explained all the weird dynamics of the previous few minutes.

Needless to say, the sisters did not go to the concert that Dubois had invited them to, but it soon became obvious that this young rock star was very interested in Beate and took every opportunity to pursue her acquaintance. At first he took to showing up at any performance where Franz Pokorny's music was to be played, knowing that his daughters would be there, and finally actually calling at their house a couple of times, much to the annoyance of Herr Pokorny, who immediately took an intense dislike to him. Nonetheless, he was undaunted and persisted in his suit, writing letters to Beate, and being a general nuisance whenever possible. Anna-Maria could even do a pretty good imitation of him.

"But enough about me!" she would say in his deep voice and Parisian accent, "How did *you* like my last solo performance?"

As his advances escalated, Beate began to loathe him more and more, and suspected that soon he would make things even more uncomfortable by making a marriage proposal. In the midst of all this he dropped by our house one afternoon.

"Bonjour Monsieur Dubois!" said Carl in a slightly amused tone. "What an unexpected surprise to see you here. What can I do for you?"

Dubois stepped into our sitting room, took off his hat and sat down as though he was an old friend, even though we had only met him very casually a couple of times.

"I stopped by to ask if you, Monsieur Türrschmidt, would be available to play second horn with me in a chamber concert that will take place Sunday two weeks from now on the *Enfants d'Appolo* concert series. We will be playing chamber music with works for horn and strings and two of the pieces require two horns."

"We aren't working that Sunday," said Carl, "so I would be happy to come and take part in the performance."

"Magnifique!" said Dubois. "Rehearsals will be the Wednesday and Thursday before at nine o'clock in the morning. I will look forward to being accompanied by one of the finest second horn players in Paris!" He left and Carl closed the door behind him.

"The young reptile is looking forward to being accompanied by one of the finest second horn players in Paris! I've never seen anything like it! But I had to accept the invitation because I've been curious about his horn playing. I can put up with a big ego for the duration of a couple of rehearsals and a concert. There must be some redeeming qualities tucked away in him somewhere that will make it a bearable experience."

Carl's optimism and friendliness, which usually resulted in his getting along with anyone and everyone, was ineffective in this case. Over the course of rehearsals, and finally the performance of the chamber concert, he developed an even deeper distaste for Jean Dubois than before. He came home from the first rehearsal in a foul mood.

"How is your new friend Jean?" I asked.

"The man is a complete asshole! Punto has one of the biggest egos of anyone I've ever met, but he uses it in a way that's fun for everyone around him and makes them feel good about themselves at the same time, as though everyone is in on the joke, but this guy is just simply annoying. If I ever agree to play with him again, promise me you'll shoot me or strangle me or something so I don't have to experience his high opinion of himself ever again!"

"But can he play the horn?" I asked, trying to calm him down.

"He's a technical wizard on the horn! He can play whatever you set in front of him, and he can even do a pretty good imitation of an actual human being with good musical taste, which makes him all the more unbearable. Someone who is that much of a self-centered jerk shouldn't be allowed to be that talented and musical!"

"But what did he do to get you in such a state of loathing toward him?" I inquired, trying to get to the bottom of his unusually agitated state.

"It was bad enough that he treated me like his hired accompanist, and talked about his many accomplishments the whole time, but the real reason why he asked me to play with him became painfully clear right away. He knew I was an old family friend of the Pokorny family, and expressed his infatuation with Beate, and wanted to ask my help and get my advice on how best to pursue a courtship with her! It was a great pleasure to nip the whole thing in the bud, and tell him it was impossible, and he should give up the idea."

"And how did you do that?"

"I told him she was already engaged to be married, and that he was too late!"

"Already engaged to be married!?" I said laughing. "Who did you say she was engaged to?"

"To you!"

"To Me!?"

"It was the first thing that came to mind."

"Well, this is going to be awkward. How are we going to explain it to Beate, and what if he mentions it to Punto and Franz Pokorny, and how do we keep up that sort of charade and keep her safe from his advances without having to announce our engagement to the entire city of Paris?! The whole idea is ridiculous!" I said, as the implications began to sink in. "You've put me into a tight spot Carl!"

"I had to do it to keep Dubois away from her. Remember that you once got me into a tight spot by getting both of us thrown into the

Bastille for what you saw as a good cause, so I think I can reclaim the debt, and put us both in an awkward situation to protect an old childhood friend from this bastard! And besides, I have the whole situation under control. I went directly to the Pokorny's house and told Franz and the girls what had happened. Beate was practically on her knees thanking me for saving her from his annoying advances, and Franz and Anna-Maria both burst out laughing when I told them how I solved the whole thing. They're all on board and plan to keep up the story until they go back to Regensburg and Beate is safely away from Paris. Punto was at the rehearsal to listen, since they were playing one of his quartets, one of a set that Rosetti wrote for him, and I caught him at the end of rehearsal to tell him what was going on."

"And what did he have to say about Dubois and his interest in Beate?"

"Oh, Punto thinks the world of Beate, and knows very well that Dubois shouldn't be let within three leagues of her without strict supervision. I got a huge earful from him about Dubois's personal qualities, or lack thereof. He's very interested in this young horse's ass as a horn player, but could do without his self-centered egotistical personality. When I mentioned to him that I told Dubois you were engaged to Beate, he thought it was the best solution to the problem, and the best joke he had ever heard."

"Well, Carl, you've definitely worked out all the details, and it looks like we're committed to act the whole thing out, though it does come as a bit of a shock that I'm going to have to act like Beate's betrothed for a while. Why does it always seem like things in this world I've been sucked into just keep happening and I don't have any say in the matter?"

Carl grinned. "Are you complaining about the success we've had as soloists?"

"Well, no."

"Or the living we're earning, which is better than just about any other horn players in Europe?"

"Again, no!"

"Are you complaining about having a fine reputation among your friends and colleagues, a network of people who would do just about anything for you at any point?"

"Not at all!"

"And if one has to pretend to be engaged to be married, can you think of a more suitable young lady than Beate Pokorny?"

"Certainly not! One could do much worse in a pretended fiancée."

"I should think so!" said Carl with another wide grin.

Chapter 44

I am as light as a feather, I am as happy as an angel, I am as merry as a schoolboy. I am as giddy as a drunken man. A merry Christmas to everybody!
- Charles Dickens, A Christmas Carol, 1843

The Pokornys, father and daughters, all got into the spirit of the pretended engagement, and I accompanied them to the Enfants d'Apollo concert that Sunday afternoon to hear Dubois and Carl. Dubois played brilliantly, and Punto was glowing in his praise of his student's performance. He and Carl played well together in the two horn pieces, which were not very virtuosic, but pleasant music.

We congratulated the performers after the concert, and as I was giving my compliments to Dubois, he pulled me aside, so the others couldn't hear.

"My congratulations to you, Monsieur Palsa on your engagement to Mademoiselle Pokorny. As you may have heard, I have been a great admirer of hers, and I hope I give no offence in saying that should the engagement break off at any point, I will be the next in line to ask for her hand."

I smiled at this bit of audacity. "Not at all, and I'm glad to hear that you have such a high opinion of Mademoiselle Pokorny, but I can assure you there is no need to consider the matter, because there is no chance of that happening."

"I wish you both all the best," he said, and turned back to the rest of his waiting admirers.

As the summer rapidly turned into fall, the sisters continued to have their regular lessons. Punto was getting more enthusiastic about the possibility of presenting Beate to the public in some way, and at the beginning of November, his chance arrived. Josef Legros announced that the Concert Spirituel performance on Christmas Eve would be devoted to some of the finest female solo instrumentalists in Paris. Punto was the first in line to suggest his student, the talented Mademoiselle Pokorny from Regensburg, the only female horn soloist of the day, and on Punto's enthusiastic recommendation, Beate was scheduled to play one of Punto's concertos.[19]

Beate wanted to play the piece that we of the 21st century know as the Rosetti Concerto in d minor, but both Legros and Punto thought this was a bit too dramatic and *Sturm und Drang* for a young lady to play, and they finally agreed on another of Punto's concertos (a concerto in F that Rosetti had composed for him) that was a more straightforward pleasant piece, and more "appropriate" musically. I thought Beate had more than enough *Sturm und Drang* for the Rosetti d minor concerto, but the general opinion of the time was that women shouldn't express such dramatic sentiments.

One of Franz Pokorny's symphonies was scheduled to open the program, and Franz wanted Carl and me to play in the orchestra, which was of course, the regular orchestra of men; only the soloists were women. Fortunately, we were able to get subs for the wind band performances for the prince that week so that we could take part in the concert. Franz's involvement in the program made it a little difficult to keep Beate's performance a secret, since he would be at rehearsals for the symphony and lead the orchestra on his piece. Punto thought it would be more fun if Franz wasn't informed in advance that his eldest daughter was one of the soloists, and none of us really knew how he was going to react to the news anyway, so Punto, in true style, made sure everyone in the orchestra, including Nicholas Capron, the concertmaster, and Legros himself, did all they could to keep the fact that Beate was performing as soloist a secret. As Punto was so fond of doing, he went to great pains, and made the most elaborate plans to get Beate to rehearsals with the orchestra without her father suspecting that anything was in the works.

On the evening of the concert, we stopped by the house where the Pokornys were living, to accompany them to the performance. Beate looked stunning in a new dress of deep burgundy velvet that flattered her petite figure elegantly and contrasted well with her flowing dark hair and the silver necklace she was wearing, from which dangled a tiny silver Waldhorn.

"My, you look absolutely beautiful this evening!" I said.

"I thought I would celebrate both Christmas Eve and Ladies Night at the Concert Spirituel with a new dress," said Beate, with a knowing sle.

"And I am proud to be accompanied to the concert this evening by my two lovely daughters, and to have them hear my latest symphony!" said Franz.

He thought the excited state of the sisters was due to the fact that their father's piece was going to be performed, having not the slightest inkling of what was actually going to take place that evening.

We walked to the Palace of the Tuilleries trying the whole time to protect Beate and Anna-Maria's festive dresses from the mud and filth of the streets, mostly in vain, and met Punto, who was waiting for us outside the *Salle des Suisse.* He had two horns in cases with him, which drew Franz Pokorny's attention right away.

"Jan, are you playing tonight in the concert?"

"Just one small encore piece with one of the soloists - nothing of any great consequence."

We entered the ballroom, which was even more highly decorated than usual, with additional tapestries and flowers, for Christmas. Chairs and music stands were arranged around the keyboard at one end of the rectangular room for the orchestra. People were slowly coming in to fill the three hundred or more stiff wooden chairs and small tables that had been set out for the audience. Soon wine glasses were clinking against bottles and decanters, fancy cakes were being cut and served, and everyone was settling in for the performance.

Beate, Anna-Maria, and Punto left us, supposedly to take their seats in the audience, and I went with Carl and Franz to the side of the room where the musicians were getting out instruments and making their way to their seats for the opening symphony. There were no printed programs, so after we were all seated, Legros stepped up and announced to the audience that this was a special holiday concert in which all the soloists had been chosen from the finest female amateur musicians of Paris. But first, the orchestra would play a new symphony, led by its composer, the visiting concertmaster of the Thurn und Taxis court orchestra in Regenburg, Germany, Monsieur Franz Pokorny.

The current music of the composers of the German court orchestras was all the rage in Paris at this point, and Pokorny's new symphony in was well received. There was even a featured moment for the winds in the minuet, which was in G major, in which the oboes, horns and bassoons played the trio section alone, trading soloistic melodic passages, a couple of which took me up into the stratosphere of the G horn accompanied by fast arpeggios in Carl's part, with quick sixteenth note answers from the oboes. Something that only happens in jazz concerts in the 21st century, but was quite common at this time, occurred at the end of this section. The audience clapped and cheered for the winds at the end of the trio as the full orchestra went back to play the minuet. Having experienced this phenomenon often in the 18th century, I think 21st century orchestra audiences would do well to revive this practice and not be so stiff and formal.

After the symphony, Legros announced the first soloist, Mademoiselle Cécile, who played a concerto for the pianoforte by J.C. Schroetter. This was followed by Mademoiselle Murdrich, playing a flute concerto. The flute concerto was accompanied only by a small string group and the rest of us went to seats at the side of the room to join Franz Pokorny, and a few other musicians. When this piece was finished, Legros once again addressed the audience.

"Ladies and Gentleman, I would now like to introduce our next soloist, and a rare treat this will be to hear the first woman Cor de chasse player to be presented to a Paris audience. May I introduce to you the student of Giovanni Punto, Mademoiselle Pokorny, daughter of our distinguished guest, concertmaster and composer Franz Pokorny, playing a concerto by Punto. Monsieur Punto and Mademoiselle Pokorny the younger will play in the orchestra accompaniment."

Franz, who was sitting between Carl and myself, stood up in surprise as Beate stepped in front of the orchestra with her horn. He looked like he was about to say something, but Carl and I each grabbed an arm and pulled him back into his seat. Carl put a finger to his lips.

"Quiet Franz! Your daughter is about to make her Paris debut!"

"You're all in on this, aren't you?" Franz whispered to everyone around him.

"Yes! - now sit down and enjoy the performance!"

The orchestra began, and during the entire opening tutti, Franz looked as though he had been played a very dirty trick by all of us, and then Beate put the horn to her lips and started to play. His frown slowly turned into a slight smile, and gradually to a broad grin. She was playing beautifully, with a sweet sound and clean technique. Her hand stopping in this rather chromatic solo concerto was precise with good intonation and tone color, and she was playing the lyrical singing phrases with an expressive range of dynamics. When some agile passagework came up, she negotiated these sections of running sixteenth notes and wide leaps with ease. The second movement, an expressive adagio, featured some lovely melodies for the solo horn accompanied by the winds only, with Punto and Anna-Maria playing the horn parts. The last movement was a rondo with a dance-like theme, passages of fast arpeggios, and a solo cadenza before the final rondo theme, all of which she played skillfully and musically.

When the piece was over the applause and cheers were by far the loudest of the entire evening. Beate took it all in as though she could hardly believe that she had just realized her dream of being a horn soloist. As she was called back for the third time, Franz came to the front, embraced his daughter, and turned toward the audience looking prouder than any other father in the history of humanity. The audience continued to cheer for this unprecedented novelty of a woman playing the horn, and playing it well, but Punto was prepared for their reaction with an encore piece, a trio by Josef Hampel in which Beate played the first part, Anna-Maria the second, and Punto the third.

The entire evening was a huge success for the Pokorny sisters and Franz took the whole situation with good humor.

"It was a wonderful concert, and you all did a superb job of keeping me in the dark. I couldn't be prouder of Beate's fine solo performance, and Anna-Maria's playing as well, but you must all understand that this great success at Legros's "Ladies night" Christmas concert does not mean that they will be accepted into the world of professional music, and I don't want to encourage them to waste their time trying."

Nonetheless, Beate was the talk of the town after her performance and received excellent reviews from the music critics in Paris.

Franz consented to the sisters continuing their studies with Punto, and twice a week they came to our house for their lessons. We would often play trios and quartets in the afternoon when we were home, so Carl, Röslein, and I spent a lot of time with the Pokorny sisters over the next few months as Franz made more connections with the preforming groups and publishers in Paris.

Everyone in the musical scene in Paris congratulated me on my engagement to Mademoiselle Pokorny, the remarkable Cor de chasse player, and I kept thinking about how I was going to explain to them that we had to break off the engagement when the Pokornys went back to Regensburg.

Chapter 45

Pokorny (Mademoiselle) – A talented virtuoso on the Waldhorn, who was heard in the Concert Spirituel in Paris in 1780, where she performed a concerto for this instrument by the famous Punto, to the great admiration of the public.
- Ernst Ludwig Gerber, Historisch-Biographisches Lexicon der Tonkünstler, 1792

Punto looked for every opportunity for Beate and Anna-Maria to play chamber music, which could only be done in groups of other women amateur musicians, but there were enough of these to give them some satisfying musical experiences. Nonetheless, Beate, being a low horn player, practiced the second parts of every new double concerto we received from Rosetti and other composers, with Punto playing the first parts in her lessons. Everyone assumed there would never be an opportunity for her to play as a soloist again, unless Legros organized another special concert for women amateurs. Then an unforeseen circumstance occurred.

In March of 1780 a symphony of Franz Pokorny's was programmed on one of the weekly concerts of the Prince of Guéméné's orchestra. In addition to the prince and his guests of the nobility and the wealthy of Paris, Franz and his daughters were invited to hear the performance. We had received by mail from Wallerstein a couple months earlier a new double concerto in E major from Rosetti. We had already performed it twice with other groups in Paris, and we were scheduled to play it that evening with our own orchestra. About an hour before the concert Carl began feeling ill.

"I'm sure it will pass in a few minutes. Probably something I ate," he said with his usual optimism. Food poisoning was all too common in the 18th century when all foods were stored at room temperature and things went bad quickly. People ate them anyway, because food was expensive. But as the time of the concert approached, he started feeling worse, and couldn't stand up due to the dizziness and nausea. Monsieur Petit started to get agitated, since the program consisted only of the symphony, our double horn concerto, and a violin concerto. Many of the important guests this evening had also been at the previous week's concert, so repeating something from that program was out of the question, and we hadn't rehearsed anything else.

At that point, Carl, who was sitting on a sofa in an alcove of the ballroom groaning and looking very pale motioned for me to come over.

"Johann, I definitely can't play tonight, but I have an idea, and I suspect you're probably thinking the same thing. The Pokornys will be here tonight, and we all heard Beate playing the second horn part with Punto in her lesson last week. She has the part down, and I think she could step in and lay it down very nicely."

"I was thinking that too," I said, "but I was hesitant to suggest it after how everyone talks about women playing music in a professional setting. I'm sure she would do a fine job. What do you think, shall I talk to her and see if she would be willing to play?"

"Oh, no problem there!" said Carl with a weak smile. "She'll jump at the chance to play, and especially in a double concerto with you. I don't think you have a bigger fan than Beate. But you'll have to sell the idea to Monsieur Petit and the prince."

Carl was beginning to turn quite green and showed every sign of being sick, so I handed him a glass of wine - water was never a good idea given what was living in the water of Paris in those days - and went to talk to our music director.

"Monsieur Petit, as you can see, Carl is in no condition to play, but we think we have a solution that will save the performance. A horn player who was recently featured at the Concert Spirituel will be here tonight, and knows the second horn part to this concerto, and would do an excellent job."

"You don't mean Mademoiselle Pokorny, who played on the Christmas Eve concert? She played remarkably well, but it would be highly irregular to have her play with our orchestra. I shudder to think how the prince would react to having a woman horn player stand before his orchestra as a soloist!"

"Yes, I do mean Mademoiselle Pokorny," I said, "but do we have very much choice?"

Before he could answer, the prince walked by and greeted me.

"We are looking forward to your concerto tonight Monsieur Palsa. We have several important visiting dignitaries in attendance, and we have told them about our wonderful Cor de chasse players."

Monsieur Petit beckoned to the prince to accompany him to a sofa and whispered in his ear for a minute or two after which they both came over to me.

"Monsieur Palsa," the prince began, "Monsieur Petit has explained the situation. Are you certain that this young lady who plays the horn can play a performance that is up to the level of our orchestra?"

"I will personally vouch for her abilities, your Excellency, as we all heard in her brilliant performance at the Concert Spirituel a few weeks ago."

"We certainly hope that will be the case this evening, Monsieur Palsa. Normally we would say that it was quite out of the question for a woman to play with the orchestra, but we have promised our guests a concerto for horns played with your usual high level of artistry, and we don't want to disappoint them. Therefore, we leave the matter in your hands."

He left and Monsieur Petit turned to me.

"No pressure!" he said with a grin. "It looks as though your young lady friend, your fiancée, I believe, is on for the concerto. I'm sure it will be a spectacular performance. If it isn't, I am equally sure the prince will have you skinned and diced up for food for his hunting dogs!"

I left him laughing at my expense and went out into the ballroom to look for the Pokorny family. It was about twenty minutes before the concert, and they had just arrived.

"Johann!" said Beate, waving to me as she saw me approaching. "I can't wait to hear you and Carl play the Rosetti concerto tonight. I didn't get to hear the first performances of it, but I know every note by heart, since I've been studying it with Punto!"

"Beate, I have to ask you a serious question. Very briefly, here is the situation; Carl is quite ill and can't play tonight. Would you be willing to play the second part tonight in his place?"

"Oh Johann!" she exclaimed excitedly, coming forward and embracing me. "I would be happy to play, and I promise I know every note of the part and will do my very best for you and Carl! Oh! This is so exciting!"

It was the first time I had held her in my arms, and I felt an unusual warmth and tingly feeling that I hadn't expected, as I took in the smell of her perfume and felt her long flowing hair against my face. She must have totally misinterpreted the confused look on my face, because she stepped back with an alarmed look.

"Oh, I'm so sorry, and I hope I didn't offend you! I should have asked first how Carl is, and what's wrong with him. Is he all right? I was just so excited by the possibility of playing with you."

"Not at all Beate. Carl will be fine. I think he just has a touch of food poisoning, or flu or something like that. I knew you would be delighted and eager to play tonight, because I know you have the part down, having learned it with Punto. But we don't have time to talk about it now. The concert starts in just a few minutes, and you'll have to play in the symphony and the violin concerto too. You can play Carl's horn. It's a Kerner, like the one you've been playing, so you'll be fine."

"I just happened to have my mouthpiece in my bag. I carry it everywhere - just in case."

"All the better to make you feel more comfortable. Let's go!"

We were walking toward the orchestra set-up at the end of the room, and I was thinking about the strange sensation I had when holding her close to me. "No! It can't be. I can't let myself go there."

We got Carl's horn and tuned our instruments together. Beate needed to add an extra tuning bit because she played a little higher than Carl due to her hand in the bell being smaller, but we got it sorted out for the four keys we needed that evening, horn in F and C for the symphony, E for the horn concerto, and G for the violin concerto. We then tuned intervals between the two of us on each crook, and took our places in the wind section, to the surprised looks of the other musicians.

The symphony was quite easy, with the exception of a couple of little duets in the adagio, and the wind section featured in the trio of the minuet, something Franz Pokorny was fond of doing, and Beate sight-read them all perfectly. Playing this symphony and the violin concerto took a little bit of the edge off the fact that we were about to play a difficult double concerto that we had never rehearsed together.

Monsieur Petit announced to the audience that because of the sudden illness of Monsieur Tierschmied, as the French were fond of pronouncing Carl's name, Mademoiselle Pokorny, who was recently featured as Cor de chasse soloist at the Concert Spirituel has graciously agreed to fill in for him on extremely short notice on the Rosetti concerto for horns. Amidst the surprised murmurings of the audience, Beate and I came to the front of the orchestra, checked the tuning of our crooks with the oboist, and the concertmaster started the opening tutti.

Beate had thoroughly learned her part, and as with most of Rosetti's double concertos, the first movement alternated between passages that we played together, and solo passages for each of us. At first I wasn't sure if I should hold back in both the solo and tutti passages, in case her sound was smaller than Carl's usual full sound that matched mine well, but it soon became apparent that she could match whatever I was doing and I went right back into the full sound and confidence with which I would have played had Carl been at my side. She negotiated each of her agile solo passages expertly, and as we finished our last virtuosic solo section in the first movement, and the orchestra was approaching the cadenza we looked at each other, realizing at the same moment that she didn't know our double cadenza.

Carl and I always worked out a duo cadenza in meticulous detail for each piece, and though Beate had heard us play the cadenza for this one at home once or twice, she couldn't possibly have memorized it. In the few seconds that remained before the cadenza, I whispered, "Just play an answer to each phrase I play, and we'll end trilling in thirds, you on a B natural." That was all I had time to say before the orchestra arrived at the fermata before our cadenza.

Beate did exactly as I suggested, playing an ornamental tag at the end of each of the phrases I played, and followed me into the trill, keeping her cool the entire way. Though the cadenza was simpler than the one Carl and I would have played, no one else knew that, and it was a fine performance all together.

Beate was the heroine of the evening, and though they had been skeptical as she stepped up to play, everyone in the orchestra congratulated her on her playing. After the weekly concerts the prince always served drinks and dessert to his guests, but the musicians weren't allowed to mingle with them. Instead, we would enjoy a drink of our own together in a servant's room off the main ballroom. As we were winding down and having a glass of wine, the Princess of Rohan, the prince's wife, entered the room.

"Mademoiselle Pokorny, would you be so kind as to come with us please." Beate left with her and reappeared about five minutes later, smiling brightly.

"What was that all about?" several people asked.

"The princess was so kind and friendly to me," said Beate. "She presented me to the guests and said that I had saved the concert tonight by stepping in to play Carl's part. She invited me to come and play at one of the chamber music evenings with Carl and Johann, and gave me this gold locket on a chain!"

She came over to where I was sitting on an overstuffed sofa.

"Johann, this evening, just like the Christmas Eve concert, was a dream come true for me. And it was so wonderful to play a concerto with you, one of the finest high horn players in the world!"

"And I enjoyed playing a concerto with you; I can't think of another horn player in Paris outside of Punto who could have stepped in and done such a superb performance."

"Thank you, Johann, for believing in me. I'm just sorry Carl had to get sick for me to get the opportunity."

"Carl was taken home by one of the prince's servants. I'm sure he's comfortably asleep in bed at this point. Röslein will take good care of him. He'll be very happy to know that you did such a fine job in his place."

Everyone was leaving us alone, thinking it perfectly natural that the two engaged horn players would want a few quiet moments together to talk about the evening's events. We were so happy and comfortable together, and I started to give in to the feelings I had experienced earlier. I knew this was the moment to come out and say what I was feeling.

"Beate, we had to pretend to be engaged to each other for the past couple of months, and all of Paris is certain it's true, and I was happy to do it to save you from the advances of Jean Dubois."

"For which I will always be grateful, Johann," she said, looking down at the floor.

"But what I'm trying to say, is that after all that time, I've rather gotten used to the idea, and we've had so much fun together, playing horn, and spending time with your father and sister, and Carl and

Röslein, and we are starting to feel like one big family, and... what I'm actually trying to say is that over the past three months, I've gradually fallen in love with you, though I haven't been willing to admit it, even to myself until tonight. Beate, will you marry me? For real this time?"

Beate was the most open and straightforward woman I had ever met. Without hesitating for a second, she looked straight at me with a bright sparkle in her eyes.

"Dearest Johann! I had sworn that I would never get married. Papa kept trying to fix me up with all sorts of nice suitors, but I knew I would just become another married lady who didn't have a life of her own, and couldn't play music the way I wanted to, or be who I want to be. And then I met you, and you were different from any other man I had ever met. I don't know exactly what it is about you, but you seem to treat me as an equal in a way I've never experienced or seen before. It's like you were born in some other world where people have wholly different ideas about a woman's place in society. And then when you and Carl helped Anna-Maria and me to get lessons and spent so much time playing trios and quartets with us, I knew you had faith in my dream to play horn in a real way. The idea of marrying someone who would see me in that way was nothing more than a wild dream until I saw it happening in front of me, when we were just pretending. But I couldn't let myself imagine that you would actually end up caring enough for me that you would want to marry me. Of course I'll marry you!"

I took her in my arms and kissed her, and despite having held onto my identity as a married man in another world for the past decade, this seemed so right for this world, and I was ready to let go of that last remaining part of the old one.

"Beate, you've just made me very happy, and I wouldn't want to change you in any way. I hope you can continue to play horn and keep working your way into the musical world as you have been doing. I wouldn't want to discourage you from pursuing that dream, and especially since you've already proven that you could play in any orchestra anywhere. I want to be part of that dream."

"And what was papa's reaction?" she asked.

"Your father's reaction?"

"I'm assuming he said yes, but was he enthusiastic? He certainly knows that you won't discourage me from playing music."

"I haven't asked him. Do you think I need to? You're twenty-three years old. Couldn't you decide for yourself if you wanted to get married?"

"Maybe that's how it works in the English colonies where you grew up, but in Germany and France you must ask a girl's father first! I know he has a lot of respect for you and I'm sure it will be okay, but it just has to be done in that order."

"Well, I'll talk to him straight away and get that formality taken care of, if you think it's the proper thing to do."

"Definitely, and the fact that you don't know the common facts of modern courtship, and are not tied down to customs and traditional attitudes makes you all the more intriguing and makes me love you all the more!"

After a little more talk, and a little more kissing, we went to find Franz and Anna-Maria, and I escorted them all home, with Franz taking one handle of the horn box in Carl's absence. It was snowing lightly, and the streets were filled with a slushy version of the usual mixture of mud and horse manure, which made it more than normally treacherous for walking. After leaving them I had to walk the rest of the way home carrying that damned horn box by myself, stumbling through the slippery pitch-black streets.

My head was still spinning with all the events of the evening, and I was thinking about the fact that I had promised Beate that I would call on them the next morning to have the obligatory talk with Franz Pokorny to ask for her hand. For the previous ten years, I had often spent sleepless nights wondering if at some point in the blink of an eye, I would find myself returned to my old life with Beth and our kids, as quickly as I had been catapulted into this one. On this particular evening, once again I lay awake far into the night watching both worlds collide again. Was I about to be a bigamist? Was this being unfaithful to Beth, my 21st century wife and lifetime partner?

Again, I felt like things were happening around me that I didn't have any control over. Remarrying after a spouse dies is not unusual, but remarrying before your spouse is born is just plain weird. Human brains were designed to live life in a consecutive order, starting at the beginning, and going along through the middle to a logical end. They weren't designed to deal with a situation like this, and mine was trying to make sense of it all. There was no question in my mind that I was in love with Beate and wasn't going to let the opportunity to marry her slip away, but I was haunted by my past, which was everyone else's future, though a future so far removed that it wasn't anyone's future here. My thoughts kept getting wilder and more confused as I lay awake. I fell asleep finally, thinking about how my old world seemed more and more like the dream, and this one had definitely become the real one.

Chapter 46

O let us be married! Too long we have tarried!
- Edward Lear, The owl and the Pussycat, 1871

The next morning it was obvious that Carl had a bad case of the flu and was going to be out of commission for a while. Having the flu in those days, before decongestants and boxes of tissues, was a miserable business, and Carl spent most of the day wrapped in blankets in front of a blazing fire, drinking tea and chicken broth that Röslein made for him. Other than perking up a little when I told him about Beate successfully playing his part in the concert, he was in a dismal mood.

"But I have some other news this morning that I want to share with you," I said.

"Wait, don't tell me. You're going to get yourself run over by an ox cart and go back to biblical times to play the shofar at the walls of Jericho?"

Röslein gave Carl a worried look. "I think the fever is affecting his brain and he's going a little out of his head this morning."

"Carl and Röslein," I said, ignoring Carl's inside joke, "I made a marriage proposal to Beate last night, and she accepted!"

"Oh! Johann we're so happy for you!" said Röslein. "We have all been hoping this would be the result of your pretended engagement, and the two of you would figure out that you are the perfect match for each other! Why, we were just talking to Anna-Maria about it the other day. She said she has been gradually dropping hints to Beate that it could happen, but Beate would always tell her to stop talking nonsense."

Carl had perked up considerably at this news and stood up, letting the blanket he had draped around him fall to the floor, and shook my hand.

"Röslein is right. We all knew it was bound to happen; not that I had it in mind to be a matchmaker when I told Dubois Beate was engaged to you. The idea was simply to stop him from pursuing Beate, but it didn't take long for us all to start thinking about it. Now we will have two low horn players in the family, and if we can train little Carl Nicholaus to be a high horn player, we'll have two of each."

"And as always, I'm the last to know what everyone has planned for me," I said, "but I'm happy to know everyone else is as enthusiastic about the idea as Beate and I. And this morning I have to go to the Pokorny house to ask Franz for Beate's hand."

"Wait!" said Röslein. "You asked Beate to marry you before you asked for her father's consent?!"

Carl came to my rescue.

"Röslein, you have to remember that Johann grew up in the English colonies in America, and the customs of courtship and marriage are very different there. Beate knows him well enough to know that, and she also knows her father will have no objections, Johann being a very successful musician and someone who he knows will be a good husband to his daughter. I may be biased because he is my closest friend, but I don't think I'm alone in thinking he is one of the most upstanding, honest men I've ever met, and Franz knows his daughter could not do better for a husband."

Carl, the only person in this world who knew my real story, was always ready to help me navigate his world, and overcome the awkwardness of my lack of knowledge of how things were done in his time. He was a master of understanding my situation and how it related to his world, and everything that would take place over a period of twenty-two years for me would not have been possible without his highly insightful watchfulness over my transition into his world. I left the house thinking about this, and how disastrous my introduction into the 18th century could have been, but for him.

My arrival at the Pokorny residence that morning was met with feigned surprise from Beate, and from Anna-Maria, who had undoubtedly been let in on the events of the previous evening, and true surprise from their father, who was still sitting at breakfast in front of the hearth drinking coffee and eating hot buttered toast that Anna-Maria was toasting in a wire basket with a wooden handle over the fire.

"My dear Johann, what on earth could bring you out so early on such a cold and icy morning as this?"

"I've actually come here this morning on a serious matter, Herr Pokorny."

"Is Carl's illness worse? How is he this morning?" asked Franz, in some alarm.

"No, No - Carl definitely has the flu, and is not very happy this morning, but he isn't in any danger that I know of. He is in the best of hands under Röslein's care. I came to talk over something else altogether, and if Beate and Anna-Maria could excuse us for a few minutes, I'll explain what it's all about."

"It sounds terribly important," said Beate to her sister. "Let's leave them alone to discuss their business and attend to a few household chores that need to be done." They left the room, trying desperately to act as though they didn't know what was going on, and leaving me with a totally puzzled Franz Pokorny.

"My dear boy, take a chair and tell me what's on your mind, though I'm beginning to have my suspicions as to what it's all about."

I relaxed a bit, seeing that he was in a good mood.

"Well sir, for the past few months, due to Carl's intense dislike for Jean Dubois, and his desire to protect Beate from him, Beate and I have pretended to be engaged to be married."

Franz smiled.

"The intense dislike of Jean Dubois has become a pleasant family pastime for us over the past few months, and thanks to the pretended betrothal, you have been able to keep him out of our hair to a great extent."

"I'm glad to have been of service in that way," I went on, "but during that time, I've spent a good deal of time with Beate, when your daughters came to our house for lessons, and more recently during preparations for her Concert Spirituel debut."

"Let's say Concert Spirituel appearance," Franz interrupted. "Debut sounds like the start of a series of performances or the beginning of a career. This was a one-time special ladies night concert, - a sort of novelty event."

"That may be true sir," I said, trying to get back on track, "but between all these opportunities for us to get to know one another, right down to last night's performance..."

"Another most extraordinary and unprecedented occurrence," Franz said interrupting me in mid-sentence again, "which I'm sure could never happen again, though I must say that she did play admirably and saved the concert."

"Yes sir, but as I was saying, during all this time, I've grown fonder of her than I can express, and have come to appreciate not only her musical talents, but really every aspect of her personality and good nature. She is the most charming and interesting young woman I've met in all of my time ..." I almost blurted out, 'in this 18th century of yours', but I caught myself just in time to say, "since I arrived in Paris some ten years ago from the English colonies. In short, Herr Pokorny, I have fallen in love with Beate, and would like to ask your permission to marry her, which would make me happier than anything that has happened during these very happy ten years, and I hope that the prospect of being my wife would bring the same happiness to her as it would to me."

He looked seriously at me for a few moments.

"I wondered if all of this play acting might result in something of the sort and was fully anticipating this moment. If I must say so myself, she is a charming, attractive, and intelligent young lady, though at times a bit headstrong with some strange ideas in her head about pursuing music as a career. Being married would certainly help to settle her down a bit and start to take seriously her role as a sensible modern woman. Have you any indication from her that she is prepared to return the affection you've just expressed as having for her?"

"I believe she does, sir, from the conversations we have had."

Franz hesitated for a moment. "At this point the father is supposed to ask a lot of questions about your background, your ability to make a decent living to support a wife and family, and about your character, but I already know you to be at the top of the music business, and one of the most prominent soloists of today. I also know you to be an honest and dignified man who would take good care of my daughter and your children, should you be fortunate enough to have children. I don't have anything else to say other than that I can't imagine a better match for Beate than yourself, and I give you my permission to ask her for her hand. The final decision lies with her, of course, but I must warn you; I've been through this process a couple of times before, having given permission to a couple other perfectly fine young men, and each time she has refused them. I sincerely hope you will be more successful than they were."

"That is my hope too. And if I'm the lucky one, I'll do my very best to take good care of her and make her happy."

Franz got a far-away look in his eye.

"My only regret in all of this is that she would stay here in Paris with you, Johann, and I will eventually have to go back to Regensburg to the Thurn und Taxis Court Orchestra. My wife died in childbirth when the girls were quite young, and they have been my family and my happiness ever since. I would miss her terribly, but she does need to live her own life, and I can't think of a better choice for a young man to be her husband. Now go and speak with her and let me know what she says."

"Thank you Herr Pokorny," I replied. "I'll go directly and have this important discussion with her."

Eighteenth century German could get overly formal and flowery on occasions such as this, and my translation of the conversation between Franz and myself doesn't do justice to the formality with which we were speaking.

The house in which Franz and his daughters lived was a rather small one in an attached row of similar dwellings, and there wasn't a lot of privacy. I stepped into the sitting room, and very nearly knocked over Beate and Anna-Maria, who obviously had their ears to the door the entire time.

"Anna-Maria, can you run along and practice some scales and arpeggios or something for a few minutes? Johann and I have some important things to talk over."

Anna-Maria scurried away excitedly, and we sat down in the ice-cold sitting room, the only fire in the house being in the kitchen. This felt awkward initially, but Beate was ready from the beginning to make me feel as though we were both in on this together, partners already.

"I heard most of the conversation through the door, and it sounds like he's enthusiastic about our getting married and gave his consent. I knew he would, but you just had to ask, because that's the way things are done."

"And now Beate," I said taking her in my arms, "I can officially ask you what I asked last night; the most important question of our lives. Will you marry me?"

She smiled the biggest, brightest smile that I've ever seen on a girl's face.

"If I sounded certain last night, dearest Johann, an entire sleepless night thinking about the prospect of being your wife has made me more certain than ever. It will make me happier than I can ever express to marry you!"

After a few more minutes of talking about our future, holding hands, and cuddling close in the cold sitting room, Beate sprang up.

"Papa! We must tell Papa and Anna-Maria!"

She ran into the other room and embraced them both simultaneously. "Johann and I are going to be married! Isn't it exciting? We're going to live here in Paris where there's music everywhere, and Carl and Röslein and Johann and I will be like a family and live in their house. And Papa and Anna-Maria, I'll miss you so much, but I'm sure you'll come back to visit us, and we'll come to Regensburg on concert tours."

She was talking at a death-defying rate of speed, as she always did when excited, while Franz shook my hand and Anna-Maria cried and laughed simultaneously.

"This is all wonderful news, but we should discuss some serious plans," said Franz, after all the congratulations. "We won't be able to have a wedding for a while, because I also have an announcement for all of you. I have received a letter from London just this morning inviting me to go there and take part in a series of concerts which will keep me and my daughters there for a couple of months."

"Oh, Papa! Beate broke in. "We can't possibly wait that long! I thought we could be married immediately. Can't we? Must we all go to London?"

"My dear, we will need to leave by the end of this week. It would be impossible to organize a proper wedding in that time, and I'm sure you want a real wedding with a wedding breakfast and dinner at which all our Paris friends can celebrate with us. Besides, after an absence of a couple of months, both of you will be even more sure of your decision and your love for one another."

"But Papa! I couldn't be surer than I am now," Beate said trembling with disappointment. "But I am also quite sure that Anna-Maria and I will be bored out of our minds while you play with all the most important musicians of London, and I'm also certain that there will be no opportunity for us to play with anyone, and we won't even have horns to play by ourselves. Oh, how will we survive it?"

I felt I needed to help the situation in some way.

"Beate you know I'll wait patiently for your return and love you all the more when you get back. Carl and I will talk to the prince and ask if we can have our wedding at the Hôtel de Guéméné in a real ballroom. And maybe Punto will let you take your horns with you on the trip. I'll ask him if he would allow you to take them along."

Beate hugged me and gave a sigh of resignation.

"I suppose we shall survive it somehow, but I'll write letters to you as often as I can, and I'll be sustained only by the fact that when we return we can be married."

"My dear, as a consolation for this time of keeping the two of you apart, I'll write a little piece for you and Johann to play at your wedding," said Franz, who was always a pushover when it came to his daughters. "I think it would only be fitting to have you play a piece that commemorates the performing that you've done and signals the beginning of your new life as a married lady, in which you obviously won't be playing the horn."

"Oh Papa! That would be wonderful, and I can't imagine a better wedding present, considering that my horn playing career will be coming to an end," said Beate, turning and winking at me so that her father didn't notice."

Before I left, we talked over plans for the wedding, which Carl and I would take care of organizing while the Pokornys were away in London. I promised we would arrange everything and do our best to convince the prince to let us use a room at the Hôtel for the wedding and dinner.

Chapter 47

Among them the two celebrated Miss Pokornys, who will blow several concertos and duets on the French Horn.
-from an Announcement in the London Morning Post and Daily Advertiser, 1780

It was about a week before Franz and his daughters left for London, during which time I spent a good deal of my free time with them. Carl was down with the flu the entire time, and despite my best efforts, Monieur Petit would not hear of Beate filling in for him with the orchestra.

"You are certainly head over heels in love with your young lady friend, Johann!" he said to me when I brought up the question. "Though she played very nicely this past week, we cannot allow such a thing to occur again. I'm sure you will be able to find a professional Cor de chasse player to play during Carl's absence."

"Oh well," I said to Beate later that day. "I gave it a good try, but Monsieur Petit wouldn't hear of it."

"It was very kind of you to ask him, Johann, though I could have predicted that if there were any other possible solution, they would not let a woman play in the orchestra. But I won't give up. Father thinks my marrying you will cool down my enthusiasm for playing the horn, but I will find opportunities to play in the future."

I knew she would not give up playing, despite this world's expectations, and called on Giovanni Punto that same afternoon to ask if the sisters could go to England with their borrowed horns.

Punto greeted me in his usual mixed style. *"Johann, mon Ami! Grüß Dich!* Please come in! How nice to see you, *mein lieber Freund!* What can I do for you on this dismal and rainy afternoon, which has been made happy and sunny by the news of your pretended engagement to Beate becoming a real one?"

"Thank you, Jan. I didn't know the news had traveled so quickly." In these days before email, telephone, and text messages, it was always astonishing how fast interesting news could get around. "I have learned that Franz Pokorny and his daughters will be going to London for a couple of months before our wedding, and I've come to ask if the sisters could take along the horns you've been so kind to loan them. They need something to pass the time while they are there. Though it seems there is little chance they would get to take part in any concerts."

"I would be happy to let them take the horns to London," he replied, "and now that I think about it, I have a couple of ideas to help them do some performing while they're there. I have a few friends I can write to in London, and I'll let them know that two extremely talented young ladies who play the Waldhorn will be there shortly, and they should not miss out on the opportunity to have them play on a concert or two. England is a different scene from France or Germany. There are a lot of amateur groups, and the novelty of women performing in them is not as completely unheard of as it is in France. It would be amusing to see Franz Pokorny's reaction when he gets to London and finds several invitations to play addressed to his horn playing daughters! It will be a nice surprise for the Miss Pokornys too, though you might want to mention to Beate that she should take a couple of solo concertos and orchestra accompaniments with her on the trip - just in case."

"If anyone can get the sisters some opportunities in the London music scene, you can, Jan."

"It's been very gratifying to promote them and their musical talents, and you must admit that Beate is playing as well as any low horn player in Paris today. I've already heard this morning from a member of your orchestra that she did a superb job as a stand-in for Carl on the new Rosetti double horn concerto at the Prince of Guéméné's concert."

"It was quite amazing how well she played on such short notice, and we even improvised a double cadenza on the spot, because in our haste, I forgot to let her know what Carl and I had worked out. But she was able to follow me and answer each phrase I played with a tasteful accompaniment."

"I wish I could have been there to hear it, and that reminds me; while Carl is recovering, and must stay at home, this would be a good time for us to sit down with him and design the new horn he has been talking about for at least the past five years. We'll get the design together, and I'm sure we can get Joseph Raoux to make it."

We had talked to Punto about the design for a new model of orchestra horn as far back as 1776, when I first met him, and now it was time to move ahead and make this new instrument, which would be a ground-breaking step in the history of the horn.

“Stop by tomorrow evening,” I said, “and we’ll have supper and a bottle or two of Bordeaux and talk it over. We can cheer Carl up by drawing him into a discussion of one of his favorite subjects.”

Chapter 48

A chapter full of technical information on the development of the horn in the late 18th century. Can be skimmed by the general reader, though students and players of the horn are encouraged to read carefully.[20]

> *In the making of simple horns for solo playing, the Paris makers are at present the most advanced. One can even have them made in silver for 100 louis-d'ors; like the excellent pair belonging to Herrn Palsa and Türrschmidt in Berlin.*
>
> *- Ernst Ludwig Gerber, Historisch-Biographisches Lexicon der Tonkünstler, 1792*

The design of the French orchestra horn, or *Cor d'orchestra,* had been on Carl's mind since the mid-1770s. The next evening, Giovanni Punto, and his dog Hans Joachim, showed up at our house to talk over the new design. He was carrying a basket with food and bottles of wine, and Hans, who had a bright red scarf tied around his neck that evening, was carrying a rather large bone that he spent most of the evening gnawing in front of the hearth, in which we had a blazing fire for Carl's benefit, and playing with four-year-old Carl Nicholaus, with whom he was a great favorite.

It was a warm cozy scene in our kitchen at the table before the hearth, in which Röslein had a fowl roasting and a pot of soup simmering. The table was spread out with bread, cheese, and wine, which Giovanni had brought, but Carl, who was still coughing and sneezing, didn't have a taste for wine that evening. Instead Röslein had made him *tea a l'anglaise*, which was hot tea with milk and sugar in the English style, a drink that was not often encountered in France at that time.

After finishing our meal, (in the 18th century we never discussed any business or important issues while eating) we got down to the task of designing the new *Cor d'orchestra.* You could, however, continue drinking while discussing business. Carl started the conversation.

"There are a few things we need to take into consideration. Orchestras are getting bigger, and with more strings in the ensemble, the wind section of the modern orchestra is getting louder. Even ten years ago the small orchestra horns of Kerner and other German and Austrian makers made enough sound to balance with a normal section of oboes and bassoons, but with the addition of clarinets and flutes, and sometimes even trumpets and timpani, it's going to require a horn with a larger bell that produces more sound without getting a harsh edge. We also want to equip it with a slide for fine tuning. Fixed pitch horns, and more recently *Inventionshorns* with crooks, work alright with tuning bits if you play in the same group day in and day out, and in a limited number of keys with time to change them, but over the past few years, composers have been using a wider range of keys for orchestra horn parts, and requiring the horns to change crooks on very short notice, especially in opera. A slide would mean you could put in a new crook and make a quick adjustment with the slide, and you're ready to go. Being able to adjust quickly when playing with different groups at different pitch levels and temperatures would be a major improvement."

"That's right," said Punto. "For orchestra playing it would eliminate fumbling around with tuning bits and couplers if you had a single crook for each key and a slide. As a soloist, however, I still prefer the simple horn. I've been thinking of having Joseph Raoux make a couple of fixed pitch solo horns for me. All the slides and crooks you're proposing may make it easier to tune and change crooks fast, but a horn like that would be too heavy and slow responding for agile solo playing. I've played concertos all over the continent, and since the group will usually tune to me, or meet me in the middle somewhere, I can function with a few bits and a pigtail or two on an acoustically clean and light fixed pitch horn."

"Exactly," continued Carl. "Since there are two distinct styles of playing - simple open note orchestra playing and chromatic soloistic playing - it only makes sense that there should be separate models of horns, one for the modern orchestra player, who needs the full range of crooks, and one for the soloist, who only plays in two or three keys and needs an easy playing horn. The few horns with slides by Werner in Dresden and Haltenhof in Hanau that I've seen have a sharp bend on either side of the slide that adds resistance. I would like to make the tubes going into the slide cross over each other, which would make a gentler bend, and add strength. Those makers have also tried a fixed mouthpipe, and crooks that go into the slide, but if you need to play the full range of orchestra crooks, that's going to be a compromise in the extreme upper and lower keys, since the mouthpipe taper would only be appropriate for the middle keys. We need separate terminal crooks for each key, with the proper taper for each, if we want them to have true octaves and good intonation."

We drank a toast to the new design and started making pen and ink drawings of the *Cor d'orchestra* to take to the Raoux shop to present to Joseph Raoux and his son, Lucien-Joseph.

The orchestra horn that Carl designed would become the standard model in France and would have an influence on horn playing and making in every other country for the next century, until the era of the valve horn. The simple fixed-pitch soloist's horn would last a few more decades, and slowly be replaced for solo playing by the French *Cor-solo* beginning in the 1790s. The Cor-solo model had a fixed mouthpipe and crooks that were inserted into the slide, and was perfected by Lucien-Joseph Raoux around the turn of the 19th century. As Carl said, one fixed mouthpipe would only be appropriate for a few of the middle keys, but the soloist only needed the middle keys of F down to D. A few soloists stuck to their simple fixed pitch horns well into the 19th century.

Three or four days later Carl was beginning to get back on his feet, and the three of us made a visit to the Raoux shop to ask them to make the new design. A couple of years before, in 1776, Joseph Raoux had joined forces with his son Lucien-Joseph. The father, now in his mid-fifties, and the twenty-six-year-old son were now the most respected makers of brass instruments in Paris. The new shop was in the rue Froidmanteau in a large house where the Raoux family lived and worked. This shop was larger than the old one I had visited in 1770, consisting of three rooms on the lower floor. The first was a sort of sitting room/office, where instruments were displayed and business was done, and the other two were workrooms. As in the old house in the rue de Petite Lion, the family lived upstairs.

The first of the two workrooms was extremely dirty with two large anvils at which a couple of workers were hammering bells by hand with a deafening noise, and a forge with hot coals where the soldering of bells and tubes was done. The second room was the assembly room, with workbenches, a lathe, cabinets, and drawers full of tools and materials, and rows of tools and wooden bending forms hanging on the walls. I also recognized from my previous visits the long bench with a winch and chain for drawing tubes through dies. It was a picturesque and noisy scene, which I had only briefly seen a couple of times since Joseph Raoux had made a mouthpiece for me after my arrival in Paris.

We were met at the door by the father and son, who took our coats and scarves and led us into the front room, which was furnished with a table, a few chairs, a desk, and a cabinet containing finished instruments.

"Giovanni! So nice to see you again!" said Joseph. "And Messieurs Pals and Tierschmiedt, what a pleasure to see you as well. I must say, Monsieur Pals, your French has improved greatly since you last visited us."

The truth was that my French was non-existent when I had last visited them.

"What a great honor to have three of the finest Cor de chasse players in all of France here in our shop today! Lucien, please ask your mother to prepare some tea and cakes for our visitors. And now, Messieurs, what can I do for you?"

We sat down at the table and spread out our drawings and explained to him our ideas about the new design. After we had presented all the details as we had discussed them a few days earlier at our house, Carl turned to Joseph.

"Monsieur Raoux, I hope, in presenting these ideas to you, we do not offend by presuming that we are experts in brass instrument design. We are horn players and bring to you what we believe to be improvements to the modern orchestra instrument in the hope that you will be willing to try the experiment of making horns on this pattern."

Joseph poured another cup of tea and looked at the drawing again.

"My dear Carl, unlike many other brass instrument makers, who think they know best what musicians need to do their work, we pride ourselves in this shop on our willingness to listen to what the player wants, and we take very seriously their opinions and feedback on the instruments we make. Giovanni has been of the utmost assistance to us in developing the proper bell shape and size for the new chromatic hand-stopping that all of you are doing and helping us to determine what sort of tapers in the crooks give the best results in stability and intonation. This working together, taking advantage of our knowledge and experience of instrument making, and your knowledge of what is required in modern orchestral and solo playing, is the best way to arrive at the optimal design for the modern horn player.

Lucien and I have been taking a careful look at the current trends toward larger groups that play in larger venues and have been adapting our designs to those needs to make the acoustical properties of the horns more appropriate to the current musical environment. The horns of twenty and thirty ago, with their small bells are no longer going to get the job done, either for orchestra players or for the traveling soloist."

"But do you think the design that we propose is likely to play well?" asked Punto.

"The design that you propose only has to do with the configuration of the horn," said Lucien, taking up where his father had left off. "After the bell design and tapers of the horn have been established, the way it is wrapped has surprisingly little to do with the playing qualities. The drawings you have shown us make a great deal of sense. Both the single piece terminal crooks and the slide with the tubes crossing over each other will create greater stability in the hand of the player. And the slide itself, which is relatively easy to make, will give the possibility of a wider range of fine tuning than was ever possible with tuning bits."

"Give us about two weeks," said Joseph, "and we will have a prototype ready to try. I can't think of any reason why it shouldn't be a fine instrument for the modern orchestra player."

We each contributed some money for materials for the new horn and left the father and son to begin their work. Since they didn't have to make new tooling for the various parts of the horn, other than bending forms for the new configuration, the work of making the prototype could happen quickly. By the end of the following week, we received a message that the new design was ready to test.

The results with this first example, made in brass, were everything we had hoped for, and we immediately put in our orders for instruments for each of us. With the larger bells, these produced a broader and richer quality of sound than our old Kerner horns, were completely tunable, and were very comfortable in the hand. And thus, the French orchestra horn with tuning slide was born and gradually became the standard horn design for the orchestra player in France for the next few generations. From that time on, we began playing these new Raoux horns for orchestra performances.

It was also at this time that we commissioned from Raoux a pair of solo horns made of silver for our double concerto performances. They were simple fixed-pitch horns in three coils, pitched in E, at the standard pitch level in Paris. They could be taken down to E flat with a small pigtail crook, or anywhere in between with a set of graduated tuning bits. We played on these beautiful silver horns for solo performances from that time onward. Punto also had silver horns made in F and E and played on them for the remainder of his career.

Chapter 49

This bud of love, by summer's ripening breath,
May prove a flower when we next meet.
- Shakespeare, Romeo and Juliet, 1595

Three more months passed by while the Pokorny family was away in London, and during this time Beate and I were able to send several letters back and forth. It often took as much as a couple of weeks for a letter posted in Paris to get to London, if it survived the journey at all, and we managed to keep each other informed of what was happening in our respective places. Beate was as excited to see and try the new horns as she was to return home to me and plan our wedding, and wrote about their musical activities in London.

Beate and Anna-Maria were surprised to find invitations to play waiting for them when they arrived in London, due to Punto's recommendation of them to both amateur and professional groups. The sisters appeared several times on concert programs, usually with Beate playing a solo concerto and Anna-Maria joining her for duets or trios with another horn player. Franz was even more surprised than the sisters at this enthusiastic reception of his daughters by the London musical world. He was certain Beate would have a fine time performing in the more relaxed musical environment of London, and having gotten the urge to play as a horn soloist out of her system, would settle down after her wedding when they were back in Paris.

The time went slowly, even though we were as busy as ever with orchestra and wind band services nearly every day through the spring of 1780, but eventually the Pokornys left London, having had as much success and income as one could expect from touring in those days. The rooms they had previously occupied in Paris had been rented to someone else in the meantime, so they would have to find a new place to live for the relatively short time Franz and Anna-Maria would remain in the city. Carl and I searched out and rented a smaller set of rooms for them in a nearby street, and had a modest household arranged for them to move into on their arrival. As usual, we didn't know on which day they would arrive, travel being quite unpredictable, and there being no reliable way to communicate while on the road. With the last letter I had sent, we arranged for them to come to our house first, and we would take them to their new lodging. Though we didn't know it, that letter did arrive in London before they set out for Paris, and the father and daughters knew we had arranged everything for their return.

As it always happened in the 18th century, when you were expecting someone to return from a trip, the sequence of events went from anxious expectation that they could arrive at any moment, to resigning oneself to the fact that it could be next week, and on to starting to be concerned because it was getting to be a couple of weeks later than you had thought it should be, and eventually on to despair and worry that something had happened along the way, and you would never hear from them again. I was just entering this last stage of despair one morning as Carl and Röslein and I were having breakfast and a cup of the best coffee in all of Paris, thanks to my now perfected coffee roasting and brewing skills. Carl would no longer drink the poor excuse for coffee that was served everywhere else in the city, and would hold out for my coffee every time.

He tried his best to reassure me.

"Johann, you really can't start worrying about the Pokornys yet. We're not even sure when they left London or if they got your last letter. More opportunities to play concerts may have come up at the last minute that they couldn't turn down. It's still early spring, and they may have decided to wait until a little later when the weather is a little more comfortable for traveling. Franz wouldn't want to make his daughters ride in drafty coaches and catch pneumonia if it could be avoided by waiting a few weeks."

"Beate's last letter sounded as though they would be on their way back at the beginning of the month," I said pacing the squeaky floorboards of our kitchen. "Anything could have happened. They could have been robbed and killed along the way or had an accident on the road."

"I'm sure nothing bad has happened and we'll be welcoming them home at any moment," said Röslein. And just as though it was a cue in the script of a play, we heard the house door open and footsteps on the stairs. All three of us were on our feet in a moment. The door opened and a second later Beate was in my arms. Close at her heels was Anna-Maria followed by their father, and before we knew it everyone was talking at once and embracing each other.

"Dearest Johann, I missed you so much the whole time and couldn't wait to get back, but the trip was worthwhile after all. Anna-Maria and I got to play with several groups and concert societies. Thanks to letters that Giovanni sent ahead of our arrival, invitations were waiting for us when we got there!"

"The concert scene in London was apparently ready for the novelty of two young ladies playing Waldhorns," said Franz. "They had a good deal of success, and I was proud of the high level of their playing. But now that they have gotten that out of their systems, we have to get down to the business of organizing a wedding in the next few weeks before Anna-Maria and I have to go back to Regensburg. And as I promised before we left for London, I have composed a piece for your wedding day. To commemorate the end of what has been an unexpected string of solo performances for Beate, I am nearly finished with a new concerto for two horns."

"Oh Papa!" exclaimed Beate. "An entire new concerto, just for us? When you said you were going to write a little piece, I thought you meant a little duet. Oh, this is the most wonderful wedding present I could imagine!"

"I'm assuming all the members of the orchestra of the Prince of Guéméné will be at the wedding celebration," said Franz, "and could be prevailed upon to accompany you and Johann. It will celebrate the end of your performing career and the beginning of your new life as a married lady."

"I'm sure all of the orchestra members will be there, and would be happy to play," I said.

"Oh, Papa, what a wonderful way to celebrate our wedding! Of course, only time will tell if it really is the end of my horn playing career," said Beate, embracing her father, with glance at Carl and me over his shoulder.

"We have your lodgings in a house nearby all arranged, and we can take you there directly," I said, trying to steer the conversation in another direction. "We'll take along food and wine and have a nice quiet supper and go over our wedding plans."

It was early spring, and still rather cool and rainy. A horse and small cart were waiting in the street with the family's traveling trunks, and Beate, Anna-Maria, and Röslein rode through the wet streets in the cart, while little Carl Nicholaus, and the rest of us walked behind, in high spirits, happy that the Pokornys had arrived home safely. We spent a pleasant evening hearing about their adventures in London and talking about our wedding.

Two weeks later, after much preparation, the celebration of my wedding with Beate Pokorny took place on April 28th, 1780. After a wedding breakfast at the Pokornys' house with a few close friends, the ceremony was held in a small chapel with about thirty guests, all of whom were musician friends. The ceremony itself would have been recognizable to 21st century observers. Common people, which included musicians, couldn't just go out and have special clothes made for a wedding, but instead wore the best clothes they owned for the occasion. For most people these were the clothes they wore to church, but for a musician, it meant our best concert attire.

Carl and I were only allowed to wear our tailor-made orchestra uniforms when performing with the prince's orchestra, but we had our second concert suits for other performances, and in these very successful times for us, we could afford to have them made to order, which meant that unlike many people you would see in the streets of Paris, they fit reasonably well. Beate wore her burgundy velvet concert dress, the one in which she had made her Concert Spirituel solo appearance. She looked absolutely beautiful, with a bouquet of the best flowers available in Paris at that time of year. Her thick dark hair was skillfully arranged with a garland of flowers, and they made her look like the most stunning bride I had ever seen.

One unfamiliar part of the wedding was the placing of the "gimmel ring" on the bride's finger. Carl had coached me on this tradition of the time, and Beate and I had gone to a jeweler in the city to work out the design and have it made. The gimmel ring consists of three parts; one for the groom, one for the bride, and one for the best man. The betrothed couple and the best man wear the rings until the wedding ceremony, on which occasion the three parts are joined together to make a single ring for the bride to wear. The rings for the bride and groom each had a hand, and the third ring had a heart, so that when the three parts were joined together with a clever little hinge and pin, the hands clasped together over the heart. In the middle of the ceremony, after saying our vows, all three of us removed our rings, and with trembling hands, I put the three pieces together and put the ring on Beate's finger.

The ceremony was short, and afterward we all went to the Hôtel Guéméné, where the prince had agreed to let us use the orchestra rehearsal room for the wedding dinner. Unlike Carl's hasty wedding at which only a handful of people took part, this was a real party. Tables were set up around the space where the orchestra normally rehearsed and food and wine were brought in from a nearby inn. In stark contrast to the prince's elaborate dinners, there was no silver on the tables, and no servants, only simple pewter, and every piece was carefully counted upon arrival by the two boys who brought them from the inn, and counted again when they took them back afterward.

There were speeches and toasts by just about everyone, but none were as eloquent and long-winded as that of Franz Pokorny. He talked at length about our future together and the grand adventure we would have here in Paris or wherever the world of music would take us, and ended by emphasizing the fact that after having had a few appearances in Paris and London as a horn player, Beate was now embarking on her life's journey as Madame Palsa, and to commemorate this happy occasion he had composed a new concerto for two horns for us to play with the members of our orchestra as a sort of swan-song to her brief horn playing career.

Beate and I had practiced our parts together, but the rest of the orchestra was reading it for the first time. It was a rather difficult piece for both solo horns, in F major, very high for the first horn, and very acrobatic for the second horn, which was the fashion of the time in horn writing. The accompaniment was string orchestra, two flutes, and two horns, played by Carl and Anna-Maria. We did a first reading, which was rather ragged, and then played it through again, with a higher rate of accuracy all around the second time. This piece remained in the repertoire that Carl and I played for the next ten years, and we got a good deal on mileage out of it on our tours. I was always disappointed that Beate and I never got another chance to perform it in a public concert, due to the attitudes of the time.

The party went on for most of the afternoon and into the evening in high spirits until all the food and wine was gone, and lots of music had been played. The last speech and toast was given by Giovanni

Punto, who could always be counted on to deliver a spectacular finale to any concert or event.

"Meine Damen und Herren! Ladies and Gentlemen! Votre Attention s'il vous plait! Ein Toast pour les newlyweds!"

Punto went on in his own peculiar mixture of French, German, and English for about twenty minutes, talking about my coming from the English colonies and my career in Paris, Beate's love for the horn and her successes as a soloist, how there had never been, in ancient or modern times, a better match than the two of us, and told several stories, including that of the clandestine horn lessons he had given the sisters leading up to Beate's Concert Spirituel appearance. As he raised his glass to toast for about the seventh time, Carl stood up and stepped forward.

"Thank you Giovanni, for the wonderful toast, and in the interest of letting the newly married couple finish the celebration of their wedding before their first anniversary, I propose we move the location of these festivities to our house. It's now time for the last part of the celebration, the bedding ceremony!" This was accompanied by cheers from everyone.

I didn't know exactly what all this could mean, but Beate obviously did, because she was turning several shades of red. Franz, who was sitting next to us saw my bewilderment and explained to the guests.

"Having grown up in the English colonies, and lived in Paris all these years, my newly acquired son-in-law might not know about the tradition in German speaking lands of the wedding party preparing the young couple for bed on their wedding night. Off we go to the Palsa-Türrschmidt residence, where the celebration will continue! Let's clear the rehearsal room, send all of the dishes and silverware back to the inn from which they came, and escort the newlyweds home!"

We left the Hôtel Guéméné and made our way through the streets with Carl and Röslein, Franz and Anna-Maria, and a few close friends who had made up the wedding party. After just a little more celebrating and making a healthy fire in the downstairs hearth, Anna-Maria, who had been the maid of honor, Röslein, and two other women, wives of orchestra musicians, took Beate upstairs to my room and prepared her for bed. The men of the wedding party did the same for me, explaining the whole time the traditional "bedding ceremony" in which the wedding party prepares the newly married couple for their first night together and places them in bed before leaving them for the night.

When word was given from upstairs that Beate and the ladies were ready for us, and the men had undressed me, we went upstairs. I was freezing in nothing but a nightshirt, and feeling highly self-conscious, while everyone else was in full party mode. Hot coals had been placed into two bed warmers that had been borrowed from somewhere - we certainly didn't own such decadent luxuries, and the bed had been warmed up in advance so that it was warm and cozy. Only rich people with servants and bed warmers got into a warm bed in the cold months in the 18th century. The rest of us had to crawl into ice-cold beds and slowly warm them with body heat all winter long. Beate had already been placed in my bed, with the women standing on her side, while the men, standing on my side, tucked me in next to her. Though it was billed as being a solemn occasion, there was plenty of joking and hilarity on the part of the gentlemen, and giggles and whispering on the part of the ladies. Wishing us both well, they finally left us in peace, and went back downstairs to continue their revelry, which traditionally included singing, drinking, and making noise by beating on pots and pans.

This was the first moment the two of us had alone together all day, and our hearts were overflowing with all the things we wanted to share with each other.

"Well!" I said, "I hadn't expected this last part of the day's festivities."

"Dearest Johann!" she said snuggling up to me and kissing me. "It's absolutely the way things are done in Germany and France, and everywhere in Europe. Our friends want to make sure we are comfortably situated before leaving us alone. Yet another tradition that apparently hasn't made it to the colonies where you grew up. But now here we are, at the end of the happiest day of my life, and finally I belong to you!"

"Beate, you've made me the happiest man in the entire world today. I love you more than I can ever express, but I don't want you to think that you belong to me. I would rather think we belong to each other."

"Oh Johann! I love you too with all my heart, and the idea of being married to someone who would think of me as an equal partner and let me play music and have an equal voice in our journey through life is something I couldn't have allowed myself to even fantasize about until I met you. You are so different from any man I've ever met. Different in the way you play music, different in the way you treat those around you, different in how you view women, different in every way! And all of that makes you the only man I've ever met who I could marry."

"Beate, you are a most remarkable woman, full of artistic ambition, thoughtful and intelligent beyond most people I know. I can't imagine ever finding anyone who I would rather spend my life with."

The candle burned low as we spent the rest of the night getting to know each other even better...

Thus began our married life, and the last step in my becoming part of this world - a world into which I had been catapulted a decade earlier. I was now unquestionably here to stay, and had a rich life full of family, friends, and music. These were the thoughts going through my mind as I contemplated the smiling face of my lovely bride in the dim candlelight.

Part III
1781- 1792

Chapter 50

So shuts the marigold her leaves
At the departure of the sun;
So from the honeysuckle sheaves
The bee goes when the day is done;
So sits the turtle when she is but one,
And so all woe, as I since she is gone.
- William Browne of Tavistock,
Memory, early 17th c.

The next two years flew past at an astonishing rate. Beate and Röslein worked their way into the scene of amateur music societies where ladies could perform, mostly at small soirees at private homes. Beate was able to perform regularly in these settings on horn, violin, and viola, and made the best of a world that wouldn't allow her to play professionally, though she played the horn at as high a level as any professional horn player in Paris. Röslein was also in demand for theater productions, being a fine soprano, and was beginning to teach singing and piano to Carl Nicholaus in the hope of getting him into the Notre Dame Cathedral boys' choir in a few years.

For Carl and myself, regular orchestra work alternated with our appearances as soloists in double concertos and as a duo for chamber music concerts. The prince was often absent from Paris during this period on business and sometimes we would have weeks at a time when we could play with other groups. During this time, we were able to polish up our act to an even higher level as a duo and solidify our repertoire of double concertos. Although orchestras and opera companies had to keep presenting new music all the time, and rarely brought out old compositions to play again, traveling soloists had a repertoire of virtuosic pieces they knew and could take from place to place. Our repertoire consisted of pieces by several composers, but by far the concertos we played most often were those of Antonio Rosetti. In 1781 Rosetti made a trip to Paris and brought new compositions with him, and like every other German court composer who came to Paris, wanted to get them played and published[21]. Due to the connection with Carl's family and our visits to Wallerstein a few years earlier, we were Antonio's main contacts in Paris, and helped him find a place to live and put him in contact with the concert organizers for the various series. He brought some of his newest horn concertos with him, and by the time we left Paris we had seven or eight of his compositions, all of which served us well on our travels for the next ten years.

Rosetti stayed in Paris for a few months promoting his compositions and doing some bits of business for the Öttingen-Wallerstein Orchestra and his employer, Prince Kraft-Ernst. During this time we often got together to dine with Rosetti and Punto. These evenings were very pleasant and would most often end with horn trios and quartets. With Beate now a member of the family, we had a good collection of horn trios by Punto, Franz Zwierzina, Rodolph, and Hampel.

Antonio knew, as did many composers of the time, that writing pieces for traveling soloists was the best way to get his name spread far and wide. A composer who stayed in his own town and wrote for the local Hofkapelle, even if he composed top quality music, would stay relatively obscure, so it was important to have people out playing your compositions. It was mutually advantageous for him to send us the latest horn concertos he had written so we could spread his fame by playing them in Paris and wherever else we might go on tour. We were sorry to see him leave Paris, but after he went back to Wallerstein, Rosetti continued to stay in contact and send us new music. In the years from 1780 to 1782, we premiered three new double concertos of his at the Concert Spirituel that he had written for the Wallerstein horn players.

This busy life of music making in one of the most important musical cities in Europe went on unimpaired during this time, with trips to Germany, Holland, and Austria each summer, which was now often a family trip including Beate, Röslein, and the six-year-old Carl Nicholaus. But in the summer of 1782 Carl and I traveled alone during the orchestra vacation due to the fact that Röslein was expecting another child and needed to stay at home in Paris. Beate wouldn't think of leaving her alone and stayed behind as well. The baby was expected at the beginning of September, and we planned to be back in Paris well before that to be there when Carl's new family member arrived.

Around the first of August we had finished performances in several cities in the Palatinate and the Duchy of Württemberg and were working our way back to France slowly by coach on roads that seemed to get worse every year as money to repair them, especially in France, became scarcer.

Our trips as well as our repertoire and arrangements for performances were now well planned out. Our reputation as a duo made it possible to book performances many months in advance, not for a specific date, but within a general period of time. Travel was much too unpredictable to nail down specific dates, but performances could be arranged after we got to our destination. By this time we had a trunk that contained most of our traveling repertoire, horn parts and orchestra parts neatly copied out, with my addition of rehearsal letters or numbers to make rehearsing music with a group more efficient. Why no one had thought of doing this previously was a mystery. We sat through many rehearsals with various groups in which a lot of time was wasted counting measures to find a starting place in the middle of a piece. With trips that were so well planned, it was possible to receive letters from home, but not with a very high degree of reliability. Both our families and the director of the prince's orchestra knew a few specific inns in various cities where we would most likely be staying, and the approximate dates when we would be there, but there were never any guarantees that a letter would find us.

At the beginning of August we were staying at one of these inns in Strasbourg, with only a couple of performances lined up in that city, and Carl was getting anxious to get home to Paris. We sat in the common room having a supper of roast pork, potatoes, and an Alsatian wine, and discussed the rest of the trip and Röslein's condition.

"There were no problems at all when she was pregnant with Carl Nicholaus," Carl said, sipping his wine, "and I'm sure she'll come through this one as easily."

All childbirths were a tense time during this period of history, because if there were any complications, there was very little a midwife or doctor could do, and as a result dying in childbirth was a far too common occurrence. The Infant mortality rate was high in the 18th century and the first few years of life were precarious for all children.

"I can't imagine it will be any more difficult than last time," I said, gnawing the meat off the last bone of the pork that we had very effectively picked clean. "Are you hoping for a boy or a girl this time?"

"I would be happy with either, as long as they're healthy and strong and likely to survive. You'll see when children start coming along; you'll be happy with boys or girls, and incredibly thankful when all goes well."

"In my time, doctors can tell you whether it's going to be a boy or girl, or whether it's going to be twins. They use a technique called ultrasound, which sends sound waves into the mother's belly that can create a picture so you can see the baby clearly. It not only tells you the sex of the baby, but also confirms that everything is going along as it should."

"Sound makes a picture, does it?" said Carl, giving me his usual incredulous look.

"That's right, and then you know what sort of clothes to buy for the child in advance and can start to think about choosing a name."

"I think I like the present way of doing things," said Carl, pouring out the last of the bottle of wine into our glasses. "Your entire 21st century seems a little too organized and predictable. Who would want to know if a baby was going to be a boy or a girl before it is born? What would be the advantage to that?"

"There are lots of advantages. They don't do the ultrasound just because they're curious. It's done to see if there are any complications that the doctors need to know about. If the pictures show some situation that looks like it will be a difficult birth, they may do surgery to remove the baby from the mother, giving it a much greater chance of survival."

"Like the way Julius Caesar was born," said Carl, draining his glass. "I read about that in a book about the twelve Caesars when I was a boy. It sounds dangerous and I still think the modern way of having a midwife present, who knows her business, and letting the whole process happen naturally is the way God intended it."

"Well, you're safe from all of the scientific advances and medical miracles of my time," I said, finishing my wine, "since I don't see that there is any alternative to the natural way."

At that moment the door to the common room opened and in came the rather portly innkeeper, with a wide grin on his face.

"Herr Palsa! It's your lucky day! A coach just arrived with outgoing mail from Paris, and here's a letter for you, addressed in a beautiful feminine hand. News from home no doubt!"

I thanked him, gave him a couple of coins, and took the letter.

"It's from Beate. I would recognize her hand anywhere. Maybe there's news of Röslein's progress," I said opening the envelope and beginning to read. Carl knew immediately that something wasn't right, from the expression on my face. It was a short note, written rather hastily.

My Dearest Johann,
I don't want you to alarm Carl unnecessarily, but I would urge you to return to Paris as soon as possible. Röslein is not doing well, and the midwife is worried that the approaching birth may be a difficult one. She is in much pain and having difficulty eating and sleeping. A doctor has been here, and he fears the worst. It would be best to keep this news from Carl, but please don't schedule any other concerts and come as quickly as you can.
Your loving wife,
Beate

"What does it say? said Carl, rising out of his seat in alarm. "Read it to me! I can tell something is wrong! Is Röslein all right?"

"Beate didn't want me to alarm you Carl, but things are not going well at home. She thinks we should cancel the concerts here and get home as soon as possible." I handed him the letter, which he read through quickly.

"We have to go now! There's no time to lose! Get a pen and some paper from the innkeeper and we'll write a letter to the band we're supposed to play with tonight and tell them an emergency in Paris has called us back and we need to leave right now."

We left the letter for the Strasbourg group that had hired us to play that evening and the next, paid our bill, and hired a rather expensive private coach to take us on our way. Coaches of this sort could be hired from one town to the next, and then you had to find another. Normally by a regular passenger coach it was about five days to Paris, but by spending a lot of money and travelling non-stop, which Carl insisted on, we made it in just over three, arriving at about noon. We had been set down by the coach at an inn in a nearby street and brought into our own street by a single horse and cart with our trunk and the box containing our silver Raoux horns.

The previous few days had been unusually hot, and the traveling had been almost unbearable. Being away in the country was always a brief respite from the smells of Paris, but returning on a sweltering day like this made the stench all the worse. Carl ran into the house and up the stairs, while I followed carrying our boxes with the help of the driver. By the time I got upstairs and into our rooms, Carl was already in their bedroom with Röslein and the midwife.

Beate fell into my arms sobbing.

"Oh, Johann, I'm so glad you were able to come so soon! You must have gotten my letter at the inn in Strasbourg. From your last letter I thought that's where I might reach you."

"How is Röslein?" I asked.

"When I wrote you, several days ago, she was in a lot of pain. I wanted to let you know that you should hasten home as soon as possible, but I didn't want to worry Carl if it was only a sickness that would pass soon. But since then her condition has grown much worse, and neither the doctor nor the midwife expect her to live another day. We've done everything we could to make her more comfortable, but nothing seems to ease the pain."

We went in to where Carl and little Carl Nicholaus were sitting next to the bed in which Röslein was lying. She looked pale and exhausted, and in great pain. It was hot in the room and Carl gently wiped her brow and face with a towel he dipped into a bowl of water that the midwife held. Carl Nicholaus held his mother's hand, and tried, not very successfully, to keep the tears from flowing. He didn't really understand what was happening, but he knew his mother was very ill and that we were all extremely worried.

The doctor was expected at any time, and as we all sat by her, I felt the helplessness of the situation, even more than the rest, because I knew that in my own time, in a 21st century hospital, they would have known exactly what to do to save the mother and child. But here in this damnable 18th century, we were all helpless to do anything, and having had my own rather unsatisfactory experiences with medicine of the time, I was sure the doctor would be just as ineffective as we were.

The doctor arrived late in the afternoon and took over the situation. He and the midwife stayed in the room with Röslein and instructed Beate and me to take care of Carl Nicholaus and stay in the kitchen to prepare food and anything else they needed for the patient. Carl went back and forth fetching things for them and generally staying busy in an effort keep himself from worrying, but it was obvious he was at his wits end and not very hopeful as the evening wore on. We could hear Röslein's groans of pain and all we could do was wait and leave the situation in the hands of the doctor.

It was a long night of sitting up, waiting, and helping as much as we could. A few friends and neighbors stopped by at intervals to see what was happening and offer their help, but there wasn't anything anyone could do. At about midnight we put Carl Nicholaus to bed and stood in the doorway watching the exhausted little boy fall asleep. As he drifted off, his troubled face relaxed into his own world of sweet dreams, leaving the sad reality behind for a few hours.

It seemed like an eternity as the hot summer night crawled slowly toward the dawn, and just as the sun was showing signs of rising over the filthy soot-covered rooftops of Paris, Carl called us into the room.

"It's time," he said simply, and without a word we all knelt next to the low bed on which the dying woman was lying. Carl and Beate recited a Latin prayer together that I didn't know, and in a few short silent minutes, Röslein took her last breath, shuttered slightly, and was still. We knelt silently for a long time, each absorbed in our own thoughts. I don't know what Carl and Beate were thinking, though I sensed the sadness, resignation, and all too familiar inevitability of death in this century, regardless of age or state of health. They knew and accepted that anyone could die at any time. In my own head there was anger at this primitive world, because I knew that even the most basic 21st century medical skills probably could have saved the mother and child. I had a different view of death. In my time death was for the very old, and only rarely for someone my own age. In my mind I didn't want to accept what they saw as a sad, but commonplace occurrence. That isn't to say the loss was any easier for them, or the sadness any less intense. We all just had our own ways of processing death, based on our individual upbringings in our different times.

Chapter 51

Innsbruck, ich muss dich lassen.
Ich fahr dahin mein Straßen,
in fremde Land dahin.
Mein Freude ist genommen,
die ich nit weiß bekommen,
wo ich im Elend bin.
- Heinrich Isaac, 1485

Innsbruck, I must leave you.
For I am traveling the road
to foreign lands.
Deprived of my joy
I know not how to get it back,
and will be in misery.

Röslein's death was hard for all of us, but especially for Carl and his son. For the previous thirteen years, I would have always described Carl as perpetually positive, optimistic, and just simply happy to be doing what he did best, which was playing the horn. But at this point he fell into a melancholy state of disinterest in anything but his son, Carl Nicholaus. The boy was his link to Röslein, and the bond between them grew daily.

We had fewer orchestra services than usual at this point, but many other appearances with groups in Paris, and Carl played as beautifully as ever, but he wasn't as excited about his work or as engaged in life as before. I knew this was a natural reaction to the circumstances, and other than being a good friend, there was nothing else I could do but wait for him to come back to life. Beate took over the care of Carl Nicholaus when we were working. Up until now, we had functioned more as a single family than two families, and therefore the transition to being taken care of by Beate and Carl and me, was easier than it might have been for him.

The reason there were fewer performances for the Prince of Guéméné was that he was in financial trouble and couldn't afford to put on the lavish parties and concerts he had for the previous thirteen years. His impending bankruptcy became more and more obvious to everyone as the year 1783 wore on. Finally, in April, Monsieur Petit, our music director, announced that the performances scheduled for the following week would be our last as an orchestra. The prince was unable to finance either the Hotel de Guéméné or his private orchestra any further and would end the existence of the group with a special concert featuring all the soloists of the orchestra, including concertos for violin, cello, oboe, flute, bassoon, and a concerto for two horns.

The orchestra had been together for nearly fourteen years at this point, and because it was one of the best and highest paid orchestras in Paris, we had some of the finest musicians in the city, and therefore few personnel changes over the years. The result was a very tight band that played cleanly and well in tune, weather conditions in the concert hall permitting, and more precisely and musically than just about any other group that Carl and I played with until we arrived at our last positions in the King of Prussia's orchestra in Berlin a few years later.

On the occasion of this farewell concert, families of the musicians were permitted to be present. This was highly unusual, since nearly all our performances for the previous thirteen years had been for the prince and his family and guests. The audience usually numbered anywhere from fifteen to fifty guests, but this evening the ballroom was packed with over a hundred people who were all there by invitation. I was happy that Beate, who had only heard the orchestra once before, on the night when she filled in for Carl in a double concerto performance, could be there to hear our last concert. Carl and I played our most recent Rossetti double concerto, one that we had premiered at the Concert Spirituel a few months earlier, and all the soloists gave fine performances that night, knowing this was our last opportunity to play together. The evening ended with a speech by the prince, who addressed the guests first, and then his orchestra.

"Messieurs, after tonight's fine performance, and many others over the past thirteen years, it is with a heavy heart that we address you this evening to bid you farewell and express our gratitude for your service and artistry. Having had one of the finest orchestras and chamber ensembles in Paris has been a great joy and a sparkling jewel for the entertainment of our guests of royalty and nobility from France and all the kingdoms of Europe. We have asked our secretary to prepare letters of introduction and recommendation for each of you, which we will sign personally, to aid in gaining employment elsewhere. We wish you all the best for your future artistic endeavors and bid you adieux."

And that was that. Not a word of the reasons for disbanding his orchestra, but he didn't have to explain. All of Paris knew of his embarrassed financial state, and that he had to greatly reduce his household and expenses to survive the upcoming bankruptcy that would probably involve retreating to his estate in Italy and leaving Paris for good.

We walked back home that evening without saying very much. I could tell Carl was not in the mood to make any plans or major life decisions, but we both knew the events of the last month were a major turning point, and that we were ready for a change of scenery.

"We'll talk about what to do next in the morning," said Carl when we got home. "I'm too tired to even think about what to have for breakfast, much less what to do with the rest of our lives. See you in the morning."

I held Beate in my arms as we talked far into the night. We were both feeling alone and fragile, and at the mercy of circumstances beyond our control.

"As long as we are healthy and can play music, everything will be okay," she said. "You and Carl are known far and wide as the best horn soloists anywhere, and there will be opportunities wherever we go."

"I'm sure that's true," I said pulling her closer to me. "We'll stick together and find new positions somewhere. But I'm afraid it means leaving Paris and being on the road for a while until something turns up."

"I'll be with you wherever that may take us," she said, before drifting off to sleep.

The next morning dawned bright and clear, and the air was fresh and clean after a spring shower during the night. It was as if the city of Paris was trying to show us her best side to try and convince us to stay there, but we knew her too well and the ploy wasn't going to lure us. Carl was in a much better mood and the three of us were ready to talk, over a breakfast of coffee, cheese, and toast. Carl started the discussion.

"So ends one of the longest running and most successful private orchestras in Paris, and here we are, top of the heap, and at the top of our game, and out of steady work."

"We've been doing a lot of solo appearances and chamber music," I said, "but we can't live off that for the long term. We need a regular gig, and after the experience of the prince's orchestra, I just can't imagine working in one of the theaters doing twice as much work for half the money with a low-quality group. We're going to have to take our chances somewhere else. If we stay here waiting for another high-end orchestra to hire us, we could wait for years before such a thing even existed and use up all our savings in the meantime."

"The two of you have a good deal of money stored away safely in the bank," said Beate. "You could go on the road for quite a while and not have to worry about earning a lot. It's been wonderful living here with all of the music and art and culture, but I'm ready to leave Paris and get back to the German speaking countries."

Carl was less nostalgic about Paris itself.

"After losing Röslein, and now with the orchestra out of business, there just isn't anything that compels me to want to stay in this filthy city. I really couldn't bear staying here with all the memories associated with this house and the orchestra. It's time to move on to something new."

"But, of course, we stick together," I said. "We are a duo - one of the best on the continent, and we'll take our chances and offer our services together."

"I didn't mean to imply anything else! We started together from the beginning and agreed that we would stay together to the end, whatever that may be."

"We hang together, or surely we shall hang separately!" I said, bringing out an old quote, though it wasn't quite as strong a statement translated into German. "Something an American guy said."

"Your friend Benjamin Britten?"

"No, it wasn't him, and Britten wasn't a friend of mine, or American. I just played his music. Very good stuff. No, it was my friend Benjamin Franklin. Remember him?"

“How could I forget him? Did he say that when we went to his soirée?”

“No. It was on another occasion.”

“Well, I think it’s decided that we’ve done everything we could possibly accomplish in Paris. We need to find a new situation and some new scenery, and hopefully someplace not as crowded and dirty and smelly as Paris.”

Carl went into his room and fetched the map of Europe and the Holy Roman Empire he had bought several years before when we had planned our first tour. We spent the rest of the morning plotting out a route that would take us into Germany, going through a few cities and courts that would be likely to have us play concerts.

Chapter 52

From C. Türrschmidt, 50 Duos, op. 3, 1795

It was easy to leave Paris. We gave a few household things to friends, packed a couple of large trunks, two Kerner orchestra horns, two Raoux orchestra horns, our pair of silver solo horns, along with a couple of violas and a violin, and began our escape. It only took a couple of days to arrange everything, pay any outstanding bills, and go to the bank to get traveling money. We left the bulk of our savings in the bank, since you didn't want to go on the road in those days carrying your life savings in cash.

It was the first week of May when we left Paris by coach. As with our other tours, which had all been done in the summer months, the weather was gorgeous, and though traveling was never safe, or easy, or comfortable, it seemed like Paris was releasing us willingly to go our ways and find our fortunes elsewhere. We hadn't taken the time, in our haste to leave, to write to anyone in advance, and therefore we thought the opportunities to play would be more difficult to come by, but we did have the advantage of a reputation in musical circles that had developed over the previous fourteen years and had spread throughout Europe. This meant that in a few places as we traveled through France and into the German speaking Holy Roman Empire, we were welcomed with open arms, and a few performances were organized on short notice, but more often the answer would be, "We are very honored to have such famous Paris virtuosi visit here, but unfortunately we don't have the money or the musical forces to have you perform a concert." In some places a wealthy landowner or businessman would have a house concert, but all in all it was disappointing to go on the road in this way, just taking our chances in whatever town we happened to visit.

After a few weeks of working our way out of France and wandering around the cities and towns of the Palatinate and into Hessen-Cassel, we were all getting tired of living in inns or local private houses of various levels of cleanliness. Carl and I had done this sort of travel before, living out of a trunk and taking our chances with whatever questionable food was available, but we could tell it was beginning to take its toll on Beate and Carl Nicholaus. We couldn't afford to have their health deteriorate while traveling, so Carl decided to take some decisive action and wrote to a couple of people he knew in the orchestra of the Landgraf of Hessen-Cassel in the hope of going there for an extended stay. The Landgraf, Friederich II, had a fine court orchestra where we might arrange a few concerts of a higher level than we had been doing, and also make some valuable connections that would help us decide where to go next, and eventually find something permanent. We slowly made our way in that direction through the German countryside, and by the end of July we found ourselves in the relatively large city of Cassel.

Cassel, which in modern times is spelled Kassel, was large by 18th century standards, with a population of just over 17,000. The city is situated on the Fulda River, and the easiest way to get there back in those days was by boat from Felsberg, which was how we arrived. Cassel was a walled city, most of which is on the north side of the river, and a smaller portion on the south side. Among its famous buildings and gardens are the Martinskirche, the Karlsaue Park, and the Orangerie Palace. The streets must have been laid out all at once, because they were arranged in neat squares, more organized than any other 18th century city I visited.

Upon arriving we thought it best to get in touch with some of the court orchestra musicians, and decided to look up Johann Braun, the concertmaster of the orchestra, and a well-known violin soloist. Braun had been in Paris a few years earlier and we had gotten to know him when he played a violin concerto in a concert in which we had also been soloists.

It was never easy to locate someone in a city in which you had just arrived. There were no phone books or directories, and the best thing to do was to go to the *Rathaus*, or town hall, and see if anyone could direct you to some musician, who would then probably know the person you were looking for. In this case we were dropped off at the Rathaus by a hired wagon from the dock on the river where the boat had let us off with our traveling trunks and instruments. After talking to about six people at the Rathaus who were way too busy with important business to talk to anyone who spoke German in an accent other than the local dialect, we were directed to a tavern where someone thought the owner's brother or son or cousin was a musician. It turned out to be the son, who took piano lessons from a local teacher who knew a violinist in the court orchestra, and by looking up that person, who was much more friendly and helpful after we told him we were from Paris, and were friends of Braun, we found out where he lived. And that's how you found your way around as a traveler in the 18th century, only it was rarely as simple as what I just described, and often meant spending the first night in a new city in the common room of a tavern that didn't have any available sleeping rooms, sharing the room with an interesting and colorful slice of the local population that was there drinking until late into the night.

We were more fortunate this time though and knocked on the door of concertmaster Braun's house late in the afternoon. Having not received our letter, which in true 18th century fashion, arrived about a week after we did, he was genuinely surprised to see us, and had to ransack his memory to figure out where he had met us.

"Oh yes! The famous Waldhorn duo from Paris! I remember you well from the Concert Spirituel, where you played the most astounding double concerto by Rosetti from Wallerstein. You played the horn using chromatic notes in a way I had never heard before. It's a great pleasure to see you again! What brings you to Cassel?"

"Well, the fact is that we've left Paris, probably for good," I said. "The Prince of Guéméné, for whom we worked, fell into financial difficulties and had to disband his private orchestra. Between that and the worsening state of life in Paris, we thought it was time to head elsewhere to look for a new situation."

Carl took up the story from there.

"The prince isn't the only one who is having financial troubles. There is a lot of unrest in Paris. The common people and nobility alike, seem to be struggling more than when we arrived there fourteen years ago, and that has made for a lot of tension between the two classes. The only stable musical scene is at court, and there are even rumors of political trouble brewing that could ultimately put those musicians out of work. The deteriorating musical scene, and the death of my wife in childbirth, seemed like clear signals that it was time to go back to friendlier German-speaking lands."

I couldn't add to the discussion that I knew for certain that Paris was going to turn into a much more unpleasant place in just a few years when the French Revolution began. I had shared some of that with Carl, but not being a scholar on the subject, I didn't really know much more about what would take place, and when, than most 21st century students learn in a European history class. I just knew that the Bastille would be stormed in July of 1789, and we didn't want to be around during the years before that as tensions built.

"I'm very sorry to hear of the death of your wife," Braun replied, "and from reports we've received here, and what you say now, it seems like a good time to come home to Germany. I have only fond memories of my few months stay in Paris, the quality of music there, and the many wonderful musicians with whom I had the opportunity to work, including yourselves. I do hope you will be able to stay in Cassel for a while. We have a fine orchestra with musicians from all over the Empire that the Landgraf, Friedrich II, has enticed to come here for good salaries."

"Do you think there are possibilities for a performance or two with the Hofkapelle of the Landgraf?" I asked. "We have a trunk full of concertos by various composers, with orchestra parts, that could be put together in a rehearsal or two."

"I think there is every possibility of arranging such a thing," said Braun. "I'll talk to our Kapellmeister and see what we can do. In the meantime, you will need a place to sleep. There is an inn just around the corner with comfortable rooms. You'll find musicians of the Hofkapelle there just about every evening, and you can get to know some of them."

"That sounds perfect!" said Carl. "We're exhausted from several days on the road. A meal, a mug of beer, and a comfortable bed would be just the thing. And it would be nice to meet some of your musicians."

Braun went to fetch his hat, and then escorted Carl, Beate, Carl Nicholaus, and me to the *"Gasthof zum Steinernen Schweinchen,"* (The Stone Piglet Tavern) which true to its name had a stone pig next to the street door. We were shown into a couple of neat sleeping rooms by the innkeeper, and then sat down in the common room where we enjoyed a meal of pork roast, roasted potatoes, and a fine beer, brewed right on the premises. There were a couple of violinists, an oboist, and a bassoonist there that evening whose acquaintance we made, and we settled in to wait for further word from Herr Braun about playing with the orchestra.

It wasn't until the evening of the next day that he stopped in to see us.

"Good evening, gentlemen! I talked to our Kapellmeister at rehearsal this morning and told him of your arrival. He was not enthusiastic about horns. He said he had some bad experiences with traveling Waldhorn players in the past and used some rather uncomplimentary words to describe your fine instrument, which I won't bother to relate to you. I tried to explain that you are two of the finest and quite a bit more refined than your average traveling horn players. But he is of the opinion that horns are a necessary evil in the orchestra and should remain in the background just to add color to the wind section, and never be allowed to play as a concertante instrument. I'm going to keep working on him to give you a chance. I'm sure if the Landgraf hears you, he will be impressed with your artistry and technique."

"Maybe there is a way to have the Landgraf hear us in chamber music or duos," said Carl. "Are there chamber concerts in which we might take part?"

"The Landgraf has private chamber music evenings, but everything is arranged through the Kapellmeister, so you can't get on one of those programs without his approval. But I have an idea that might work, though it will take a little time. As I said yesterday, there are always a few musicians here at the *Schweinchen* every evening, and within a few days, just about every member of the orchestra will stop in for a drink at some point. Let's talk to the innkeeper and see if he would let you play duets in the common room in the evenings in trade for a supper. As the musicians get to know you and your playing, word will spread, and if we can get the Kapellmeister to come to hear you, we may be able to change his opinion about horns."

We approached the innkeeper, a jolly, red-faced man, who wore an apron that had probably once been white, and he was absolutely on board with the idea.

"*Jawohl!* I'm happy to have some music in the common room for the entertainment of the guests! I'll even print an announcement to be put in the window saying that there will be Waldhorn music every evening this week."

He was rather proud of his ability to write, and made a neatly printed sign that read: *"This week, at the Steinernen Schweinchen – Waldhorn duets by two famous masters from Paris – every evening at seven o'clock."*

Chapter 53

There is nothing which has yet been contrived by man by which so much happiness is produced as by a good tavern or inn.
- Samuel Johnson, from James Boswell, Life of Johnson, 1791

Starting that very evening we played duets off and on for a couple of hours, and Beate joined us for trios. The first night there were only a few people, including three or four musicians in the common room, drinking beer and talking. As so often happened when we played duos or trios, they actually stopped and listened. Unless one had heard us, Punto, or just a few other horn players who were doing chromatic hand-horn playing, this was a totally new sound. After a couple of *Petit airs* as they were called in Paris, consisting of minuets, slow airs, and rondos, the musicians in the room wanted to see how we were able to play chromatically on the horns, and asked us to play more.

The next night there were more people there, including the two horn players from the orchestra, whose names were Borliebner and Klimmenhagen. They were very friendly and wanted to know all about the current developments in horn playing in Paris, and our hand stopping technique.

The third night the common room was packed, and the innkeeper did as much business as he had the previous week. It wasn't until the fourth night that Herr Braun showed up with Kapellmeister Rochefort, director of the orchestra and opera. He looked skeptical as he sat down at a table and ordered a beer. At that point we played the six little duets that Mozart had written for us for the party at Legros' house after a Concert Spirituel performance in Paris in 1778. As we played, Kapellmeister Rochefort's features began to soften, and after a couple of pieces, he raised his glass and called out to us.

"Bravo! Wunderbar! I've never heard anything like it!" We played a few more duets by various composers, after which Braun brought us to the table at which they were sitting. Rochefort stood up and shook our hands.

"Welcome to Cassel! What a great pleasure to hear you play! Members of the Hofkapelle who were here the past few evenings convinced me that it would be worth my while to come and hear you myself, and I must say, it is astounding what you are able to do on your horns. Herr Braun had suggested last week that you play a concerto with the Hofkapelle, but I was not enthusiastic, given some previous experiences I have had with horn players. But this evening you have absolutely changed my mind! The Landgraf will be very pleased to hear you in a concert, and I imagine he will be as taken with your skill and artistry as we all have been. Will you join us for this week's concert?"

"We would be happy to play for the entertainment of the Landgraf," said Carl. "Your orchestra enjoys a fine reputation everywhere and it would be a great honor to play with you and with such an outstanding group."

This seemed to please him even more, and it was true; the Cassel Hofkapelle did have a reputation as being a top-notch group.

"And in anticipation of having you perform with us," said Braun, "I have sketched out the score to a concerto for two horns that you can play with us. I believe your silver horns are in the key of E, is that right?"

"We have a pair of silver solo horns in E, made by a famous Paris maker," I replied, "and also Viennese orchestra horns with crooks that can play in all keys. We can play whatever you would be so kind as to compose for us, but E is our best solo key."

"Then a concerto in E major it shall be!" exclaimed Braun.

The next week was a busy one. In addition to working with Braun on his double concerto, trying out sections of it to make sure it was playable, we continued playing each evening at the Steinernen Schweinchen. The proprietor was so enthusiastic about our music, and the large amount of business that it brought to his house, that he offered us our meals and rooms for free as long as we wanted to stay if we kept on playing each evening. So, we kept on playing.

The concerto that Braun composed for us was not terribly difficult technically, but idiomatically written for the horns with some nice melodies distributed democratically between the two horn parts. After the first rehearsal Kapellmeister Rochefort was convinced that the whole idea of having horn soloists was going to be successful, and since Braun's concerto was rather easy for the orchestra to put together, it was decided that we would also play one of our Rosetti double concertos on the program. This gave us some more virtuosic material to play for the entertainment of the Landgraf and his guests. Concerts here were much like those in Mannheim. The performances were not open to the public, but rather only to the family, court, and guests of the Landgraf, who would send out invitations to a select group of friends and important people in Cassel.

The orchestra was about the size of the group we had played with in Paris for thirteen years, and almost as skillful and musical. We got to know them all, and especially the wind players during that first week of rehearsals. The horn players were surprisingly friendly and welcoming, and we spent a good deal of time with them, talking shop and playing together. They were of the old school of orchestral players, quite skillful, but played open horn exclusively. The orchestra and wind band music they generally played didn't require hand-stopped notes, and though they knew how to produce them, they were not part of their regular way of playing the horn. The orchestra had pairs of horns in B flat alto, F, and D for them to play on, and crooks to take these down by half, and whole steps to play the other keys, in the same way that we could add a pigtail crook to our fixed pitch solo horns in E if we needed to play in E flat. Tuning bits of various lengths would allow us to tune to groups in different cities. During my entire 18th century career, I never knew what pitch level we were playing at, since there were no electronic tuners to tell us, only that this group was higher or lower than that group. On a couple of occasions, with a group that played very low, we had to copy out new orchestra accompaniments in F major, because our solo horns in E were called F horns at the local pitch level. Pitch was a complicated mess, especially for wind players in those days, and a real challenge for those who traveled.

Rehearsals went smoothly and we quickly earned the respect of not only the Kapellmeister, but also the rest of the orchestra, and they were doing their best to give us a good accompaniment and polish up the pieces for the concert. As in many other places, performances took place in a large room in the Landgraf's palace, with the orchestra in the middle and the audience sitting at tables all around, eating and drinking, playing cards, and talking. The audience was enthusiastic, and as attentive and polite as any 18th century audience, which is to say that they didn't listen terribly carefully, but cheered and clapped with great enthusiasm after each piece. As was usually the case with evenings like this, it was a long program of symphonies, arias, chamber pieces and concertos. Our concertos were sandwiched between several other pieces with lots of time in between for people to eat and drink. All together it was a successful performance, both for us and for the orchestra. Kapellmeister Rochefort seemed very pleased, Braun was overjoyed at the success of his horn concerto, and we made a lot of new friends among the orchestra of twenty members. Friedrich II, Landgraf of Hessen-Cassel sent his compliments on our performance through Kapellmeister Rochefort, and there followed a pleasant evening of beer with the wind players at the Steinernen Schweinchen to round out the festivities of the day.

The next morning we sat in the common room, slightly hung over, drinking coffee from the steadily dwindling supply I had brought from Paris, and discussing our future plans.

"A regular position with the orchestra here doesn't seem to be a possibility," said Carl. "Borliebner and Klimmenhagen are perfectly fine horn players, and I wouldn't want to suggest to anyone here that we displace them."

"Certainly not," I replied, "but it was still worth the effort to come here and see what the situation was, and we were able to get a solo performance and a new concerto out of it. But it looks like we'll have to head elsewhere and keep putting out feelers for a place that needs a pair of horns. Something will turn up eventually, but it feels as though we're going to be on the road for a while."

"It's too bad," added Beate. "I liked the town and could see some possibilities for teaching music lessons and getting an amateur music scene going here. You'll have to be part of the world of traveling virtuosi for now, but you can only do that so long before it starts to wear you down. A nice long-term position and a permanent place to live would be wonderful."

Beate was right, we were well equipped to make a living as traveling soloists, but it was a hard life and there were many out there trying to make a go of it. You had to have a solo repertoire that you could play well at a moment's notice, which we had, and a reputation that would help you get concerts wherever you went. But those kinds of musicians generally burnt out after just a few years. Some of our friends and acquaintances, such as Carl Stamitz and his brother Anton, were beginning to show signs of wear from many years on the road. We really didn't want to end up destroying our health and our love of the music by having no particular home base.

We were just discussing where our next destination would be when a messenger came into the common room with a note inviting us to the Landgraf's palace to meet with his highness and the Kapellmeister at eleven o'clock that morning.

"Please take this note back to the palace and tell his Highness that we will be there at the appointed time," Carl said, writing out a short reply accepting the invitation and handing it to the servant, who immediately put it in his hat and left.

Carl turned to us. "Well, this could only mean that the Landgraf is interested in taking us into his service, but as I said, I won't be part of putting anyone else out of work. We'll go and see him, and just as we had to do in Mannheim, we will thank the Landgraf for his good opinion of us and decline his offer, no matter how generous it may be."

We finished our breakfast, put on our hats, and walked over to the Landgraf's palace, which was only a few minutes away in this relatively small town. We were taken into a highly ornamented sitting room with tapestried walls and chandeliers and were invited to sit down in two overstuffed carved chairs. Kapellmeister Rochefort was already there.

"Good morning gentlemen," he said standing to shake our hands. "Once again I would like to thank you for your fine performance last night. The audience was delighted to hear how you could play chromatically on your instruments. We were transported by the sweet melodic playing in the high range, Herr Palsa, and the technical agility and precision of your low passages, Herr Türrschmidt."

We thanked him for his kind words and were just about to sit down when the Landgraf himself, Friedrich II entered the room, and as always in the presence of nobility, we remained standing until invited to sit.

"Gentlemen, good day to you," he said rather formally. "We've invited you here this morning to propose that you join our musical establishment. Please take a seat and listen to our proposal. Your reputation as soloists and as members of the orchestra of the Prince of Guéméné is not unknown to us here. We understand that you have left Paris and are now at liberty and traveling until you can find a permanent situation. We would like to offer you that opportunity here in Cassel, where we have taken the greatest pains to assemble a fine group of artists from all over the Empire."

"And a fine group it is, your Excellency," said Carl. "As fine a group as we have played with anywhere. But there is one point we would like to make clear before we go any further in the discussion. It would be a great honor to play with this group of fine musicians, but if it means that the current horn players in your orchestra would be let go, we would, out of respect for them, have to decline your offer and continue on in our search for a new situation."

"That is very noble of you, and a sign of high character to be concerned about the well-being of Herrn Borliebner and Klimmenhagen, who are outstanding members of our orchestra, and with whom we are extremely happy. No, you misunderstand our proposal. We have in addition to the orchestra performances, many chamber music concerts here in our private residence, involving a small group of musicians, most, but not all, of whom are members of the full orchestra. We also have our chamber musicians perform as soloists with the orchestra in festival weeks in the summer months, and it is in this capacity, as members of our private chamber music and as soloists that we wish to engage you."

"This is a great relief, your Excellency," I said, speaking for the first time, "to hear that you would add us to this smaller group and retain your horn players. In that case, I think I can speak for both Herr Türrschmidt and myself, that such a position would be worlds beyond any situation we could have dreamed of."

"We are glad to hear that you are enthusiastic about our proposal. We understand that as soloists, like others in our service, you need to travel, and we would encourage you to continue to do so, not only for your own artistic satisfaction, but to spread the reputation of our musical establishment. Here are the terms of our proposal to you. You will be required to be in Cassel a least half of the year, and we will determine when those periods will be for the purpose of special chamber music and solo performances that will be planned well in advance. The other half of the year you will be free to travel wherever you would like to perform as soloists. Kapellmeister Rochefort will need to know how to contact you wherever you are in case we need to call you back to Cassel. For making yourselves available on those terms, and for taking our musical reputation to other courts and cities, we will match your Paris salary, and of course, you will be entitled to keep all the money you earn on your travels. May we come to an agreement on those terms?"

"With the greatest of pleasure we accept your Excellency's most generous offer!" said Carl. "We thank you for the opportunity of playing for you in the company of such a fine group of artists."

"Excellent! And we look forward to enjoying your music at the earliest opportunity. My secretary will now take you to his office to make the final arrangements and draw up a letter of agreement for your service. And here is a small token in appreciation of your concert last night. Good day!"

With that he handed us each a small silk purse, rose and left the room. Immediately the secretary entered and led us to another room where he drafted a contract for us in a beautiful round hand with a quill pen on parchment. Though it was hard to compare the value of the money in this area to that of France, and the cost of living in Cassel to that of Paris, the amount he named seemed to be equal to, or better than, our previous Paris salaries. We left the palace quite dazed by the swiftness of the entire interview with the Landgaf, which didn't last more than ten minutes, and also by the efficient, businesslike secretary who seemed quite accustomed to drawing up papers of this sort.

Carl first broke the silence.

"Was I just dreaming, or were we just offered a gig as soloists and chamber musicians with half the year free to travel and do solo concerts, and all at a handsome salary?"

"Unless I had exactly the same dream, I think it all really happened," I said. "We are now set with our dream job and we don't have to worry about the effects of constant travel on all four of us. We can now make a stable existence for ourselves and for Beate and Carl Nicholaus."

"And we can take our time to arrange our tours well in advance," Carl said, finishing my thought, "rather than the usual seat-of-the-pants trips in which you go somewhere with no particular expectations and hope something turns up."

We came back to the Steinernen Schweinchen to tell Beate what had taken place. She was overjoyed to hear the news and glad that her dream of having a place to settle down, create a home, and develop her own musical scene of performing and teaching was becoming a reality.

Chapter 54

When a man is tired of London, he is tired of life,
for there is in London, all that life can afford.
- Samuel Johnson, from James Boswell,
Life of Johnson, 1791

We spent two blissful years in Cassel playing music with the other chamber musicians and orchestra members and traveling to other courts in Germany and Austria to play double concertos. Beate didn't waste any time in finding other women who were skillful musicians with whom she established a fine amateur chamber music scene. She also assembled a group of children in the town to whom she gave piano and violin lessons. The two other horn players from the orchestra, Borliebner and Klimmenhagen, lived in the same street, and became good friends. Often, we would have them over for a meal and horn quartets, of which we had several among our scores. Beate joined in playing with us, and they soon found out that she could do everything on the horn that Carl and I could do.

"How did you learn to do that, Frau Palsa?" asked Klimmenhagen after our first evening of playing trios and quartets with them.

"Lessons with Punto, and lots of practice!"

From then on Borliebner and Klimmenhagen had the utmost respect for Beate, never before having encountered a woman who could play the horn at such a high level, and in the new chromatic style.

In the summer of 1785, just after arriving home from a trip to Koblenz where we played with the orchestra of the Elector, we received an invitation from Carl Friedrich Abel, the famous viola da gamba player, to go to London to take part in the famous Salomon Hanover Square Concerts the following spring. The opportunity to appear on this prestigious series was difficult to pass up, and more so because Carl and I had never played together in England. Beate had visited London with her father and sister in 1780 and was enthusiastic about the idea.

"We really must go to London! Father and Anna-Maria and I had such a wonderful time there. The Salomon concerts you and Carl have been invited to are of the highest quality, and there is such an active amateur music scene. We could make an extended trip of it and stay for a few months and take part in all sorts of music!"

Beate had played as soloist in a few concerts in London and had always dreamed of going back and taking advantage of the musical scene in a city that was slightly more open to the idea of female musicians. This was because in addition to the professional musicians, there were many groups in which amateurs and professionals played together, and any number of wealthy people who sponsored house concerts and other events involving music.

Carl was enthusiastic too, having made a trip to London with his father a few years earlier.

"I think it's a great idea. We'll ask the Landgraf for a leave of absence to go there and see what sort of opportunities come up in addition to the Salomon concerts."

We asked for leave to go before replying to Abel's letter. The Landgraf was in favor of us taking part in the London concerts, but said he couldn't possibly let us take such an extended trip until the end of the year, since he had several musical events he wanted us to take part in during the winter concert season. After that we could go to England as long as we were back in Cassel for the big music festival he was planning for August of 1786. The time frame seemed to work, so we wrote to Abel that we could be in London sometime after the first of the year and would be happy to take part in the concerts.

Through the fall we wrote more letters to concert organizers in London, and soon got a handful of favorable replies, saying that we should look them up as soon as we arrived there, and they would work us into their programs at some point. I wrote the letters in English, and the replies that we received all complimented my command of the English language in the way that you would compliment a foreigner who was using your language properly, but awkwardly and unidiomatically. I had no idea how unidiomatic my English was going to be until we actually got to England and I had the opportunity to try it out. I understood them only very poorly at first, and they were at a loss to make out much of what I said.

Like the groups in most cities at the time, the London orchestras and chamber series didn't determine programs in advance, but would most often put the programs together the week before, or even during rehearsals. The difference between 21st century programing and 18th century programing was that in modern times, there is a canon of standard literature, and an audience would know months in advance that they could hear Beethoven's 9th Symphony, or Handel's Messiah on a specific date, while in the 18th century, when all music was new music, the most advance notice the audience got was an announcement the week before that they could hear "A New Grand Symphony by Dr. Boyce and arias from the most popular operas", or in our case "Concertos and Duets performed by two visiting French Horn Players, newly arrived from Germany". This is how we appeared on a concert announcement for our first London appearance at the Anacreontic Society, a weird mixture of amateur musicians, who paid to play in the group, and professional players who got paid to lead the sections.

In the midst of these preparations, we received another invitation to go to Vienna to play with the Orchestra of the Vienna Court Theater sometime early in the summer, and though the schedule would be tight, we agreed to go directly from London to Vienna in May or June, play some concerts there and be back in time for the Landgraf's music festival. In those days, we thought of it as a tight schedule if we needed to be in London early in the year, in Vienna by May or June, and back in Cassel by August. Due to the long and unpredictable travel, you didn't just pop in for a visit to some far-off place; you often went there and lived for a couple of months.

We finished up all the chamber music evenings the Landgraf had planned before letting us leave for England, and early in January were on our way, at about the most miserable time of year that could be imagined for traveling. We made our way across Germany and into France, and gradually to Calais, where we could take a ship across the English Channel to Dover. We still had current traveling papers and documentation that would allow us to travel relatively trouble-free through France, which would not be the case even a couple of years later as the revolution was approaching. The biggest difficulty of going across borders was being thoroughly searched and questioned by customs officers, though all they were interested in at that point were valuables that we might be transporting from one country to another that could be taxed. Usually when we identified ourselves as traveling musicians, they assumed immediately that we didn't have anything of value. The only thing that drew their attention was the pair of solid silver horns, but we got through alright with them and only had to pay small bribes to the customs people.

After extremely uncomfortable coach rides in the cold and rainy weather, dirty inns, or whatever lodging we could pay exorbitant highway robbery prices for, we finally arrived at Calais. Both Beate and Carl Nicholaus had bad colds, and we were all tired of traveling and happy to be only a couple of days out of London now. After a damp cold night at an inn near the docks, we went early in the morning to book our passage on the packet ship across the English Channel. There were no boats leaving the next morning, so we booked passage on one for the following day, only to be informed the next morning that the winds weren't right and a storm appeared to be coming up, and the ship wouldn't leave until the next day. The 21st century reader will undoubtedly think; "How was anyone able to do any kind of business when you couldn't rely on getting anywhere on any sort of predictable schedule?" The fact was that everyone knew about the unreliability of travel and built it into their business. There was almost no activity, including concerts, that couldn't be put off by a day, or a week, or a month for that matter if you had to travel to get there. News was much the same; a battle, coronation, or death of a prominent person in Austria or Italy would make it into the London newspapers two or three weeks after the fact and still be considered "the latest news."

After three days of delay in Calais, we finally boarded the ship for the journey, which took about six hours that day. It was a rough day on the channel, and poor little ten-year old Carl Nicholaus was seasick the entire time, and for a few hours after. He spent most of the time with his head over the rail at the side of the ship, Beate holding onto him to prevent his tumbling overboard. When we did arrive, the ship was not able to go into the harbor for some reason that no one who we talked to was able to fully explain, and we had to pay some very rough looking seamen who came out in a boat to bring us and our belongings into the harbor.

We arrived at the docks in Dover, only to be worked over by yet another set of customs officials, who when told we were musicians, left us in relative peace, thinking we probably had little to offer in the way of things to tax. The silver Raoux horns, as well as the pair of brass Kerner horns attracted their attention, but a couple of silver coins we had picked up somewhere along the way, and weren't quite sure of the value of, got us through. This reminded us that the French and German money we had would have to be taken to a bank to be changed into British pounds.

It was late afternoon when we were finally free to travel onward. The way to get to London was by the stagecoach, which would get us to Canterbury by the evening, then on the following morning going through Rochester and arriving in London that night. I detail this portion of our journey to illustrate the tedious and inconvenient nature of travel at this time in history, though the 18th century traveler had nothing else to compare it to, and therefore accepted the whole business as absolutely normal, which it was.

And finally, we were in the metropolis of London. Every city I visited in the 18th century had a different and distinctive smell to it. Paris smelled of sewage and perfume, Cassel smelled like there was a bakery and a meat market around every corner, Berlin, where we lived later smelled like stables and farm animals, and London had its own peculiar smell. It was that of breweries, probably because there was a pub in every street that was continually brewing beer. As always, you noticed it when you first arrived in a city, and then it became normal and you forgot about it. I don't remember 21st century cities having such distinct, recognizable aromas.

We had only a vague notion of where we were going, in the form of an address in the letter from Friedrich Abel, and another from William Park, a London oboist. We stayed the first evening at an inn in Grosvenor Square where the coach let us out, and it being late in the day, had to wait until the following morning to search out our connections. Unlike many other concert tours we took in our early years together, this time we were not arriving in this city not knowing a soul and having to convince the local musicians who we were. This time we had been invited and were expected. We sent a messenger from the inn to the address of Abel to see if he would be home that day, and within a couple of hours, shortly after noon, received a reply asking us to visit him at four o'clock in the afternoon, and giving us very detailed directions to his house from our inn. Without these directions, with their many landmarks in place of street names, it would have taken us days of wandering the streets of London to find him. We left all our worldly possessions in the care of Beate and Carl Nicholaus at the inn, and Carl and I set out toward Abel's house.

My first impression of London was that it was a cleaner city than any I had visited before. The streets were swept regularly, and some of them were paved with bricks, making them easier to navigate than those of Paris. It wasn't until we were on our way home later that evening, that we experienced another surprise, - street lamps! The city had lamps in many of the streets that dimly lit one's way when going about at night.

Abel lived only a few minutes away, but his directions took us through a winding maze of small streets and lanes, some paved with cobblestones, and some just muddy paths. We got to his house to find that William Park, the oboist, and violin virtuoso Johann Peter Salomon were there as well to greet us.

Since Abel and Salomon were German, the conversation proceeded in that language, under the assumption that Carl and I would be most comfortable communicating that way. Park understood very little of the conversation, but Abel and Salomon translated for him. I kept out of the English conversation, since the others probably assumed I couldn't understand English very well, having not yet heard my made-up story of having been born and raised in 18th century Boston. I was also reluctant to speak English very much until I had heard a little more of how it was spoken in London at this point in history. Though I did my best to imitate what I heard, when I did speak English on this trip, I would always receive odd looks and smiles at my quaint and unorthodox use of the King's English. The one thing that made it easy for me to be convincing in German speaking lands in the 18th century was that there were so many hundreds of local dialects in German, and people would just assume that you "weren't from around here". In England it was even easier, because everyone assumed I was a foreigner who wasn't supposed to use their language properly. The way people spoke in London was just one of the many different regional dialects in the British Isles.

These three men seemed to be the organizers of Salomon's concerts, which were held in Hanover Square. This meeting was meant to fill us in on what they had in mind for our stay in London, and to make arrangements.

"Gentlemen," began Salomon. "Welcome to the London musical world! We are delighted to have you here to play in the Hanover Square concerts this season. There will be six concerts, beginning on the second of March, and we would like to feature you right away in the first programs. What sort of music do you have with you?"

Carl took up the conversation.

"We brought all of our traveling repertoire and can play double horn concertos by Rosetti and Josef Fiala from the Öttingen-Wallerstein Hofkapelle, and a few others. We have clear, well-copied orchestra parts for each, and lots of small unaccompanied duets."

"Excellent! said Abel. "We should be able to make some very interesting programs, and of course you can play in the symphony and aria accompaniments when there are horn parts. It was my idea to invite you, having heard of your reputation for many years. We wanted to add some new artists from the continent to this year's programs. Mr. Park has also arranged for you to give lessons to the horn players of the King's band and a few other London horn players. Horn playing here is not what it is in France and the German States. Punto was here a few years ago and tried to teach them about his method of playing in tune, using the hand, but in the 1770s there was resistance to the new methods. We hope that fifteen years later you will have better success in bringing them around to your playing techniques."

"That sounds very agreeable," I said, "since it's just the beginning of February, and we won't have anything else to do until the concerts in March."

"Oh, on the contrary, there are plenty of other things you can do to warm up the London concert-going public to your horn playing, and advertise our concerts," said Salomon. "We've already spoken to the Anacreontic Society, and a couple of other amateur groups who would be happy to have you play on their concerts, as well as a few private chamber music concerts at the homes of wealthy patrons of music in London and at coffee houses in the city. You are our guests, and we'll make sure you won't be bored while you're in London!"

Here Park joined in on the conversation in English.

"We also want to advertise the fact that you'll be playing on your solid silver Paris-made horns.[22] That will be a big selling point for the audience. They love things of that sort and will come out to see fancy instruments as happily as to hear the music. You will be playing on them?"

"Yes," I replied. "The silver horns are in E, and if the pitch here matches them fairly well, we'll do fine with our double concerti, which are all in E. If the pitch level here in London is too high or too low for our horns, we also have parts for each piece in E flat and F, and then we use tuning bits to match the group. We also have brass orchestra horns with crooks for tutti orchestra and chamber music."

"Oh! You speak excellent English for a foreigner," said Park in surprise. "Where did you learn to speak so fluently?"

"In the American Colonies. It's a long story. I'll tell you all about it sometime."

Though we didn't know it until now, these three had made all the contacts we needed, and had paved the way for a busy time in London by presenting us in advance to the London concert organizers and groups as a grand opportunity to have a state-of-the-art German horn duo for their concert audiences this season.

Chapter 55

To Anacreon, in Heav'n, where he sat in full glee
A few sons of harmony sent a petition
That he their inspirer and patron would be.
- Anacreontic Song, John Stafford Smith/Ralph Tomlinson, The Vocal Magazine, 1778

Over the next few days we found furnished rooms to rent in Grosvenor Square, and got settled in for a new adventure in a new city. Within a couple of days we were visited by the horn players of the King's band, four friendly Englishmen, who said they had been sent by the leader of the band to have lessons. These lessons consisted of taking us to a quiet pub in the neighborhood twice each week, drinking the ale they made there for about an hour, (to get them into the right frame of mind to play horn, they said) and then playing duos, trios, and quartets until well into the night and telling jokes and stories. Occasionally we would do some bit of chromatic playing and one of them would stop short, amazed.

"Well, I'll be goddamned! Show us how you do that!" and then to the barmaid, "My dear, fetch another pint each for these two agreeable and talented Dutchmen!"

Over the course of our stay, we got them doing some rudimentary hand-stopping, and definitely improved their intonation and articulation, but the whole thing was much more of a drinking party than a lesson. A few times the lessons went on so successfully that our new friends had to have us sent home in the most ridiculous mode of transportation that this ridiculous 18th century ever thought up - the sedan chair. The London horn players, who seemed relatively unaffected by a larger volume of beer than we had drunk, would give the chair men the address, and they would whisk us away at a respectable and bumpy trot. It's unlikely we could have found our way home under our own power, intact with horns, on those particular nights.

The Anacreontic Society was the strangest mixture of amateur and professional musicians we had ever encountered. Reasonably talented and skillful businessmen and independently wealthy people of no particular trade paid a fee to take part in the concerts, and because keeping the ensemble together was much like herding drunken cats, it was necessary to hire a few professional musicians to lead each section. The group was a string orchestra of about thirty-five players that sounded like fifteen, because at any given moment a certain number were lost, and another portion were scrambling to find the right notes. It was billed as being a serious musical experience for the amateur musician, but it was actually an opportunity for them to get together on a Sunday afternoon, invite their friends and families to enjoy the music, and just have a good time. It was all extremely informal, and you could never tell with any degree of certainty at what point the rehearsal ended and the concert began.

We were the featured soloists on a Sunday afternoon in February, and we dug deep in our trunk of music to find solo horn pieces with the easiest and most trouble-free string parts. The whole experience was highly entertaining, and everyone enjoyed themselves immensely. And, of course, everyone had to crowd around us to see our silver horns that were now the talk of the London musical world.

Over the next few weeks, before the Salomon concerts, we played chamber music at a couple of coffee houses with some professional string players for not much more than a meal and a few shillings, and some performances of horn duets for small select audiences at wealthy private houses around London, for which we were paid handsomely. We probably could have stayed in London for a good long time and taken advantage of being the novelty of the season, but our stay was of a definite length, leading up to the Hanover Square concerts in March, and Salomon, Abel, and Park had arranged things for us so that everything we did was an advertisement for their upcoming concerts.

Beate had made the acquaintance of an entire circle of women musicians in London, and had joined a couple of chamber music societies in which she played horn, violin, or viola as needed. These resulted in some kind of performance just about every weekend, and she was thrilled to get to play that often. Even ten-year old Carl Nicholaus was pulled into the thriving musical world of London and was singing in a boys' choir and taking voice lessons with an Italian singing master.

As the Hanover Square concerts approached, we decided with Johann Salomon which of our concertos we would play. We chose two of the more spectacular concertos that Antonio Rosetti had written for us, and the one by Josef Fiala. One of these Rosetti concertos was known for most of the 20th century as the Haydn Double concerto, until the musicologists figured out that it was actually written by Rosetti. I could have cleared up the entire mystery of who composed it, but none of the musicologists knew to ask me about it, nor would they have believed me if I told them how I knew. We played all three of the concertos in E on the fixed-pitch silver solo horns, one concerto per concert, and used the orchestra horns for the other pieces on the programs.

The orchestra was a group of about thirty musicians, all from the top ranks of professional players in London, and it was as tight and polished an ensemble as we had played with anywhere. Unlike the rather global style of 21st century orchestras, every city in Europe in the late 18th century had its own style. Modern musicians and listeners would disagree with me on that and talk about the differences between orchestras around the world, and rightly so, but they would not have heard the very stark differences between music making in Germany, France, Italy, and England in this time. I remember many years later, (about 250 years later) hearing a period instrument group play Couperin's *"Apotheose de Lully"*, in which the musicians play alternatingly in the French and Italian styles of the early 18th century, and thinking, "Those are the kinds of different musical personalities and styles I remember having to get accustomed to when we would travel to different cities and countries."

Our orchestra in Paris was refined, expressive, and emotional, willing to stretch time in ways that 21st century listeners would hardly be able to understand. They played with a rather transparent sound in the upper voices, and very heavy in the bassline, sometimes using four cellos, a contrabass, and two or three bassoons. In Germany the orchestras were more disciplined and precise, a little less flexible with time, and their sound was fuller top to bottom. In England the general feel of the music was much less serious in nature, and the players seemed to be in it simply for the fun of it, chasing each other through a piece and doing mischievous things musically like excited English schoolboys. Articulation and phrasing also varied wildly from place to place. Every city had its own pitch level and concept of intonation too. It was always a challenge to try to fit into the local style.

Rehearsals began late in February, and the plan was to rehearse all the music for the six concerts of the series and then distribute the pieces we had prepared into the various programs. We had our three concertos to rehearse with the orchestra, and several other symphonies, concertos, overtures, and arias from favorite operas of the time. It was a lot of music to rehearse all at once, but the London musicians were fast learners, and Salomon was very efficient and focused in the way he rehearsed with the group. No time was wasted during rehearsals, and it reminded me of the efficient way Christian Cannabich rehearsed with the Mannheim orchestra when we played with them a few years before, only Salomon was a good deal friendlier and less authoritarian in the way he worked with the musicians.

Each evening after a long day of rehearsing, we would dine with Salomon, Abel, some of the other vocal and instrumental soloists, as well as some of the wealthy patrons of the series at an inn in Hanover Square. Among the company was a lawyer from Edinburgh named James Boswell who was living and working in London at the time. Boswell had one subject that he loved to talk about, and that was to tell stories about his late friend, Dr. Samuel Johnson, the writer, lexicographer, and literary critic who had died just about a year before. Boswell was preparing to write a biography of Johnson while working on some high-profile criminal cases in London. He was just one example of the array of colorful and eccentric wealthy people who supported Salomon's concerts.

Flyers started appearing in shops in London advertising the concerts and giving the address at which tickets could be had. The flyers gave the names of the soloists, including ourselves, and stated that "Messers Palsa and Thurschmit, virtuosi from Germany will perform concertos and duets on their Paris-made solid silver French horns."

Chapter 56

Hell is empty and all the devils are here.
- Shakespeare, The Tempest, 1612

On the third evening of rehearsals, we left Hanover Square and started on our way home after a meal with the group. It was quite late, after eleven o'clock at night, and the streets were deserted. Carl, who understood very little English, was a little uncomfortable walking around the streets of London even in broad daylight and being out at night made him even more apprehensive.

"Walking through these streets late at night with our horns makes me nervous," he said, "especially since there are advertisements in all the papers and in shop windows that say we play on solid silver horns of great value."

"I know," I said. "I don't like it either that they've made such a big deal out of the silver horns, but I don't think anyone would recognize us in the street. We just look like a couple of guys carrying a wooden box between them. No one would necessarily know there were horns of any kind in it. Nonetheless, I'll feel better when we get to the main street where we can hail a cab that will drop us off at our door. I don't know how much of the conversation you caught, but that lawyer, Boswell was talking most of the evening about the criminal world of London, and how organized the gangs are. He seemed to be familiar with a lot of them, and how they operate. He described some of the famous robberies that have taken place in London, and how the crimes have been solved, and what horrible things were done to the criminals."

"Thanks Johann. That makes me feel ever so much better, and I'm sure I'll sleep well tonight for hearing that."

We were walking down the small street in which the inn was located and were planning to catch a cab at the next corner.

About halfway down the narrow street a voice came out of nowhere from behind us.

"Evening, my good foreign horn blowers! I'm sure you don't understand a word I'm saying, but you'll understand the universal language of the pistol that I'm pointing at your backs! Stop right there and set that box down in the road."

"We do understand you," I said. "We don't have very much money, but whatever we have in our pockets we'll gladly give you if you'll let us go on our way."

"I'll be happy to take whatever you have in your pockets too, but what we came on purpose for was that box of yours, since all the adverts for those fancy concerts say it contains a couple of solid silver French horns." At that moment three other men stepped out of a doorway and approached us.

"Now," said the first ruffian, "just to keep everything nice and tidy, I'll keep this here pistol pointed at you, to prevent you from making any quick moves that could get you hurt, and my good friends will relieve you of whatever you have in your pockets and give you a hand with that heavy box. Go ahead mates, I've got 'em covered."

The three others helped themselves to the few coins in our pockets, picked up the box and were off and around the corner into the darkness of the city in seconds.

"Very good scholars!" said the man with the pistol, with a friendly smile. "You followed your instructions perfectly. Now your next task is to walk down the lane here in front of me. I hope you won't take this chance meeting of ours personally. It's all in a day's work in our line of business. And now, just like good soldiers - Forward! March!"

We started walking slowly down the street in silence. After about a minute I was pretty sure I was no longer hearing his footsteps behind us. I glanced around and he was nowhere to be seen. He must have ducked down one of the alleys we had passed.

"Quick! Back to the inn!" said Carl in a frightened whisper. "Everyone will still be sitting at the table eating and drinking."

In another minute, running at top speed, we were back at the inn, out of breath and still trembling from the encounter. We found William Park, Friedrich Abel, and the lawyer Boswell still at the table finishing off a bottle of port. They all stood up at once seeing the state we were in.

"What's happened? Is everything all right?" Park said, coming toward us.

"The horns are gone! Taken by robbers!" I managed to get out, trying to catch my breath. "One pointed a pistol at us, and three others took the box with the silver horns and were gone in an instant! We need to get to the police and report the robbery!"

All three immediately raced into the street, looked in every direction, and went around the corner to where we told them the robbery had taken place, but of course there was nothing to see. They came back and made us sit down and tell them the entire story.

"Second time this year already that musicians have been robbed of valuable instruments," said Park. "A violinist had a valuable Cremona violin taken from him in the street after a concert, and my friend Besozzi, the oboist, who was here in London in January was robbed of a Denner oboe and a flute. Unfortunately, these things are not uncommon in London, and before anyone can do anything about it the instruments are whisked off to Paris or Amsterdam where they'll not be recognized and sold again at a high price. It's a big business."

Boswell sat down next to me and started asking questions in a professional tone about the appearance of the men, the direction they had gone, and any other details we could give. I asked Carl each question in German so we could each recount what we had seen and heard. After I finished our story Boswell turned to the company.

"Gentlemen, the London police will be of little help in this matter. They will take a statement and make a report, and 'Follow any leads and look into the matter'. I know much of the London criminal world. I've defended many of the worst, or best, depending on how you want to look at it. Some have been sent to the gallows and a few I've managed to get off scot-free. A few of the latter feel they are in my debt, and it's just possible they can make inquiries and put us on the trail of this band. It's also possible that they would be willing to accept a ransom rather than trying to sell such identifiable instruments. There probably isn't another pair of silver horns in all of England. On the other hand, they wouldn't be very identifiable if they were melted down into silver bullion, which is often done with stolen silverware and vessels that could be traced. Inquiries could be made, and certain people sent out into the streets to gather information. In the meantime, friends, do not despair! Similar cases have been brought to a happy conclusion often enough in the past."

He seemed to know his business and the scene well enough to give us some encouragement, but we weren't hopeful of ever seeing our favorite horns again. We exchanged addresses with him, and the company broke up for the evening.

Carl was curious about what Boswell was saying at the end.

"Having to do with the law and criminal courts, is there anything he can do?"

"He talked as though he would send out word to every criminal in London to be on the lookout for the horns," I said. "He wasn't very enthusiastic about making a police report, but we'll report it to the police anyway and approach the thing from both sides, official and unofficial."

"Well, if we don't get them back, we can play any concerto on the brass Kerner horns as we used to do before the silver ones were made. But when you play on a really fine instrument and develop a relationship with it, it feels like a part of you, and then when something like this happens you feel like you've lost a part of yourself, lost your voice somehow."

"I know what you mean," I said, "like a family member has been kidnapped and you know they're out there somewhere and in danger but there's nothing you can do. At least the criminals didn't do us any harm, as they easily could have. Imagine how badly it could have gone with four of them, and one pointing a pistol at us! I've never had a gun pointed at me before. It's a terrifying feeling."

"I nearly soiled my breeches!" said Carl in English.

"Soiled your breeches? Where did you pick that up?"

"I heard a man in the street say it when he narrowly avoided being run over by a coach the other day. I'm not exactly sure what it means, but it seemed to fit our situation too."

"It means you almost shit in your pants."

"Well then, it was very accurate. I'll master this English language yet."

In the 21st century, people all over Europe, and all over the world learn English and use it as a rather universal language, but that was not the case in the 18th century. England was a small island with its own language that wasn't of great importance to the rest of the continent. French was the important second language to know. A standard French worked just about everywhere you went and was understood by most well-educated people, and all wealthy people or nobility.

Beate was waiting up for us and we told her the whole story, which upset her greatly.

"Oh Johann, this is terrible! I'm always so worried about you and Carl when you're out late at rehearsals or having lessons with the horns of the King's band. How will I ever be able to sleep again until we are safely away from this dangerous city?"

"We'll all be on our guard as we move around the city," I said, trying to reassure her.

The three of us talked things over for quite a while before going to bed.

I woke early the next morning, and the memory of the previous evening came back to me like a heavy weight set down on my chest. More than the loss of the horns, I felt a sense of having been violated and pulled unwillingly into a world of low criminal activity that had very little regard for its victims. He could have shot us then and there with no hesitation or remorse if we had not been cooperative. I found Carl already at breakfast, obviously feeling the same way.

"I don't know how you felt last night Johann, but I wasn't able to sleep for the longest time thinking of what a dangerous situation we were in last night, and about the loss of the horns, and what we should do."

"It was the first time in my life that I've thought I was facing someone who was willing to kill me," I said sitting down at the table to a platter of bread, meat, and cheese that Beate, who was already up, had prepared.

"I thought about that most of the night too," she said. "To think of being attacked at night by a gang that was lying in wait for you! It made me nervous when I saw those advertisements that mentioned your 'valuable silver horns'. I thought they were making too much of the horns and not enough of the players."

A few minutes later a messenger knocked on the door and delivered the following note to us.

Dear Messers Palsa and Türrschmidt,
Once again, let me express my deepest condolences on the loss of your remarkable silver French horns last night. I'm sure the loss of them was a crushing blow to you, as well as the manner in which you were accosted. It seems to me that the gang of criminals had seen them advertised and were watching you closely for a most vulnerable moment to make their move. They chose a particularly dark street at a late hour to make their attack, and this is an indication that these are some of the most experienced and organized criminals in London. With the freshness of the event heavy on your minds last night, I didn't want to be so bold as to offer you my professional services, but this morning, when we are all in a calmer state, and with clearer heads, I will take the liberty of doing so. As I said last night, the London police will be of no help whatsoever in recovering the instruments, but a privately hired investigator, like myself, who knows well the layer of society in which these ruffians function could be of great service to you in locating and reclaiming them. For acting on your behalf, I will not ask for a fee up front, but rather take the case on speculation, which is to say I will only ask a fee if the horns are recovered.

If you wish to contact me in regard to this offer, you will find me in my office in Gray's Inn. It is my sincere wish to be of assistance and to hear you play on them in Mr. Salomon's concerts.

Until we meet again, I remain,
Your most humble and obedient servant,
James Boswell Esq.

"Well, what do you make of that?" I said, after I had read it out loud and translated it for Carl and Beate.

"I think he might be somehow involved in the theft," said Beate. "How well do you know this man? How can you tell if he's really looking out for your best interest, or if the whole thing was set up with the criminals to extort some sort of ransom, or to get you to pay him to get them back?"

"It does seem that he knows an awful lot about the criminals of London, and was suspiciously ready to help us," said Carl. "If we consider engaging him as a private investigator, I think we should ask around a little to find out what others know about him, and if he can be trusted."

After talking this over for a while, William Park showed up to see how we were doing after the events of the previous evening, and whether we had reported the theft to the police. Over the past weeks we had gotten to know him well, and during the previous few days in rehearsals for Salomon's concerts, we had developed quite a friendship.

"Good morning William!" I said, welcoming him into our breakfast room and offering him some coffee and a seat at the table. "I'm glad you stopped by, because we need to ask your opinion about a note that was delivered to us this morning."

I handed him Boswell's letter, and he began to read while sipping the freshly brewed coffee I had brought with us from Germany. After reading about half the letter he looked up.

"My goodness! This is excellent coffee. Where did you get it?"

"I roast it myself and brew it in a special way," I said.

"Well, if the market for horn soloists ever dries up, you could come to London and open a coffee room. If you could serve up coffee like this, you would have an instant success on your hands! But I'm distracted from Mr. Boswell's note." He read to the end and looked up at us smiling.

"Classic Boswell! We've all known him for years and I could have predicted that he would step in to take charge of the situation - for a small fee, of course."

"But can he be trusted? Is he somehow mixed up in the whole thing?"

"My dear Johann, I wouldn't call our friend Boswell an honest man, he is a lawyer after all, but he knows better than to get involved with criminals. The penalty for the theft of your French horns, should the criminals be apprehended, could range from transportation to Australia, to many years in prison, to hanging. Boswell knows it's safer, and more lucrative, to be on the other side of that equation, in the shoes of the one solving the crime and bringing the culprits to justice. No, Boswell is simply one of the sharpest lawyers and, I might say, private investigators in London. He jumps at the opportunity to not only make some money, but to get publicity in the papers for solving a daring and spectacular crime. He is right in saying that the London police will be of no assistance at all, and I'm sure anyone you ask who knows him will tell you that Boswell knows the ins and outs of the criminal underworld of London. He is your best hope for recovering your horns."

"So, you would recommend engaging him?" I asked.

"I think it would be your best course. In the meantime, can you play the rehearsals and concerts on your orchestra horns?"

"That's not a problem, we played double concertos on those horns for years in Paris before the silver ones were made."

After Park left, we decided to go and see Boswell at his office. Beate insisted that from then on, instead of finding our way through the city on foot and getting lost, and having to ask people all along the way, we would take a cab wherever we were going, and not to think about the expense. The cab drivers knew the city so well that you would be there in no time, and cleaner and safer than on foot.

We were expected at rehearsal in Hanover Square at one o'clock, and there was just enough time to find Boswell at his office and go with him to the alehouse downstairs to have a meal and beer and discuss his investigations.

"So, gentlemen, you would like me to formally become your agent in solving the disappearance of your French horns?"

"Yes, very much so," I replied. "Everyone tells us that you are better equipped than anyone to help us recover them."

"And to bring this dangerous band of criminals to justice!" he added.

"Yes, of course, that too, but we're mostly interested in getting our horns back."

"If it is in my power to do so, Sir, you shall have them back, and in time for the Hanover Square Concerts, of which I am a subscriber and patron, so I consider it in my own interest, as well as yours, to bring this matter to a satisfactory conclusion."

"And you mentioned being willing to take up the case on speculation, receiving a fee only if you recover the horns?"

"Certainly, Gentlemen, and for a trifling fee, in comparison to the value of these remarkable instruments. Very nominal indeed.

Shall we say twenty pounds sterling? Of course, in any case there will be some out-of-pocket expenses that will need to be covered whether the horns are recovered or not, certainly not to exceed another ten pounds. If that sounds agreeable, I'll just have my clerk, who happens to be sitting at the bar, fortifying himself for the afternoon's work, draw up a letter of agreement to that effect."

That amount was about as much as we had earned already at private concerts and would be about half of the total we were hoping to earn on the entire trip, after our expenses, but it was still much less than we had paid for the silver horns. The clerk, through long practice of copying out legal documents while mildly drunk, wrote out a letter of agreement in a beautiful flowing script that expressed in flowery legal terms everything we had just talked about.

"Gentlemen!" said Boswell, "I must be off now to contact a few professional friends and acquaintances on your behalf. I will keep you informed of my progress daily as important developments take place. Good day to you!"

On the way to the Hanover Square Rooms where we were rehearsing, Carl wanted to know all the details of the conversation.

"It reminded me of your first year in Paris, when you didn't understand French, and I would have to keep you up to speed on what was being said. Now I'm the one in the dark and am dying to know what he's going to do for us."

I explained everything as we walked to rehearsal.

Chapter 57

A plague upon it when thieves can not be true to one another.
- Shakespeare, The Tempest, ca. 1611

Over the next two days we continued to rehearse using the brass Kerner orchestra horns, which weren't as impressive looking, but worked almost as well as the silver solo horns. The only difference was that the silver horns had a darker, richer sound, and the brass ones were brighter in their tone color.

Each morning I sent a messenger to Boswell's office asking how the inquiries were going, and if he was making any progress. The reply would come to the rehearsal rooms each afternoon, worded something to this effect:

Dear Mr. Palsa,
As much progress as one could hope for, but slowly and carefully, given the delicacy of the situation. More information soon.
Yours in haste,
Boswell

We proceeded with rehearsals and the music was coming together well with this fine group of musicians. On the first of March we finished the final dress rehearsal for the opening concert of the series, which would take place the following evening. Apparently things were happening behind the scenes, because we got a note from Boswell that we should meet him at the alehouse below his office at five o'clock to get some important information. We went there directly after rehearsal to wait for him, and just before five o'clock he and his clerk came in.

"My dear Sirs!" he said shaking our hands. "Things have been proceeding nicely, and I believe we are closing in on the whereabouts of your French horns. Take a seat please and I'll fill you in on everything that has transpired in the past couple of days. My dear, a pint each for our friends, and a bottle of port for Mr. Winch and myself!"

We sat down and the barmaid soon placed foaming pints of ale in front of us and Boswell began detailing for us his researches and sleuthing.

“Though there is an amazing amount of honor and solidarity among thieves in London, if you are willing and able to give the right amount of money to certain people, they will put you in contact with other people who you can pay for valuable information about the most secretive criminal activities in the city. It only took a few pounds placed in the palms of a couple of select individuals, and oaths of secrecy as to where I obtained the information, to get to someone in a rival gang who was happy to give me, also for a small fee, information about the gang who robbed you of your instruments. It seems the gang that stole the horns has been encroaching on the territory of this rival gang, and passing on information to their disadvantage could possibly get them out of the way permanently and clear the area of competition. And that’s how business is done in those circles. The information I was able to get is that Bill Hartman, the man who pointed the pistol at you, and his business associates, thought the instruments would be too identifiable and traceable in their present form, and decided not to take any chances, but to have them melted into silver ingots.”

“Have they melted our horns!?” I said in alarm.

“Not yet. That isn’t something that can be done on a moment’s notice. First they had to find a foundry that could do it, but of course you can’t walk in off the street and say, ‘We’d like to have these beautiful solid silver French horns melted into bricks and expect to have it done with no questions asked. They had to locate a worker at the foundry who they could bribe to do the work after hours, and they’ve only managed to make the arrangements this very day.”

“When will they do it, and where?” I said, almost spilling my beer in my excitement and anxiety.

“Please, please, be calm! We don’t want to make a disturbance that might be overheard by other people here in the taproom. You never know who might be within hearing distance. The metal worker who they’ve taken into their scheme has made an appointment to meet them at midnight tonight at the foundry. He will get there about half an hour before to get the fire in the furnace hot enough to melt silver, and when Bill Hartman and his gang arrive, he will be ready to melt the horns."

"But what can we do to stop them?" I said, my agitation and excitement getting the better of me.

Carl was unable to contain himself at this point, and I had forgotten that he could understand almost nothing of the conversation other than the excitement in our voices. I took a minute to translate what was being said. Then Boswell took up his story again.

"I have it all in hand, and everything is arranged. I will arrive with eight or ten armed police officers before the foundry worker gets there, and we'll secure him first and then wait for the others to arrive. I doubt they should be armed with more than a pistol or two, and it will be easy to surprise them and get them to lay down their arms to avoid being shot by several armed men. I imagine the element of surprise will make it very easy to recover the horns and apprehend the criminals. Everything should be taken care of by midnight, and if you will meet me and my party of police officers there, you may take your horns home with you. Here is the address of the foundry, but I don't want you to hire a cab to take you there. We can't be too careful in a business such as this. You never know who might be friends with whom, and who knows more than they should about other people's business. I'll send a private coachman who I can trust to pick you up and deliver you there."

With all arranged we went home and waited anxiously for the appointed hour. It was a tense evening and Beate didn't want us to go.

"Couldn't you just let Boswell and the London police take care of the whole thing?" she asked.

"Boswell says it will all be over before midnight and we'll be able to recover our horns on the spot," I assured her. We really want to be there to get them ourselves."

"And after all these thieves have put us through, it will give us great satisfaction to be there to see them captured by the police and taken to jail," added Carl.

The evening dragged on for an eternity until finally, just as the local church bell had chimed half past eleven, the private carriage Boswell had ordered for us arrived, driven by two men. We got in, gave the driver the address, and sat tensely on the cushioned seats, in great anxiety about what we might find when we got there. What if the gang arranged to meet earlier and we were too late to save the horns? What if Boswell and the officers were met by a larger party of criminals than they had anticipated? What if Boswell's informant had sent us all off on a wild goose chase? What if the whole thing was a trap? These were the thoughts that were going through our heads, and the topic of our whispered conversation on the short ride.

As we approached the vicinity the driver stopped at a corner and got down from the box.

"Gentlemen, you'll have to get out here. I can't go any farther into the narrow lanes of Whitechapel. Mr. Boswell instructed me to wait for you, but I'll have to wait here, and Johnny will show you the rest of the way. I don't like the looks of this here dark street at this time of night, so I'll just pull around the corner into the next street, what has a streetlamp and wait for your Lordships there."

We got out, rather reluctantly, and the driver was off and around the corner. His companion led us through several dark winding lanes before we got to the door of the dingy industrial looking building.

"Here you are mates! You're on your own from here. This place don't look safe. I'm going back to the carriage to wait." He took off at a run, and we found ourselves alone in front of the brick workshop building, staring at an imposing black iron door with a filthy window on either side. A tall chimney was protruding prominently from the peak of the roof, and out of it was coming smoke and sparks.

"I thought they were going to stop the whole business before they could start a fire to melt the horns," said Carl.

"I've heard they often leave a foundry furnace going all night because it takes so long to fire it up the next day if the fire goes out," I said trying to convince myself that this was the explanation."

"I certainly hope you're right," Carl's whispered.

The windows were so dirty that we could only see a faint glow from within the building, but couldn't see what was going on inside. I lifted the bolt of the door and slowly opened it inward. The room was large and long, and perfectly dark except for the glow of the wood or coal fired furnace at the opposite end. The whole length of the room was filled with workbenches, tools, and other machinery, which helped us stay out of sight. We couldn't see what was going on, but we could make out that there were people by the furnace at the other end. We assumed it was Boswell and the London police officers, but moved forward slowly in the darkness just in case we were mistaken. The furnace was noisy and drowned out any noise we made when entering the building, so no one noticed us. As we got closer, we could make out that it wasn't Boswell and his friends and my blood turned to iced water when I heard a voice that I wasn't likely to forget for a long time - that of Bill Hartman. You don't forget the voice of someone who has pointed a pistol in your face and made it very clear that he was willing to use it.

"Let's get out of here! Something has gone terribly wrong!" I whispered. I didn't have to say it twice. Carl knew that voice too and had already turned around and was heading back through the dark room toward the door. We were two or three yards from the door when it was suddenly opened, and in walked two of the men who had assisted Bill Hartman in the robbery. One had a lantern and the other a pistol, which was instantly raised and pointed in our direction.

"Well, look what we have here! If it ain't our two friends from t'other night, the German French horn blowers. Come to fetch your horns back, have ye? Very clever to figure out where to look. But don't leave now! You'll want to see the nice silver bricks that Bill and his mates have made from those horns. This way, back into the foundry you go. And Bill will need to decide what to do with you now that you've seen so much!"

He prodded us back into the room with his pistol and marched us back to where some men were crouched over the wooden horn box. The man who was obviously the foundry worker they had enlisted was talking.

"We're almost up to temperature for melting silver. You can tell by the color of the glow. These look to be coin silver, slightly lower silver content than sterling, and with a higher melting point."

"Quiet! Who's there?" said Bill in a tense voice as he heard us approaching.

"It's us, Nigel and Tony, and look what we picked up along the way! A couple of French horn blowers. They say they dropped by to ask you if you would be so kind as to give them back their horns."

Everyone laughed. The German for "soiling one's breeches" is "*in die Hose machen*" and both Carl and I were on the verge of doing that, we were so petrified with fear for our lives, and wondering what the hell had happened to Boswell and his troop of London police.

"Let's make them watch while we melt their hunting horns," said Tony.

"But then they'll know much more than they should, and we can't have them walking the streets talking about what they saw here," said Nigel, poking the barrel of his pistol into each of our stomachs by turns.

"That's right," said Bill. "They already know far too much for my liking."

"Shoot 'em and throw 'em in the furnace, I say!" added Tony.

"No! No!" said the foundry worker, whose name was Daniel. "If you burn a body in this furnace the whole street would be out of doors in a minute at the smell of burning flesh and would want to know the reason, and then we're all dead men! Besides, you'd have to cut 'em up small, like we'll have to do with these French horns."

"He's right," said Bill. "We need to do this quick and not draw any more attention to the business than necessary. Nigel and Tony, take 'em down to the river and get rid of them. But first put a red-hot iron to their feet or whatever it takes to find out how they knew to come here. I smell something awfully fishy about them turning up."

"Off you go boys. Boss says you're going for a swim tonight," said Nigel pushing us forward with the barrel of the pistol. Bill took no further notice of us and we were pushed roughly toward the door at the other end of the room. I was more terrified than I had ever been in my life, knowing that they were taking us out to kill us to keep us quiet and out of the way. Carl was pale and trembling and looked as though his shaky legs weren't going to take him much farther.

They instructed me to open the door and we went out of the dark room into the even darker street, which seemed to be deserted. Nigel and Tony were behind us, Nigel with his pistol, and Tony beside him with the lantern, which was now closed so that it only sent out a small ribbon of light. After just a few steps, suddenly the noise of something heavy coming down on Nigel's head was followed immediately by his pistol going off and the ball whizzing past my right ear between Carl and me. I turned around immediately to see Nigel fall to the ground from the blow of the butt of a musket on the back of his head, applied by a rather ragged looking London police officer. Nigel was out cold. Tony was standing stock still with his hands in the air, another officer pointing a musket at his head. Behind them were about six more of their colleagues, all armed, and James Boswell, Esq.

"Mr. Palsa! Mr. Türrschmidt! Are you hurt? asked Boswell running up to us out of breath.

"No, just very shaken and in fear for our lives," I said. "What the hell happened? Where have you been? These guys were about to take us somewhere and shoot us! And Bill Hartman is in the foundry ready to melt our horns!"

"I'll fill you in later, there isn't a moment to lose!" shouted Boswell. "Two or three of you, take care of these ruffians, and the rest, follow me!"

One of the officers was tying Tony's hands behind his back, and another was doing the same to Nigel, who was just beginning to regain consciousness. We left them to their work and followed the rest into the foundry. We went quietly down the length of the long room, and just as we came into the light of the glowing furnace, we looked on in horror as Bill opened the wooden box, took out both silver horns, and walk toward the furnace, where Daniel, the foundry worker, was waiting with a hammer and a large pair of metal shears.

"We'll need to cut 'em into pieces small enough to fit into this crucible before we can put 'em in the furnace," he said, taking one of the horns. Their backs were turned to us, facing the furnace, as we stepped into the light.

"Stop!" cried Boswell. "Don't make a move or you're dead men! There are several armed officers here, so take that pistol out of your belt, Bill Hartman, and lay it down on the floor, very slowly."

Bill did as he was told. In the commotion of our encounter with Hartman a couple of minutes earlier, I was pretty sure there was a third man, but I didn't see him now. I was about to warn the others, when a pistol barrel appeared from behind the furnace and a shot rang out that scared the living shit out of everyone, and one of the officers clutched his arm swearing.

Then, while Bill and Daniel were being held at gunpoint, two other officers went behind the furnace and came back with the third man, whose name I never heard. I thought it incredibly dangerous to go behind the furnace after him, but they knew that having fired his pistol, which would need to be reloaded with powder and ball before being able to fire a second time, he wouldn't be able to shoot again. They brought him out into the open, and he chose to come along peacefully. All three men stood with several muskets pointing at them as their hands were tied. Bill and the other members of his gang were silent, but Daniel wasn't going to go without a few choice words for Bill.

"I knew this whole business was going to go wrong somehow! How did you talk me into getting involved in this? We're all going to hang now because I was stupid enough to be taken in!" he said with tears running down his face. Bill looked calm.

"What I want to know is, who tipped you off Boswell? Who did you pay to find out we were going to be here tonight with these damned French horns? They've been more trouble than they're worth the whole way along."

"You'll get to hear the entire story in great detail in court in a day or two, and until then, you'll be well taken care of as guests of the city of London police!" said Boswell. "Take them away!"

Carl and I, now greatly relieved, rushed over to where the horns were sitting on the floor. They were almost too hot to handle from being so near the intense heat of the furnace, and appeared to have sustained a few dents, having been set down rather roughly on the floor when the thieves were surprised. Carl carefully picked up one of the horns and I turned to Boswell.

"So, what took you so long to get here?"

"My dear Palsa, it was a most unfortunate comedy of errors."

"A most unfortunate comedy of errors that almost got us shot and thrown into the Thames!"

"Yes, yes, my most sincere apologies for leaving you in such a tight spot, but it was quite unavoidable. I arranged to meet the eight city policemen at the Kings Arms Tavern early enough to be here by eleven o'clock, but my clerk, Mr. Winch, copied the note that I dictated to him incorrectly, writing down King's Coach Tavern instead, a favorite of his, and that is where they assembled to wait for me. I waited at the King's Arms until well after eleven o'clock, when it occurred to me what might have happened, and I set off at a trot toward the King's Coach. In the meantime, Mr. Winch had received an answer to his message at my office. The officers had written their reply, saying that they would be there waiting, on the back of Mr. Winch's original note. Upon seeing it, he recognized the mistake, and immediately went off to the King's Coach to tell them to go to the King's Arms, which I had just left to look for them. I took a different street than they did, and therefore didn't meet them on the way. Suffice it to say that it took some time for us to locate each other. The entire time I was terrified to think of what might be happening to the horns and to yourselves! We rushed here as fast as our feet would take us and arrived just in the nick of time."

I was now beginning to regain at least a tiny bit of my composure.

"Well, we're grateful that you arrived when you did, to save our lives and our horns."

"And first thing tomorrow morning I'll make a point to have Mr. Winch flayed alive and deliver his tanned hide to you as a token of my esteem, and as a slight restitution for the harrowing experience you and Mr. Türrschmidt have been put through."

"Leave Mr. Winch alone. Shit happens," I said, lapsing into a 21st century idiom that I'm sure was unfamiliar to him, but was quite understandable under the circumstances. "At least no one was injured or killed other than one of the officers being grazed on the arm by a pistol ball."

By this time Carl had collected the horns, which could now be touched (silver, which is an excellent conductor of heat, warms up, and cools down quickly) and had brought the wooden box away from the area of the furnace.

"Everything seems to be here," he said in German. "The bell of yours got a little misshapen, and both have a few dents, but they should be playable until we can get to a horn maker to have them fixed. But the best news is that the mouthpieces are still there!"

After the horns were stolen, I had to play on the mouthpiece that Carl had loaned me during my first days in Paris, and Carl had been playing on an extra-large low horn mouthpiece, both of which were in the brass Kerner horns' box. Neither fit us as well as our regular silver mouthpieces, but we were getting by with them. It would be a huge relief to be playing on our silver solo horns, and on our regular silver mouthpieces, which fit us like comfortable old shoes.

Boswell insisted on accompanying us back to our lodging in his hired carriage, and it was well after one o'clock in the morning when we arrived home to Beate, who after having put Carl Nicholaus to bed, was sitting up waiting for us, sick with worry about what might have happened to keep us away so long. She ran out to the carriage and folded me in her arms.

"Oh Johann, I'm so glad to see you alive! I was so worried the whole time! Tell me what happened. Are both you and Carl unhurt? And are the horns safe?"

Boswell went on his way home, promising to meet us in the morning, and we went into the house to tell Beate the entire adventure, and make some tea to calm our shaken nerves. None of us could go to bed or sleep until late into the night, and had very unsettling, unpleasant dreams when we did sleep.

Chapter 58

The most striking part of their exhibition was their horns, which were made of silver.
-William T. Parke, Memoirs, on Palsa and Türrschmidt, 1830

The story of the previous evening spread quickly, and by nine o'clock in the morning Boswell had arrived, first to inquire about how we were doing after the excitement of our adventure, and then to present us with his bill for the agreed upon twenty pounds, plus a rather hefty sum for bribes, travel, and other miscellaneous expenses. We settled with him, and shortly thereafter we received a visit from Johann Salomon, Friedrich Abel, and William Park. They didn't stop asking questions until they had heard the entire story about three times over in all its details. After determining that we were none the worse for the experience, they wanted to see the condition of the horns.

"Just a few dents here and there," said Carl. "A nasty one in the mouthpipe of mine that will probably inhibit the flow of air a bit, and some creases in the bell of Johann's. We haven't tried them yet to see how they play."

We proceeded to do that and discovered that Carl's horn was quite resistant, due to the deep dent in a rather narrow part of the mouthpipe. Mine felt better, but the misshapen bell made it hard to play the stopped notes in tune.

"I have just the solution!" said Park. "I know one of the best horn makers in London. We can go and see him this morning and have him put the horns back in good order for the concert tonight."

Since everyone was interested in seeing the horns repaired, all five of us proceeded to the shop of George Henry Rodenbostel in Piccadilly.

Rodenbostel had learned from a maker by the name of Christopher Hofmaster, originally Christoph Hofmeister, from Vienna, where he had learned to make horns with crooks in the Viennese style like our Kerner horns. Rodenbostel, as his apprentice, had married Hofmaster's daughter and inherited the shop upon his death, and he now produced some of the best brass instruments in London.

"Very pretty work!" he said as he ironed the creases out of my bell and drove small barrel-shaped balls through the tubes of both horns and tapped the surface with a small polished hammer to remove the dents. "We rarely get to see instruments made in Paris. Mr. Raoux is known for the high quality of his horns and these are quite extraordinary in their workmanship. Trumpets are often made of silver, but the only other French horns of silver I've seen are a pair of horns made in Vienna for an English nobleman about fifty years ago by a maker named Leichnamschneider who my master knew. Not an easy metal to work with."

He talked easily and continuously the whole time as he deftly reshaped the metal and polished the surface until the repairs were invisible and the horns looked as good as they had the day they left the Raoux shop in Paris.

We got home early in the afternoon, and our three friends left us to rest for the concert. Carl and I needed to play some on the silver horns to make sure they would be comfortable for the concert in the evening, and having determined that they were in top condition and their playing qualities had not suffered, we both rested for the remainder of the afternoon, having not had very much sleep the previous night.

We could have used more rest, but soon enough it was time to dress and find our way to Hanover Square. Tickets for Salomon's series were expensive, and not very many free tickets were given away, but we managed to get two "ladies tickets" as they were called, so that Beate and Carl Nicholaus could hear the concert.

The Hanover Rooms consisted of a large house on the east side of Hanover square, onto which had been built rooms large enough for concerts and other meetings. The main concert room on the upper level appeared to be about eighty or ninety feet long and about forty feet wide with a high arched ceiling that had been painted with elaborate murals by a famous Italian artist named Cipriani. Below on the ground floor was a room where audience members could go to have tea and food before, during, or after the concert. Both the Salomon Concerts, and its rival series, the Professional Concerts, led by German violinist Wilhelm Cramer, were attended by the highest levels of society, including King George III and Queen Charlotte who had her own private tearoom off the main concert room upstairs, elegantly furnished by the king.

The room in which the concert took place was filled with well-dressed ladies and gentlemen, and though it was a bit cool and foggy outdoors, the crowd brought the temperature up to a comfortable degree in the room, which was advantageous for intonation on wind and string instruments. It was rarely just the right temperature so that the pitch of the strings and the winds didn't go off in opposite directions, and this was one of those rare nights. The concert started at eight o'clock and lasted about two and a half hours. We played in an Overture by William Boyce, the only English composer on the program, a symphony in A major by Haydn with very high and delicate horn and oboe passages in the opening Adagio and in the trio of the Menuet, (known in modern times as Symphony no. 5), a violin concerto played by Salomon, and another symphony by Johann Christian Bach, as well as a few opera arias that had horn parts. In the middle of all this, came our Rosetti double horn concerto. Years later, whenever I heard a recording or performance of the piece known to 21st century horn players erroneously as the "Haydn Double Concerto", it would bring up fond memories of this performance on the Salomon concert series in London.

The story of the theft of the horns and their recovery had spread among the concert goers, and to make the event even more exciting for them, Salomon asked James Boswell Esq. to give a full account of the entire affair, which he told as dramatically as possible, emphasizing his own cleverness and heroism, but not mentioning that he was also responsible for our coming within a hair's breadth of being murdered and thrown into the Thames. The audience hung on his every word, as he described the daring robbery, his sleuthing, the capture of the criminals, and the saving of the horns. Though its real purpose was to puff up the ego and reputation of James Boswell Esq., it was actually a very effective introduction to our concerto, and all eyes were on the newly repaired and polished silver horns, which were undoubtedly the most impressive looking instruments in the room.

Salomon then talked about Rosetti, horn playing on the continent, and about us and our careers as soloists. He then turned to the orchestra and began the opening tutti of the concerto. It was a pleasure to play with such a fine group whose precision and intonation made it easy to negotiate the highly technical passages in the solo horn parts. Being back on our silver solo horns and mouthpieces made everything more comfortable and the performance was better than any of the rehearsals.

This was in the mid - 1780s, and horn playing in England was still in a rather primitive state. The art of playing chromatically on the natural horn was a totally foreign sound, except to the few who might have heard Punto when he had played at Covent Garden in the 1770s. The audience was spellbound by what they were hearing, and broke into wild applause after each movement, led by our friends, the four horn players from the King's band, who would not have missed the concert for the world. After the piece was finished, the audience wanted to hear more, which they expressed by unison clapping and the cry that one of the King's band horn players started of "More French Horns! More French Horns!" We had no choice but to play a suite of unaccompanied duets consisting of a short allegro, a minuet, an air, and a rondo from a set published in Paris a few years earlier by a composer by the name of Chiapparelli. Finally, the audience was satisfied, and they allowed the concert to move on to the next piece on the program, the Haydn symphony in A major.

It was a highly successful opening concert to the series, both musically, with rave reviews in the London papers, and financially, selling out the Hanover Rooms for each of six programs. Pay for the musicians was based on the profit that was left over after all costs of the series were paid. We appeared as soloists in three of the programs and played in the orchestra for the other three, and received thirty pounds for each appearance as soloists, and fifteen pounds for each concert as orchestra horn players. One hundred thirty-five pounds each was equal to the yearly salary of a good deal of respectable professions in London at that time, and definitely worth the trip. There was however, a great disparity between wind players, who might receive what we did, and a violin soloist who would receive twice as much, and a singer who might be paid five times that amount, - a disparity that continued to be the norm right up to the 21st century.

The other concerts we played, both public and private before the Hanover Square concerts, had covered our travel and lodging costs and Boswell's fee, and the Salomon concerts were pure profit, making this the most profitable tour of our careers. It was with mixed emotions that we left London at the beginning of May 1786. Mixed because we had played some of the most high-profile and musically rewarding concerts of our lives, but almost lost our lives twice, - once during the theft of our prized silver horns, and once in the recovery of them.

Beate also had mixed emotions about leaving London. She had played on several amateur chamber concerts, and even played a solo sonata with pianoforte that she transcribed for horn from a Mozart violin and piano sonata. But after the terrifying experience of the horn theft, she was constantly worried about Carl and me traveling around the city and felt extremely uncomfortable in this place where she knew very little of the language. Fortunately, she had made friends with a few German women musicians with whom she played regularly. By May, she too was ready to leave London, which she considered the most dangerous place she had ever been.

On the second of May we set out on the long journey to Vienna, where we were expected by the first week of June. The trip, like all long journeys in the 18th century, was exhausting and uncomfortable with long days on bumpy roads in coaches, long hot nights in inns of various qualities and levels of cleanliness, money changing, border crossings, customs officers, and the hit or miss availability of food that was fit to eat. As a boy who grew up in Boston around the turn of the 21st century, I was amazed that by 1786 I was so used to all these inconveniences that I hardly thought of them as inconveniences.

The trip was relatively uneventful until we had to stay a few extra days in the city of Schärding, on the border of Bavaria and Austria, due to all of us falling ill with stomach cramps and fever. It was probably a case of food poisoning, but in those days you rarely knew what sort of ailment you were experiencing. Fortunately, it passed in a couple of days and we were able to proceed on to Vienna. Even with that delay, we were still able to arrive there before the first of June.

Chapter 59

There was music every day, during dinner, and in the evening at the inn, where I lodged, which was the Golden Ox; but it was usually bad, particularly a band of wind instruments, which constantly attended the ordinary. This consisted of French horns, clarinets, hautboys, and bassoons, all so miserably out of tune, that I wished them a hundred miles off.

- Charles Burney, The present state of Music in Germany, The Netherlands, and the United Provinces, London, 1775

Earlier I mentioned the characteristic smells of each European city, and when we stepped out of the coach in the city center of Vienna, I was immediately hit with the smell of coffee, spices, and pastries, and that was the aroma that surrounded us the entire time we were there. We went to an inn called the *Goldener Ochs* (Golden Ox) near St. Stephan's Cathedral, which had been recommended to us by the director of the orchestra of the Vienna court theater. It was with this group that we would be appearing as soloists in several performances at the famous *Burgtheater*.

It was early in the day when we arrived, and after safely storing all our baggage and instruments in the inn, Beate and Carl Nicholaus wanted to rest from the trip, but Carl and I decided to take a walk around the city and get a feel for where things were. We set off in the direction of the Burgtheater, curious to get a look at the building where most of our performing would take place. To entice us to make the trip to Vienna, the director of the theater orchestra had promised to spread the word that we would be there and look for some other concert opportunities for us in the form of private house concerts, or possibly even at the court of the Emperor, Joseph II.

The Burgtheater was a comfortable walk of just a few minutes, and on the way, we were able to get a good feel for the city. Vienna had some of the tallest buildings of any city I visited in the 18th century, mostly made of white stone, and very durable and ancient looking. The Burgtheater was in the *Michaelerplaz*, next to the palace of the Empress Maria Theresa. Arriving at the theater, we found it closed, and not being able to enter, we started reading the posters and announcements of upcoming plays and operas.

"Carl! Look at this! The Marriage of Figaro just opened last night! The second performance is tomorrow! We have to see it! This is an important historic event!"

"What are you so excited about? What's the Marriage of Figaro?"

"It's one of the most famous operas of all time, by Mozart! It will be a standard in the opera repertoire all over the world for the next several hundred years, and we get to see the first production of it! We have to get tickets!"

I was beside myself with excitement at seeing this, and wasn't going to miss it if it were humanly possible to get in.

"Oh, a new opera by our friend Amadeus Mozart, who we met about ten years ago in Paris? You've been going on about the brilliant career he's going to have ever since. He certainly played the pianoforte well and composed some pretty duets for us, but is he really better or destined for more lasting fame than some of the other composers listed on these posters? Look at all of them – Hasse, Salieri, Vanhall, Gassmann, Wagenseil, Haydn, Gluck, Ditters. These are some of the most famous composers in a city that's crawling with famous composers. Surely he's not that much more talented than all of them."

"All I can tell you is that by my time, most of those names will be known only by students of music history, but Mozart and Haydn will be the two whose music stays in the standard repertoire. I've played their music all my life. We have to see this opera."

"Okay Johann," said Carl, obviously thinking he was humoring my sudden flight of fancy. "The poster gives an address in this street where we can buy tickets, and we have nothing planned for tomorrow evening. We may even see if the precocious little prodigy has grown up at all during the past ten years. It says here that he will direct from the keyboard. He didn't make a very good impression on the Paris musical world ten years ago. I've heard that after he left Paris, he went back to Salzburg and did some touring, and has now settled down in Vienna, but he still hasn't landed a Kapellmeister position."

"I tell you he's one of the most important and influential composers ever. It won't be long before the world acknowledges that. Let's hurry over there. I hope it isn't sold out."

We walked down the street and entered the house where tickets were on sale. This was the business office of the theater and the opera. A disinterested looking man sitting at a table with boxes of printed tickets for the various plays, operas, and concerts was absorbed in a book, and it took a while to get his attention.

"Grüß Gott!" I said, using the standard Austrian greeting that I learned in my 21st century German classes. It literally means; "Greet God" but is meant as a blessing and greeting. Carl looked oddly at me, and the man at the table slowly lifted his eyes from his book and looked me up and down.

"Should I happen to run into our heavenly father, I'll certainly pass your greeting on to him. What can I do for you?"

Apparently, this standard greeting wasn't in use yet in the 18th century.

"We want to buy four tickets for the opera tomorrow evening at the Burgtheater," I said. "I hope it isn't sold out."

"Let's see here. Yes. Mozart, Marriage of Figaro," he said finding the right box, which was full of tickets. "Nope. Lots of tickets left. Would you like a box over the stage for four? I have several still empty."

"That sounds fine. I'm surprised there are seats available."

"Only Gluck and Hasse ever fill the place. It's only his second opera in the Burgtheater. If he gets as famous as those two, he'll get better audiences. Here are your tickets."

I paid for them and we headed back to the inn to tell Beate and Carl Nicholaus the news that we were going to see the opera the following night. I was about as excited as I could be, but as with Carl, Beate wasn't particularly impressed with my choice of a performance to attend.

"I remember hearing you talk about this Mozart," she said. "Couldn't we see something by Gluck instead? I'm sure he's very good, but coming all the way to Vienna I would have thought you would want to see something by one of the famous Viennese opera composers!"

I couldn't explain it in the same way to Beate who knew nothing of my knowledge about Mozart's future fame.

"From things I've heard about the music he's been composing, I just have a hunch it will be worth going to see."

That evening we ate in the common room of the inn and were entertained by the worst wind band we had ever heard. It was an octet of street musicians made up of oboes, clarinets, horns, and bassoons, and quite ragged and out of tune. We survived it by concentrating on the food, which was excellent, and the beer, which was made in a softer, sweeter style than the beers of the German parts of the Empire that we were more familiar with. After we finished eating, we introduced ourselves to the horn players, who played with their horns straight up in the air, hands out of the bell in hunting horn fashion.

"Good God!" said the first horn player. "Had we known that the finest horn duo in the Empire was here tonight we would have been more attentive to our playing. I've never played so badly!

"Oh, cheer up Hans!" said the second player. "Sure you have. I've heard you do it many times." At which they both burst out laughing. We invited them to sit down and have a beer with us and talk about horn playing in Vienna. Though they were common street musicians, these two pleasant and entertaining guys knew all the horn players in the city, and we had a nice friendly chat.

The next day was filled with business, changing money, buying a few essential things, and connecting up with the director of the Burgtheater orchestra, who had indeed made some other contacts for us for private house concerts. By the evening we were ready to sit down at the theater and see the opera.

The Burgtheater, which was eventually replaced by a larger building late in the 19th century, was ornate inside and out. We had a box that was stage right in the second level, and therefore almost directly over the stage. As was usual in 18th century opera, the orchestra was not in a lowered pit, but rather on the floor in front of the stage so that the stage was at about shoulder level to the sitting musicians. Unlike the way they did things in the Paris theaters, where the orchestra sat at a long table, some facing the stage and the other side with their backs to it, the pianoforte was in the middle facing the stage, and the musicians were gathered around, more or less facing the keyboard player, who led the group, but able to see the stage at the same time.

There were twenty-five or thirty musicians, including strings and a full wind section of pairs of flutes, oboes, clarinets, horns, bassoons, trumpets, and tympani. Sitting at the piano conducting the performance mostly by nodding at the singers while playing, was our old acquaintance Wolfgang Amadeus Mozart. He was now almost ten years older, just over thirty, but he had the same boyish gestures and demeanor and looked to be having the time of his life conducting the performance. He also had his hands full keeping very this obviously under-rehearsed orchestra together. He didn't need a score, having every note of his own work in his head, and his eyes were on the stage, and also in the orchestra to cue musicians who clearly weren't totally familiar with the music. It's a difficult score compared to other operas of the time, and they played it like skillful musicians reading it for the first or second time and relying heavily on Mozart's cues for entrances and tempo changes. Working by candlelight in a dark theater, reading handwritten parts, and watching the keyboard player conduct only with his head while trying to listen to the singers made opera difficult work in this period. Modern lighting, and a conductor with a stick who isn't busy playing an instrument makes opera performances a lot easier in modern times.

One of the striking features of the performance was the way the orchestra played the overture. It was the first bit of orchestral music we had heard in Vienna, and as with every other European city, Vienna had its own flexible style. Everything they played had a relaxed dance-like quality, and the overture, which every classical musician knows, was played not with the fast intensely driving equal eighth notes that are so familiar, but rather with relaxed, unequal notes that reminded me of the way a 20th century big band would interpret it, "swinging" the eighths. Somehow it seemed more appropriate for the overture of this comic opera than the intensity with which it's played in the 21st century.

I'm sure Carl and Beate enjoyed the performance, but they were hearing it fresh, while I, who was very familiar with the opera, having played a run of several performances of it in 2016, was waiting for each familiar aria and marveling at the interpretation I was hearing in this dark candle-lit theater. The only downside was that the Viennese audience was even noisier than Paris and London audiences during the performance.

After the performance was finished and the applause and curtain calls were over, we went down to the orchestra to say hello to Mozart.

"Ach! Meine Gute!" he said, recognizing us immediately. "Carl and Jojo the famous Paris Waldhorn duo! What a surprise! What brings you to Vienna, the musical capital of the world!?"

"We left Paris last year and are now in the service of the Landgraf of Hessen-Cassel," said Carl. "We're just returning from a tour to London and got an invitation to play with the Burgtheater Orchestra next week, so we came to Vienna on our way home."

"On your way home to Cassel? There are more direct routes from London to Cassel!" said Mozart laughing.

"It wasn't really on the way home," I said, "but we had never been to Vienna, so as long as we were still on leave from the Landgraf we took the opportunity, even though it's been a long trip already. We did six programs with Johann Peter Salomon at the Hanover Rooms in London."

"I've been meaning to check out the scene in London," said Mozart without missing a beat. "If nothing comes of this new opera, and things don't pick up for me here, I may go there this year. I've heard the professional music scene works much as it does here in Vienna, no permanent posts, only freelance gigs. I would love to break into the London Hanover concerts and get some of my music played there. Could you guys recommend me to Salomon? He's been inviting Papa Haydn for the past few years, but apparently doesn't know about my existence yet. Haydn is always too busy to go, but I would drop everything here for the chance to go and show them some of my recent pieces. Speaking of which, how did you like my Figaro? Pretty entertaining, eh?"

Carl was holding back his laughter. Mozart hadn't changed a bit and was still as awkward and socially clueless as when we had met him in Paris in 1778.

"It's wonderful music," I said. "We enjoyed it very much."

"Something tells me this one is going to pass the test of time," Mozart went on, not giving me a chance to elaborate. "It wouldn't surprise me if they're still playing it ten or even twenty years from now."

I thought to myself that even Mozart's very self-assured ego would have been surprised to hear that he was only off in his estimate by about two hundred fifty years to my certain knowledge, and it was by no means losing its popularity in my time.

"By the way, if one of you are free this coming Saturday, I've been engaged to organize some chamber music for a house concert for a rich patron, and my horn player cancelled. Could one of you join us? It will be chamber music with pianoforte, and we'll do a quintet for piano and winds that I wrote last year."

"I know that piece!" I blurted out before thinking. "I'll do it!" This was unusual for me, because normally Carl and I would talk it over when an opportunity came up for only one of us and divide things up democratically. Carl smiled, apparently amused at my strange fascination with this young upstart composer.

"That's fine - Go for it, Johann."

"You know it, do you?" said Mozart. I'm happy to hear that it's made its way to Paris somehow. It was only printed last year here in Vienna."

I couldn't explain to him that I had played it as an undergraduate student, and a couple of other times over the years. It's such a standard of the chamber music repertoire that most horn players have played it a few times and know it well.

"Umm... someone in Paris got hold of a copy," I said, rather unconvincingly.

"Well, all the better that you have played it," said Mozart, "because there won't be any time to rehearse. We'll just read it down. I've played it with the other three players before."

He gave me the address and the day and time, and we left him to greet other audience members, including the Emperor, Joseph II and the Empress Maria-Teresa.

Chapter 60

A concert and lawn bowling party with Wolfgang Amadeus Mozart, and a large dose of horn history

from Mozart Duo #6, K. 487/496a

We went home, and instead of concentrating on the actual work of the week, my mind was full of the anticipation of playing the Mozart Piano and Wind Quintet (K. 452). That week we rehearsed with the Burgtheater orchestra, which was not a bad group, and had our first performance with them. They played well and caught on fast enough that we could do some of our most difficult double concertos, including the Rosetti concerto we had played in London. But the whole time I was focused on this relatively unimportant house concert where I would get to play Mozart's piano quintet with the composer at the piano.

It was strange that throughout my sixteen years in the 18th century thus far, I had played music by dozens of composers, but only on a very few occasions pieces I had played in my 21st century career. One of the few exceptions being the Rosetti concerto that I had known in my youth as the Haydn double concerto. The reason for this was that, in the 21st century, the classical repertoire was represented by Mozart and Haydn, and almost no one else. The truth of the matter was that there were composers everywhere turning out music all the time. Mozart and Haydn were just two out of the many hundreds of composers, but the two who ultimately rose to the top and remained there, and for good reason. I met so many composers whose names I wouldn't have recognized in my 21st century life, but this was different. This was Mozart, and a piece I knew well. Being now a natural horn player and being part of this time had become quite normal in my mind, but this brought back the weirdness of the whole experience, because the Mozart piano and wind quintet related to my old life, and I watched the whole performance unfold as though I was watching a movie in which I was taking part.

Since this was at the house of a wealthy music lover, Mozart had recruited some of the best wind players in the city, and they were excellent! Especially the clarinet player, whose name was Anton Stadler, (pronounced "Stodla" in Vienna by Mozart and the others). Stadler and the oboe and bassoon player were all members of the Burgtheater orchestra that we had been playing with all week, and had heard in the opera.

The wind parts were handwritten and belonged to Mozart, who sat at the piano with just a few sheets of manuscript paper on the music desk. As happened so often at less formal house concerts, the eight or ten guests of our patron liked the piece so much that they insisted we play it again from beginning to end. The first time through I was pretty sure that I heard things in the piano part that were not familiar, and the second time he played it even more differently, improvising out of his head most of the time, but so precisely and well organized that if what he played that day had been printed in the published modern edition, it would have been every bit as well composed and perfect as the version we have. The wind players were used to his spontaneity, and got into the spirit, ornamenting their parts too. What a surreal experience to play this standard of the repertoire with them, in a style that would be quite foreign to present day musicians. All through this narrative I've attempted to describe the music we played and how it sounded, but as everyone knows you can't describe music in words, and that's the beauty of music.

After the performance, Mozart was in a good mood due to the fact that everyone liked the piece, and was his usual overly energetic self.

"*Wunderbar! Wunderbar!* Thank you for playing with us! You fit in with the group as well as if you had known the piece all your life and we had played it together for years! We will be paid handsomely if I know our patron as well as I think I do, but to thank you even better, I'd like to invite you and your charming wife, who I met at the opera, and Carl and his little boy, to my house tomorrow afternoon. I'm having a little garden party with some friends. Could you make it at six o'clock in the evening?"

"Carl and I are playing duets at another house concert at three o'clock, but I'm sure we'll be finished in time. We'll come directly from there."

"Ah, so you'll have horns with you? Maybe I'll dash off another set of *Petit airs*!"

"We still have the ones you wrote in Paris," I said, "and play them regularly. That would be wonderful to have more. Where do you live?"

"Number 5 Domgasse, first floor. Just go to St. Stephan's and ask the first person you meet on the street."

Armed with that information, I went back to our inn with my head still swimming from the experience.

"Was the opportunity of playing with your favorite composer everything you had hoped for?" asked Carl later that night. "Has he grown up at all since we last saw him in Paris?"

"He's exactly the same, but his music is wonderful! I hope you get to play more of it someday."

"We know a lot of fine composers, but I've never seen you get this excited about any of them," said Carl, laughing. "It makes me wonder if this Mozart of yours might really make a big impression on the world of music when all is said and done."

"Just wait about two hundred fifty years," I said. "You'll see." We could talk like this when Beate, who was just bringing in food from the kitchen of the inn with Carl Nicholaus at her heels, was out of earshot.

The next afternoon, after playing an hour of duets for a wealthy Viennese businessman and his family and guests, set up for us by the director of the Court Theater Orchestra, we met Beate and Carl Nicholaus, who had been waiting at a coffee house for us, and we all set out in the direction of St. Stephan's Cathedral.

Right in front of this towering edifice we did as Mozart had suggested and asked the first person we met where we could find the house at number 5 Domgasse. This happened to be a rather slow-moving old gentleman with a cane and wild white hair, wearing a threadbare tailcoat that had obviously been in service every day since it had gone out of style a good twenty years before.

"Number 5, Number 5... Yes! That's where that damned pianoforte player lives. Plays the goddamned thing at all hours of the day and night! Sometimes there are clarinets, oboes, singers, and all sorts of other noisemakers squawking away with him. Damned nuisance!"

"Yes, that's the one," Carl said patiently. "Where can we find it?"

"Down that street about halfway on the right. Just follow the noise and you won't miss it."

We thanked him, and he went harrumphing off, mumbling about drunken musicians, and we went on to find Mozart's house. We knocked, and as he opened the door, a tortoise-shell cat, who turned out to have the unlikely name of *Gürkel*, (little pickle) shot out, followed closely by a fox terrier, who turned out to have the equally unlikely sounding name of *Bimprel* (the equivalent of Spot). Mozart let us in and went out to retrieve the animals, coming back with one under each arm. The first thing that caught our eyes, and ears, was a starling that was perched on top of a birdcage, singing a tune that sounded like the rondo of one of Mozart's piano concertos[23].

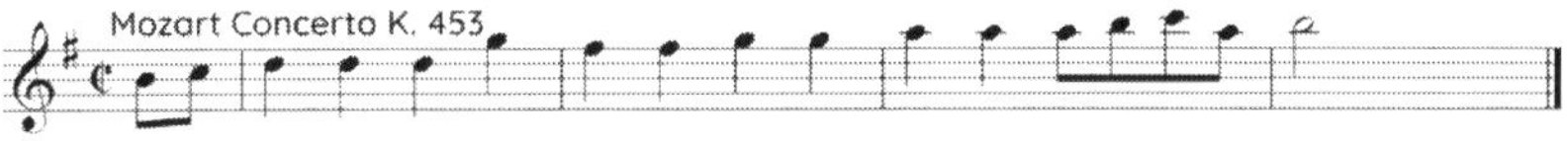

"You've noticed my bird! That's a very special bird. He gave me the theme for my most recent pianoforte concerto. I was walking around the city one day trying to think up a theme for the last movement when I walked by a shop and heard him singing that melody. I ran home and wrote and orchestrated the entire movement that evening and went back the next day and bought the bird, in gratitude for having given me the theme."

I looked around the room, and it was a total expression of his personality. Papers were strewn around the floor, mostly unfinished pieces that he had laid aside to start on another, a pianoforte with empty wine glasses and bottles on the floor under it, a tray with remnants of a meal, a viola sitting on a chair next to a quartet stand, the kind that has four desks facing each other so four people can see their music and each other, stacks of music in every corner, mostly in bundles tied together with string, a couple of pairs of shoes, each separated from its mate randomly around the room, a stand that held a lady's coat and shawl and a gentleman's waistcoat, a desk covered with papers, pens, inkwells, sealing wax, blotting paper, knives, and letters, and a few children's toys.

At that point a petit young woman with dark flowing hair came into the room carrying a child that looked to be about two years old.

"Constanze, meine liebe! Let me introduce you to my friends, the famous Palsa/Türrschmidt Waldhorn duo from Paris. And Frau Palsa, and Carl's son, - um...., what was your name again my fine little man?"

"Carl Nicholaus, mein Herr," said the boy bowing politely.

"A regular little gentleman!" laughed Mozart.

"Oh, please excuse the condition of our sitting room," said Constanze. "This is where Wolfie works, and often eats and sleeps. When he's in the middle of composing something important he will not leave this room for days at a time."

"I've been working on a symphony, and a piano concerto, and a wind divertimento all at the same time this week, and they're all getting mixed up with each other in my head, so I thought a break for a lawn bowling party in the garden downstairs would clear the brain and reset things to go at them again tonight."

As he finished, Constanze approached Beate and hugged her with the baby between them.

"My dear Frau Palsa! I've heard that you are also a horn soloist and have played a concerto at the Concert Spirtuel. I would never have dreamed that I would meet a woman who played the horn! You must tell me all about how you managed to learn and find your way into the top of the musical world of Paris! Come with me into the kitchen and help me gather the wine and cakes that we'll take downstairs to the garden."

Constanze and Wolfgang were the perfect pair, absolutely childlike, full of energy and talking non-stop. Before she could get in a word, Beate was swept into the kitchen and we soon heard the voices of both chattering away merrily."

"I hear a knock! That must be the others who will join us this afternoon," said Mozart, going to the door and inviting in two more pairs of ladies and gentlemen. Anton Stadler and his brother, Johann, and their wives entered, and Mozart greeted them as though they were old friends he had not seen for years, though Anton had been part of the quintet concert the day before, and both brothers had played clarinet in the Figaro performance we had attended.

The party was completed by the arrival of the two horn players we had seen in the opera orchestra, Martin Rupp, and Jacob Eisen. They were the horn players in the Wiener Hofkapelle as well, and considered to be the most skillful horn players in Vienna at the time. They certainly played well in Figaro, which has substantial horn parts.

In the meantime, Constanze had enlisted all the ladies to help her bring wine, glasses, plates and cakes downstairs to the garden. This wasn't so much a garden as just a shaded and pleasant plot of grass at the back of the house away from the street noise. The gentlemen brought chairs and a table, Carl and I carried our horn box between us, and Mozart followed with a chest filled with wooden bowling pins and balls just a little bigger than a softball for lawn bowling. The table and chairs were set down and a space was cleared for the *"Kegelbahn"* or bowling green.

Everyone was familiar with the thirteen rather complicated rules of nine pin lawn bowling, or *"Kegeln"* except for me, but they were good enough to tell me when it was my turn, and I seemed to do all right by simply trying to knock over as many pins as I could in a single throw. The childlike silliness of Wolfgang and Constanze was absolutely contagious, and the game proceeded with very imprecise scorekeeping, lots of cakes, a local red wine called *Zweigelt*, and enough laughter and jokes to distract everyone's attention for an afternoon from the difficult life of being a musician in Vienna at this time of history. Carl Nicholaus took charge of the Mozart baby, two-year-old Karl Thomas, and the two of them chased each other around with the cat and dog at their heals, sometimes tumbling like a single ball of children and animals, adding to the entertainment of everyone.

As the game went on, and got less and less organized, Wolfgang stood up and addressed us all.

"I have promised our two guest Parisian horn players (for some reason he always referred to us that way) I would write a set of duos to commemorate their visit to Vienna. Horn duos are best composed in just the right state of drunkenness - not too little and not too much. Conditions appear to be perfect at the moment for good horn writing, so I had better start now before the particular muse responsible for horn music goes over the edge, or rather under the table, to sleep off her fit of creativity! That's how I've always composed for my good friend Leutgeb."

"I don't know if you've heard," said Martin Rupp, addressing Carl and me, "but that drunken horn writing muse has inspired Wolfgang to write some very nice concertos for the horn, and a quintet for horn and strings for his friend Joseph Leutgeb. Do you know him?"

I certainly couldn't tell him that I was intimately familiar with every note of solo horn music Mozart had written, or would write in the future.

"I've never met Leutgeb, but we've heard he's a fine horn player and made a grand impression when he played as soloist at the Concert Spirituel in Paris in the early 70s. Is he still active?"

"He still plays, but he is a member of an earlier generation of solo horn players," said Mozart. "He came to Salzburg in the '60s to work with my father in the court orchestra, and that's where I got to know him. He's so much fun that I had to write concertos for him. He was on the road a lot and played them everywhere. As a composer, if someone goes all over playing your music, it's the next best thing to being in all those places yourself, so I keep writing things for him. I've just started a new concerto in E major, but when I showed him the sketches of the first movement, he said his high range wasn't up to it anymore. I may scrap that one and start over on a lower one in D major instead."

"He's already over fifty-five, and his teeth aren't what they used to be," added Jacob Eisen. "He's lost a lot of high range and power, but you should have heard him ten and twenty years ago when he was at the top of his game! He had the most beautiful singing adagio you've ever heard."

I knew that fragment of a concerto in E major, which Mozart had abandoned. Had Leutgeb's upper range still been intact, it would have been an even more beautiful concerto than the others, judging by the opening tutti and first solo section that he did complete. It had always been a mystery, and now I knew why he never finished it. Mozart's last pieces of horn music were the first movement of a concerto and a Rondo in D major with a very limited range. Jacob Eisen's remarks about the decline in Leutgeb's skills had cleared up the mystery of the very easy range and endurance of those pieces too.

Mozart sat down and dashed off the first duo, a short allegro, in about four minutes, and Carl and I got the silver horns out of their box. We set the separate parts on the horn box facing each other and played this first piece.

"Charming! Well-done! Bravo! Wunderbar!" were the shouts as everyone clapped. The bowling continued and Mozart spent a few more minutes working on a minuet. It was my turn to bowl when he set the music down on the horn box.

"Let Beate play one!" said Constanze. "We want to hear Beate play!" Beate stayed in good shape, playing horn every day, whether there was a performance to prepare for or not, and was always ready to step up and play. She blew a few notes on my horn, and then she and Carl played the newly composed minuet while I took my turn. From then on, Mozart kept writing short pieces and setting them in front of us, and whichever two of the three of us were not taking our turn at the game, would play it. We even pulled Martin and Jacob into the fun and let them have a go on our silver horns, which they had been curious about. They pronounced them to be excellent, and took to them immediately, being the skillful players they were.

Carl and Beate were both low horn players, and I'm a high horn, and so he wrote several of the duos in a range comfortable for two low players to play together, and a few with almost over the top high horn writing in the first horn, going up to the G above high C in a few cases. I could see he was testing the waters, first writing up to high C, and in successive duos pushing the range until ascending to the G above, when I finally laughed and said, "Stop! That's my limit! If we go any higher we'll get to a range that only little Bimprel will be able to hear!"

Mozart looked at me quizzically for a moment, and then burst out laughing at what he thought was just a piece of absurd nonsense, which pulled everyone else into a wine-induced laughing fit. It hadn't occurred to me at the time that this bit of science about dogs' hearing was probably something that had not been discovered yet.

All together he composed six little pieces that day, which turned out to be the most artistic and pleasant of all the duos that we collected from many different composers over the years. Mozart later published them in Vienna, along with the six he had written for us in Paris ten years earlier. A Paris edition of the twelve duos also appeared around the same time, which Mozart may never have heard about, and from which he probably never earned a penny. We got a lot of mileage out of those twelve little pieces over the next five years of touring, using them as encores after concerto performances, and in chamber music concerts[24].

As to the extreme upper range of some of these duos, there were a few players at the time who specialized in that range, and a few composers who wrote for them. Carl Franz, in the service of the Prince of Esterhazy, was one of them, and inspired Joseph Haydn to write all sorts of daring high horn parts for him. Once when we were in Dresden on a tour in the late 1770s, the concertmaster of the Hofkapelle there, Johann Neruda, gave me a little concerto in E flat he had composed that stayed up in the range from written high C up to G a good deal of the time. It's possible to squeak out those notes, but it loses its effectiveness to write a whole piece up in that range.

Haydn wrote more sensibly by only going that high very occasionally, as a special effect. Rosetti knew that anything above written E was risky and didn't go there. He saved his highest passages, only touching the high E occasionally, for the musical high points in the movement, which is a better use of that range. I only performed the Neruda concerto once, and that was enough for me.

The garden party at the Mozarts' house was an experience I will never forget. Modern horn players read about his joking relationship and good-humored banter with the horn player Leutgeb, but that was his way with everyone he knew and worked with. Though it might get old as a regular diet, the laughter of Wolfgang and Constanze, the antics of the children and animals, the afternoon's festivities, and the new duos, kept us in a good mood for the rest of our time in Vienna. It was the last we saw of Wolfgang Amadeus Mozart, who was the greatest musical genius, and quirkiest, goofiest human being I've ever met.

Chapter 61

Lexicographer; A harmless drudge. A maker of dictionaries.
- Samuel Johnson, Dictionary of the English Language, 1755

We had three more successful concerts at the Burgtheater, and a couple more private chamber music concerts before leaving Vienna. We weren't able to play for the court of the Emperor, Joseph II, but that was fine with us. The public concerts at the theater, and the informal and friendly house concerts both paid well, and were much less trouble, and more enjoyable than the stiff, formal concerts at court for royalty.

By mid-July we were finished with all our obligations in Vienna and began the trip back to Cassel for the grand music festival that the Landgraf, Friedrich II, was organizing. We were ready to be home again in our own house and our own beds after seven months straight of traveling and sleeping in inns in London and Vienna and everywhere in between. We had to travel directly back, since we were expected in Cassel by the first of August in time to prepare for this special musical event.

It was well known that the Landgraf's health was failing, and he wanted to have this one last grand music festival to surround himself and his court with the best music and musicians of Europe before he died. Groups large and small from France, Italy, and all around the German speaking Empire had been invited, and for four weeks the different groups performed concerts nearly every day alternately in the two theaters in town, known as the small and large opera theaters. Concerts were open to the public for free and were well attended by the people of Cassel and visitors from far and wide. Music of all the best composers was heard almost daily. Hasse, Gluck, Cannabich, Mozart, Schweizer, Holzbauer, Paeseillo, Martini, Rosetti, and many others were represented on the programs. It was a showcase of the most current music from all over Europe, but primarily from Germany, Austria, and Bohemia.

The Landgraf's own orchestra, the Cassel Hofkapelle, performed a concert every Sunday afternoon, and that was the Landgraf's chance to show off not only the orchestra and its soloists, but also to feature his chamber musicians, to which Carl and I belonged.

We were soloists on most of these programs and played lots of chamber music other evenings and afternoons at the Landgraf's residence and other venues in town during this non-stop month of music. On the first of the Sunday concerts in the *"Hofassemblee"*, a large ballroom in the palace, we played one of our several Rosetti double concertos and the double concerto of concertmaster Johann Braun, who led the orchestra that afternoon. The other soloist on the program was our good friend, oboist Christian Barth, another of the small group of Cassel court chamber musicians. He played a concerto of his own composition, and another by Ignaz Holzbauer.

These Sunday programs were meant specifically to showcase the Cassel soloists and singers, and therefore would consist mostly of concertos and arias. This one started with an opera overture from *"Piramo et Tisbe"* by Hasse, then Carl and I alternated with Christian Barth, playing our respective concertos. The program concluded with a Mannheim symphony by Cannabich.

It was at this first Sunday concert that we met Ernst Ludwig Gerber, composer, writer, and author of the famous *"Historisches-Biographisches Lexicon der Tonkünstler"* (Historical -Bibliographical Dictionary of Musicians) which was published in the early 1790s. He had devoted several years already to his research for this monumental work, and had come to Cassel to the festival, or *"Musikmesse"* to interview as many musicians as he could and document their life stories and music.

We had just left the stage after our second and final piece, the Rosetti concerto in E, when we found ourselves shaking hands and exchanging bows with a tall academic looking gentleman dressed in black waistcoat and breeches, with an unusually bright and clean white ruffled shirt and cravat, and small oval gold-rimmed eyeglasses. He had a large shiny bald forehead with long white hair flowing down at the sides into curls over the ear, and was wearing a scarf, despite the warm summer weather.

He introduced himself, told us about the dictionary he was working on and asked if he could spend a little time with us to get some information about our careers up to that point.

"We would be happy to tell you about our travels and the music we love to play," said Carl. "We can go to our rooms and sit comfortably. My friend Johann can make his special coffee for us, and some of the other Cassel chamber musicians will stop by. You can interview them as well."

"How very friendly and generous you are with your time!" replied Gerber, bowing again. "I never know what kind of reception I will get from the most famous artists. Some are quite unapproachable, and I'm grateful for your openness and hospitality."

"Horn players are generally friendly types," I said. "The horn is such an unpredictable instrument, that it keeps you humble. As the old saying goes, 'God only knows what's going to come out of the horn, and he's not telling.' You take your chances every time."

I have no idea if that was an old saying, but it sounded awfully good, and got across the point that horn players didn't usually have big egos. The one exception of course, being our Paris acquaintance, Jean Dubois, who had enough ego to supply all the horn players in Paris with enough self-assuredness to last for years and not run low on the item himself.

Gerber was very eager to talk, so we packed the horns into their box, and led the way to our house, where Beate was just arriving home from an afternoon chamber concert in which she had played viola in a program of string quartets with a group of women from Cassel. As often happened after Sunday afternoon concerts, several others stopped by, including Christian Barth, and a couple other woodwind players, as well as the other players from Beate's string quartet. I brewed coffee for everyone, and Gerber scribbled furiously in his notebook as each person told him the story of their musical life.

All the others had a real story to tell of where they came from, where they had studied, and other details about their performing careers, but I told my own story, which had been fabricated sixteen years before by Carl, of having been born in Jemeritz, Bohemia on June 20th, 1752, where I studied the horn, and about our time in Paris. I was so used to it now that it flowed out as easily as if it were all true.

One of the group stepped out to an inn down the street and came back a few minutes later with hot sausages, bread and beer, and the evening turned into an informal chamber music party. Gerber was fascinated by what he had heard in the horn concertos in the concert that afternoon. He wanted to know how we were able to play chromatically and modulate into other keys within the pieces. We showed him how hand stopping worked and ended up playing duets in several major and minor keys. He was full of questions, and by the end of the evening had filled a small notebook with information. Eventually I got to see what he wrote about us in his dictionary. He wrote a longer entry for each of us than most of the other musicians in the book and included many of the details about where we had been and what we had told him about chromatic solo horn playing. He also included in his book a description of a curious little picture that Beate had displayed in our house in Cassel.

Before we left Paris, I was going through some things in a small box of personal papers and items I hadn't looked at in years, among which were a few pictures that had been in my 21st century wallet, including a wallet-size color photo of me in black tie and tails with my modern horn, standing under a tree outdoors which had been done as a publicity picture for my website. Beate happened to be walking by as I flipped through them and snatched it out of my hand.

"What's this?" she said, examining it. "A miniature of you in a strange looking waistcoat! Who painted it, and when?"

"That was in America, before I came to Paris," I said nervously as she was looking at it. I couldn't remember if you could see that it was a modern valve horn. If the valves had been visible I would have had some very complicated explaining to do, but fortunately I was standing with the bell facing out under my right arm, and the rest of the horn behind me, so the valves weren't in sight.

"It's very skillfully done. It looks exactly like you. Is that an American orchestra uniform?"

"Yes, the standard dress for our orchestra in America."

"How very strange! And your hair is short; is that the style in America?" she said looking even more closely.

"Just a passing fad that was in style at the time."

"It's a beautiful little painting. So delicately done. May I keep it and have it put into a frame?"

"If you like it, of course you can have it, my dear Beate!"

Before we left Paris, she took it to a shop and had it put into a small wooden frame, and from then on it was displayed wherever we lived and was examined and commented on by everyone who saw it. I've often wondered what happened to that little photo, and if it survived somewhere for people to wonder about in the coming centuries.

When Gerber, who was familiar with painting techniques, saw it on our fireplace mantel, he was fascinated and wanted to know how the artist had painted it.

"My dear Palsa!" he said, with his eyes fixed on the little photo. "This is one of the most extraordinary miniatures I have ever seen! It looks precisely like you, and the brushstrokes are so fine as to be completely invisible. I did some oil painting and drawing in my youth and have studied a lot of paintings by the great masters, but I've never seen anything as exquisitely done as this!"

He stared at it a good long while, and it must have made a lasting impression, because he mentioned it in my biography in his book.

Gerber stayed in Cassel for the entire four weeks of the music festival, and we saw him and talked again several times. Each time he mentioned the remarkable "miniature painting" that he saw in our house.[25]

Chapter 62

In 1785 they traveled to London and returned in August of 1786 to Cassel to perform at the music festival there. This was the high point of music making in Cassel, the time when the most prominent musicians there celebrated their last great triumph.
- Ernst Ludwig Gerber "Historisches - Biographisches Lexicon der Tonkünstler" Leipzig, 1792

The grand music festival concluded at the end of August 1786, and life in Cassel got back to normal. The court orchestra went back to regular performances in church and the opera, but the concerts of orchestral music and concertos were fewer and farther between due to the Landgraf's failing health. He also had fewer private chamber music evenings than ever before, and everyone could see the writing on the wall. We were all going to be at liberty to look for new work soon, because it was well known that neither Friederich's wife, the Princess Mary, daughter of King George II of England, or his eldest son, Wilhelm, who would succeed his father, were interested in supporting the large and expensive musical establishment that Friederich had assembled in Cassel. In the days and weeks before his death, most of us among the chamber musicians started putting out the word that we would soon be available, and we began writing to a few people we knew in orchestras in other parts of the Empire asking if anyone needed a pair of horn players.

Friederich II, Landgraf of Hesse-Cassel, died at the end of October, and with his death, the court went into mourning. This meant that after a performance of a grand Requiem Mass, there was no more music in Cassel for the foreseeable future. All we could do was send out more letters in the hope that something would come up. The idea of leaving Cassel with no destination in mind wasn't appealing to any of us after the experience of being on the road for an extended period after leaving Paris.

As we sat at breakfast one rainy morning at the beginning of November, Beate, Carl and I were, as usual, discussing our options.

“I just can’t see going back to Paris,” said Carl. “Not without a steady position.”

“And neither of us wants to play in a theater orchestra or even the Paris opera, where you’re buried musically,” I said. “And though they’re happy to have us play, both as soloists and in the orchestra at the Concert Spirituel, they don’t play often enough to make our living that way, or as freelance soloists in Paris.”

“Both you and Carl were tired of everything about Paris,” added Beate. “You really wouldn’t be happy going back, for many reasons.”

I could tell she was thinking of Carl’s bitter memories of the death of Röslein.

“No, no,” Carl went on. “We want to stay in the German speaking Empire in a place where we can have a steady income from orchestral playing in a group of high enough quality that it will be musically satisfying and be able to pursue solo playing too.”

“We have to keep touring and playing double concertos,” I said. “We’ve already lifted the level of solo horn playing a good deal over the past sixteen years, and there’s still a lot to do in showing the musical world the possibilities of the horn as a solo instrument.”

“But you don’t have to hurry,” said Beate. “We’ve saved a good amount of money already here in Cassel, and you have enough in the bank in Paris to live comfortably for years. You can wait until the right opportunity presents itself, and not feel like you have to jump at the first offer that comes along.”

A few minutes later there was a knock at the door, and Beate rose to answer it. A delivery boy handed in a letter.

“Guten Morgen Frau Palsa!” he said pleasantly. “The post just arrived at the *Rathaus* and there’s an urgent letter addressed to Herr Palsa and Herr Türrschmidt!”

The boy was off in a flash, and Carl took the letter and looked at it in astonishment.

“It has the seal of the Prussian court in Berlin! The court of Friedrich the Great, King of Prussia!”

“Open it! Quick! What does it say?” I said, rising out of my chair in anticipation.

“It’s from Johann Friedrich Reichardt, the composer, and Kapellmeister of the Berlin court orchestra,” he said while reading.

"Read it out loud!" said Beate. "Otherwise the suspense will be the end of us!"

Carl began reading:

Berlin, November second, 1786

Herrn Palsa und Türrschmidt,

I have been informed by several of our colleagues here in Berlin that you are soon to be at liberty to take a new position due to the death of Friederich II of Hesse-Cassel and the consequent changes in the Hofkapelle in Cassel. Though I have not had the honor of hearing your fine artistry on the horn personally, your reputation as the leading horn duo of the present day has been related to me by those who have worked with you in Paris and heard you on your tours of the musical centers of the Empire. The consensus of everyone with whom I have been in contact is that you are the first horn players I should approach in the present matter.

Let me first explain the current musical situation here in Berlin. His highness, Friedrich II, King of Prussia, passed away earlier this year, which was a great loss to all. His grandson and successor, Friedrich Wilhelm II is now in charge of the entire musical establishment. As is well known, the late King was a great lover of music, a fine player of the flute, and a skillful composer. He was enthusiastic about his orchestra and opera but was rather old-fashioned in his musical taste. He engaged Johann Joachim Quantz as his flute teacher, court composer, and music director in 1741, and engaged many of the most important composers and musicians of the time, including Franz Benda, C.P.E. Bach, Carl Heinrich Graun, and a host of others. These men were at the forefront of the musical style of their day, but the King's taste in music did not keep up with the changing times. By the time of Herr Quantz's death in 1773, the orchestra and opera were sadly behind stylistically, and in a state of decline. From that time up to the present the King insisted on continuing to have performances of antiquated orchestral music and opera productions from as much as thirty and forty years ago.

Since his grandfather's death, his Highness Wilhelm Friedrich II has made it his mission to bring music at the court of Berlin back to the high level it enjoyed thirty years ago and has engaged the best modern composers and musicians. He has called me back from Vienna, where I had been working, to reestablish the reputation of the orchestra and produce operas in the current style. I have been authorized by his Highness to spare no expense in engaging the finest musicians in the Empire and therefore I am offering you positions with the newly reestablished orchestra and opera, which I believe will be of the very highest quality. And in case you are concerned about your freedom to tour as soloists, there will be certain periods in the year during which you will be able to request permission to travel, as will be the case with many of the fine artists we are engaging. It will be, as the famous Charles Burney said of the Mannheim Orchestra in its heyday, "an army of generals."

I would request that you send your reply to this invitation by return post, and if agreeable, come to Berlin as soon as is convenient.

I remain, your most humble and obedient servant,

Johann Friedrich Reichardt
Kapellmeister, Königliche Hofkapelle, Berlin

"Heaven has answered our prayers!" said Beate.

"This is exactly what we're looking for!" said Carl, and we each read the letter two or three times over again to wrap our minds around this unexpected piece of good fortune.

"Everyone is talking about the reorganization of the Hofkapelle in Berlin, and how they're pouring huge amounts of money into hiring the best instrumentalists and singers. This will be without a doubt the best orchestra in the Empire."

"And maybe finally a stable position that we can settle into for the rest of our careers." I said.

"And a large modern city with lots of performing and teaching opportunities for me, and a place where Carl Nicholaus can have a good musical education," added Beate.

Berlin was a thriving city of 150,000 residents, and the musical scene was undergoing big changes. Plans were underway for a new opera house, and there was much talk about the coming revival of music and the arts under the new monarch.

"No question," I said. "We have to go there and join the orchestra. It will be a bit of a change to go back to full-time orchestra playing, but he did mention time off for touring."

"The court of Friedrich the Great was known for its chamber music at court, in which the most famous musicians in the Empire took part. There will be chamber music and solo opportunities everywhere!" said Carl, as he started to consider the possibilities of one of the largest cities in Germany.

The three of us bent over the kitchen table and put our heads together to draft a letter to Reichardt accepting the position, which Carl wrote in his best *Kurrentschrift*, the formal German handwriting of the time that one learned in school, and which I never came close to mastering during my 18th century time. The letter was posted before noon that day.

We spent the next couple of days packing, taking care of any unfinished business in Cassel, and taking leave of all our friends there, who were pleasantly surprised to hear that we had landed new positions so quickly. The rest of the chamber musicians eventually found new situations, mostly in high quality orchestras, since they were all fine musicians, but we were among the most fortunate.

Carl Nicholaus, was the most reluctant of all of us to leave Cassel. He had made some good friends in the school choir of the cathedral where he studied and sang at services, and he was sad to leave his singing master, who had helped him to greatly improve his voice and singing abilities. The boy had a fine voice, and there was every indication that he could make a career as a singer. It was only after we all convinced him that Berlin was much larger, and a major musical center where he could study and sing with the best, that he consented to leave Cassel where he had spent the previous three years.

Chapter 63

Several months later, death took the Landgraf, and with him, the supporter of music in Cassel up to that time. Palsa and Türrschmidt were among the first to leave, and went to Berlin, where they immediately went into the service of the current highly esteemed King, who was at that time crown prince.
- Ernst Ludwig Gerber, "Historisches-Biographisches Lexicon der Tonkünstler" Leipzig, 1792

We set off from Cassel in the second week of November, which was a terrible time to travel in the northern part of the Empire. It was slow going due to the weather, and we were traveling with all our possessions and instruments. After a couple of unpleasant weeks on the road, we arrived in Berlin, the capital of the Kingdom of Prussia.

As with London, it was a pleasant experience to go to a city where we were expected and didn't have to explain who we were and what we wanted. On the morning after we arrived, Carl and I presented ourselves at the royal opera house, where we were immediately treated like special artists. The first person we met apparently knew that we were expected and called to one of the servants.

"Go and fetch Kapellmeister Reichardt and the Herr Musik-intendant. The new Waldhorn players have arrived!"

There was much bustling around and within a couple of minutes, a large man with a pleasant round face, red nose, white hair, and a large expanse of forehead entered.

"Let me be the first to welcome you to Berlin and the court of his Highness, Friedrich Wilhelm II," said Reichardt shaking our hands. "I hope the trip from Cassel was not too unpleasant at this time of year."

"It was, in spite of the weather, a trip made pleasant by the prospect of joining this famous orchestra under your leadership, Maestro," I said, sensing that this was the way to start our relationship with this man, who while pleasant enough, was obviously quite formal and full of his own importance.

"Indeed, it is our honor to receive you here. After the death of our beloved King Friedrich, I have been charged by his successor, Friedrich Wilhelm, to completely restructure the orchestra and opera. The first order of business in that process was to seek out the finest musicians in the Empire. Given your celebrated reputation as a horn duo, and the fact that you have played together orchestrally and as chamber musicians for many years, there was, in my mind, no better choice for our orchestra."

"The honor is all ours, Maestro," said Carl, bowing, "and we will do our very best, artistically and as colleagues, to further the fine reputation of the Prussian Court Orchestra."

"Very well spoken!' said Reichardt. "I am pleased to have not only fine artists, but also well-bred gentlemen in my orchestra. We will be putting you to work right away, since we have just opened a production of my most recent opera, a lyric tragedy entitled *'Tamerlan'*. We have borrowed a couple of horn players from a nearby court orchestra to play the first few performances, but now that you're here you can take over. Our next performance is tomorrow night."

"It will be a great pleasure to join in as soon as possible," I said.

"And for us as well," he said with a bow. "I will now introduce you to the music intendant, Herr Engel, who will show you where to go tomorrow evening for the performance and take you to the theater's tailor shop where you can be fitted this afternoon with orchestra uniforms. You will also need to meet with our oboist, Herr Ebeling, to check the pitch level of our group and make sure your instruments are compatible with our wind section. Herr Schramm, our harpsichordist, will give you the horn parts to the opera and familiarize you with the music, which I think you won't find difficult. I will see you next at the performance tomorrow evening. Wait here and I'll summon Herr Engel. Good day, and welcome to the finest orchestra in the Empire!"

"Efficient, isn't he?" said Carl, after Reichardt had left.

"Very formal too," I said, "but he seems happy to have us here, and friendly enough."

"He didn't waste a moment in getting us right into the thick of things. We've been here about twelve hours, and we're getting orchestra uniforms and horn parts for a performance tomorrow of an opera that we've never heard or rehearsed!"

"I guess he wants to see if we can land on our feet and get with the program quickly," I replied.

Reichardt turned out to be a pleasant colleague to work with and a good orchestra leader, but he expected everyone to jump at his orders, as we had just experienced. His compositions, mostly stage works, were as good as, or better than those of many composers we had worked with over the years, but he was, from that day onward, as long as we worked with him, just as stiff and formal on all occasions.

Herr Engel, who took care of all business and logistical matters arrived to take us to see the theater and accompanied us to the tailor shop. He talked non-stop the whole time.

"I think you'll like the orchestra uniforms. They are black and white with gold trim - the Prussian national colors. You'll get two full suits and linen at the court's expense."

"That's very generous. Thank you, and do we..."

"And we issue shoes to match the suit, but that will have to wait until another day when there is time to sit down with the shoemaker we use to be measured for shoes that fit properly. Whatever you have will be fine for tomorrow's performance, and then we'll get new ones sorted out."

"Thanks, that sounds..."

"And did anyone talk to you about lodgings?"

"No, for the moment we're..."

"The court will pay for your lodgings in addition to your salary. Many of the musicians live in a street that's an easy five-minute walk from the theater. I'll show you a nice little house in that street that's empty at the moment when we are finished here. Maestro Reichardt may have mentioned that chamber music takes place in Potsdam at the Sanssouci Palace, which is half a day's ride from the city center. The court will arrange and pay for your transportation there when you are required for chamber music evenings."

"Is there a good deal of chamber music? We love..."

"Oh yes! And his Highness has already given you both the title of "*Kammermusicus*", in addition to your orchestra service, which adds substantially to the salary."

"We're happy he has a high opinion of..."

"Without a doubt! Ever since we received your letter accepting the positions, his Highness and Kapellmeister Reichardt have been talking as though they have acquired the best horns in the Empire, which I'm sure, is the case."

This whirlwind tour took us into the theater and to the tailor shop, where he continued to tell us about each member of the orchestra and all the singers, the history of music in Berlin, descriptions of recent opera productions, and on and on, as we were measured for our clothes, met with the secretary of the orchestra and signed an agreement of engagement, and found out what our salaries were to be. The pay, which did indeed include extra for chamber music duties, was higher than we had received in Paris or Cassel, simply because the King of Prussia had more resources than our previous employers. Engel then took us to see the house, in a connected row of houses in a relatively clean street.

We picked up Beate and Carl Nicholaus at the inn along the way so they could be in on the decision of our living quarters. We all agreed that it was a fine house and went directly back to have a wagon bring our trunks from the inn. After these had been deposited in the new house, and we had unpacked a few things, we left Beate and Carl Nicholaus to arrange our new abode, and we went with Herr Engel back to the theater. We brought our Raoux orchestra horns back with us to meet with the first oboe and the harpsichordist and were shown to an orchestra rehearsal room to wait for them.

"I have arranged for Herr Ebeling and Herr Schramm to meet you here in just a few minutes. And before I take my leave of you, do you have any other questions?"

"No," I said. "I think you've covered everything we could ever want to know, and taken care of all of our needs, right down to a place to live, for which we are very grateful."

"My pleasure completely to be at your service. Now I wish you a pleasant day, and look forward to seeing, and hearing you tomorrow evening!"

With that he left, and after the door closed, Carl looked around in silence for a few seconds.

"Johann, do you hear a weird, unfamiliar sound?"

"No. What is it?"

"Ah. I have it! It's the sound of Herr Engel not talking!"

"Right! Silence! I'd almost forgotten what it sounds like."

After we had a good long laugh, fully worthy of Wolfgang Mozart, Ernst Ebeling, the principal oboist, and harpsichordist Johann Christian Schramm arrived and introduced themselves. We discovered that the pitch here was just a bit lower than that of Cassel. We could get along with our regular crooks for the time being, thanks to the tuning slides on our Raoux orchestra horns, but as soon as we had some time to ourselves, we would need to visit a horn maker and have a few important crooks made that more exactly matched the Berlin orchestra's pitch level. Then Herr Schramm gave us the horn parts, which were very straight-forward, and played a few of the arias and choruses for us so we could learn the tempos.

"These people don't mess around," said Carl, as we walked back to the new house. "They get right down to business."

"They sure do! In three hours they've gotten us ready to step into the opera orchestra."

"And it will be interesting to hear what the musical personality of this band is," said Carl.

"I have a feeling it isn't the poetic, flexible Parisian style, or the fun, devil-may-care style of London. I expect it's more formal, like the Cassel orchestra, but with a couple of mugs of your strongest coffee."

Carl's guess was accurate. The Prussian court orchestra's style was stricter in its concept of time, by 18th century standards, which is to say that you still couldn't put a metronome on anything they played except the very fastest movements. Intonation in both the strings and winds was some of the best we had encountered anywhere. Top to bottom, the orchestra was an all-star team collected from all parts of the Empire.

We went home that afternoon to find that Beate had not only made this new house into a comfortable living space, but had also supplied us with firewood, bedclothes, and linens, and had a pork roast, bread, and beer on the table ready for us all to have our evening meal, knowing that we hadn't eaten since breakfast that morning at the inn. We filled her in on all that had happened during the afternoon, and the few orchestra members we had met.

Over the next few days Beate began meeting some of the other families in the street. Herr Engel was right that there were several orchestra members who lived there. There were a few wind players, a couple of trumpets from the trumpet ensemble, and some string players. Beate was already putting out feelers about the amateur scene and checking out who among the wives and family members of the musicians in the street were also musicians, with whom she might be able to play chamber music. She was planning to take Carl Nicholaus the next day to check out the school and choir at St. Peter's Church, which was close by. Things were already coming together, and all four of us were excited and enthusiastic about this new city with its wide range of possibilities.

Chapter 64

The orchestra of the Royal Theater and Opera was a high-class group in every respect. Everything was precise and well in tune, parts were clearly and meticulously copied by the court copyists, and there was a good working relationship between Reichardt, who conducted the orchestra mostly with a baton, but occasionally led from the violin, and Herr Schramm, who conducted the recitatives from the harpsichord. The wind section phrased like a single person, which made it possible from that first opera performance to blend into the orchestra as though we had been playing there for years.

The number of members would vary for different purposes, but the opera orchestra generally consisted of about a dozen violins, four violas, four cellos, two flutes, two oboes, two bassoons, two horns, and harpsichord or pianoforte.

Friedrich Wilhelm II and his friends and guests sat in the first row of boxes nearest the orchestra, while his wife, the Queen, Frederika Luise and her ladies sat in the next row of boxes. There were other boxes that were reserved for nobility and foreign visitors. Otherwise, the seating was open with no admission fee. Anyone who was decently dressed could enter free of charge until the house was full - and it was always full. To be assured a seat at the performances, which started at six o'clock in the evening, it was necessary to arrive at least an hour early.

One tradition that surprised us the first night was the announcement of the entry of the queen and her company of ladies by an ensemble of trumpets and kettledrums, arranged in two groups stationed on either side of the stage in the top row of boxes. They sounded a brilliant fanfare which was composed specifically to last from the moment the queen's party entered the theater until they were seated in their box. This took place at every performance.[26]

The singers were of a very high quality all together, though a couple members of the cast were sixty and seventy years old, and their voices were probably no longer what they had been. What these lacked in strength, they made up for in their expression and acting. Much expense had been put into costumes and sets, which were elaborate and impressive.

This first opera was an easy one for the horns and gave us an idea of how this group did things, how they shaped phrases, their concept of note lengths and spaces between notes, and their way of perceiving pulse and interpreting rhythm. By the second act we felt like we were at home, and that feeling persisted for the next several years of playing with them.

Concerts of purely orchestral music and concertos, known as *Academia,* took place less often than opera performances, but still occurred frequently. For these, Herr Reichardt conducted with a stick, and there was no keyboard instrument in the orchestra, both of which were very "modern" innovations that he had recently introduced.

Up until the death of Frederick the Great, music of the previous generation was often heard, including works of C.P.E. Bach, Graun, Benda, and Quantz. Some of these appeared occasionally on the programs during our time with the group, but Reichardt generally programmed more modern composers, including a lot of his own recent works. It was in Berlin though, that I became acquainted with the horn parts of C.P.E. Bach, who wrote in the most unidiomatic way for horn of any composer ever. From Mozart and Haydn to Strauss and Mahler, when the best composers of orchestral music wrote difficult things for the horns, it was worth the effort you had to put forth to play them, but C.P.E. Bach wrote difficult and awkward horn parts for no particular reason, though the music itself was always well-composed, inventive and interesting.

The other component of our positions was that of *Kammermusicus*, members of the private chamber musicians of the court. These evening performances of chamber music for a small and select audience took place in the town of Potsdam, which was situated on the River Havel, about fifteen miles, or a two-hour coach ride from the city of Berlin.

During the time of King Frederick the Great, or "*der Alte Fritz*" as he was known, there were private concerts just about every evening at the summer palace of Sanssouci in Potsdam. Friedrich was, from all the reports of the musicians who took part in those evenings, an excellent flute player, and the concerts would consist mostly of flute concertos by Quantz, his flute teacher and court composer. Quantz wrote over three hundred flute concertos for Friedrich, and the king would cycle through them during the year, playing two or three each evening. These were almost all scored for flute and strings, and were usually played with one on a part and harpsichord. These concerts were relatively informal, with no rehearsal, just show up and read the pieces down with the king as soloist. It seems almost inconceivable that a composer could write that many concertos, but this was common with court composers. Haydn wrote well over one hundred baryton trios for the Prince of Esterhazy, and as many symphonies. Telemann wrote more pieces than he could remember, and Bach produced a cantata for just about every Sunday of the year, and none of them ran out of musical ideas.

Now that Friedrich Wilhelm II was at the helm, the chamber concerts didn't take place every evening, but still two or three times a week, and were much more varied in the music played. This involved more contemporary chamber music, and more use of wind instruments. When the pieces required horns, or the king and his friends wanted to hear horn duets, we were called upon to come and take part.

The road from Berlin to Potsdam was not a very good one, but as you entered the town, they went from mud and sand to stone paving, and suddenly you found yourself in a road going through a beautifully manicured forest and into gardens that led to both the *Neue Schloß* and the palace of Sanssouci. At the gates of the town there was a guardhouse, manned by soldiers of the garrison, which consisted of about eight thousand troops. If it was one of the regular guards, they would recognize the chamber musicians and just wave us through the gate, but if it happened to be a soldier who hadn't seen us before, we would have to stop and present a letter from Herr Reichardt authorizing us to enter the town. On more than one occasion one of us would forget to bring his letter along, and the rest of us would have to vouch for that person, explaining to the guard that all hell would break loose if the beginning of the concert was delayed because one of the court chamber musicians was held up at the gate. The guard's fear of getting in trouble always outweighed the fear of letting an unauthorized person into the town, since the former was much more likely, and we were usually able to talk our way through the gates in cases like that.

Most of the concerts were in the music room at Sanssouci, but occasionally we would play at the Neue Schloß, which was a large building, highly ornamented, with Corinthian columns, a classical-looking statue in front of each, and featuring an ornate fountain in the open courtyard in the middle. This was the royal family's summer residence, and there were plenty of rooms and suites for visiting dignitaries and other guests. Concerts in either palace would start at six o'clock in the evening and sometimes last over two hours. The musicians would then stay overnight in some of these guest rooms at the *Neue Schloß* and travel back to Berlin the next morning.

The main music room at Sanssouci was large, with wall hangings, oriental carpets, fine furniture, and a domed ceiling painted with a mural of classical figures. The harpsichord was at one end and the musicians would stand around it at ornate wooden music stands with candle holders. This is where we played some of the highest quality chamber music of the late 18th century and got to play it with the best musicians of the day. It seemed as though every year another prominent musician would join this group, such as Georg Wenzel Ritter, the bassoonist we had known in Paris and Mannheim, who arrived in Berlin in 1788.

This was our musical life in Berlin, and we settled into this busy, but comfortable schedule very quickly. Beate became active in all the best amateur chamber music settings, playing horn, violin, or viola, and giving music lessons at our house to an entire troop of children and ladies. I never really got over my annoyance at the musical world of this time for being so closed-minded about women playing music professionally, but in the end, I had to resign myself to the fact that this was the attitude of the time, and no one could wrap their minds around my 21st century ideas about equality. It was their loss that one of the finest low horn players of the time was sitting right under their noses and they couldn't take advantage of her talents. Had she lived in the 21st century, she would undoubtedly have been a prominent professional player.

It was also in Berlin that Carl Nicholaus came into his own musically. He studied singing with a famous Italian voice teacher, played horn with all three of us, sang in the choir at St. Peter's church, and attended its fine school. He would spend the rest of his long life as a well-respected singer, horn player, and teacher in that city.

Chapter 65

Liberté, égalité, fraternité!
- Motto of the French Revolution

From July of 1789 onward reports started appearing in the Berlin papers about the unrest in Paris. I knew, from my world history class in high school, that the French Revolution would start in 1789 with the storming of the Bastille, but somehow, even though I had seen first-hand the circumstances and attitudes that sparked the revolt, it seemed like a far distant historical event, until the full reality of the situation stared us in the face. Even when we lived there, the signs were clear that the common people of France had been crushed under the feet of the aristocracy for too long, and it was just a matter of time before they would rise up and fight back - and the common people greatly outnumbered the aristocracy.

In March of 1790 we had been established very comfortably in Berlin for almost four years when it occurred to us that this might be a good time to retrieve the savings we had left safely in the Paris office of Barclays Bank when we left in 1784. It would have been foolish at the time to withdraw more than ten thousand livres and carry it with us on the road with no fixed destination in mind, given the unsafe conditions on the roads and in strange cities.

Carl started talking about it one evening on our way home from an opera performance.

"Johann, we really need to retrieve our money from Paris before things get worse there. If what you tell me about the next few years is true, and a 'Reign of Terror' by a revolutionary government is coming, we should go there and get it as soon as possible."

I had been talking about what I knew about the French Revolution ever since our brief but eventful stay in the Bastille in 1770, and Carl was impressed by the picture I had painted for him of current and future events.

"The royal family is only going to last another year or two, and ultimately King Louis XVI and his family will be executed, and the revolutionary government will go on a campaign of searching out aristocrats and sending them to the guillotine."

"Sending them where?" asked Carl.

"The guillotine. It's a machine used for punishing people. I'm not sure if it's been invented and in use yet, but it will become very popular in the next few years, and I don't really want to go into the details of how it works."

"Sounds awful," said Carl. "I don't care to hear the details. I'm sure we'll hear more of these things all too soon."

After much discussion, we determined that the only way to protect our substantial savings, which would help take care of us and our families in our old age, was to go to Paris and get it ourselves. We asked for a leave from the orchestra for a couple of months to go to Paris, which was readily granted as an early beginning to our usual summer tour. Summer was the best time to travel, and musical activities were slower in the Berlin orchestra, so it was the best time of year to get away. Since it was a volatile time in France, we thought it would be best if our families stayed at home in Berlin.

"Johann, are you sure this is a good idea?" said Beate, the day before our departure. "It may be a good deal of money, but I don't want anything bad to happen to you. All of Europe is in such an unpredictable state, and France is the most unstable of all."

"Not to worry, - Carl and I know how Paris works, and we have a lot of friends there who can advise us as to what to do and what not to do at this point. We've arranged for solo spots at the Concert Spirituel and Concerts des Amateurs where I'm sure we will be received as old friends, and then we'll do our business, get our savings and be out of the country as soon as possible."

"I won't breathe easily until you're both safely back here in Berlin," she said, with great concern in her voice.

"It will all work out well," I said, kissing her, "and our financial future will be much more secure with the money we earned while working in Paris for thirteen years."

We left by coach the next day and traveled for nearly two weeks through Germany and into France. The weather was perfect for traveling, and we could afford at this point to travel in a higher class *"Berliner"*, which was a four-wheeled coach drawn by six horses. The trip was also more expensive than previously in another way. As soon as you crossed the border into France you had to pay small bribes to the officials at the many customs barriers along the way.

After paying a fee of a twenty-four *sous* coin, or as much as one *livre*, and assuring them that you weren't a merchant or nobility, they would usually let you pass without further trouble. In addition to the customs barriers, we had to show our official French and German traveling papers to soldiers and officials at the heavily guarded limits of each city. My French papers had been made out for me shortly after my arrival in Paris back in 1770 and had served me well for traveling since then. Now here I was, nearly twenty years later entering Paris again, and the scene we found there was almost as unfamiliar as it was to me in 1770. The city had changed greatly in the few years since we had left.

The streets were even filthier than I remembered, the beggars and street people looked even poorer, and everyone seemed to be more anxious and on their guard than ever before. Women in the streets wore tricolor dresses of red, white, and blue, or tricolor scarves, and most of the men wore red hats, which were a symbol of liberty and equality. Women's hats were called "milkmaid caps" and had a tricolor cockade. We were surprised by a lot of other changes too; people addressing us with *Citoyen*, meaning citizen, instead of Monsieur, and everyone addressing each other with the informal "*Tu*" instead of the formal "*Vous*" as a sign of social equality. Everyone wanted to show their allegiance to the new revolutionary government, even to the point of women wearing jewelry made from bits of stone from the Bastille. Inflation had made everything more expensive, especially bread and other foods, while wages had not kept up. There were tens of thousands of unemployed, and many people had to rely on charity or begging to get food for their families. This was the unsettling and unwelcoming scene that lay before us on our arrival.

Though we knew the city well, we found it a little hard to find our way around, because street names had been changed. The *Place de Louis XVI* was now *Place de le Révolution*, the *rue Madame* had become the *rue des Citoyennes*, and weirdest of all, *Nôtre Dame* Cathedral was now known as the *Temple of Reason*.

We found lodgings in the Hôtel de Monaco in the rue Varenne and started looking up some of our old musician friends.[27] The first person we visited was Josef Legros, director of the Concert Spirituel. He no longer lived in the lavish house where he had given parties at the end of each season of the concert series, the mansion where we had witnessed Mozart torpedo his chances of making a career in Paris by offending several prominent and influential musicians in one fell swoop in 1778. We found him at his new house which was much more modest and less ostentatious.

"It wasn't that I couldn't afford to live in the old house, though the economy in Paris is pretty bad, and virtually everyone is poorer than they were when you lived here. I still have enough money, but it just isn't advisable to make any show of wealth these days. Everyone is running scared. Many of the more prominent and successful musicians have left town to protect their assets and their skins. They've started arresting or killing not only aristocrats, but also people who have worked for aristocrats and royalty, including artists and musicians. Most of the court musicians have fled, knowing that at any moment they could be hauled in to be questioned by the leaders of the Revolutionary Constituent Assembly who are working on forming a new government and ousting the royal family."

"We had no idea things were this bad," I said. "How does the future of the Concert Spirituel look?"

Legros looked tired and worn out from the events of the past year. He shook his head in despair. "We're going to have to cancel the rest of the season. Other theaters and smaller series are still in business for the time being, but we were much too high-class to go unnoticed by the ringleaders and the crowds who might show up at any public event and carry off or kill anyone who looked like an aristocrat. You remember the high society flavor of our audiences during your time in Paris. I can't afford to put on concerts that will put the lives of both the concert goers and musicians at risk, so we're putting the series on hold until this all blows over and things get back to normal."

I couldn't tell him that it wasn't going to "blow over" and that France was in for many years of hardship, suffering, and violence before life would stabilize, and that the old way of life of the 18th century would never return again.

"So, you see how things stand," he went on. "When you wrote to me a couple of months ago, it looked like we could continue, and I could offer you some performances while you were here, but the situation has deteriorated recently, and all we can do now is retire quietly and wait. Do you have anything else lined up musically while you're here?"

"We've been in touch with Gossec, and he's scheduled us to play with the *Concerts des Amateurs* Orchestra," Carl said. "Do you think it's safe to play there at this point?"

"You're probably safe there for the moment since the smaller series generally draw a lower level of audience and look a little less overtly wealthy and aristocratic. But my advice for you is to do your business in Paris, have a good story ready about why you're here for the authorities when you want to leave again, and get back to Germany as soon as possible. It's getting harder to leave France these days, so don't delay too long."

This was all sobering news, and it was beginning to look like we needed to change our plan, which had been to spend a couple of months in Paris, playing performances with all our old friends and colleagues. We next sought out Gossec, to find out if we should still plan on a performance with the *Concerts des Amateurs*.

We found him also in more modest lodgings than he had during our time in Paris, and for the same reasons as Legros, and many other musicians and concert organizers; to stay below the radar.

"Yes, we're still having performances during this difficult period," he said, "and I would like to have you play in the next set of concerts this coming week. But we need to be careful and advertise you as visiting soloists from the Orchestra of the King of Prussia, and not mention the fact that you had been members of the private orchestra of the Prince of Guéméné. The prince has fled France, and he and his family are now living in their castle in Bohemia. He's not very popular in Paris these days, and your association with him could cause trouble, so we aren't going to bill you as "*les Cors de chasse de la Prince de Guéméné*", as they used to when you were in the thick of things in Paris ten years ago. Keeping a low profile and showing support for the Revolution is the best way to stay out of trouble these days. I don't know if you've heard, but Punto has become the leader of a theater orchestra and composed a "Grand Hymn of Liberty" for one of the revolutionary spectacles. He knows where his bread is buttered, so he's put on his red hat and joined the crowd, which we will all have to do before it's over."

We made arrangements to rehearse with the orchestra, and before leaving, gave him the orchestra parts for the concertos we wanted to play. We thought we could get an even better picture of the musical situation from Punto and looked him up next. We found him after a performance at a small theater of the sort that were springing up all over the city, and offering what were billed as operas, but were really variety shows of singing and dancing with little or no plot to hold them together. Punto was playing violin and leading the orchestra, something he had always wanted to do, but since he was a terrible violinist, it took something as cataclysmic as the fall of a major European government to make it possible.

"Carl und Johann, mon Amis! Quell une Überaschung to see you wieder ici dan le greatest city der Welt, Paris!" He hadn't changed his way of expressing himself in the seven years since we had seen him last, nor had he lost any of his characteristic enthusiasm or charisma. "What brings you back to the city that made your fortunes and reputations?"

"We're going to play with Gossec and the *Concerts des Amateurs* next week and do some financial business before heading back to Berlin," said Carl. "We had planned to stay for a couple of months, but Paris doesn't seem quite as friendly as we remembered it, so we're not going to hang around very long."

We went to a wine shop in St. Antoine, and spent the rest of the evening with him, drinking wine, catching up on the news in the musical scene in Paris, discussing the current state of horn playing, and talking over old times.

"So, you came back to fetch the money you left here when you went to work for the Landgraf of Hesse-Cassel?" asked Punto. "It may not be so easy to retrieve it, since there is very little money in Paris nowadays, and taking money out of the country isn't allowed. Banks and financial institutions have been failing and businesses have been going under for the past couple of years. Fortunately, people still want entertainment though, and some of us who decided to stay and keep playing have adapted. I've been writing music for the new government and got a position as leader of this theater orchestra, something I've always wanted to do. Unlike a lot of the court musicians, and members of private orchestras, I've been pretty safe from any trouble with the Revolutionary Constituent Assembly because I've been a poor freelance musician, part of the oppressed working class, for the past fourteen years."

Punto, one of the most celebrated and popular soloists of the time, was anything but poor or oppressed, but as Gossec had said, he knew what was good for him, so he was now a member of the "Third Estate" red hat and all.

"I was in the same position as you with a substantial amount of money invested in the Paris stock market. Leaving France when the revolution broke out would have meant losing it all, so I decided to stay and protect it. When you find yourself between two large and angry crowds, put on the colors of the one that's larger and louder. That happens to be red these days." He refilled his glass and raised it. "So here's to *liberté, égalité, et fraternité!*"

Chapter 66

I hope we shall never be so totally lost to all sense of the duties imposed upon us by the law of social union, as, upon any pretext of public service, to confiscate the goods of a single unoffending citizen.
- Edmund Burke, Reflections on the Revolution in France, 1790

The next morning we went to the Paris office of Barclays Bank to retrieve our savings. Barclay's was an English bank that did mostly English business with wealthy English residents of Paris and businesses from either country that traded with, or had offices in the other. Our contact there was an English banker by the name of Nigel Bangham, who recognized us immediately, and in the past always liked to address me in English, as he said, "to enjoy Mr. Palsa's quaint and unusual, but very fluent use of the King's English."

The tall lanky Englishman rose slowly from his desk in the dusty, poorly lit office. His suit of green breeches and waistcoat was ornamented with a tricolor cravat, and he wore thick reading glasses that made his eyes look twice life-size. These he quickly perched on the top of his forehead to get a better look at us. "Messrs. Palsa and Türrschmidt! What a pleasure to see you again my good sirs, after quite an extended absence from Paris. I trust you are both well and you and your families are thriving in your new situation in the service of the Prussian monarch?"

"Very well, thank you," I said, as we shook hands warmly, "and I hope business is going well for you and your associates."

"Not particularly well, I must say. As you know, these are very unsteady times, both financially and in every other imaginable way. Communication is slow and difficult with our London headquarters, and the safe transfer of funds between England and France is extremely unreliable and problematic at present. But Barclays is a strong institution, and we will weather these difficult times."

After these preliminary words of greeting in English, he proceeded to business and switched to the French language.

"What brings you back to the French metropolis in the midst of this great upheaval? And what can I do for you *Citizens*?"

"We've returned to Paris for the purpose of retrieving our savings and bringing it back to Berlin, which is now our permanent home and base of operations. I believe we each have sums in the neighborhood of five thousand *livres* deposited with you."

His look altered immediately, as though he was about to make a speech that he had made many times in the past few months.

"Please take a seat. I see that you have not been in Paris for some time and are unaware of the true gravity of the situation, both financially and socially. The official policy of the National Assembly, who are now making the laws, is that no money shall be taken out of the country. Anyone who is apprehended at a border crossing with large amounts of money, I can assure you, will be arrested and tried by one of the provisional courts of the assembly, who are in a frenzy of sniffing out rich aristocrats and anyone who isn't sympathetic to the revolution. Last year we had a great number of withdrawals, both by our French customers and by English nobility and businessmen living in Paris who become skeptical of the banking institutions and the political climate, but that is no longer possible with the new laws. If any of them try to flee the country with their fortunes, I shudder to think of the consequences."

"Is there any other means of sending money elsewhere?" I asked. "Could it be sent to England and deposited at Barclays in London for safe keeping until we could make arrangements for it to be sent to Germany or get it ourselves on a concert tour?"

"The assembly allows money to come into France from abroad, but not to be sent out. And in any case, with the great number of withdrawals we've had, we don't have sufficient funds here in our Paris office to be able to either pay out a withdrawal of ten thousand *livres* at present, or to transfer money to London, even if it were allowed. The best I can do is to give you each one hundred *livres*, which given the current rate of inflation of the French currency, would not arouse too much suspicion with the authorities who audit our books almost weekly to find out who is trying to transfer wealth out of the country."

"What options do we have in that case for protecting our savings?" Carl asked. "It's becoming clear that we should not stay in France, and that we will not be able to take our money with us."

"It's difficult to say what the future may bring *Citizen* Türrschmidt. Your money is safe for the present at Barclays, but I can give you no guarantees. There have been instances of the new government confiscating the assets of certain of our noble clients who have attracted their notice and displeasure by trying to flee the country, and in those cases, we have been powerless to resist. Your only option is to leave your money here, in the hope that as conditions stabilize, and a new government forms, it will remain intact and become accessible to you in the future. I'm sorry I can't do more for you, and I hope you understand that we - you and I, as foreigners, are at the mercy of the current powers that be and have no choice but to wait for conditions to improve."

We left the banking office with a hundred *livres* each feeling like our trip to Paris was all in vain and that we may as well play the one set of concerts that were lined up and leave for home as soon as possible.

"Well, that's great news! A hundred *livres* will be just about enough money to pay out bribes to border guards and customs agents along the way," Carl lamented when we were out in the street again.

"It's probably best that he didn't have any money to give us," I said, "because we would have been tempted to take it and find some way of traveling home with it, which could have gotten us into a lot of trouble. From what we've heard so far, you can't leave the country without being searched at several checkpoints and customs barriers, so it's best that we just get out of the country with our clothes, our horns, and our lives."

Thinking there might be some risk in going into France at this point with our valuable silver horns, we had decided to take the old Kerner horns on the trip, and the advice we were getting indicated that this had been a good move. Costly silver items would not have looked good at the customs stops.

Carl was a gentle soul and couldn't wrap his mind around conflict. In his book, people should simply be nice to each other.

"Couldn't the revolutionaries, the aristocrats, and the common people just sit down and talk these things over and come to some kind of agreement as to how to live together in peace?"

"Carl, I can tell you that over the next two hundred fifty years there will be people who will express that same sentiment, and despite those few sensible voices, there will be more wars and other unfortunate events for humanity than you could possibly imagine."

We started rehearsing the next day with the orchestra of the *Concerts des Amateurs*, which had slipped a little in the quality of its performance since we had last played with them. We played a concerto by Rosetti which we had done many times before and could do in a couple of rehearsals with a decent group. We still knew some of the musicians in the group, both French and German, though it seemed as though there were fewer German musicians in Paris than there were ten years earlier. It was now unpopular and, in some cases dangerous, to be a foreigner, and many of our German, Austrian, and Bohemian friends had gone back to their homelands, with the exception of some who couldn't afford to leave, or a few, like Punto, who didn't have a homeland to go to, and wanted to protect their assets in France. Before the concert we talked with a few of the musicians who we had known earlier, and most were baffled by our coming back to Paris at this point. Jean Sieber, one of the horns from the Paris Opera, was playing in the orchestra and was truly concerned.

"What brings you two back to Paris at such an unsettled time? You escaped some of the worst times these past few years in France and got a comfortable gig in one of the most stable courts in Europe. I think I would have stayed there rather than risk traveling back to France at this point."

"We had a good deal of money in the bank from our Paris days," Carl explained, "and we knew that if we didn't retrieve it now it would probably disappear. What we didn't know until we got here was that, as of very recently, it isn't allowed to take any money out of France. So we're giving it up as a lost cause, and leaving for Berlin in a couple of days."

"I noticed you're playing on your Kerner horns, you didn't bring your silver Raoux horns with you, did you?" asked Sieber.

"No," I replied. "We knew it probably wouldn't be a good idea to travel with them, not after what happened in England a couple of years ago when our silver horns were stolen. That was an adventure that we didn't want to repeat!"

"That story made it back to Paris, and all the horn players were relieved to hear that you got them back, though at peril of your lives. It might have been easy to enter France with French-made silver instruments, but it would have been very difficult to leave again with them. It would have taken some very fast talking, and a lot of bribes to get them across borders and customs barriers. They would have been viewed as silver art objects, wealth that you were trying to smuggle out of the country. Much better idea to travel with a couple of older-looking brass horns. And don't even think of mentioning to anyone that you came with the intention of taking money back with you. You'd better have a good story ready for when they start questioning you."

"Man! Everyone here is running scared," Carl remarked as we went into the ballroom where the performance was about to take place. "I don't know if everyone has just gotten into a paranoid mind-set in recent times, or if we really are in much more danger than we anticipated."

"Well, Carl old friend, we're leaving the day after tomorrow, so tonight let's do what we do best for one last time in our old stomping ground of Paris, where we had such a good run for the better part of fourteen years, and then leave France for good."

Gossec had been very vague in his advertising of the concerts, not mentioning our previous employment in Paris by the Prince of Guéméné, but nonetheless word got around that we were back in town, and many concertgoers who remembered us from the 70s and early 80s came to the concerts to hear us one last time. Despite being a bit out of shape from travel, the weirdness of the situation we found when we got there, and the disappointment of not achieving what we had come for, we played two very respectable concerts on consecutive evenings. We felt as though we gave the audience memorable performances, and we were bidding farewell to the musical world of Paris in fine style.

We were just about to leave the ballroom after the second concert, and were saying our goodbyes to Gossec and a few other musicians from the orchestra, when we were approached by four rough looking men in red hats who looked like they had been doing a bit of heavy drinking that evening.

"*Citizens* Tierschmied et Pals, formerly *Cors de chasse* de la Prince de Guéméné, we hereby place you under arrest by order of the Revolutionary National Assembly! Please come along with us quietly and there will be no trouble."

Everyone present was taken aback by this sudden intrusion. Carl stepped forward and addressed the spokesman of the group, who was swaying slightly.

"On what charge does the assembly order our arrest, and how do we know that you scruffy-looking bunch really were sent by them?"

"We were not told what the charge is. That you will find out when you appear tomorrow morning before a judge of the assembly. As to our authority, our revolutionary guard badges and these pistols are enough to convince you to accompany us back to the assembly office in St. Antoine."

There was no arguing with that sort of reasoning. We had no choice but to go with them, despite the loud protests of all present. I turned to a bassoonist friend who we had known since our first opera performance with the Opera Comique back in 1770.

"Jean-François, take our horns and get them to Punto. He'll take care of them until we can clear up this mess."

It felt very much like that dismal afternoon in 1770 when we were escorted roughly by a similar band of ragged Paris police officers to the Bastille for having offended the French ambassador to England.

After a sleepless night in a rat-infested jail cell, which was the norm for jail cells of the time, we were brought before a judge and a group of grim looking men, including the ones who had brought us in the night before.

"Citizens! What is the charge that brings these despicable foreigners before this court?"

One of the men handed him a piece of paper which he read quickly and turned gleaming eyes toward us.

"Despicable foreigners?" I said. "We were residents of Paris for many years, and musicians in the service of the ..."

"Shh!" hissed Carl in my ear.

"Ah ha!" said the Judge, "So you admit that you spent fourteen years as close associates with Henri Louis Marie de Rohan, Prince de Guéméné, enemy of the Revolutionary National Assembly?"

"We were musicians, little more than servants in his house during those years!" said Carl.

"We were paid members of his orchestra," I added.

"We have information that you were present and participated in high level gatherings of foreign diplomats and aristocrats at his private residence, and accumulated large sums of money which you have recently attempted to withdraw from Barclays bank in Paris, and take out of the country. I started to speak;

"But your Honor, we were only ..."

"Silence! Your trial will take place as soon as possible in front of a jury of citizens. Take them back to their cell to await the fate of traitors to the National Constituent Assembly!"

With that, we were taken roughly back to our new abode to wait for further developments.

Chapter 67

If you give me six lines written by the hand of the most honest of men, I will find something in them which will hang him.
- attributed to Cardinal Richelieu, chief minister to Louis XIII of France

They must have put together a case against us and assembled a jury overnight, because the next morning we were dragged down the street in front of jeering crowds who waited each morning to see the well-dressed prisoners who were taken from the prison to the courtroom. When we arrived, we found a hostile scene waiting for us. A group that was obviously an aristocratic family was leaving, accompanied by soldiers. They were bound together, in pairs, husband and wife, and four teenage children, all in tears and in great distress.

"What do you suppose they're going to do with them?" said Carl, shuddering.

"I hate to even imagine," I said. "I've read too many stories and seen movies about this time period, and we're right at the beginning of one of the worst decades France has ever experienced."

"We don't have time for one of your futuristic history lessons, Johann. We need to deal directly with the present, and our present doesn't look very good."

We were brought into the makeshift courtroom, which had been arranged in the ballroom of a hotel that had been taken over by the assembly. The same unsympathetic looking judge from the evening before was staring at us maliciously from behind a large desk that was on a dais raised above the rest of the assembled chairs. The jury consisted of a group of eight or ten men in red hats, and the rest of the room was filled with upward of a hundred spectators, who came daily to see aristocrats and other traitors tried, sentenced, and executed.

"This is it, my friend, we don't stand a chance with these people. They've made up a case against us, and they have an angry crowd to cheer them on," I said to Carl as we looked around the room.

"When they're not watching trials here, I'm sure they're burning down chateaus and churches and hunting down landowners and rich people," Carl said, as we approached the judge's desk.

"The prisoners will refrain from conversing in German in this court! All communication will be addressed to the judge and shall be held in French!" bellowed the soldier who presented us to the court, pushing us roughly forward. The judge started the proceedings without ceremony.

"The prosecutor will read the charges."

One of the jurors stood up and began to read.

"Your honor, the prisoners are charged with a long association with the Prince of Guéméné, Henri Louis Marie de Rohan, lately sentenced to execution in absentia after he fled the country with his family and fortune. They are further charged with attempting to take a sum in excess of 10,000 *livres* deposited with Barclays Bank in Paris out of the country in direct violation of national financial preservation laws passed in January of this year."

"Thank you, Citizen Dupont, and now you may call the witnesses for the prosecution."

"I've never heard of the prosecuting attorney being a member of the jury!" Carl whispered to me. "And where's our lawyer, and our witnesses?"

"They make their own rules here, and in a year or two there won't even be any juries, just a judge who pronounces sentences," I whispered back.

A soldier ushered a small nervous looking man into the room and placed him in the witness stand.

"The first witness is Citizen Jacque La Plante, formerly a servant in the service of the Prince of Guéméné."

"Citizen La Plante!" roared the prosecutor in a stentorian voice. "Tell the court if you recognize the prisoners, and where you have seen them before."

He looked nervously at the judge.

"Your honor, during my time in the service of the prince as a menial servant at very low pay, the two prisoners often attended dinners and musical evenings at the prince's private residence at the Hôtel Rohan-Guéméné. I remember them mingling with the other guests of the prince and playing music with them."

"I remember him, he's the one who was thrown in jail for stealing spoons at the Hôtel," I whispered.

"They probably let him out of jail to testify. They're going to find as many ragged beggars as they can who will testify against us," said Carl between clenched teeth.

The judge stood up from his desk, red in the face. "Silence! The prisoners will refrain from speaking to each other, or anyone else, and if I hear one more word of the German language out of you, I will pronounce sentence immediately, just to get you out of my sight! Citizen Dupont, please proceed."

"Your Honor, I would like to call to the witness stand Citizen Jean-Philippe Drolet, of the Revolutionary Guard." A tall red-capped man with a long hooked nose in an incredibly dirty and threadbare red waistcoat took the stand.

"Citizen, please tell us where and when you have seen the prisoners."

"I was at a wine shop in St. Antoine last week and overheard them conversing with another foreigner with a big yellow dog. They looked suspicious, so I asked a friend who understands their language what they were talking about, and he assured me that they were plotting how to take a large amount of money from Paris back to their home country. My friend and I then followed them back to their lodgings and took turns watching through the night to see what they might do next. In the morning we followed them to Barclays Bank in the rue des Citizens, and watched outside as they entered and had a long interview with an English banker."

"Thank you, Citizen Drolet. You may step down. And now your honor I would like to call to the stand Citizen Gaston Blavet, financial auditor of the National Assembly.

A business-like man in an old-fashioned powdered wig and long waistcoat, which was long out of style, but neat and clean, took the stand and waited expectantly for his first question.

"Citizen Blavet, please tell us what you discovered about the banking transactions of the prisoners who stand before us in your weekly audit of the accounts of Barclays bank."

"Citizen Dupont, in my weekly audit, I was asked by the Assembly to be especially watchful for the financial activities of the two prisoners, Pals et Tierschmied, based on information gathered by the surveillance of your previous witness. I discovered that the prisoner Johann Pals has the sum of 6541 *livres* in an account at

Barclays, and the prisoner Tierschmied 5670 *livres* and 24 *sous*. These are considerable amounts your honor, and it is known from my office's interrogation of customers of the bank who overheard their interview with the English banker, Nigel Bangham, that the prisoners' plan was to withdraw the aforesaid amounts and transport it out of the country."

"Thank you, Citizen Blavet. You may step down. And now your Honor, the prosecution rests its case."

The prosecutor now sat down, confident that he had done his best to convict us and send us to immediate execution. At this point the judge turned his eyes toward us, and in a condescending voice asked if we had anything to say in our defense. We knew that anything we had to say would be in vain, given the evidence that had been presented, but we had to at least make a statement on our behalf.

I began to speak, having no idea what I could possibly say to help our case.

"Your honor, let me tell you very simply and honestly the real story." There was a low murmur in the room, and quite a number of people laughed. "You see, your Honor, we are at a disadvantage, not having a defense lawyer or witnesses of our own, due to the fact that we were brought here on such short notice and were not allowed to communicate with any friends..."

At this tense moment, the door of the room opened and several people came quietly into the chamber, and as they did, a commanding theatrical voice rang out.

"I represent the defense of the two foreign prisoners, and wish to call several witnesses on their behalf, if it please the court!"

The judge, the prosecutor, and all the jurors sprang to their feet, and the judge addressed the stranger.

"This is most irregular, not to say unprecedented in a court of the Revolutionary National Assembly. To date, a defense representative has never been present or allowed to call witnesses in these hearings! Who are you, and by what authority do you intrude on these proceedings?"

"I am Giovanni Punto, your Honor, leader of the orchestra of the *Theatre de Liberté* on the *Place de le Révolution*, and composer of the famous "*Hymn de Liberté*." To our utter astonishment, he was speaking perfect French with a flawless Parisian accent. He took off his red hat and made a low bow. The prosecutor and jurors all crowded around the judge's desk, and among the audience could be heard the murmured name of "*Citizen* Punto!" and "*Hymn de Liberté*!" The judge and jurors knew that with such a prominent citizen and revolutionary supporter as Punto asking to be heard, the crowd would never accept their turning him away. They had no choice but to let him speak and present his defense.

"Thank you, your honor, and now I would like to call my first witness, Citizen Charpentier, to the stand. Please state your name and under what circumstances you know the accused."

"My name, Citizen Punto, is Pierre-Antoine Charpentier. I was the harpsichordist in the orchestra at the Hôtel Rohan-Guéméné from 1770 until its disbandment in 1783 due to the bankruptcy of the Prince of Guéméné. The two citizens who stand before you were members of that orchestra with me, and we were all hired servants who performed in concerts at the Hôtel or played chamber music for events at his private residence. The prince was a difficult and demanding employer who worked us hard, and the wind band, in which these two were the *Cor de chasse* players, worked especially hard and long hours, providing "*Musique de Table*" for banquets and other functions for the prince. They were valued little more in the prince's eyes than his cooks, maids and livery servants, despite their superior musical talents which were acknowledged everywhere else. During the first several years of their service to him, the prince refused to allow them to play elsewhere, and it was not until some of his music-loving peers insisted, that he finally relented and allowed them to appear as soloists at the famed Concert Spirtituel, where they were received with great applause, finally receiving the notice of the Paris concert going public of which their oppressive employer had for so long deprived them. Contrary to the testimony of the previous witnesses, these men were not guests of the prince, but virtually owned by him for the better part of fourteen years."

Punto came up close to the witness stand.

"Just one more question, if I may. How well was the orchestra paid in those days? Is it reasonable to assume that these two *Cor de chasse* players could have amassed the amount of money that the National Assembly auditor quoted earlier?"

"Citizen Punto, the orchestra was reasonably well paid in those days, and our two horn playing friends being unmarried, and being upright and frugal young men, worked hard and saved their money one sous at a time. Over those fourteen years they scraped together this savings that they needed to support themselves, and in later years, their families when they found themselves out of work in Paris upon the prince's financial demise. They left their hard-earned savings in Paris, as the safest place during their travels as poor free-lance musicians over the next several years, and came back to Paris in great need, having worked for the ruthless nobility of the capitals of Europe, who for many years took advantage of their talents for their entertainment with but scant remuneration."

"Thank you Citizen Charpentier; you may step down from the stand. Your honor, I would now like to call Citizen Jean-Pierre Petit."

Petit, director of the orchestra of the Prince of Guéméné, who we had known since 1770, now took the stand and Punto forged ahead.

"Citizen Petit, please tell your honor and the jurors about the events that took place in the month of November 1770, when you first met the *Cor de chasse* players, Palsa and Türrschmidt."

"Your honor, and citizens of the jury, I first met these two talented and upstanding young artists in November of 1770 when they applied for the positions of *Cor de chasse* in the orchestra of the prince. We saw immediately when they played their music for us that they were extremely gifted performers, and engaged them on the spot, but an unfortunate event postponed their joining the group for some time. After leaving the Hôtel de Rohan-Guéméné, they were on their way to a shop that fitted newly engaged servants of the prince with new clothes, when they encountered a blatant example of the arrogant brutality of the aristocracy and took matters into their own hands in the name of liberty, equality, and fraternity. The coach of Adrien-Louis de Bonnières, Comte de Guînes, French ambassador to England, was careening recklessly through the streets of Paris at breakneck speed, with no regard to the well-being of anyone in the streets, an all too common occurrence that I'm sure we all have experienced, when an innocent child who happened to be crossing the street was brutally mowed down by the four white horses and heavy ornate coach. The two citizens standing before you, unable to contain their outrage at this injustice, attacked the coach and the

Comte de Guînes, breaking the windows and attempting to assassinate the Comte and his daughter who were inside, knowing full well the consequences of such an act."

"He's laying it on rather thickly," whispered Carl, "Do you think the jury is buying it?"

"I don't know about the jury, but the crowd is eating it up," I replied.

Monsieur Petit proceeded in his testimony.

"But your honor and citizens of the jury, this meant nothing to our two heroes, weighed against the feeling of joy it gave them to finally speak out with their actions against decades and centuries of oppression of the common people by the First Estate. The consequences, however, were grave, your honor. They were soon subdued by the livery servants of the Comte and by a crowd of police officers. The Comte ordered the prisoners to be taken directly to the Bastille to be imprisoned until he could press formal charges, resulting in severe punishment, or even execution. But as we have all seen during those years, accused criminals would often languish forgotten in the Bastille and never get their day in court, and so it was for these citizens, that they remained there for a protracted period until finally, after a time of great hardship, deprivation, and sickness experienced in a filthy cell of the Bastille, by an unprecedented effort on the part of the musical community in Paris, they were finally released. After a most humiliating reprimand and promises to 'flay them alive if they ever rebelled against the aristocracy again,' the two physically and mentally broken men were taken back into the service of the prince, who was not interested in their personal well-being, but merely in their talents as players of the *Cor de chasse* for the amusement of his guests, like trained animals."

There was a cheer from the audience, which had grown in the meantime as rumors of something spectacular taking place in the courtroom had circulated in the surrounding streets. The prosecutor, Dupont leapt to his feet.

"Your honor, I object to this ridiculous testimony, and demand some proof of its veracity!"

Punto stepped forward again, cool as a cucumber, and confident as Julius Caesar.

"Your honor, in addition to Citizen Petit, I have several other prominent Parisian musicians, who were present for the events just outlined, and were instrumental in the long and arduous process of freeing the Bastille prisoners. May I present concertmasters of the Concert Spirituel, Capron, and Leduc, the violin virtuoso Le Chevalier de St. Georges, the composer Guiseppi Cambini, Josef Legros, director of the Concert Spirituel, and several others, who are prepared to testify that these events took place exactly as recounted by Citizen Petit."

One by one each of the witnesses, nine in all, verified, and all being fine performers, expanded in theatrical style on the story of our imprisonment in the Bastille, and the cheers of the audience, which had now grown to at least two hundred, became more and more enthusiastic with each testimony.

When all were finished, Punto strode up to the judge's desk again to make his final statement.

"And so your honor and citizens of the jury, it becomes obvious that these two patriotic citizens, Palsa and Türrschmidt, were two early voices who were brave enough to speak out against inequality and oppression, and their story, which was so well known in the musical and artistic circles of Paris at the time, is still remembered, and has become almost legendary as having contributed to the history of events that have resulted in the recent uprising and reclaiming of the rights and dignity of the common people! These men, and their brave acts, and the hardships they endured as Bastille prisoners, should be raised up as shining examples of patriots and heroes in the quest for liberty, equality, and fraternity!"

The crowd went wild with shouts of "*Liberté, égalité, et fraternité!*", "*Vive Pals et Tierschmied!*" and "*Vive le Révolution!*"

Dupont and the judge knew they were absolutely powerless with an enthusiastic crowd of over two hundred people now cheering and chanting our names as heroes of the revolution. They stood at the judge's desk and talked furiously and gestured to each other, but we couldn't hear what they were saying over the noise of the crowd.

Finally, the judge, who knew the consequences of opposing a frenzied revolutionary mob, banged his gavel on the desk to restore order, which took a full minute, stood up, and began to speak.

"Prosecutor Dupont and I are still highly skeptical of the history and intentions of the two prisoners." This elicited angry murmurs from the crowd, some of whom were beginning to get to their feet.

"But under the circumstances," he went on quickly, "and given the body of information presented by such a distinguished group of citizens, not the least of which is the celebrated musician Giovanni Punto, a citizen of unquestionable loyalty, I hereby dismiss the charges against the prisoners and pronounce them free to go."

The room erupted in cheers and patriotic songs and chants of "Long life to the Bastille prisoners, enemies of oppression and brave supporters of the people!"

Before we knew it, we were raised off the floor and were being carried out of the courtroom on the shoulders of a wave of people. It was not until we were well out of the building and halfway down the block that our feet touched the ground again. At that moment we were overtaken by the judge and prosecutor. Dupont shook his fist in both of our faces and, in a low voice that couldn't be heard by the crowd, addressed us.

"You have the safety of an enthusiastic crowd around you now, but I will rebuild my case against you and disprove the testimony of these low musician friends of yours! I know where to find you, and I'll have you yet!"

With that he stormed away, just as Punto and the other musicians caught up with us.

We shook all of their hands, and Carl hugged Punto.

"Jan, you were brilliant! How did you get all of these friends together and assemble such a convincing case so quickly?"

"My dear Carl, it was almost not quick enough, for as you saw, we only arrived in the nick of time. After your arrest we had to work fast and find people who really were with you in your early days in Paris to testify legitimately to the Bastille story. I knew the fact that you had been Bastille prisoners would resonate with the crowd, and these days there is no arguing with an angry mob! But we had to make a convincing presentation of it, and we all rehearsed our lines as though we were rehearsing a symphony. Bringing it all to the stage and performing it was just the sort of theater audiences go for these days. But you heard the parting words of our good friend Citizen Dupont, He's not going to give up trying to get a case going and I predict you'll be back in that court in a matter of days. The danger to your lives is real and immediate, and those of us here have arranged everything for you. Here are your tickets for a coach that leaves from an office around the corner from Notre Dame Ca.... or I should say 'The Temple of Reason' in one hour. If you are on that coach, the chances of the revolutionary guard preventing you from leaving Paris are slim, but there is no doubt that Dupont and the National Assembly will put out the word to detain you, so your best chance is to travel faster than their orders will travel. I will accompany you to the coach office myself, and I won't breathe easily until I see the coach leave with both of you safely on it. Let's go!"

Chapter 68

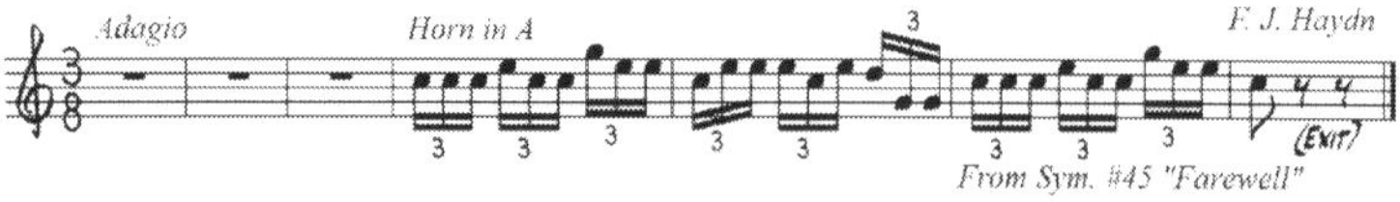

We hurried through the streets with Punto and a few other friends who had testified at the trial, talking the whole way.

"I'm invested in the whole scene and the revolution and all, so I'm staying to see this thing through and help to salvage the musical community, which is in a sorry state at this point," said Punto, out of breath as we almost ran through the streets. "But you walked right into the worst of current events, and immediately aroused suspicion by being recognized from your days in the orchestra of the Prince of Guéméné, and by making inquiries at Barclays Bank. We knew the only way to save you was to make you into temporary revolutionary heroes and get you into the fastest coach we could find leaving Paris. Two nights ago, when you were taken prisoner, your horns were brought to me, which tipped me off that we needed to get things organized quickly. We don't have time to fetch them now, and in any case, you could be identified easier if you had them with you. They can stay in Paris with me for the moment, and when things are calmer, you can get them back and we'll share a bottle of wine together and have a good laugh about today's adventure."

"We normally play on our silver Raoux solo horns and the Raoux orchestra horns, so we won't miss them in the meantime," said Carl, panting, as we all trotted down the street.

We arrived at the coach office as the coach was being loaded for its departure. At that point yet another party of musician friends showed up to see us off, and with them was old Hans-Joachim, Punto's dog and constant companion, who was now quite gray and slow-moving. He was wearing a tricolor scarf around his neck and a small red hat tied around his head with a ribbon.

"Hans has come to bid adieux his old friends!" exclaimed Punto. We all crowded around to pat him on the head and say goodbye.

"Take it easy Hans and take good care of your master!" I said as we climbed into the coach.

"Jan, we can't begin to thank you enough for everything you've done for us over the years and especially for your stellar performance this morning in court, and the case you organized in our defense," said Carl.

"All in the line of duty, my dear Carl, and I would do it again in a minute for two such fine friends as you have been, and two of the finest Waldhorn players in the world! Oh – I almost forgot one more important detail! I've given you your tickets for the coach already, but here are your traveling papers, which should get you safely out of France."

"But we have traveling papers already," said Carl.

"Yours won't get you past the city limits," said Punto. "These, which were made this morning by a friend of Monsieur Petit in the Foreign Office, state that you are two brothers, merchants from Nürnberg, who are on their way home after their business closed in Paris. You are going home penniless because you lost everything, and the only thing you have to remember is which one of you is Fritz and which one Heinrich Knödel. Careful! The ink may still be wet, though they are dated June 1789. You can use your own papers again as soon as you cross the border into Germany at Strasbourg."

As Punto finished speaking, a friend who knew where we had been staying ran up breathless with our small traveling bags, in which we had a few clothes, the hundred *livres* each that we would undoubtedly need along the way, and our small store of German money that would take us through the rest of the trip through the Empire to Berlin.

"Jean-Louis!" cried Punto. "You are just in time! I was hoping you would get my message and bring our friends their bags. It will look much better if they have very modest traveling bags with them. Travelers without luggage arouse suspicion."

"Again, we must thank you," I said. "You've thought of everything and unquestionably saved our lives!

"I hope they have been saved. The rest of the story will depend on fast horses, slow revolutionary guards, and a few bribes to the border watchdogs to slow down any pursuers."

"I'm puzzled about one thing," said Carl, leaning out of the coach window. "This morning in the trial, you spoke to the court and the audience in perfect French with a Parisian accent. How were you able to do that?"

Punto had been his old linguistically mixed-up self ever since we had left the courtroom.

"Carl, my old friend, we are all nothing more than illusions that we make up and sell to the world. Some of us realize the power in that concept, while most don't. Those of us who understand that secret can consciously create who we are and how we want the world to see us. It works in speaking, playing music, and everything else we do. Today it was vitally necessary, in order to capture the crowd and win the case, to speak their own language as they speak it, and to be one of them. I would have done precisely the same thing for you in Italian, German, English - or Latin for that matter, had we stood before the Pope at the Vatican! But the coach is leaving, so *adieux, meine liebe Waldhornisten! I wish you eine bon voyage! Und until we meet again, auf Wiedersehen, mon Amis!"*

And that was the last we ever saw of our good friend, the celebrated Giovanni Punto, who was, without question, the most remarkable man and consummate performer I have ever met, with or without a horn.

Chapter 69

Thou sure and firm-set earth, hear not my steps, which way they walk, for fear the very stones prate of my whereabouts.
- Shakespeare, Macbeth, 1606

After what felt like an excruciatingly long delay the coach departed and we were off and running - running in a very real sense. The next half hour was truly frightening as we traveled at what seemed to be a snail's pace, looking out of the back window of the coach for any signs of pursuit. We crawled through the crowded rue St. Antoine, starting at the *Place de la Bastille* and made our way down its length into the rue Denis, turned into the rue Honore, which seemed as though it would never end, passed by the *Jardin des Tuileries* and finally through the *Place de la Revolution* and over the *Pont Royal*, the bridge crossing the Seine. At this point we met our first customs barrier and checkpoint.

A guard ambled slowly out of his guardhouse, carrying a musket.

"Stop! Citizen driver, who are you carrying in this coach?"

Paying passengers, foreigners leaving Paris," was the reply from the driver's box.

"Please step out of the coach and show your papers, Citizens!"

We stepped out, scared to death of what was about to happen, and handed him the papers.

"German merchants, Fritz and Heinrich Knödel, from Nürnberg," said the guard, absolutely mangling the German pronunciation of the names. "And where are you going?"

"We are going back to our own country after a very unsuccessful business trip in which we lost everything," said Carl putting on a heavy German accent.

"And what is your line of business?"

"Hats!" said Carl, at the same moment I said;

"Oil lamps!"

The guard looked hard at us for what seemed like about half a minute.

"So, which is it going to be, lamps or hats?"

"Hats with lamps fitted to them, said Carl.

"Yes, like the hats miners wear," I said.

"We thought they would be popular in the dark streets of Paris," added Carl.

"But it turned out to be a very bad idea, and we lost all of our money trying to sell them." I said, bringing this improvised farce to a very unconvincing end.

"I think we should sit down in our guardhouse with some of my fellow guards and have a nice quiet little chat about your unlikely sounding business," said the guard, obviously enjoying watching us fidget nervously. I decided it was time to hint at a bribe.

"Let me tell you very honestly that we have had a very bad time of it in Paris. We want nothing more than to leave France quietly and as soon as possible and go home. Is there anything we can do to expedite our departure?"

"Possibly, possibly...," was the reply. "Are you carrying any taxable goods with you - any tobacco, wine, precious art objects, jewelry, large amounts of money, or hats fitted with lamps he said with a smile?"

"No, nothing of the kind, whatsoever. Only the few clothes and personal items that you will find in our bags," said Carl.

"Well, in that case, for a small consideration, say a *livre* or two, I think we can grease the wheels of your coach and 'expedite your departure' as you say."

I handed him a one *livre* coin, which he took with a look of distain.

"Citizens, let me give you your lesson for the day. When a border guard says 'a consideration of a *livre* or two' it is always best to choose the larger sum mentioned. It saves so much unnecessary time and trouble!"

I handed him a second coin.

"Now off with you! And heed my advice about border guards. If you want to find your way back to Nürnberg, be very nice to all border guards and customs officials in these troubled times. Bon Voyage!"

He walked back to his guardhouse murmuring to himself.

"Hats fitted with lamps! I should have sent them directly to the Revolutionary Guard!"

It was a tense few minutes, one of many in the next few days, and neither of us said a word or so much as breathed until we were over the bridge, across the river and into the rue de Bourgogne in St. Germain, where the city became a little more spread out and sparsely populated. But we were by no means out of the woods yet. We met with guards and customs barriers at least four more times before leaving the city. And each time we got a little more convincing with our story, though still having to grease the palms of virtually everyone we encountered.

We headed south from the city and were soon on rough country roads, no better than cow paths, and at an alarmingly slow pace began the five days journey to Strasbourg, paying more "fees" at the city limits of each town to customs officers, having our bags repeatedly searched, paying exorbitant prices for lodging and bad food at inns, and high prices for each new coach and horses. It wasn't at all like the "good old days" of travel fifteen years before. Then they simply robbed you blind, poisoned you with bad food, and infested you with bedbugs after jarring your bones loose on the bad roads, but at least they were friendly about it in those days. Now, on top of all the old inconveniences they needed to search you and threaten to throw you in jail or kill you if you didn't pay a ransom on your life.

The traveling was uneventful for the next two days as we went through the French countryside. On the third night, after a long and difficult day of traveling, we stopped at a country inn outside the city of Nancy. All we wanted was a meal and a bed to prepare us for the next day's journey. The innkeeper was a big burley man with jet black hair and a full bushy beard that framed a perpetually good-natured face. I'm not sure we ever actually learned his name. He was dressed like a farmer, and though he was quite friendly, he looked like the type who didn't take any nonsense from anyone.

"Messieurs, what can I do for you?"

It struck us both immediately that he said "Messieurs" rather than "Citizens".

"We are traveling from Paris back to our home in Germany, and are tired and hungry from a long day on the road. Can you give us a meal and a bed and fresh horses for tomorrow?" asked Carl.

"You've come to the right place," he said in a jolly tone. "I can give you all those things for a decent price. I'm willing to give as much help as I can to anyone who wants to escape all the craziness that's going on in Paris. I've never been able to abide by the aristocracy's terrible treatment of the common people, but the reaction of simply killing every rich person in sight is just as bad. It's turned into an absolute witch hunt there with people getting arrested and executed and no one feels safe unless they go around singing patriotic songs and making sure the very snot that drips out of their noses is red, white, and blue! I tell you it's total insanity and I for one am not buying into that sort of propaganda and mob mentality. You're smart to get back to a civilized country. Why, just today some soldiers from the revolutionary guard were in the village here asking about a couple of guys that the National Assembly wants to bring back to Paris to put on trial and execute."

"What are they accused of?" I asked.

"Nothing at all! Trying to withdraw their own money out of a bank and take it home with them. Can you imagine being so rabid and crazed as to send people halfway across the country to chase down someone who just wanted to claim their own money! But enough of my ranting about the insanity of these times. You gentlemen want a hot meal and a place to sleep."

He showed us into another room off the common room where there was a comfortable fire in the hearth, and within minutes a supper of roast beef, roasted potatoes, boiled turnips, and an almost drinkable wine was sitting before us. We settled down to our meal and were a good way into the roast beef when we heard a commotion in the common room. A loud group of men had entered the house and were making inquiries of the innkeeper. We decided it would be a good idea not to go out and see what was going on.

"Citizen! We are looking for two travelers, Germans who are wanted by the Revolutionary National Assembly on charges of attempting to transport wealth out of France in violation of financial preservation laws. They are either traveling under their real names, Pals and Tierschmied, or under some alias with forged traveling papers. It was reported that they may be traveling on this road. Have you seen anyone fitting that description?"

"No, I have not!" was the prompt reply from our host. "I run a quiet and respectable house and would not allow any disreputable or suspicious characters here. I've had no guests all day and don't expect any at this time of the night."

"Nonetheless we will have a look around the house and see if there are any suspicious signs," said the leader of the group of four soldiers.

Carl and I slipped into the kitchen, which communicated with the room in which we were eating.

"What have we here?" exclaimed the leader. "It looks like a comfortable supper for two with roast beef, potatoes and wine! Citizen innkeeper, who was eating here, and where have they gone?"

"My wife and I were trying to enjoy a quiet meal in front of the fire when you and your men burst in to disturb our peaceful evening. Now may I offer you all a glass of ale before you go on your way and disturb us no more?"

"Not so fast," was the reply. "We need to check out the rest of the house and stables."

Carl and I weren't sure what to do at this critical moment, and just when it looked like we would be discovered, since the only escape route was down a set of stairs that went to a cellar, where we would be cornered, the innkeeper's wife, a plump French country woman, with black hair flowing out of a dirty white bonnet and blood spattered apron from cleaning and preparing chickens for roasting, came halfway up the stairs and beckoned to us with her finger to her lips to follow her back down the stairs. We did and when we got to the bottom in the pitch-dark cellar, she whispered;

"See the speck of light yonder? That's a trap door leading up to the yard behind the house. We use it for bringing food into the cellar. Go out that way, go straight to the barn, and behind the barn you'll find a path into the woods. Quickly! Not a word! Heavens, they'll flay us all alive if they find you! Stay in the woods until we come to fetch you. Your lives, and ours, depend on it!"

With that she pushed us forward into the darkness and we crawled out of the small opening, scurried under cover of the darkness over the barnyard to the barn, onto the footpath, and into the dark woods to wait until the coast was clear.

We didn't want to go too far into the forest, so we stayed in a thicket within sight of the barn that had a well-concealed path deeper into the forest if we needed it. We waited so long that we were sure they had forgotten about us. The night was beautiful, though a bit cool, and it was beginning to look like we were going to have to sleep on a bed of leaves and pine needles. The thick, soft bed of pine needles was actually quite comfortable, and we lay down to wait until we got the signal that the soldiers had gone.

Just as we both started to doze off, there was a clap of thunder and large drops started falling that soon turned into a torrential downpour that soaked us to the bone. A cool night of about fifty-five degrees Fahrenheit is bearable out in the woods if you have a comfortable place to sleep, but that same temperature when you're soaking wet is decidedly not.

Though we were sure it would never happen, the sun rose as usual the next morning. We were about as chilled and miserable as any two horn players have ever been and lived to tell about it. After another hour or so the innkeeper and his wife came out to the path behind the barn and called to us.

"Messieurs! It is now safe to come back! The coast is clear!"

We came out of the forest looking much the worse for wear.

"What happened? Why did we need to stay out there all night and half the morning? I asked.

"I'm very sorry, but it was unavoidable," said the innkeeper. "They searched the house, and then sat down to drink in the common room. They drank until after midnight and after they were all completely drunk and unable to leave, they wanted rooms for the night, which I couldn't refuse without suspicion, because as you know, the house is empty. We would have come out after they had gone to bed and invited you into the barn before the storm came, but we couldn't take the chance, because their horses were in the barn, and we didn't know how early they would leave in the morning. Please come in and dry off your clothes by the kitchen fire and we'll give you a hot breakfast that will bring you back to life."

We followed them into the kitchen where a comfortable fire was crackling in the hearth and listened to him pontificate about the revolution while we ate our breakfast of fresh eggs, bread, weak beer, and the rest of our roast beef from the night before, while warming our chilled bones, and drying our clothes. It seemed like the best breakfast in the history of mankind.

"I expect you are the two gentlemen they were after. Am I right? You need have no fear, we will continue to protect you and help you on your way. Are you from noble families, trying to escape the revolution?"

"We are the ones they were looking for, but we are by no means members of the aristocracy," explained Carl. "We are common musicians who left France seven years ago and came back only to retrieve our savings which we had left for safety, or so we thought, in a Paris bank. And all of a sudden, we find that we are enemies of the new government, and they want to execute us for wanting our own hard-earned money."

We went on to tell them the entire story of who we were, where we were going, and what had brought us back to France at this inopportune time.

"I thought it was something of the sort," said the innkeeper. "This whole revolution madness has gone too far, and they are all acting like hungry animals. Where will it end? I'm as pissed off and angry about the attitude of the upper classes as anyone, but let's not start killing people wholesale just to take out our frustrations. The best solution would be to trade places with the landowners for a while and let them experience the life of the common people. A few years of laboring in the fields, mending roads, hauling water, or weaving cloth on an empty stomach would do them a world of good, and they would gain a real appreciation for the hardships they've inflicted on us for centuries."

He went on like this for a good while before addressing our situation and what we should do next.

"But Messieurs, now that I know your true story, and the fact that you were innocent bystanders, so to speak, who got caught up in the revolutionary frenzy of Paris, it is all the more important that we get you safely on your way and choose an obscure route. Main roads will not serve at all for your purposes. The men who were here last night were local soldiers, not from Paris. They had received orders by the mail to look for you, and all along the main roads similar orders have gone out. That's why we are going to send you by back roads. They can't have soldiers on every cow path in France watching for you. From here it is about two day's journey to Strasbourg and the border into the Dutchy of Württemberg."

They arranged for horses and a coach for us to the next inn on a less traveled road, and by noon we were ready to depart, in dry clothes again and well fed. The innkeeper's wife prepared food for the road, and though we were burning through the two hundred *livres* that we had between us very quickly, we gave them more than they asked for in appreciation for all their help. Our money would hold out through the rest of the trip in France, and after crossing into the Holy Roman Empire we could use the small supply of different currencies we had that would work in the various German speaking lands and principalities between Strasbourg and Berlin.

"Bon Voyage, and safe travels back to your home. Don't tarry, but don't go suspiciously fast either. Strasbourg is a hotbed of revolutionary activity. After the storming of the Bastille in Paris last July, the people of Strasbourg almost tore the city apart in a frenzy of support for the crazed mob in Paris that now calls itself the Revolutionary National Assembly. So be careful there and stay on the outskirts of the city to find your way to the bridge over the Rhine. Word may get to the local guard there before you arrive." He shook our hands heartily. "We'll be praying for your safety along the way. And we hope to see you again in better times."

"There's no way I'm ever going to set foot in France again," said Carl after we were well underway on the bumpy and muddy road. "France has seen the last of the Palsa - Türrschmidt duo."

Chapter 70

Exit, pursued by a bear.
- Shakespeare, The Winter's Tale, ca. 1611

Two more relatively tense but uneventful days on the road passed, and I don't think I've ever looked all around me for signs of danger as often as I did all through the journey to Strasbourg. The roads were some of the worst that 18th century travelers were ever asked to endure. On the second night after our narrow escape in Nancy, we stayed at an inn in an obscure little town outside of Strasbourg, and the next morning ventured toward the city. We made sure to keep the curtains of the coach closed as we passed by several groups of soldiers on our route around the southern part of the city. There are several branches of the river that need to be crossed to get to the Rhine, which is the border between France and Germany. At almost every bridge, there were barriers with guards who needed to see our papers and check our bags, and each time we held our breath as we told our story again. Other than extracting a *livre* or two from us, they didn't give us any trouble or seem overly suspicious. Had we gone through the city center, which would have been quicker, we might have run into soldiers who had orders to watch for us. As the innkeeper had said, there was a lot of revolutionary activity in Strasbourg, and a lot of communication with the National Assembly in Paris. We had traveled fast, but the trip that we made in five days could have been done in three by a single messenger on horseback, or by a mail coach that traveled almost continuously, stopping only for fresh horses.

After some of the longest hours I've ever experienced, the coach we had hired early that morning at a country inn pulled up to the one and only bridge that crossed the Rhine over to the German city of Kehl. The driver got down and opened the door of the coach.

"Citizens, this is as far as I can take you. You'll have to cross the bridge on foot from here and find some other conveyance when you get to the other side."

We paid him and took our small bags and started off toward the customs house on the French side of the bridge. The Rhine at this point appeared to be about a quarter mile wide, and on the other side we could see the thatched roofs of the houses in the sleepy little border town of Kehl. We were almost there with just one more group of customs officers and border guards to contend with. The border guards came out of the shabby guardhouse to work us over first before handing us over to the customs officers to take their turn. This was a little more thorough than elsewhere, since people crossing the bridge were actually leaving France, and they knew this was their last chance to give foreigners a final scrutiny and extract money from them.

"Citizens! Your papers please!" shouted the border guard.

We successfully fielded all the usual questions about where we were coming from, where we were going, what our business was, and how much money we were carrying. After he was satisfied, and paid off, the customs officers looked through our bags, as about a dozen other customs officers had done since we left Paris. Two more *livres* later, we found ourselves walking over the bridge in the clean pure spring air and warm friendly sunlight that we hadn't noticed up until that point in our anxiety. But now we laughed and talked easily for the first time in many days. About halfway across the bridge, we heard horses and voices back at the French guardhouse. We turned around to see what was happening, and to our horror, half a dozen soldiers had arrived were pointing at us and shouting.

"There they are! After them! Stop, enemies of the people!"

"Run for it Carl!" I shouted. "If we can get to the German side before they catch up to us we're safe!"

The horses and foot soldiers started onto the bridge, and we took off at a run toward the German guardhouse at the other end. The German guards came running out of their guardhouse when they heard the noise, and within a minute, we came up to them panting and out of breath.

"Stop Gentlemen! French or German Citizens?" I had never been so happy to hear the German language in all my life.

"German!" We both cried in unison, "And we're being pursued by the revolutionary guard!" shouted Carl. "Please protect us!"

"This way! To the German side, and we will examine your papers and see if everything is in order for your entering the country under these unusual circumstances!"

The French soldiers were now catching up to us, shouting all the way.

"Stop them! Give them to us! These men fit the description of two prisoners of the Revolution who are trying to escape their punishment for breaking French laws, and we have been ordered by the National Assembly to send them back to Paris. We demand that you hand them over to us!"

"Not so fast my hasty Frenchmen! These gentlemen are standing on German soil and are in the custody of German border guards for the moment. Your jurisdiction ends at this bridge, which belongs to both countries, and if they can prove to us that they are citizens of one of the lands of the Holy Roman Empire, they are free to go their way."

We were off the bridge and surrounded by German guards. The French guards were holding muskets and pistols and looking menacingly at us, as though they weren't going to take no for an answer.

"Let's see their papers and see if they are not the men we are pursuing, though it is likely that they were traveling with forged documents."

At this point we created a sensation among both the French and German guards. I took a razor out of my bag and cut the seam at the back of Carl's waistcoat, and out fell our actual German and French issued traveling papers – the French ones that we had received in 1770, and our current documentation, stating that we were musicians in the service of the King of Prussia, on an approved leave of absence to travel to France. On Punto's advice, as soon as we had left Paris we had taken the precaution of sewing them into the back of Carl's coat to avoid detection, since we knew that our bags would probably be searched several times along the way.

I handed them to the German guards who looked them over for a minute.

"Messieurs of the French Revolutionary Guard, if you were looking for Johann Palsa and Carl Türrschmidt, Cor de chasse players of the King's band in Berlin, you have indeed found them. But unfortunately we cannot hand them over to you, as you have so rudely demanded of us."

He turned and addressed us.

"Gentleman, welcome to the Holy Roman Empire! And welcome back home to the safety of a civilized country where a sensible civilized language is spoken!"

He was obviously aiming these remarks at the French guards. He turned to their leader again.

"And you, Messieurs, can go back to hunting down the French aristocracy and whatever else it is you do for fun. Off with you!"

The French soldiers were still holding their weapons and didn't want to give up their pursuit. Everyone stood in silence for a few moments, but as a few more German soldiers had arrived, the numbers were now about twenty to six, and the leader motioned to his men to turn around and retreat back over the bridge, but not without a few choice insults and threats that were passed back and forth.

"It looks as though you've had quite a time of it staying ahead of those stinking Frenchmen over the past few days," said the guard, after we had told our entire story. "We of the border guard would be happy to invite you into the guardhouse and we'll send out for a pitcher of good old fashioned German beer to raise your spirits and prepare you for the rest of your trip."

We were more than happy to buy a round for all the guards who had helped us at that last tense moment. After resting and talking to them for a while, we went into the town and arranged for the rest of our trip back to Berlin. From Strasbourg to Berlin was a trip of nine or ten days, and the tedious travel home from there was a welcome relief after the frightening events of the previous couple of weeks.

Nearly three weeks after leaving Paris, having lost our faithful old Kerner horns, our Paris savings, and nearly our lives, we were back in Berlin, I in the loving arms of Beate, who had been sick with worrying about us the whole time, and Carl with his son Carl Nicholaus, and our lives proceeded on in the orchestra of the King of Prussia.

Chapter 71

Through the devotion of the Bohemians, we see this instrument, after a hundred years of its development, brought to a level of perfection that leaves nothing more to be desired.
- Ernst Ludwig Gerber, Historisch-Biographisches Lexicon der Tonkünstler, 1792

After many years of playing concerts with the best orchestras and musicians in Europe and preforming for royalty and nobility, Carl and I settled down into our positions in the court orchestra of Berlin, and Beate established herself as a music teacher and performer in the amateur chamber music scene. The work in the orchestra was relatively easy, the pay was very good, and we were featured as soloists often enough to keep us in good shape as a duo. There was also ample opportunity to play chamber music and horn duets for concerts and other events at court.

We were still in demand as soloists elsewhere too and made a couple of trips every year to play at other courts and in public concerts. In 1791 we made our last tour, which took us to cities not far from home to play double concertos mostly, and a few chamber music evenings of our favorite repertoire; duets by various composers. These included the twelve short duos of Mozart, pieces by Punto, Chiaparelli, Hampel, and Haudek, as well as Carl's collection that he published in Paris before we left there in 1783. There were many others who composed horn duos, and no one in the 21st century has any idea how much music for horn there was during the heyday of the horn soloists and duos. More was lost than preserved, and I would give much to have the library of music I possessed back then.

Our last tour was successful both artistically and financially, and we were at the top of our game as horn players. Normally we wouldn't have traveled in November and December, but there was a break in performances in Berlin, and we had received invitations to play in Hamburg, Lubeck, Wismar, Rostock, and other cities in northern Germany. It was a lot of traveling over a period of almost two months from the middle of November to early January. The weather was damp and cold, with a lot of rain, and even a bit of snow and ice which made the traveling by coach treacherous. We were both getting a little tired of being on the road and were getting to an age where we would rather be at home with our families in Berlin than sleeping in dirty inns and riding in cold coaches on bumpy roads, always on the lookout for robbers and other dangers along the way. But the offers from various cities and courts kept coming, and they were too tempting, both musically and financially, to turn down.

I had a bit of a cold for most of the trip which didn't stop me from playing, but I didn't give it much thought, since in the 18th century, colds, coughing and sneezing, and runny noses were normal business in the winter. We left Rostock where we played our last concert and started by coach for home, a trip of several days. That day I started having chills and symptoms of the flu and spent most of the time in the coach wrapped up in blankets with a fever. The only real relief would come when we stopped at an inn where they had a roaring fire in the kitchen hearth, and I spent most of my nights dozing in a chair there rather than risking sleeping in an ice-cold bedroom without a fire as we had always done. Carl started to be seriously concerned about my condition as we got closer to home and tried to make me as comfortable as possible.

"We'll get you home and into your own bed and keep you nice and warm until all this passes," he said. "We're due to start work in the orchestra in the second week of January, and you'll need to rest and recuperate until then. Beate and I will take good care of you until you're on your feet again".

Carl had written to Beate as we left Rostock asking her to arrange for a doctor to be there when we arrived home and preparing her for the fact that I was quite ill, but as often happened in the 18th century, the letter got to our house in Berlin a couple days after we did, so my arriving home very ill was a complete surprise to everyone.

We were fortunate enough to be able to afford to have doctors and nurses stop in each day, and Beate, Carl and Carl Nicholaus watched over me the rest of the time. They did their very best to get me through my illness, and the doctors who visited did their very worst, and in the end the doctors and Mother Nature were clearly winning. I could tell that I was developing pneumonia, which in those days was deadly to all but the strongest and youngest, and I was neither of those at this point. I tried to eat and drink, but the coughing fits prevented me from getting much nutrition or sleep. During my better waking hours, they would try to cheer me up with stories and reminiscences of some of our adventures.

"Remember the time in London when James Boswell helped us recover the stolen horns?" recalled Carl.

"Yes. I'll never forget the look on the faces of the criminals when he entered the foundry with the London policemen, all with muskets, and made them put down the horns they were about to melt in the furnace and marched them off to jail. We've had some grand adventures."

"And all our travels, and all the concerts, and my being arrested in Mannheim, and of course the Bastille! You tried to start your own personal French Revolution before anyone else thought of throwing stones at nobility."

"We do have a lot of great stories," I said, "and who else has done as much as we have to move forward the art of solo horn playing, or made so many people happy by playing horn music? I hope we can continue spreading the art and entertaining people for a while yet."

"We're not finished yet, my good friend," said Carl. "There's plenty yet to be done; there's music to be written and commissioned, places to go, and lots of music to be played. We'll get you back in shape and the Palsa-Türrschmidt Duo will be back in business again!"

Beate entered the room with a hot bowl of broth for me, and we all talked over our years together, each remembering our favorite scenes and events. I think we all had tears in our eyes as Beate talked about my rescuing her from the advances of Jean Dubois, and of our finally being married in a ceremony with our musician friends and Beate's father and sister in Paris in 1780, ten years before.

My last memory was of Beate sitting next to my bed holding a cup of warm soothing tea to my lips.

"Try to drink this, Johann my dear. The honey in the tea will soothe your throat and help ease the cough. The doctor will be back in the morning."

"I don't want any more doctors and medicine," I said. "I just want to sleep."

"Sleep dearest, and you'll feel better in the morning. I want to hear you play the horn so beautifully again, and to see you smile again. I love you Johann."

"I love you Beate," I said and closed my eyes. I felt my right hand, which was outside of the counterpane of the bedclothes, in her hand.

Carl came back into the room and asked Beate how I was doing.

"Not well, but he's calmer now after a bad fit of coughing. I think he'll sleep quietly now."

I began to drift off, but I knew instinctively that this time I was drifting farther away than into sleep. It was a very calm and peaceful experience. I felt the sensation of floating above myself and seeing them sitting on either side of the bed. As I moved farther away, I could feel the intense love that was going back and forth in waves between myself and these, the most important people in the world to me. I was sorry to go, but at the same time it was clear that it was time. It was easy to let go, and I left them sitting quietly in the peaceful twilight of the room, watching the snow falling slowly and silently on the dirty streets of Berlin.

* * * * * * * * * * * *

Chapter 72

"Where to Bud?
"Um... I think I'd like to go home. Can I do that?"
"Up to you man, I just drive this thing."
"Yes. I think I'd like to go home."
"Okay. You sit back and relax. I'll have you there in no time."

Chapter 73
The Last Chapter

By that hidden way
My Guide and I did enter, to return
To the fair world: and heedless of repose
We climbed, he first, I following his steps
Till to our view the beautiful lights of heaven
Dawned through a circular opening in the cave:
From there we stepped forth to see the stars.
- Dante Alighieri , The Divine Comedy,
End of Chapter 34

After a long and deep sleep, and this scrap of a dream about climbing into a New York City taxi, I woke feeling totally exhausted, wondering if I had even enough strength to open my eyes. Around me I could feel soft smooth bed sheets, and my head was resting on a fluffy pillow. My first thought was "Am I dead?" The air smelled clean with hints of flowers and some chemical smell that seemed vaguely familiar, but something I hadn't smelled for a very long time. Then I opened my eyes. The ceiling of the room was white and smooth, and the only thing in my line of sight was a window trimmed in polished metal with light blue curtains. Through the window only a piece of sky was visible. I stared at this trying to make some sense of these surroundings for some time, and after a few minutes I noticed a small silver dot in the sky that was moving, leaving a strip of white cloud behind it. I couldn't figure this out, and then it flashed into my head; an airplane! That's a jet airplane up in the sky!

"Where am I?" I said in German.

"Monsieur! You are awake!" said a voice in French.

"Yes, I am awake. Where am I, where is Beate?" I replied in French.

"You are in a hospital in Paris," said the voice, which was now nearer, and a young woman with short blond hair dressed in a spotlessly clean white dress came into view over me.

"How did I get here?"

"An ambulance brought you here two days ago. You had an accident and had to undergo emergency surgery to stop the internal bleeding from your injuries. You have had several blood transfusions. How do you feel? Are you comfortable? You are on a lot of pain medication."

I didn't completely understand a couple of the words, but I caught the meaning of what she was saying.

"I have a lot of pain on my left side, and I'm very tired."

"Don't try to move," she said, as I tried to turn my head. "The doctor will be here in a few minutes to give you your pain medicine.

"I don't want any more doctors or medicine. I just want to sleep."

"What's he saying?" said another voice in the room, in English.

It was a familiar voice.

"He says that he is feeling a lot of pain in his side, and he is very tired, Madame," continued the neatly dressed young woman, this time in English.

"But he can't speak French!" said the familiar voice.

"Madame, he apparently can speak French. Does he come from Canada? His French sounds Canadian."

"Beth! Is that you?" I said trying to turn my head to the left, which immediately sent a lightning bolt of sharp pain down my neck. In a moment she was standing over me with tears in her eyes. My wife from many years ago! Beth! As young and beautiful as I had remembered. Was I dreaming of her as I had done so many times over the years? No! I was back home - back in my own time. But was I twenty-eight years old and badly injured, or nearly fifty and deathly ill with pneumonia?

"I flew over yesterday and got to the hospital in the morning just as you came out of surgery. I stayed here all day and through the night praying that you would wake up. I'm so happy to see you alive! Do you remember what happened?"

"I'm so happy to see you too – happier than I can tell you. I remember a whole lot of things that are very confusing in my head, and I need to sort them out. But I'm so tired I can't keep my eyes open. Will you stay here with me? It seems like years since I've been awake and myself."

"I'll be here." she said.

"Madame, I think we should let him sleep now," said the nurse. I closed my eyes, and felt my right hand, which was outside of the blankets and sheets in hers. But I didn't go to sleep immediately. Instead, lying awake, I let a lifetime of memories flood back into my head, engulfing my tired brain like waves crashing into the shore during a storm at sea. It was all so clear and immediate in my memory. I felt that if I blinked Carl and Beate would be at my bedside, but they were gone, and my previous life was back. Was I hallucinating or was this real? Or was the other life and all of the people in it just a dream I had manufactured while struggling to stay alive after the accident? I couldn't be sure of anything at this point as worlds collided in my head.

I dozed off and on all that day, and each time I opened my eyes, the new world was still there, with Beth smiling lovingly at me and giving me words of encouragement and comfort. I was fascinated to see her after what seemed like many, many years. Doctors and nurses came in and out and discussed my case in French, and I could understand most of what they were saying, with the exception of a few words - modern words. How was it that I could understand French if it had all been a dream? Before the accident I had known hardly a word or two. The French from many years of living in Paris, and the German from my years in Germany, and daily life with Beate, Carl, and his family, and with many German and Bohemian musicians, was all there and as fresh and alive as could be - one bit of evidence that it wasn't a dream. But what other proof did I have?

For a few days after my surgery, I was only able to move a little, and with help, so I was mostly left to my own thoughts about my 18th century life. I didn't have to let the memories come to me; they were as clear as the memories anyone has about what they had been doing for the past twenty-two years. A lifetime that was longer than the adult lifetime I had experienced in the modern world was stored away in my head with all the vivid details of people, places, and music. Lots of music, and lots of friends, who I was already missing terribly. Along with the pain of my physical injuries, I was experiencing a deep sense of loss – the loss of my entire life, my identity, and a world that had defined that identity. Twenty-two years ago, when I found myself in a strange world, I had no context with which to identify myself. But this time it was different because the world I found myself in now was familiar. It was the world in which I had grown up, and it made sense to me already. There wouldn't be the steep and severe learning curve there had been in the fall of 1770 in Paris. Everyone knew me and expected me to be here, but the transition was going to take some time, since I was mourning the disappearance of everyone I had known in the other life. What had happened to them? After my "death" in the 18th century; what had happened to Beate, Carl and his son, and all the people we had known and worked with in Paris, Mannheim, Wallerstein, Cassel, London, Vienna, Berlin, and all the other places we visited and lived?

Beth went over all the details of what had happened during the previous few days. I had been hit by a bus in the street I had been crossing, and the injuries, due to internal bleeding, were considered to be immediately life threatening by the emergency room doctors in the hospital in Paris. I was lucky enough to have the emergency surgery I needed immediately upon entering the hospital, which probably saved me from bleeding to death. The rest of the orchestra had left Paris to return to the states the next morning and traveled all the way home before finding out whether I had survived the surgery, which was very much in question that morning. I was now getting messages from them by every imaginable means, and expressions of relief and wishes for a speedy recovery were all around me. It felt much like when you hear from old high school friends who you had all but forgotten about over the intervening years. But in reality - this reality in any case, I had seen them two days before.

"What happened to all of the things I had with me?" I asked Beth a few days later.

"Your horn is safe," she said. "Katy picked it up out of the street when you were hit, and miraculously, it was absolutely unharmed. They took it back with them and it will be there for you when you get home. I'm sorry to say, from what the doctors tell me, that you won't be able to play it for a while. You've got a lot of healing and some physical therapy ahead of you before life gets back to normal."

"And a whole world of new things to get used to," I added before thinking.

"Oh, they're expecting you to recover fully, and with no physical impairments if all goes well. You're one lucky guy to be so close to death and then have a prognosis of full recovery!"

Oddly enough, that wasn't what I was thinking at all when I mentioned adjustments to be made. I was thinking about Beate,

Carl, and Carl Nicholaus. Nor had I given much thought to my horn, though I was relieved to hear it was safe. I was thinking about a silver natural horn made by Joseph Raoux in Paris and wondering what had happened to it. I was also thinking about my phone, and what was stored in it at that moment.

On a cold, rainy October morning in 1770, in the sitting room of a dark, dusty old house in Paris, I had held it up, and practically scared Carl Türrschmidt to death with the flash of light it had emitted. The photo of the bewildered young man, who had already heard and seen much more than he could wrap his mind around that day, had been stored there when the phone had run out of power the next day. Was the picture still there?

I was in the hospital in Paris for about two weeks before they decided I could travel back home. I was still not very mobile, but recovering steadily, and the trip to Charles De Gaul Airport and the flight home took all the energy I had. But Beth and I finally made it home - a home I hadn't seen for twenty-two years, and never expected to see again. Even though I now knew that no time had passed, it was a shock to see our kids, Ana and Christopher, who, to my surprise, were still four and six years old. As I held them both close to me, we all had tears in our eyes – they because they had thought they might not see me again because of the accident, and I, because I thought I had lost them and they had grown up over the years I had been away.

I hadn't felt good enough in the hospital to really notice my physical condition, but it began to occur to me in the days and weeks that followed that I was not almost fifty years old, as I thought – I was twenty-eight again. My hair was no longer gray, as it had turned over the years in the 18th century, and it was cut in a 21st century way that looked unfamiliar and artificially short and sculpted. The teeth I had lost, despite my best efforts to keep them clean over the years with no dental care, other than having them pulled when they went bad, were all there again, but in my mind I still held the terrible memories of having them extracted without any sort of anesthetic. My limbs and joints no longer suffered from the arthritis that had set in from long coach rides in every imaginable kind of weather, sleeping in uncomfortably cold rooms, and from simply getting old. The better I started to feel, the more my return felt like a second youth; a second chance to not squander the great gift of a healthy body and a comfortable life to live in a friendly world - friendlier than the one to which I had become accustomed. I decided there was very little to complain about in this one.

I never stopped missing my dear Beate, and my good friend Carl. Often I would remember both the good times and the bad times we all shared, and wonder if I was the most unfortunate of men to have lost everything and everyone who I loved in that world, or if I was the most fortunate of men to be blessed with having lived two lives in two worlds, both filled with love, friendship, and music.

Epilogue

By Christopher Paulson

This manuscript, which ends quite abruptly, was found among the personal papers of my late father, John Paulson, who was a prominent French horn player and teacher of the first half of the 21st century. He was appointed to the position of third horn in a major symphony orchestra in 2016 and played there for nearly forty years until his retirement in 2055. He was involved in an accident in the early years of his career with the orchestra, apparently having been hit by a bus in Paris while on a European concert tour, and this piece of writing; memoir, fantasy novel, dream journal, hallucination of a near death experience, or whatever it might actually be, seems to have been written during the several months of recovery that were necessary before he was able to go back to work. This was also during the time of the great COVID pandemic of 2020-22, during which orchestra performances around the world were put on hold for more than a year, presumably giving him even more time to complete this work.

Just to set the record straight before discussing the mystery of the manuscript itself, my father, as I remember him, was a very straightforward and sensible man, the finest father a family could wish to have, a loving husband to my mother, who survived him by several years, an inspirational and highly effective teacher, and well-liked member of the horn section of his orchestra. He was respected and admired by all who knew him. He was not prone to telling fantastic and unbelievable stories, and the fact that he never once mentioned the events he writes about to anyone makes the story all the more intriguing. I was born when he was twenty-two, but I can't say that I really remember him or appreciated him until he was in his thirties and well established as a musician and teacher. I, of course, knew about the accident as a piece of family history that I and my sister passed on to our own children, but I have no clear memory of him before that time, so I don't know what changes he might have undergone as a result of that unfortunate event.

As a musicologist, research has always been a passion of mine. In my research and writing I have specialized in music at the courts of Europe in the 18th century, partly due to my father's love for the music of the classical era in particular. He was a big fan of the mainstream composers of the period, such as Haydn and Mozart, but also loved to seek out the music of lesser-known composers to listen to and play. As a horn player, he seemed to have a special affinity for the period and the style, and on numerous occasions performed solo pieces and chamber works by composers such as Antonio Rosetti, Carl Stamitz, Leopold Mozart, and many others. Did the events outlined in his writing inspire his interest in the period, or did his interest in the music and the period inspire the writing?

In the appendices to this volume, I have assembled and translated the few primary sources that document the lives and careers of the horn duo of Johann Palsa and Carl Türrschmidt. The life of Türrschmidt, with variant spellings of Thürrschmidt, Türrschmid, Dürrschmiedt, Tierschmied, among others, is well documented from his birth to his death. He was born in the German town of Wallerstein on February 24th, 1753, and spent much of his early life in Regensburg, where his father played first horn in the court orchestra of Thurn und Taxis, and where Carl undoubtedly also received some of his own early training. He went to Paris at the age of eighteen, in the year 1770, and there began playing as a duo with the talented Bohemian high horn player, Johann Palsa. No information about the life of Johann Palsa before 1770 can be found, other than a reference by Ernst Ludwig Gerber in his *Historisch-Biographisches Lexicon der Tonkünstler*, Leipzig, 1792, that states that he was born in the town of Jemeritz in Bohemia on June 20th, 1752, information that he must have obtained directly from Palsa when they met at a music festival in Kassel in 1786. The lack of any other information about him before that date seems to suggest that Palsa literally appeared out of nowhere in Paris in 1770 and immediately began working as a professional horn player in the company of Türrschmidt.

Many of the musicians and composers named in the manuscript were actually in Paris, London, and the several cities in Germany and Austria at the times my father mentions having known them and worked with them, though many other names were not to be found in sources from the time. This would not be unusual, since musicians from elsewhere in Europe often went to Paris to try to make their fortunes and reputations, and many were undoubtedly not documented for posterity in any way. There is mention in the records of the Concert Spirituel programs of 1779 that a "Mademoiselle Pokorny" performed a concerto by the Bohemian horn soloist Giovanni Punto on the program of December 25th, 1779. Though the relationship is not clear, evidence suggests that Beate Pokorny could have been the daughter of Franz Xavier Pokorny, violinist and composer in the Thurn und Taxis court orchestra in Regensburg, and secondary sources on the history of the horn speculate that she may have studied with Punto. After that date there is only a handful of other sources that mention her name or performing career. Among them is a concert advertisement from London in the year 1780, which announces that the "Miss Pokornys" would play concertos and duets on French horns.

Giovanni Punto was well known to Palsa and Türrschmidt, and was, by all indications, a close friend. The information my father relates about Punto's life, horn playing career, and character seem to agree with the information available about him. Jean Dubois, the student of Punto mentioned in the text, does not appear in any of the sources from the time. Other musical and non-musical figures, such as Johann Wendling, the flute player from Mannheim, Antonio Rosetti, and even Benjamin Franklin and Samuel Johnson's biographer, James Boswell, appear in the story, and in many cases these people can be documented as having been where my father placed them in his narrative. If this is due to his own research for a piece of historical fiction, it was an amazing feat of scholarship, and demonstrates a very thorough knowledge of daily life and music in the 18th century.

The compositions mentioned are also an intriguing part of the mystery. My father mentions a number of pieces of music from the time that are still extant, and a few that apparently did not survive. Double horn concertos that are still known today by Leopold Mozart, Franz Pokorny, and Josef Fiala appear in his story in the early 1770s. By the end of that decade the duo, according to programs of the Concert Spirituel, had double horn concertos by Rosetti, and had built up a repertoire of unaccompanied duos, many of which must be part of the collection of duos published by Türrschmidt in Paris, (now lost) and another published later in Berlin, which has come down to us. Particularly interesting is his account of the composition of twelve horn duos by Mozart, six of which he states Mozart composed in Paris in 1778, and six in Vienna in 1786. These are presumably the set of twelve duos that were published in Vienna by the *Bureau d'Arts et d'Industrie n.d. [Plate 46].* The manuscript of three of the duos is extant and the top of the first page bears the inscription: "Composed by Wolfgang Amadeus Mozart, July(?) 27th 1786, while bowling. (*untern Kegelscheiben*)". My father's manuscript doesn't give a specific date for the bowling party at the Mozart house, but seems to imply that it took place at the end of June or early July. This may be explained by the fact that the date on the Mozart duo manuscript was scrawled quickly and is messy and open to interpretation.

Sources from Paris, as well as Gerber's *Historisch-Biographisches Lexicon der Tonkunstler*, confirm that the two horn players were engaged by Henri Louis de Rohan, Prince of Guéméné, for his private orchestra and chamber musicians in 1770, and remained in his service until 1783, when the prince suffered financial losses that forced him to disband his orchestra. Their participation in a large music festival in Kassel and engagement by the Landgrave of that city, Friedrich II, their extended tour to England, and engagement in the court orchestra at Berlin are all well documented. But the visits to Mannheim, Öttingen-Wallerstein, and Vienna that my father describes, have not, as yet, been confirmed, though I continue to search for evidence in sources of the period.

There were a few other interesting, but by no means conclusive, bits of evidence connected with the 18th century narrative of my father. He did own a natural horn, a French instrument of the early 19th century, and on several occasions played it with local period instrument orchestras when time permitted, and from what I am told, played it well. Whether he played it as well as Johann Palsa, three hundred years ago, I am not in a position to judge, but he did enjoy doing it as a musical diversion from his work in the orchestra.

His foreign language skills were also a mystery. On just a few occasions I heard my father speak French, which he seemed to do with ease, though the reaction of the people he spoke with was always the same as that of the nurse in his last chapter; "Are you originally from Canada?" The French of Quebec still contains many elements of the language as it was spoken in the 18th century, when it was brought to Canada from France, and differs in many respects from modern French, as it is spoken in France today. His German, which was also much more fluent than one would expect for someone who had taken a couple of years of college-level language courses, gave the impression of coming from a local dialect of southern Germany or Austria, rather than the *"Hoch Deutsch"* or High German that one learns in school. One German friend described his use of the language as "very fluent, but rather quaint and archaic, as though he had spent most of his school years devouring Goethe and Schiller".

My mother was alive and well when my father passed away, and after finding the present manuscript, which I never showed to her, I asked her a few questions.

"Where there any unusual occurrences connected with his coming home after the accident in 2019?"

"Oh yes," she replied. "He was not very concerned about his horn, and said that his friends from the orchestra would take good care of it, but he became particularly anxious to get back the things he had in his pockets on the day of the accident. I was surprised, because all he had with him was his mobile telephone, his wallet, keys, and a horn mouthpiece."

"And did he get them back?"

"Yes - and there were two very odd things that happened. When he opened the bag that contained the items, he gasped as though he had seen a ghost, and quickly put the silver horn mouthpiece in his pocket. Then he tried to turn on the phone, which was apparently damaged, and seemed terribly disappointed when it didn't work. I told him we could get him a new phone to replace it, but he insisted on taking that one to get it repaired when we returned home. When he took it to someone who could repair it, they told him there was some defect in the battery that had made it corrode, as though it had been left in a damp place for a very long time unused, and it had corroded the electronics of the phone so badly that nothing on it was retrievable. I don't remember him ever looking so disappointed about anything before or after that."

Then I asked her if he had changed in any way after the accident. She sat silently for a few moments before replying.

"He did change subtly in his outlook on life, which one might expect in someone who had experienced a close brush with death. He had a greater appreciation of the people and of the things around him. He became more thoughtful and philosophical. I would often find him deep in thought, as though he was somewhere far away, and when I would ask him what he was thinking about, he would smile and say, 'just reminiscing about old friends and bygone days.'"

Those are the inconclusive scraps of evidence I have been able to assemble in my several years of sporadic research in an effort to solve this intriguing mystery. Anything further can only belong to the realm of speculation and fantasy, and ultimately we are left with our own thoughts and conjectures on the question of whether my father left behind a remarkably well-researched work of fiction, or even an intentional hoax, or if he really was Johann Palsa, one of the most celebrated horn virtuosi of the 18th century.

Christopher J. Paulson, PhD
Bloomington, Indiana
August 9th, 2075

Author's Notes

A few notes for the serious student of the horn and the history of its playing technique.

In addition to the fictional story of John Paulson's twenty-two year career as a natural horn soloist in the 18th century, and the adventures that I put the Palsa/Türrschmidt duo through in the course of this narrative, which can be enjoyed by any reader who is interested in music and life during this period, my goal was to paint an accurate picture, as far as our current research can determine, of the horn and how it was played, the life of court orchestra musicians and traveling soloists, and the state of music in the last quarter of the 18th century.

With sincere apologies to the general reader, whose patience I hope I've not overly taxed, I have, for the benefit of horn playing readers, and especially the natural horn specialist, sprinkled the text with details of a more technical nature about the instrument, how it was played and how it functioned in orchestral, solo, and chamber music. Many of the impressions that Mr. Paulson gives about his adapting to the 18th century natural horn and learning how to play it in a classical wind section and soloistically are taken from my own experiences playing the horn in period instrument ensembles for more than forty years and teaching natural horn to my students. The historical information I've presented on the development of playing technique and the physical state of the instrument is based on current research that has appeared in brass instrument and early music books and journals in recent years.

The most recent research on the subject would suggest that all, or nearly all, horns in use in musical settings until well after the middle of the 18th century were fixed pitch horns, and were played for the most part with the hand out of the bell. An examination of late 18th, and early 19th century writings and iconography suggest that this way of playing the horn orchestrally was practiced in some places until the end of the century, or longer. (See www.hornicono-graphy.com)

Shortly after the middle of the 18th century, however, a new kind of soloistic horn playing began to develop using chromatic hand stopping that transformed the horn into a refined solo voice that could compete well with other winds and strings as a solo and chamber music instrument. Initially taught around the middle of the century by teachers such as Anton Joseph Hampel (1710-1771), and refined and developed further by the next generation, which included Giovanni Punto, Palsa, Türrschmidt and many others, this technique was probably seen as a distinctly different method from orchestral playing and was reserved for solo and chamber music only. It was into this class of solo players that Mr. Paulson finds himself catapulted when he arrives in the 18th century and makes the acquaintance of Carl Türrschmidt.

I also wanted to give the impression that the horn was played in many different ways in different places. For example, there is some written evidence that the players in the Mannheim orchestra played almost exclusively with the hand out of the bell, while in Wallerstein, where Rosetti was writing virtuosic and chromatic solo and double concertos, it is more likely that hand technique was in use, though likely not for all purely tutti orchestral playing. My goal was to show that this was a transitional time for the horn that eventually led to the fully developed hand horn of the 19th century

Endnotes

Chapter 4

1. For information on the Anton Kerner Orchestra horn, see: https://www.seraphinoff.com/reinventing-the-classical-horn
2. For a discussion of early horn mouthpieces, see: https://www.seraphinoff.com/early-horn-mouthpieces
3. For a detailed study of the two styles of horn playing, soloistic hand stopping technique and orchestra open horn playing, see the upcoming article *18th Century Horn Performance Practice: A Re-evaluation of the Role of the Hand* by John Manganaro (presented at the Historical Horn Symposium, part of the International Horn Symposium, Ghent, Belgium, 2019)

Chapter 11

4. For information on the several generations of the Raoux family of instrument makers, see *The New Langwell index of Wind Instrument Makers* by William Waterhouse, Tony Bingham, London, 1993, and the article on the Raoux family in the *New Grove Dictionary.*

Chapter 13

5. Documentation on the engagement of Palsa and Türrschmidt to the private orchestra of Henri Louis de Rohan, Prince of Guéméné can be found in the biography of Palsa in Gerber's *Historisches-Biographisches Lexicon* in the section "Primary Sources from the 18th and 19th Centuries..."

Chapter 14

6. It was common in the 18th century for brass instrument players to also play a stringed instrument, and many horn players doubled on the viola. Heinrich Domnich, in his *Methode*, 1807, makes the suggestion that a horn player should have skill on another instrument in case they have to stop playing the horn due to loss of teeth or other accidents or illnesses.
7. This is a reference to Dr. Alexandre Mannett, a fictional character in Charles Dickens' *A Tale of Two Cities*. In the Dickens

novel the Doctor was imprisoned in the Bastille for offending a nobleman and was allowed to make shoes there to earn his food.

Chapter 15
8. Carl Türrschmidt, *50 duos Op. 3*, C. C. Menzel, Berlin, 1795. In this set there are three duets composed by Johann Palsa, all in unusual key signatures for horn duos of the time.
9. The *Three Trios for Flute, Violin, and Cello, Op. 3* by Wendling, published in 1772, were dedicated to the Comte de Guînes, who was an amateur flute player. In 1778 the Comte commissioned Mozart to write the *Concerto for Flute and Harp, K. 299*, for himself and his daughter who played the harp.

Chapter 19
10. The opera *Tom Jones*, by François André Danican Philidor, was first produced in Paris in 1765 at the *Comédie Italienne.*

Chapter 23
11. Anton Dimmler composed a concerto for two horns in E major *Concertante a due Corni*, which has been issued in a modern edition by Hans Pizka Edition, 1983. It is not known for whom it was written.

Chapter 29
12. There is very little documentation of the life of Beate Pokorny, but it has been speculated by some writers that she was the daughter of Franz Xavier Pokorny, violinist and composer of the Turn und Taxis court orchestra in Regensburg. See the section "Primary Sources of the 18th and 19th centuries..." and the article *Pokorny Vindicated* by J. Murray Barbour (Musical Quarterly, Vol. 49 No. 1, Jan. 1963) Other sources point to the possibility of her having been Franz Pokorny's sister.

Chapter 30
13. The Regensburg *Musikindendant,* Baron Theodor von Schacht, may indeed have changed the title pages on many of Franz Pokorny's symphonies in the Thurn und Taxis orchestra library. See the above-mentioned article by J. Murray Barbour.

Chapter 31
14. For more information on the life and work of Antonio Rosetti and the Öttingen-Wallerstein Orchestra, See Sterling Murray's biography of Antonio Rosetti, *The Career of an 18th Century Kapellmeister; The life and Music of Antonio Rosetti*, Univ. of Rochester, 2014.

Chapter 35
15. It is documented in the *Histoire du concert spirituel 1725-1790* by Constant Pierre, Paris 1900, that Palsa and Türrschmidt played a set of "Petit airs" for two horns at the Concert Spirituel on December 24th, 1776, and Punto played a concerto of his own composition on December 25th.
16. This is a reference to Ernis Defarge, a fictional character in a *A Tale of Two Cities* by Charles Dickens. In the Dickens novel, Defarge is the wineshop owner in St. Antoine, Paris who is high up in the inner circle of initial organizers of the French Revolution.

Chapter 38
17. Benjamin Franklin was appointed by the congress of the United States in 1776 to be a "Commissioner to France" and lived in Paris 1777 - 1785.

Chapter 40
18. Mozart's trip to Paris in 1778 is well documented, and the events covered in chapters 49 and 50, are based on passages from Mozart's letters to his father.

Chapter 44
19. For historical documentation on Beate Pokorny's solo performance at the Concert Spirituel on Christmas day, 1779, see "Primary Sources of the 18th and 19th Centuries..."

Chapter 48
20. My depiction of the designing of the French orchestra horn by Carl Türrschmidt and the making of silver horns by Raoux for Palsa, Türrschmidt and Punto, goes against the traditional story as

told by previous writers such as Reginald Morley-Pegge and Horace Fitzpatrick. These writers assumed that the instrument designed by Türrschmidt and made by Raoux around 1780 was the French cor-solo of the end of the 18th century, which became popular as a solo instrument in the early part of the 19th century. It is most likely that the term "Inventionshorn" simply meant a horn with terminal crooks, as opposed to a simple horn with fixed mouthpipe, into which tuning bits and small coiled crooks could be inserted into the mouthpiece receiver. The term does not necessarily mean a horn with tuning slide in which crooks are inserted into the slide. In the description of the instrument in the article on the history of the horn in Gerber's Lexicon, he states clearly that soloists at the time played on simple horns without crooks or slides, i.e., fixed pitch horns. It is more likely that Türrschmidt's work with Raoux resulted in the French orchestra horn with tuning slide and terminal crooks, which remained a standard design through the next century.

Chapter 50
21. Rosetti's trip to Paris in 1781 is documented in Sterling Murray's book *The Career of an 18th Century Kapellmeister; The life and Music of Antonio Rosetti* citing letters from Rosetti in Paris to his employer in which he mentions the generosity of Herr and Frau Palsa.

Chapter 54
22. The silver horns were mentioned both in Gerber's *Historisches-Biographisches Lexicon* and in William T. Parke's "Musical Memoirs". See "Primary Sources..."

Chapter 60
23. The story of Mozart having heard the starling in a shop in Vienna singing a melody, and then using the melody as the theme for the last movement of his *Piano Concerto no. 17, K. 453* comes from Mozart's letters to his father. He then went back to the shop and bought the bird and kept it as a pet. Mozart did actually have a dog named Bimprel, who is also mentioned in letters to his father.

24. The Mozart *Horn Duos, K. 487/496a* were published in Vienna by the Bureau d'Arts et d'Industrie n.d Plate 46, and a second printing appeared in Paris shortly thereafter. The manuscript of duos 1, 3, and 6 is dated 27, July(?), 1786, and according to the inscription on the manuscript, were composed at a lawn bowling party. We do not know for whom they were written, or if Palsa and Türrschmidt actually made a trip to Vienna.

Chapter 61
25. The events in this chapter are taken from the articles on Palsa and Türrschmidt in Gerber's *Historisches-Biographisches Lexicon*. See Primary Sources..."

Chapter 64
26. Charles Burney, in his *The Present State of Music in Germany, the Netherlands, and the United Provinces* London, 1775, vol. 2, p.100, gives a description of the trumpet and kettledrum fanfare that announced the entrance of the Queen and her entourage at each performance at the opera in Berlin.

Chapter 65
27. Palsa and Türrschmidt apparently were in Paris for a period of time at the end of the 1780s. Nicolas Étienne Framery, in his *Calendar Universal Musical* for 1788 and 1789, p. 275, lists Palsa and Türrschmidt (spelled Tierschmidt) as residing in the rue Varenne, Hôtel de Monaco, Paris.

Excerpts from primary sources from the 18th and early 19th centuries that document the lives of Johann Palsa, Carl Türrschmidt, and Beate Pokorny.

Relatively little is known about the actual lives of the principal characters of this story, Johann Palsa, Carl Türrschmidt, and Beate Pokorny. We are indebted to Ernst Ludwig Gerber (1746-1819), the German composer and musical lexicographer who met Palsa and Türrschmidt in Kassel in 1786 and wrote lengthy biographies of both, as well as a long article on the horn. This information, which included where they worked at different periods, and even their dates and places of birth, was copied by subsequent writers in musical dictionaries in France, England and Germany. A chance mention in the "Musical Memoirs" of London oboist William T. Parke documents where they played on their tour to London in 1786, and the *Histoire du concert spirituel* of Constant Pierre tells of their many appearances as soloists in Paris. Their names appear from time to time in other books, newspapers, and periodicals of the time, more than almost any other horn players, which gives us a hint of how active and popular they were, and how far and wide they traveled as a duo.

Beate Pokorny, as a horn soloist, is only mentioned in a couple of sources, and it is unclear whether she was actually related to Franz Pokorny. The name Pokorny was a popular Bohemian surname. These selections from primary sources, in translation, will help the serious student to sort out what is fact and what is fiction in the story.

Documentation of the lives of Johann Palsa and Carl Türrschmidt (selections)

Constant Pierre, "Histoire du concert spirituel 1725-1790" Paris 1900

In the programs of the Paris Concert Spirituel, Johann Palsa and Carl Türrschmidt are listed as having performed duets and concertos for two horns on numerous occasions between 1770 and 1783.

Ernst Ludwig Gerber "Historisches-Biographisches Lexicon der Tonkünstler" Leipzig, 1792 (English translation by R. Seraphinoff)

Palsa (Johann) One of the best and most prominent high horn players, with his no less great and artistic second horn, Herr Türrschmidt, in the service of the Prussian King in Berlin, was born in Jermeritz in Bohemia on June 12th, 1752. In 1770 he went, along with his second horn colleague, into the service of the prince of Guéméné in Paris, as well as the Concert Spirituel. They remained there thirteen years, and always to the same applause. Eventually, in 1783, they undertook a trip to Germany, and on this trip passed through Cassel. There they played for the late Landgraf and received much well-deserved applause, so that the Landgraf took them into his service with a substantial salary, although the horn positions in his orchestra had already been filled.

In 1785 they traveled to London and returned in August of 1786 to Cassel to perform at the music festival there. This was the high point of music making in Cassel, the time when the most prominent musicians there celebrated their last great triumph. The important guest artists who came to the festival performed alternatingly with the French and Italian musicians in the small and large opera theaters in masterpieces by Hasse, Gluck, Mozart, Cannabich, Schweitzer, Holzbauer, Martini, Paesello, etc. continuously for four weeks. On Sundays Heuzé, Barth, Palsa, Türrschmidt, and others performed in the *Hofassmblee* to the great applause of the listeners.

Here it was that I was able to not only hear these great artists on the horn daily in performances, but also, thanks to their friendly, open, and agreeable character, I had the good fortune to hear examples of their fine talents at their place of residence.

There they played a double concerto accompanied by the entire court orchestra, under the direction of its concertmaster Braun. It is impossible to describe the noble singing style of Herr Palsa, or the fire, agility, and wonderful passagework of Herr Türrschmidt. They played both concertos in E major on their two silver horns, made in Paris, whose value is estimated at 100 *louis-d'ors* each. In the rondos, they modulated into e minor, G major, g minor, etc. with the precision of a pianist. They presented their astonishing technique so easily, and so assuredly, and in such a refined way, that it left me wanting more.

Several months later, death took the Landgraf, and with him, the supporter of music in Cassel up to that time. Palsa and Türrschmidt were among the first to leave, and went to Berlin, where they immediately went into the service of the current highly esteemed King, who was at that time crown prince.

In Herr Palsa's room, I found a marvelous miniature painting, which captured his likeness perfectly. In Paris, under the names of these two artists, six duos for two horns have been printed. These are written in a manner of which D. Forkel has said: "One cannot hear anything more beautiful than these little duets, especially those written in minor keys."

Türrschmidt, (Carl) Royal Prussian chamber music virtuoso and second hornist with Herr Palsa, who plays the first horn, was born in Wallerstein on February 24, 1753. His history is bound together with Herr Palsa's up until the present time, as already stated in the article on Palsa. These two great masters enhance the quality of the Royal Court Orchestra in Berlin, which already enjoys an excellent reputation.

François Fetis "Biographie universelle des musicians" Paris, 1837 (English translation by Pierre-Antoine Tremblay)

Palsa (Jean), horn virtuoso, was born in Jermeritz, Bohemia, on June 20, 1752. He was only 18 years old when he went to Paris with Turschmidt, who, in their duets, played the second horn part. After hearing them at the *Concert Spirituel*, the Prince of Guéméné took them in his service. They published in that city two sets of duets for two horns. In 1783, these artists returned to Germany, and entered the chapel of the Landgrave of Hesse-Cassel. Two years later, they made a trip to London, where they received widespread admiration.

Back in Cassel, they stayed there until the death of the Landgrave. In 1786 they entered the service of the King of Prussia. Palsa died of a chest dropsy, on January 24, 1792, at the age of 38. This distinguished artist published a third book of duets for two horns, with Turschmidt, in Berlin, at Groebenschütz and Seiler. The talent of Palsa showcased a particularly beautiful manner of singing on his instrument.

Turrschmidt (Charles), horn virtuoso, was born in Wallerstein, on February 24, 1753. After being befriended by Palsa (see his entry), another distinguished horn player, he became his second, and at age 18, they both traveled to be heard in foreign countries. It can be seen in the record of Palsa what the main events were in the lives of these two artists. Türrschmidt, who in 1785 entered into the orchestra of the King of Prussia, outlived his friend by about 5 years, having died in Berlin on November 1st, 1797. Until his last days he stayed in the service of the King of Prussia, and was the second horn of Lebrun, who succeeded Palsa. In Paris, Türrschmidt published with Palsa, two collections of duets for two horns at Sieber's. We also have under his sole name : Fifty duets for two horns, Op. 3, in Berlin, 1795. This artist had a son, born in Paris on October 20, 1776, who he personally taught until he died, at which point his son went on to receive lessons from the virtuoso Lebrun (see this entry). This son of Charles Türrschmidt, named *Charles-Nicolas*, was a music teacher in Berlin, but doesn't appear to have been in the service of the court of Prussia.

He had married *Augusta Braun*, daughter of a musician of the court, born on November 20, 1800, who was a remarkable singer at the Singing Academy of Berlin. From this union came *Albrecht Türrschmidt*, born in Berlin on May 16, 1821, pupil of his father and of Neugebauer; he went on to make a name for himself as a composer of several collections of Lieder.

"Dictionary of Musicians" London, 1830

Palsa, (Johann) a very celebrated performer on the horn, in the service of the king of Prussia at Berlin, was born at Jermeritz, in Bohemia, in 1754. In 1770, he performed with his colleague Türrschmidts at the *concert spirituel* at Paris, in which they both remained till 1783, when they travelled into Germany, and were engaged by the Landgrave of Hesse-Cassel, at a high salary. In 1785, they came to this country, where they were much admired. The following year they returned to Cassel. The editors of the French Dictionary of Musicians say that it is impossible to give an idea of the beauty and purity of the cantabile of Palsa, or the vivacity, quickness, and skill of Türrschmidts. Accompanied by the orchestra of the theater at Cassel, they performed on their silver horns (manufactured at Paris, and each valued at one hundred louis-d'ors) two concertos in E major; and, in the rondos, passed to the keys of E minor and G major with as much facility as performers on the piano-forte. On the death of the Landgrave they proceeded to Berlin, where they were engaged by the court, and where Palsa died in 1792, in the thirty-eighth year of his age. In the name of Türrschmidts there were published, at Paris, "Duos à 2 Cors de Chasse," Ops. 1 and 2.

William T. Parke - Musical Memoirs; Comprising an Account of the General State of Music, from the Commemoration of Handel, in 1784, to the year 1830. London 1830, p. 63.

1786 - Salomon gave six subscription concerts in Hanover Square, the first of which took place on the second of March; Madame Mara, Miss Chenu, and Mr. Harrison were the singers. Two new French horn players, Messers Palsa and Thurshmit , who had only played previously at the Anacreontic Society, made their first appearance in public in a concertante for that instrument. The most striking part of their exhibition was their horns, which were made of silver.

Wilhelm Schneider "Historische Technische Beschreibung der musikalischen Instrumente" 1834. P. 36 (English translation by R. Seraphinoff)

Carl Türrschmidt improved the Inventionshorn in 1781 by crossing the tubes over each other, so that the air flows through the horn unhindered, rather than in the tubing of a (normal horn) with circular bows, where the flow of air is more difficult. An instrument of this type was first made in Silver by Raoux in Paris. A further invention of Türrschmidt's was a new type of horn mute, different from that of Hampel, on which the half-steps and stopped notes can be produced with the same precision as with hand stopping.

Ferdinand Simon Gassner "Universal - Lexicon der Tonkunst" 1847 (English translation by R. Seraphinoff)

Türrschmidt, - a family of famous horn virtuosi. Often written Thürrschmidt, which is incorrect.

1) Johann, the father, born in Leschgau in Bohemia on June 24h, 1725, was one of the most prominent horn virtuosi of his time. He was in the service of the Prince of Öttingen-Wallerstein and died there around 1780.

2) Carl, son of the aforementioned, born in Wallerstein on February 24th, 1753, studied first with his father, and then made several trips, went to Paris, and ultimately to Berlin, where he held a position as royal chamber musician along with Palsa. Together these two undertook a concert tour through all of France and Germany around 1780. His reputation spread over half of Europe, and few hornists have ever had such a beautiful tone on their instrument as his or possessed such a remarkable technique. He was truly a virtuoso and artist. In 1781 he made improvements to the Inventions horn, after which he had a horn made in silver, which he always used for solo, playing. In 1795 he invented a mute on which one could play chromatically with perfect intonation on the instrument. He also

composed several duets and other pieces for his instrument though few were published. He died on December 1st, 1797.
3) Carl Nicholaus, son of the aforementioned Carl, born in Paris on December 20th 1776, and studied first with his father, and after his death, with Brue (Lebrun) in Berlin. He never achieved the fame of his father, but was, nonetheless, a fine musician.

Documentation for Beate Pokorny from primary sources (selections)

These sources are all documented in the online article on Beate Pokorny on the website of the Sophie Drinker Institute, Bremen, Germany (*Europäische Instrumentalistinnen des 18. Und 19. Jahrhunderts*) https://www.sophie-drinker-institut.de/pokorny-beate

Constant Pierre, "Histoire du concert spirituel 1725-1790" Paris, 1900

In the programs of the Paris Concert Spirituel Mlle. Pokorny is listed as having performed a solo concerto on the horn on Dec. 24, 1779. Other soloists on the program included Mlle. Mudrich, playing a flute concerto by Stamitz, and Mlle. Cécile playing a pianoforte concerto by J.C. Schroetter.

"Mercure de France" 1780 p. 32 (English translation by Pierre-Antoine Tremblay)

"Those who like 'novelties' found enjoyment in an exhibition as unusual in the past as it is today, where novelties are not exactly rare. They were able to hear a woman, Mademoiselle Pokorny, play a concerto for Cor de chasse by Punto, with charming sounds and fine intonation, for which she was applauded. This took place in 1779."

London Morning Post and Daily Advertiser, June 2nd and July 5th, 1780

Announcements appeared for performances by the "Celebrated Miss Pokornys" in London on June 2nd, and July 5th, 1780. The June 2nd concert took place at Carlisle House in London and the announcement included the following:
"... A concert of Vocal and Instrumental Music. By several performers who never appeared in England. Among whom are the two celebrated Miss Pokornys, who will blow several concertos and duets on the French Horn..."

A list of actual historical figures who either appear in the story or are mentioned in the text. Any character who does not appear in this list was invented by the author.

Abel, Carl Friedrich (1723 - 1787) German composer and viola da gamba player, worked in Dresden and London
Augusta, of Duchess Würtemberg (1734 - 1787) Wife of Prince Karl Anselm, 4th Prince of Thurn und Taxis
Agustinelli, Fiorante (1741 - 1809) Italian flute player, worked in the Thurn und Taxis court orchestra
Bach, Carl Philipp Emanuel (1714 - 1788) German keyboard player and composer in the service of Frederick the Great in Berlin, later moved to Hamburg, fifth child of J.S. Bach
Bach, Johann Christian (1735 - 1782) Composer and youngest son of J.S. Bach, worked in London
Baer, Johann Joseph (1744 - 1812) Bohemian clarinetist and composer
Barsanti, Francesco (1690 - 1772) Italian flutist, oboist, and composer, worked in London
Barth, Samuel Christian (1735 - 1809) German oboist, worked in Rudolstadt, Weimar, Hannover, Kassel, and Copenhagen.
Baumann, Hermann (1934 -) German horn soloist, teacher, and composer
Beecke, Franz Ignaz von (1733 - 1803) German keyboard player and composer
Beethoven, Ludwig van (1770 - 1829) German composer and pianist
Benda, Franz (1709 - 1786) Bohemian violinist and composer, worked at the court of Frederick the Great
Besozzi, Gaetano François Marie (1727 - 1804) Italian oboist, worked in Naples, Paris, and London
Bimprel (dates unknown) Mozart's dog, mentioned in letters to Leopold Mozart
Boccherini, Luigi (1742 - 1805) Italian cellist and composer, worked in Spain
Borliebner, Carl Franz (dates unknown) Horn player and cellist in Cassel Court Orchestra

Boswell, James (1740 - 1795) Scottish biographer, diarist and lawyer, most famous for the *"Life of Samuel Johnson"*, 1791
Boyce, William (1711 - 1779) English composer and organist
Brahms, Johannes (1833 - 1897) German composer, conductor and pianist
Brain, Dennis (1921 - 1957) British horn soloist
Braun, Johann Friedrich (1759 - 1824) German violinist and composer, worked in Cassel
Britten, Benjamin (1913 - 1976) British composer
Burney, Charles (1726 - 1814) English music historian, composer and musician
Cambini, Giuseppi (1746? - 1825?) Italian violinist and composer, worked in Paris
Cannabich, Johann Christian (1731 - 1798) German violinist and composer, Kapellmeister of the Mannheim Orchestra
Capron, Nicholas (1740 - 1784) French violinist and composer, concertmaster of the Concert Spirituel
Carl Theodore (1724 - 1799) Elector of the Palatinate, underwriter of the Mannheim Orchestra, amateur flute player
Mademoiselle Cécile (dates unknown) Pianist who performed at the Concert Spirituel in the 1770s - 1780s
Charlotte of Mecklenburg-Strelitz, Queen of England (1744 - 1818) German born wife of King George III of England
Cipriani, Giovanni Batista (1727 - 1785) Italian artist, worked in England
Cramer, Wilhelm (1746 - 1799) German born violinist, worked in London
Couperin, François (1668 - 1733) French composer and harpsichordist
Damm, Peter (1937 -) German horn soloist
Danzi, Franz (1763 - 1826) German cellist and composer
Danzi, Innocenz (1730 - 1798) Italian cellist, worked in the Mannheim Orchestra
Dargent (dates unknown) Paris horn player mentioned in the orchestra roster of the Concert Spirituel
Davies, Peter Maxwell (1934 - 2016) British composer and conductor

Dawes, William (1745 - 1799) American revolutionary war patriot who took part in the midnight ride with Paul Revere to warn the colonial minutemen of the approach of the British army.
Denner, Jacob (1681 - 1735) German maker of woodwind instruments, worked in Nuremberg
Dimmler, Franz Anton (1753 - 1827) German horn player and composer, worked in Mannheim
Dimmler, Josef (dates unknown) Mannheim Orchestra horn player
Dittersdorf, Carl Ditters von (1739 - 1799) Austrian violinist and composer
Ebeling, Ernst (dates unknown) Oboist in the Berlin court orchestra
Eck, Georg (dates unknown, active 1765 - 1782) Mannheim Orchestra low horn player
Eisen, Jacob (1756 - 1796) Viennese horn player, second horn in the Vienna Hofkapelle
Elisabeth-Augusta (1721 - 1794) Wife of Carl Theodore, Elector of the Palatinate
Ernst, Alois (1759 - 1814) Flute player in the Wallerstein orchestra from 1775
Esterhazy, Prince Nikolas I (1714 - 1790) Hungarian prince, employer of Joseph Haydn
Fiala, Josef (1748 - 1816) Wallerstein oboist, viola da gambist, cellist and composer, joined the Wallerstein Orchestra in 1774
Fields, W.C. (1880 - 1946) American comedian, actor and writer
Forkel, Johann Nikolaus (1749 - 1818) German musician, composer, musicologist, and music theorist
Franklin, Benjamin (1706 - 1790) American diplomat, one of the founding fathers of the United States, printer, scientist, writer, politician, philosopher, inventor, postmaster, Freemason, etc.
Franz, Carl (1738 - 1802) German horn player, worked in Esterhazy court orchestra and Munich
Fränzl, Ignaz (1736 - 1811) German violinist and composer, worked in Mannheim Orchestra
Friederich II, Landgraf of Hessen-Kassel (1720 - 1785) Supporter of music and the arts, married to the Princess Mary,

daughter of King George II of England, succeeded by his eldest son, Wilhelm
Frederick the Great (Friedrich der Grosse) (1712 - 1786) Prussian king and military leader, amateur flute player and supporter of music and the arts
Friederich Wilhelm II, King of Prussia (1744 - 1797) grandson of Frederick the Great
Frederika Luise von Hessen-Darmstadt (1751 - 1805) wife of Frederich Wilhelm II, king of Prussia
Fritch, Josef (dates unknown, active 1752 - 1775) Wallerstein and Turn und Taxis Orchestra horn player
Fürall, Franz Xavier (? - 1780) Wallerstein Orchestra oboist, joined the group in 1774
Galvani, Luigi (1737 - 1798) Italian physician, and physicist
Gassmann, Florian Leopold (1729 - 1774) Bohemian opera composer
Gaviniès, Pierre (1728 - 1800) - French violinist, concertmaster and composer
George III, King of England (1738 - 1820) British Monarch
Gerber, Ernst Ludwig (1746 - 1819) German composer and author of *"Historisch-biographisches Lexicon der Tonkünstler"*, a dictionary of 18th century musicians
Georgi, Brigida (Bigida Banti) (1757 - 1806) Italian soprano
Geminiani, Francisco (1762 - 1787) Italian violinist and composer
Le Chevalier de St. Georges (1745 - 1799) French violinist, composer, and fencing master. The first known classical composer of African ancestry.
Giroust, François (1737 - 1799) French composer and Maître de Chapelle at the Chapelle Royale at Versailles
Gluck, Christoph Willibald (1714 - 1787) German composer of Italian and French operas
Gossec, François-Joseph (1734 - 1829) French composer of operas and instrumental music
Graun, Carl Heinrich (1704 - 1759) German composer of Italian operas, Kapellmeister at the court of Frederick the Great

Grimm, Jacob Ludwig Karl (1785 - 1863) and **Wilhelm Carl** (1786 - 1859) German academics, cultural researchers, collectors and publishers of folklore and fairytales
Guéméné , Princess Victoire Armande Josèphe de Rohan (1743 - 1807) wife of Henri Louis de Rohan, Prince de Guéméné
Guéméné, Prince Henri Louis de Rohan (1735 - 1809) French nobleman, appointed Grand Chamberlain of France in 1775 by Louis XVI
Guînes, Adrien-Louis de Bonnières, Comte de (1735 - 1806) French nobleman, ambassador to England and important member of the court of Louis XVI, amateur flute player, commissioned the *Concerto for Flute and Harp* from Mozart for himself and his daughter, Marie-Louise-Philippine (1759 - 1796)
Haltenhof, Johann Gottfried (ca. 1703 - 1783) Brass instrument maker in Hanau, Germany, credited by Domnich with developing the tuning slide
Hampel, Anton Joseph (1710 - 1771) Second horn in the Dresden Court Orchestra, early proponent and teacher of hand stopping on the horn
Handel, George Frederick (1685 - 1759) German opera, instrumental and oratorio composer, worked in England
Hasse, Johann Adolph (1699 - 1783) German opera composer
Haudek, Karl (1721 - 1800) German high horn player, worked in Dresden Court Orchestra
Haydn, Franz Josef (1732 - 1809) Austrian composer, court composer and music director for the Prince of Esterházy
Haydn, Michael (1737 - 1806) Austrian composer, worked in Salzburg
Heuzé, Jacques (1738 - ?) Violinist and Kappelmeister of the Cassel court orchestra
Hindemith, Paul (1895 - 1963) German composer, worked in United States
Hoffmann, Leopold (1738 - 1793) Austrian composer, worked in Vienna
Hoffmeister, Franz (1754 - 1812) German composer and music publisher
Hofmaster, Christopher (? - 1764) Brass instrument maker, worked in London. Possibly of German or Austrian origin

Holzbauer, Ignaz (1711 - 1783) German composer, worked in Mannheim
Hutti, Johann Anton (1751 - 1785) Violinist, worked in Kassel Court Orchestra
Jandoffsky, Franz Joseph (dates unknown) Bassoonist in the Wallerstein Orchestra
Janitsch, Anton (Janič, Antonín) (1753 - 1812) Czech born German violinist, member of the Wallerstein Orchestra
Jarnowick, Giovanni (Jarnović) (ca.1740 - 1804) Italian/Croatian violin soloist, Worked in France and many other countries in Europe, soloist at the Concert Spirituel
Johnson, Samuel (1709 - 1784) English writer, literary critic and lexicographer
Joseph II (1741 - 1790) Holy Roman Emperor, Archduke of Austria
Karl Anselm, (1733 - 1805) Fourth Prince of Thurn und Taxis, Postmaster General of the Imperial Reichspost
Kerner, Anton (1726 - 1806) Austrian brass instrument maker, worked in Vienna
Klimmenhagen, Johann Moritz (dates unknown) Horn player and violinist in Cassel court orchestra ca. 1780s
Kraft-Ernst (1748 - 1802) 1st Prince of Öttingen-Wallerstein
Lang, Franz (dates unknown) Mannheim Orchestra horn player
Langlé, Honoré François Marie (1741 - 1807) French music theorist and composer
Leduc, Simon (1742 - 1777) French violinist, soloist at the Concert Spirituel, Composer and music publisher
Legros, Joseph (1739 - 1793) French singer, composer and director of the Concert Spirituel
Leichnamschneider, Johannes (1679 - 1725) and **Michael** (1676 - 1748) Austrian brass instrument makers, worked in Vienna
Leutgeb, Joseph (1732 - 1811) Austrian horn soloist for whom Mozart wrote most of his solo horn music
Lloyd, Frank (1952 -) English horn soloist and professor at the Folkwang Hochschule in Essen, Germany
King Louis XVI (1754 - 1793) Last king of France before the French Revolution

Mahler, Gustav (1860 - 1911) Austrian composer and conductor, worked in Vienna and New York
Empress Maria Theresa (1717 - 1780) Archduchess of Austria and Queen of Hungary and Bohemia
Maria Theresia (1757 - 1776) daughter of Karl Anselm, Fourth Prince of Thurn und Taxis, married to Prince Kraft-Ernst of Öttingen-Wallerstein
Martini, Giovanni Battista (Padre Martini) (1706 -1784) Italian composer, music theorist, music historian and teacher
Matiegka, Joseph (dates unknown) Horn player and teacher in Prague
Meltel, Joseph (dates unknown) Bassoonist in the Wallerstein Orchestra
Mozart, Constanze (1762 - 1842) Austrian singer, married to Wolfgang Amadeus Mozart
Mozart, Karl Thomas (1784 - 1858) son of Wolfgang Amadeus Mozart
Mozart, Leopold (1719 - 1787) German composer, violinist and Kapellmeister in Salzburg, father of Wolfgang Amadeus Mozart
Mozart, Wolfgang Amadeus (1756 - 1791) Austrian composer and pianist, worked in Salzburg and Vienna
Mozer (dates unknown) Horn player in the Paris Opera and Concert Spirituel in the 1770s and 80s
Mademoiselle Mudrich (dates unknown) Flute player who performed at the Concert Spirituel in the concert in which Beate Pokorny performed a solo horn concerto
Neher, Johann (dates unknown) Innkeeper in Wallerstein Germany
Neher, Rosina (? - 1813) Daughter of Johann Neher, married to Antonio Rosetti in January 1777
Neruda, Johann Baptist Georg (ca.1708 - ca.1780) Czech violinist and composer, concertmaster of the Dresden Court Orchestra
Newman, Robert (1752 - 1804) Sexton of Christ Church, Boston during the American Revolutionary War
Nisle, Johann (1750 - 1802) Wallerstein Orchestra horn player
Paisiello, Giovanni (1740 - 1816) Italian opera composer

Paganini, Nicolò (1782 - 1840) Italian violinist, violist, guitarist and composer
Palsa, Johann (1752 - 1792) Bohemian high horn player, first horn of the Palsa - Türrschmidt duo, worked in France, (private orchestra of the Prince of Guéméné) and Germany, (Cassel and Berlin court orchestras)
Park, William Thomas (1761 - 1847) English oboist and composer
Philidor, François-Andre Danican (1726 - 1795) French opera composer and chess player
Phillip Karl (1745 - 1766) Count of Oettingen-Wallerstein, father of Prince Kraft-Ernst
Pokorny, Beate (dates unknown) Horn soloist, performed a concerto by Punto at the Concert Spirituel, 1779, and appeared as soloist and in duets with her sister in London, 1780. Relationship to Franz Pokorny uncertain
Pokorny, Franz (Pokorný, František Xaver) (1729 - 1794) Bohemian composer and violinist. Worked in Regensburg at Thurn und Taxis court orchestra
Punto, Giovanni (1746 - 1803) Bohemian horn soloist and composer
Quantz, Johann Joachim (1697 - 1773) German flute player and composer, worked at the court of Frederick the Great
Rameau, Jean-Philippe (1683 - 1764) French opera composer and music theorist
Ramm, Friedrich (1744 - 1813) German oboist, worked in Mannheim Orchestra
Richter, Franz Xaver (František Xaver) (1709 - 1789) German composer, singer, conductor, and music theorist, worked in Mannheim
Reicha, Josef (1752 - 1795) Czech cellist and composer, member of the Mannheim Orchestra
Reichardt, Johann Friedrich (1752 - 1814) German violinist and composer, Kapellmeister of Berlin Court Orchestra
Revere, Paul (1735 - 1818) American silversmith and patriot in the American Revolution

Riepel, Joseph (1709 - 1782) German music theorist, composer and violinist, Kapellmeister of the Thurn und Taxis Court Orchestra
Ritter, Georg Wenzel (1748 - 1808) Mannhein Orchestra and Prussian Court Orchestra bassooninst
Raoux, Joseph (1725 - 1787) French horn and brass instrument maker, worked in Paris
Raoux, Lucien-Joseph (1753 - 1821) French horn and brass instrument maker, son of Joseph Raoux, worked in Paris
Rochefort, Jean Baptiste (1746 - 1819) French composer, contrabass player and Kapellmeister in Kassel, 1780 - 1785
Rodenbostel, George Henry (? - 1789) London brass instrument maker, apprenticed with Christopher Hofmaster, continued business after Hofmaster's death in 1764
Rodolph, Jean-Joseph (1730 - 1812) Alsatian horn player, violinist and composer, worked in Stuttgart and Paris
Rosetti, Antonio (c. 1750 - 1792) Bohemian composer and double bass player, worked in Wallerstein Court Orchestra
Rupp, Martin (1748 - 1819) Austrian horn player, worked in Vienna Court Orchestra
Saint-Saëns, Camille (1835 - 1921) French composer, pianist, organist, and conductor
Salieri, Antonio (1750 - 1825) Italian composer, conductor and teacher, worked in Vienna
Salomon, Johann Peter (1745 - 1815) German violinist, composer, conductor and musical impresario, worked in Germany and London
Schacht, Baron Theodor von (1748 - 1823) German composer, worked in Regensburg in the Thurn und Taxis Court Orchestra
Schindelarž, Jan (1715 - 177?) Bohemian horn player and teacher, worked in the Mannheim Court orchestra 1742 - 1756
Schramm, Johann Christian (1711 - 1796) Keyboard player in the Berlin Court Orchestra
J.S. Schroetter (1752 - 1788) German pianist and composer, worked in England
Schuller, Gunther (1925 - 2015) American composer, horn player, conductor, teacher, and writer
Schweitzer, Anton (1735 - 1787) German opera composer

Sieber, Jean Georges (1738 - 1822) German born horn player, worked in France
Stadler, Anton (1753 - 1812) Austrian clarinet and basset horn player for whom Mozart wrote his clarinet concerto
Stamitz, Anton (1750 - 1812) German violinist and composer, brother of Carl Stamitz
Stamitz, Carl (1745 - 1801) German violinist and composer born in Mannheim, Germany
Stamitz, Johann (1717 - 1757) Bohemian composer and violinist, one of the founders of the Mannheim School, and father of Carl and Anton Stamitz
Strauss, Richard (1864 - 1949) German romantic composer and conductor
Stärtzer, Carl (1730 - 1791) Austrian horn and trumpet maker, worked in Vienna
Sterkel, Johan Franz Xaver (1750 - 1817) German composer and pianist
Stich, Jan Václav or Johann Wenzel (see Punto, Giovanni)
Steinheber, Johannes (1721 - 1807) Church music director in Wallerstein and violist in the Wallerstein Orchesra (his daughter Röslein in this story is fictional)
Tartini, Giuseppi (1692 - 1770) Italian violinist and composer
Tchaikovsky, Pyotr Ilyich (1840 - 1893) Russian romantic composer
Telemann, Georg Phillip (1681 - 1767) German composer and musician
Toeschi, Karl Joseph (1731 - 1788) Mannheim composer and violinist in the Mannheim Orchestra
Touchemoulin, Joseph (1727 - 1801) French violinist and composer, worked in Thurn und Taxis Court Orchestra
Thun-Hohenstein, Count Johann Josef Anton (1711 - 1788) Bohemian nobleman for whom Giovanni Punto worked in his youth, and from whom he ran away in 1768
Tuckwell, Barry (1931 - 2020) Australian born horn soloist and conductor
Türrschmidt, Carl (1753 - 1797) German low horn player, second horn of the Palsa - Türrschmidt duo, worked in France, (private

orchestra of the Prince of Guéméné) and Germany, (Kassel and Berlin Court Orchestras)
Türrschmidt, Carl Nicholaus (1776 - 1862) German horn player, singer, and teacher, son of Carl Türrschmidt, worked in Berlin
Türrschmidt, Johannes (1725 - 1800) German horn player, first horn of the Wallerstein Orchestra, father of Carl Türrschmidt
Türrschmidt, Joseph (dates unknown) Younger brother of Carl Türrschmidt, worked as a horn player in Paris
Tylšar, Bedřich (1939 -) Czech horn player, member of the Czech Philharmonic Orchestra, recorded many double concertos with his brother, hornist Zdeněk Tylšar
Tylšar, Zdeněk (1945 - 2006) Czech horn player, principal horn of the Czech Philharmonic Orchestra, recorded many double concertos with his brother, hornist Bedřich Tylšar
Othon Vandenbroek (1758 - 1832) Dutch horn player, teacher and composer, worked in Paris
Vanhal, Johann Baptist (1739 - 1813) Czech composer and musician, worked in Vienna
Voltaire (François-Marie Arouet) (1694 - 1778) French writer, historian and philosopher
Wagenseil, Georg Christoph (1715 - 1777) Austrian composer, harpsichordist and organist, worked in Vienna
Washington, George (1732 - 1799) First American president and American Revolutionary War general
Weber, Carl Maria von (1786 - 1826) German pianist and composer of operas and instrumental works
Wendling, Dorothea (1736 - 1811) Mannheim Opera singer, wife of Johann Wendling
Wendling, Elisabeth (1752 - 1794) Mannheim Opera singer, daughter of Johann Wendling
Wendling, Johann Baptist (1723 - 1797) Principal flute of the Mannheim orchestra and composer
Werner, Johann Georg (? - 1772) Brass instrument maker, worked in Dresden
Wallendorf, Klaus (1948 -) German horn player, member of the Berlin Philharmonic Orchestra

Willis, Sarah (1969 -) American horn player, member of the Berlin Philharmonic Orchestra
Zwierzina, Franz (1750 - 1825) German horn player, second horn in the Wallerstein Orchestra

Bibliography

Anon., *The Compleat Tutor for the French Horn, London, John Simpson, 1746*
Anon., *New Instructions for the French-Horn, London, ca. 1770*
Anderson, James, *Daily Life During the French Revolution*, Greenwood Press, 2007
Barbour, J. Murray, *Pokorny Vindicated*, Musical Quarterly, Vol. 49 No. 1, Jan. 1963
Burke, Edmund, *Reflections on the French Revolution*, 1790
Burney, Charles, *The Present State of Music in France and Italy*, London, 1773
Burney, Charles, *The Present State of Music in Germany, the Netherlands, and the United Provinces*, London, 1775
Carse, Adam, *The Orchestra of the 18th Century*, Cambridge, Heffer, 1940
Dickens, Charles, *A Tale of Two Cities*, London, 1859
Dimmler, Anton, *Concerto for Two Horns in E major (Concertante a due Corni)*, Hans Pizka Edition, 1983.
Domnich, Heinrich, *Méthode de Premier et de Second Cor*, Paris, 1807, (Translation by Darryl Poulson, Univ. of Western Australia, 2019)
Fetis, François, *Biographie universelle des musicians*, Paris, 1837
Fiala, Joseph, *Concerto per due Corni in E flat*, Hans Pizka Edition, 1983
Fitzpatrick, Horace, *The Horn and Horn Playing in the Austro-Bohemian Tradition*, London, Oxford Univ. Press, 1970
Forkel, Johann, *Nicholaus, Musikalischer Almanach für Deutschland, auf das Jahr 1782-1784*, Leipzig
Framery, Nicolas Étienne, *Calendar Universal Musical* for 1788 and 1789
Gerber, Ernst Ludwig *Historisches-Biographisches Lexicon der Tonkünstler*, Leipzig, 1792
Hampel, Anton Joseph/Punto, Giovanni, *Méthode pour Cor*, Paris, J.H. Naderman, ca. 1794 (in Methodes & Traités 21, Cor, Éditions Fuzeau, 2003)
Haydn, Joseph, *Quintet, for Piano, Two Horns, Violin, and Cello*, Hob. XIV:1, G. Henle Verlag, 1987
Laborde, Jean-Benjamin de, *Essai sur la musique ancienne et modern*, Paris, 1780 (in Methodes & Traités 21, Cor, Éditions Fuzeau, 2003)

Manganaro, John, *18th Century Horn Performance Practice: A Re-evaluation of the Role of the Hand.* Article based on lecture presented at the Historical Horn Symposium, Ghent, Belgium, 2019.
Manganaro, John, www.horniconography.com
Mercur de France, 1780
Morley-Pegge, Reginald, *The French Horn*, London, W.W. Norton, 1960
Mozart, W.A., *Twelve Horn Duos, K. 487/496a*, Bureau d'Arts et d'Industrie, Plate 46, Vienna, n.d. (www.imslp.org)
Mozart, W.A., *Concerto for Flute and Harp*, K. 299, 1778
Mozart, W.A., *Letters of Mozart and his Family*, Macmillan, 1986
Mozart, W.A., *Marriage of Figaro*, 1786
Mozart *Musikalischer Spaß*, First edition, Offenbach, a/M: André, Paris, ca. 1797 (www.imslp.org)
Mozart, W.A., *Quintet in E flat for piano and Winds*, K. 452
Mozart, Leopold, *Concerto à 2 Corni Principali in Dis*, 1752 (www.imslp.org)
Murray, Sterling, *The Career of an 18th Century Kapellmeister; The life and Music of Antonio Rosetti*, University of Rochester, 2014
Murray, Sterling, *The Double Horn Concerto: A Specialty of the Oettingen-Wallerstein Court,* Journal of Musicology, Vol. 4, No. 4, 1985
New Grove Dictionary of Music, Article on the Raoux family, musician bios, etc.
Olsen, Kirstin, *Daily Life in 18th Century England*, Greenwood Press, 1999
Parke, William T., *Musical Memoirs*, London, 1830
Philidor, François André Danican, opera *Tom Jones,* Paris, 1765 (www.imslp.org)
Pierre, Constant, *Histoire du concert spirituel 1725-1790*, Paris, 1900
Roeser, Valentin, *Essai d'Instruction a l'usage de ceux qui composent pour la clarinette et le cor*, Paris, 1764 (in Methodes & Traités 21, Cor, Éditions Fuzeau, 2003)
Rosetti, Antonio, *Concerto in E flat for Two Horns*, M.C56, (www.imslp.org) (priously attributed to Joseph Haydn)
Rosetti, Antonio, *Concerto in E flat for Two Horns*, M.C57, (www.imslp.org)
Rosetti, Antonio, *Concerto in E for Two Horns,* M.C58, Robert Ostermeyer Musikedition

Rosetti, Antonio, *Concerto in E flat for Horn and Orchestra*, M.C48, (www.imslp.org)
Rosetti, Antonio, *Concerto in E flat for Horn and Orchestra*, M.C49, (www.imslp.org)
Rosetti, Antonio, *Concerto in F for Horn and Orchestra*, M.C53, Robert Ostermeyer Musikedition
Schneider, Wilhelm, *Historische Technische Beschreibung der musikalischen Instrumente*, 1834
Seraphinoff, Richard, *Reinventing the Classical Horn*, https://www.seraphinoff.com/reinventing-the-classical-horn
Seraphinoff, Richard, *Classical Horn Mouthpieces*, https://www.seraphinoff.com/early-horn-mouthpieces
Sophie Drinker Institute, Bremen, Germany (*Europäische Instrumentalistinnen des 18. und 19. Jahrhunderts*) https://www.sophie-drinker-institut.de/pokorny-beate
Spitzer, John and Zaslow, Neal, *The Birth of the Orchestra*, London, Oxford Univ. Press, 2004
Türrschmidt, Carl, *50 duos Op. 3*, C. C. Menzel, Berlin, 1795 (www.imslp.org)
Waterhouse, William, *The New Langwell Index of Wind Instrument Makers*, Tony Bingham, London, 1993
Wendling, Johann Baptist, *Three Trios for Flute, Violin, and Cello, Op. 3*, 1772, ca. 1769, (www.imslp.org)

Printed in Great Britain
by Amazon

72036640R00293